WITHDRAWN

THE
BAKER STREET
PECULIARS™

CREATED BY **ROGER LANGRIDGE** AND **ANDY HIRSCH**

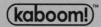

TH

BAKER

PECUL

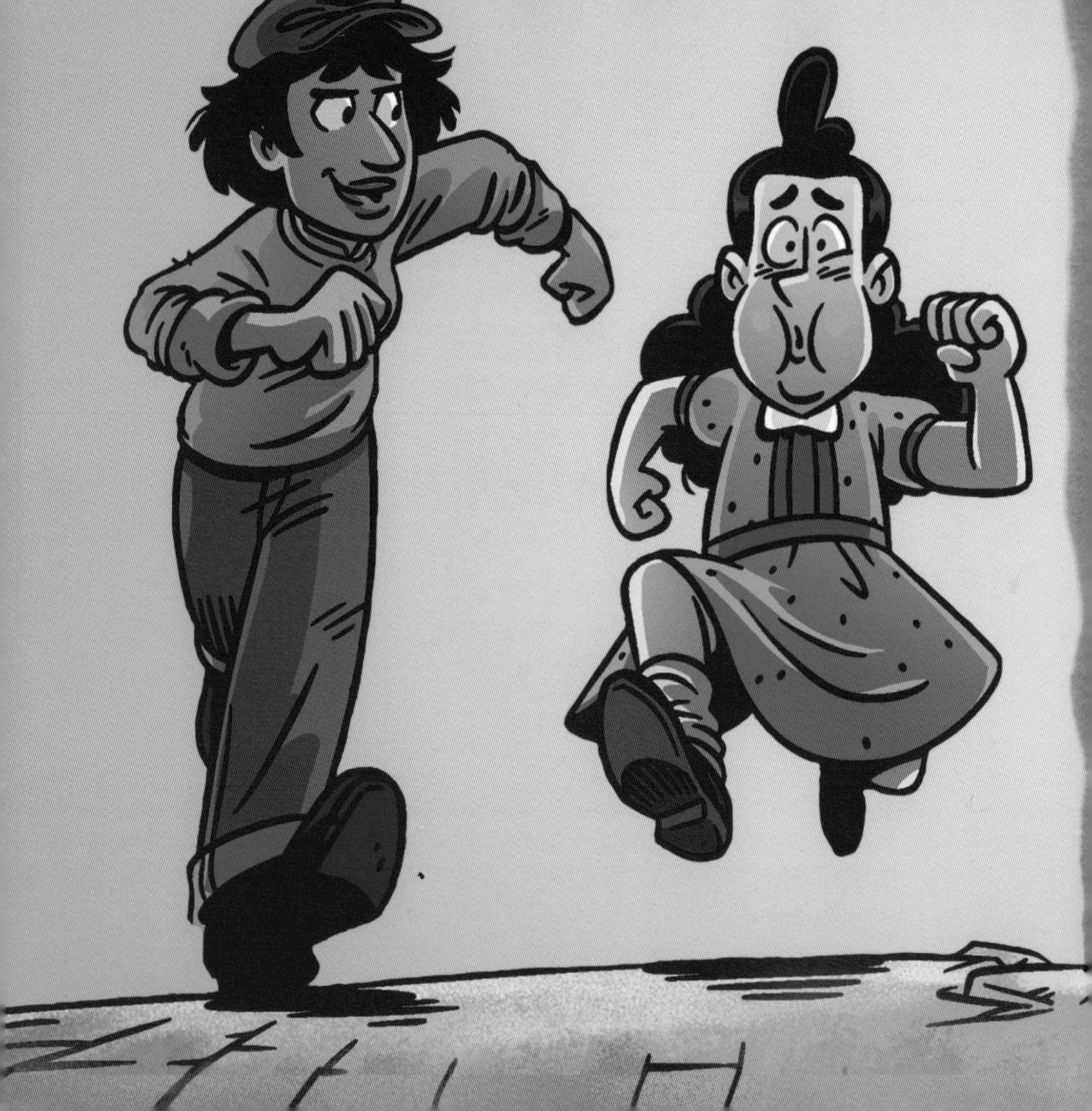

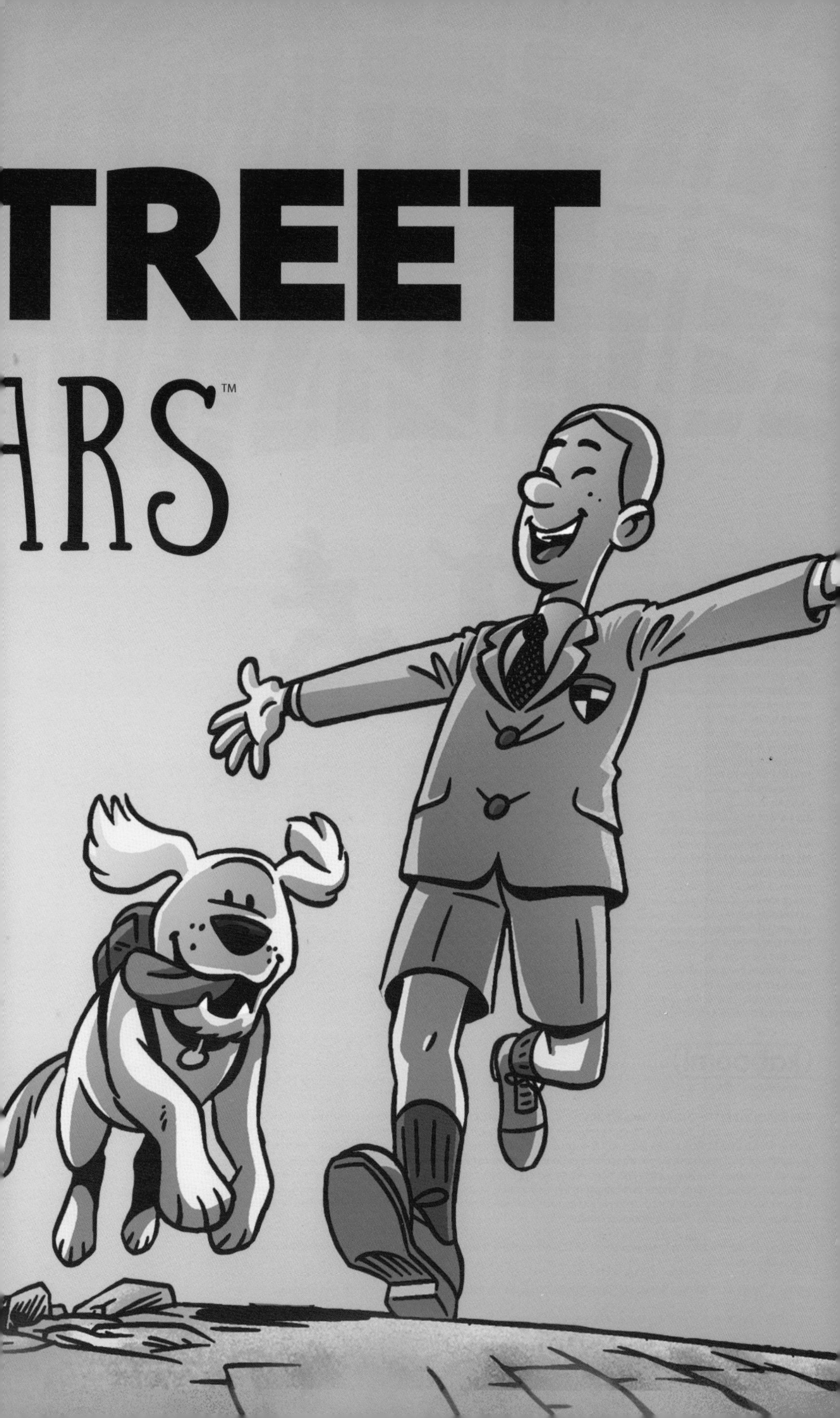
TREET
ARS™

ROSS RICHIE CEO & Founder
MATT GAGNON Editor-in-Chief
FILIP SABLIK President of Publishing & Marketing
STEPHEN CHRISTY President of Development
LANCE KREITER VP of Licensing & Merchandising
PHIL BARBARO VP of Finance
BRYCE CARLSON Managing Editor
MEL CAYLO Marketing Manager
SCOTT NEWMAN Production Design Manager
IRENE BRADISH Operations Manager
SIERRA HAHN Senior Editor
DAFNA PLEBAN Editor, Talent Development
SHANNON WATTERS Editor
ERIC HARBURN Editor
WHITNEY LEOPARD Associate Editor
JASMINE AMIRI Associate Editor
CHRIS ROSA Associate Editor
ALEX GALER Associate Editor
CAMERON CHITTOCK Associate Editor
MATTHEW LEVINE Assistant Editor
KELSEY DIETERICH Production Designer
JILLIAN CRAB Production Designer
MICHELLE ANKLEY Production Designer
GRACE PARK Production Design Assistant
AARON FERRARA Operations Coordinator
ELIZABETH LOUGHRIDGE Accounting Coordinator
STEPHANIE HOCUTT Social Media Coordinator
JOSÉ MEZA Sales Assistant
JAMES ARRIOLA Mailroom Assistant
HOLLY AITCHISON Operations Assistant
SAM KUSEK Direct Market Representative
AMBER PARKER Administrative Assistant

WWW.BOOM-STUDIOS.COM

THE BAKER STREET PECULIARS, January 2017. Published by KaBOOM!, a division of Boom Entertainment, Inc. The Baker Street Peculiars is ™ & © 2017 Roger Langridge & Andrew Hirsch. Originally published in single magazine form as THE BAKER STREET PECULIARS No. 1-4.™ & © 2016 Roger Langridge & Andrew Hirsch. Inc. All rights reserved. KaBOOM!™ and the KaBOOM! logo are trademarks of Boom Entertainment, Inc., registered in various countries and categories. All characters, events, and institutions depicted herein are fictional. Any similarity between any of the names, characters, persons, events, and/or institutions in this publication to actual names, characters, and persons, whether living or dead, events, and/or institutions is unintended and purely coincidental. KaBOOM! does not read or accept unsolicited submissions of ideas, stories, or artwork.

A catalog record of this book is available from OCLC and from the BOOM! Studios! website, www.boom-studios.com, on the Librarians Page.

BOOM! Studios, 5670 Wilshire Boulevard, Suite 450, Los Angeles, CA 90036-5679. Printed in China. First Printing.

ISBN: 978-1-60886-928-2, eISBN: 978-1-61398-599-1

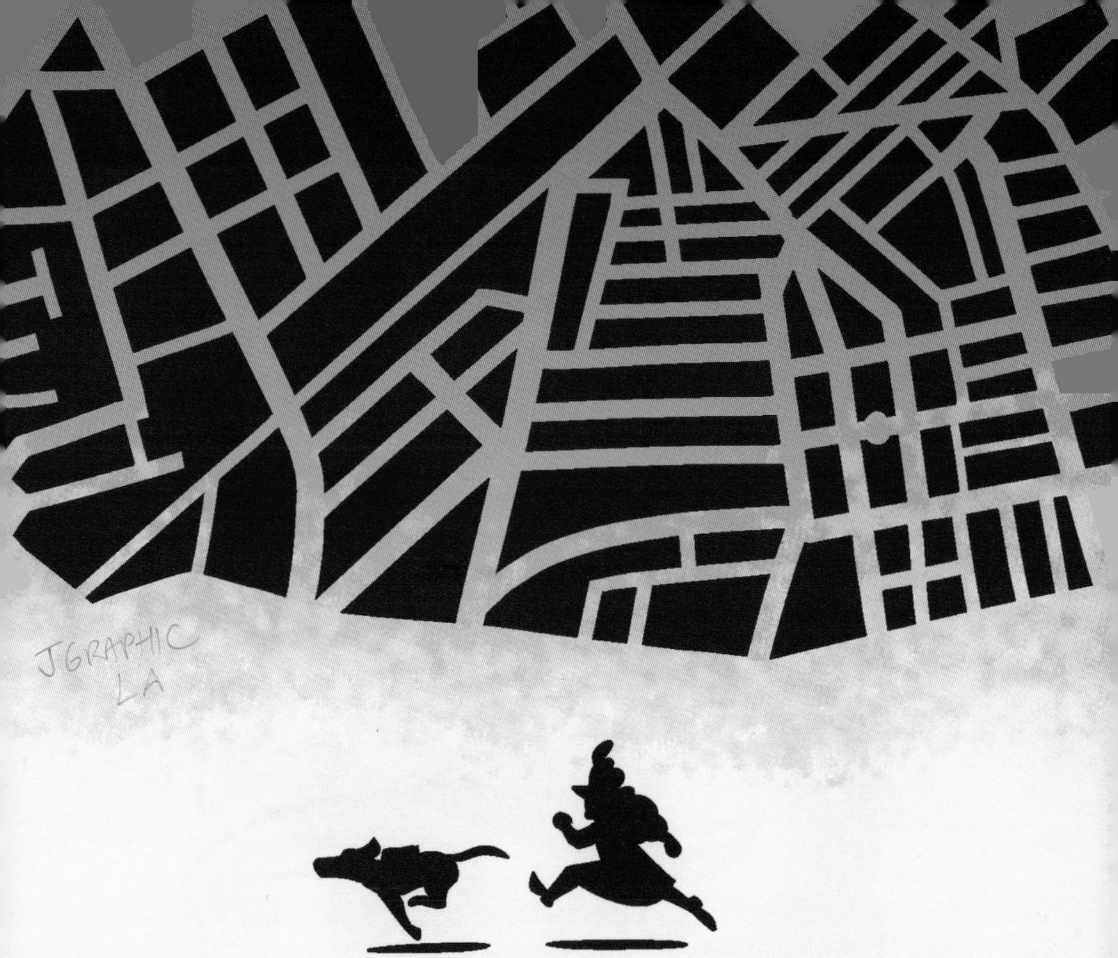

BROUGHT TO YOU BY DIRT-ENCRUSTED STREET URCHIN
ROGER LANGRIDGE

WITH ILLUSTRATIONS BY SCRUFFY PAPER BOY
ANDY HIRSCH

AND CHROMATIC EFFECTS IN ALL-NEW STRESINGCOLOR™ BY
FRED STRESING

COVER BY
ANDY HIRSCH

DESIGNER
MICHELLE ANKLEY

ASSOCIATE EDITOR
CAMERON CHITTOCK

EDITOR
SIERRA HAHN

CHAPTER ONE

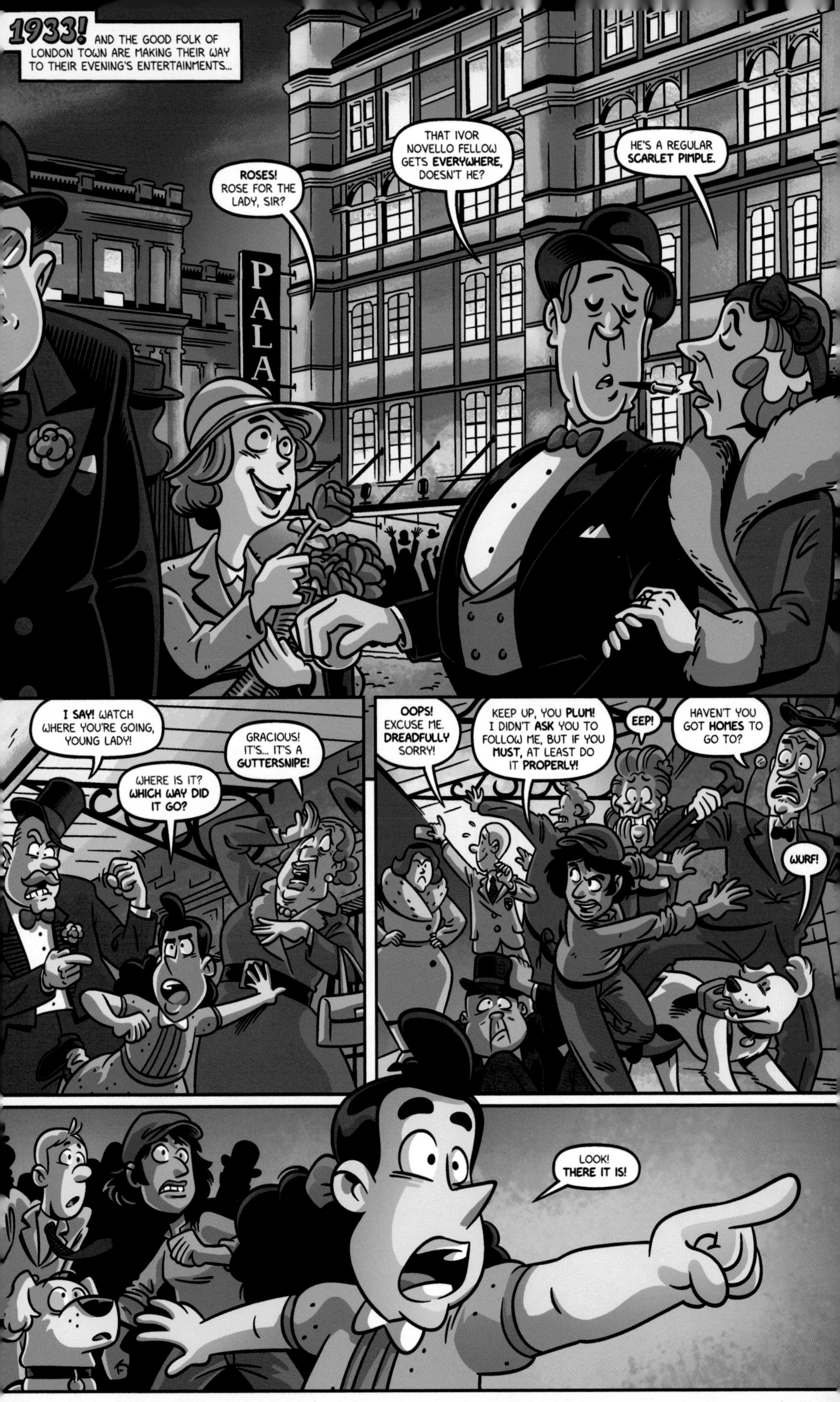
1933! AND THE GOOD FOLK OF LONDON TOWN ARE MAKING THEIR WAY TO THEIR EVENING'S ENTERTAINMENTS...
ROSES! ROSE FOR THE LADY, SIR?
THAT IVOR NOVELLO FELLOW GETS EVERYWHERE, DOESN'T HE?
HE'S A REGULAR SCARLET PIMPLE.
PALA
I SAY! WATCH WHERE YOU'RE GOING, YOUNG LADY!
WHERE IS IT? WHICH WAY DID IT GO?
GRACIOUS! IT'S... IT'S A GUTTERSNIPE!
OOPS! EXCUSE ME. DREADFULLY SORRY!
KEEP UP, YOU PLUM! I DIDN'T ASK YOU TO FOLLOW ME, BUT IF YOU MUST, AT LEAST DO IT PROPERLY!
EEP!
HAVEN'T YOU GOT HOMES TO GO TO?
WURF!
LOOK! THERE IT IS!

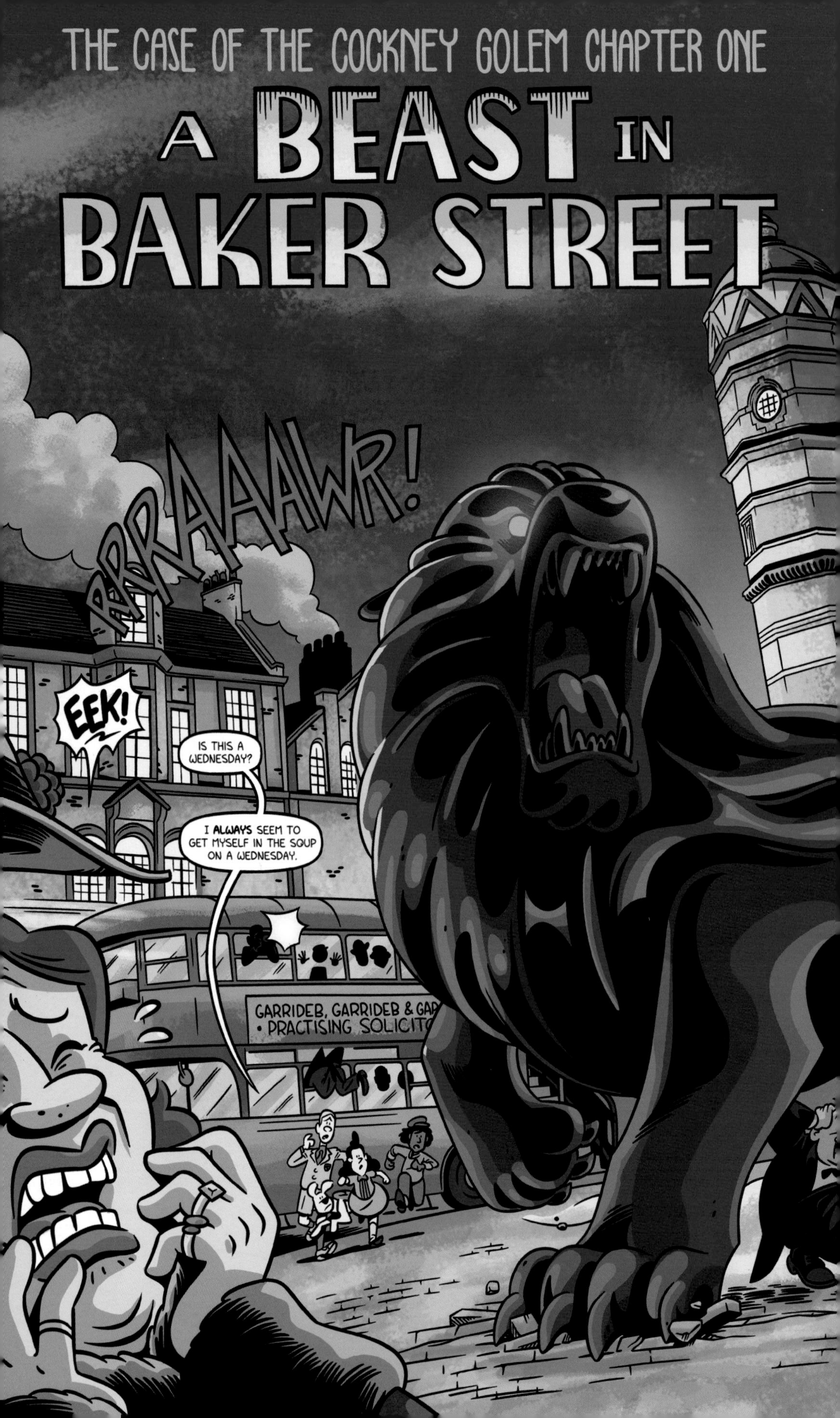
THE CASE OF THE COCKNEY GOLEM CHAPTER ONE
A BEAST IN BAKER STREET
RRRAAAAWR!
EEK!
IS THIS A WEDNESDAY?
I ALWAYS SEEM TO GET MYSELF IN THE SOUP ON A WEDNESDAY.
GARRIDEB, GARRIDEB & GAR
• PRACTISING SOLICITO

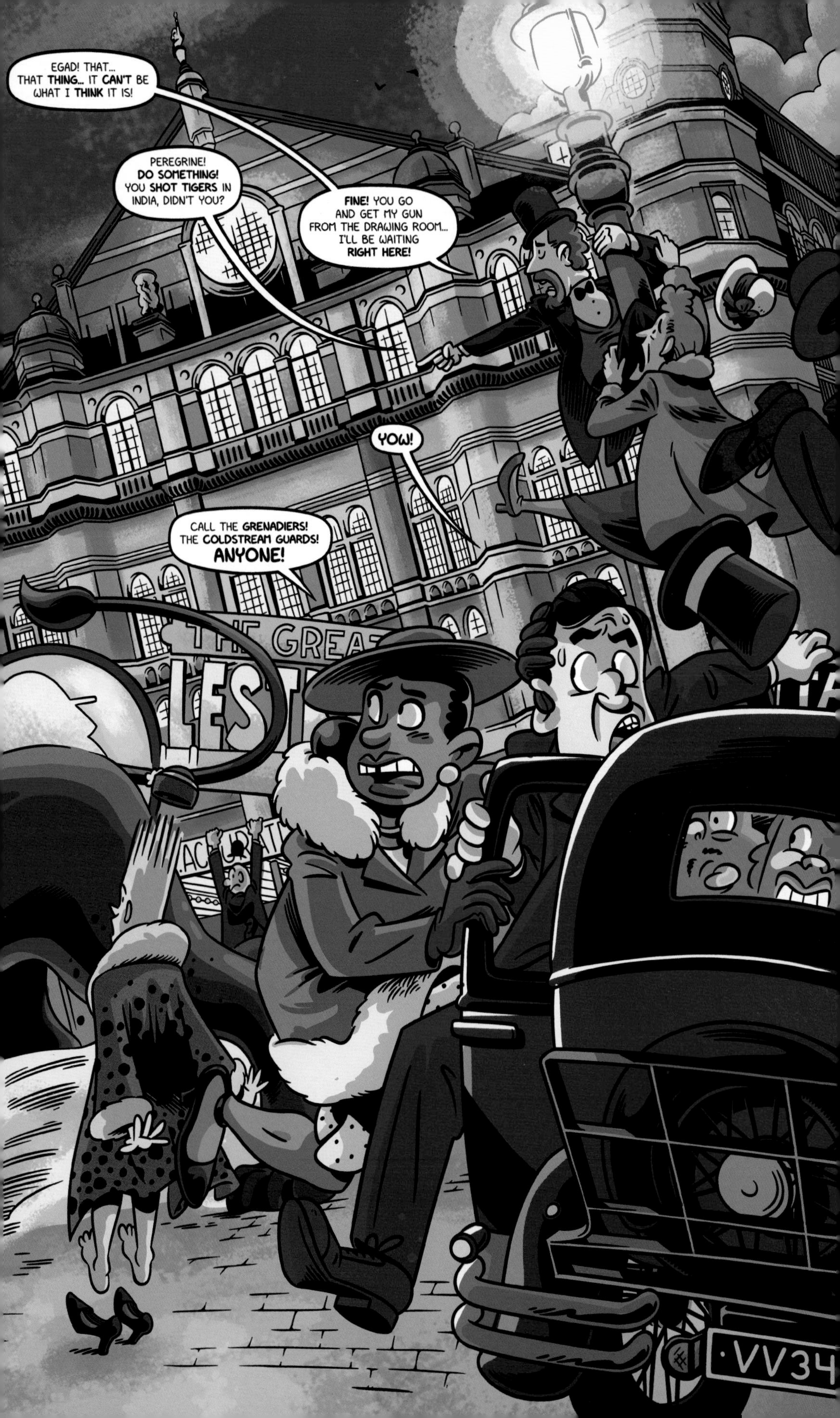
EGAD! THAT... THAT THING... IT CAN'T BE WHAT I THINK IT IS!
PEREGRINE! DO SOMETHING! YOU SHOT TIGERS IN INDIA, DIDN'T YOU?
FINE! YOU GO AND GET MY GUN FROM THE DRAWING ROOM... I'LL BE WAITING RIGHT HERE!
YOW!
CALL THE GRENADIERS! THE COLDSTREAM GUARDS! ANYONE!
VV34

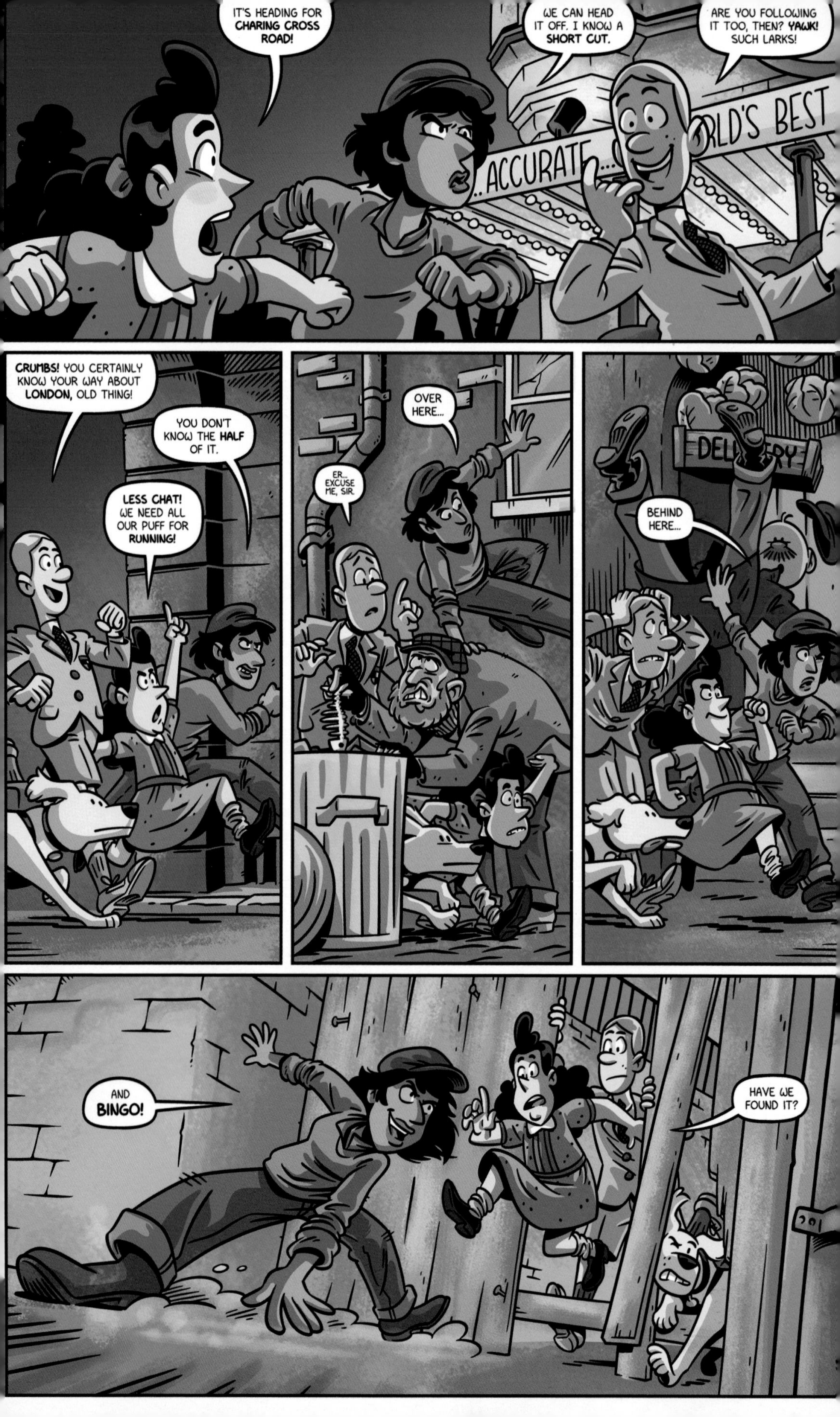
IT'S HEADING FOR **CHARING CROSS ROAD!**
WE CAN HEAD IT OFF. I KNOW A **SHORT CUT.**
ARE YOU FOLLOWING IT TOO, THEN? **YAWK!** SUCH LARKS!
...ACCURATE... ...RLD'S BEST
CRUMBS! YOU CERTAINLY KNOW YOUR WAY ABOUT **LONDON,** OLD THING!
YOU DON'T KNOW THE **HALF** OF IT.
LESS CHAT! WE NEED ALL OUR PUFF FOR **RUNNING!**
OVER HERE...
ER... EXCUSE ME, SIR.
BEHIND HERE...
AND **BINGO!**
HAVE WE FOUND IT?

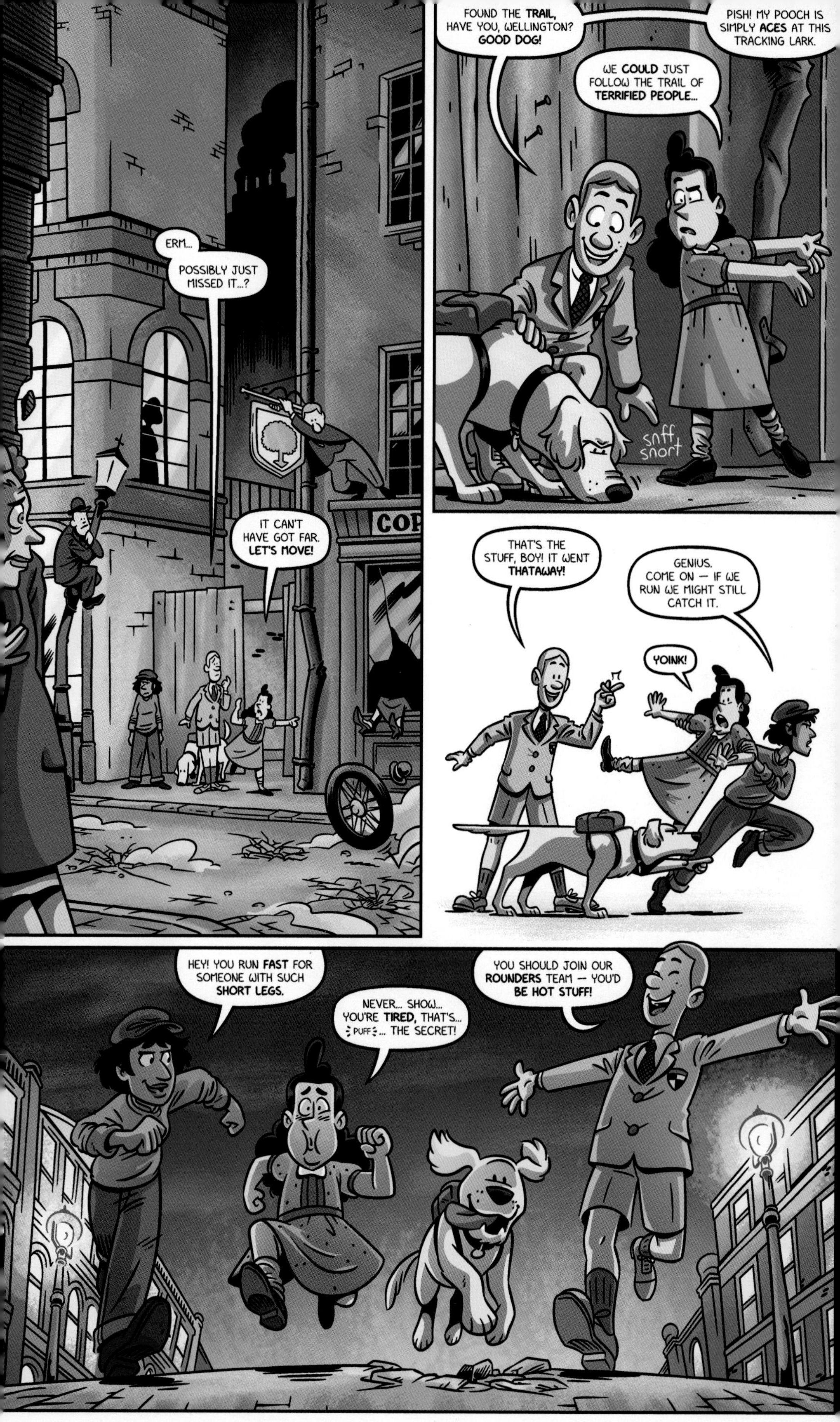
ERM...
POSSIBLY JUST MISSED IT...?
IT CAN'T HAVE GOT FAR. LET'S MOVE!
COP
FOUND THE TRAIL, HAVE YOU, WELLINGTON? GOOD DOG!
PISH! MY POOCH IS SIMPLY ACES AT THIS TRACKING LARK.
WE COULD JUST FOLLOW THE TRAIL OF TERRIFIED PEOPLE...
snff snort
THAT'S THE STUFF, BOY! IT WENT THATAWAY!
GENIUS. COME ON — IF WE RUN WE MIGHT STILL CATCH IT.
YOINK!
HEY! YOU RUN FAST FOR SOMEONE WITH SUCH SHORT LEGS.
NEVER... SHOW... YOU'RE TIRED, THAT'S... PUFF ... THE SECRET!
YOU SHOULD JOIN OUR ROUNDERS TEAM — YOU'D BE HOT STUFF!

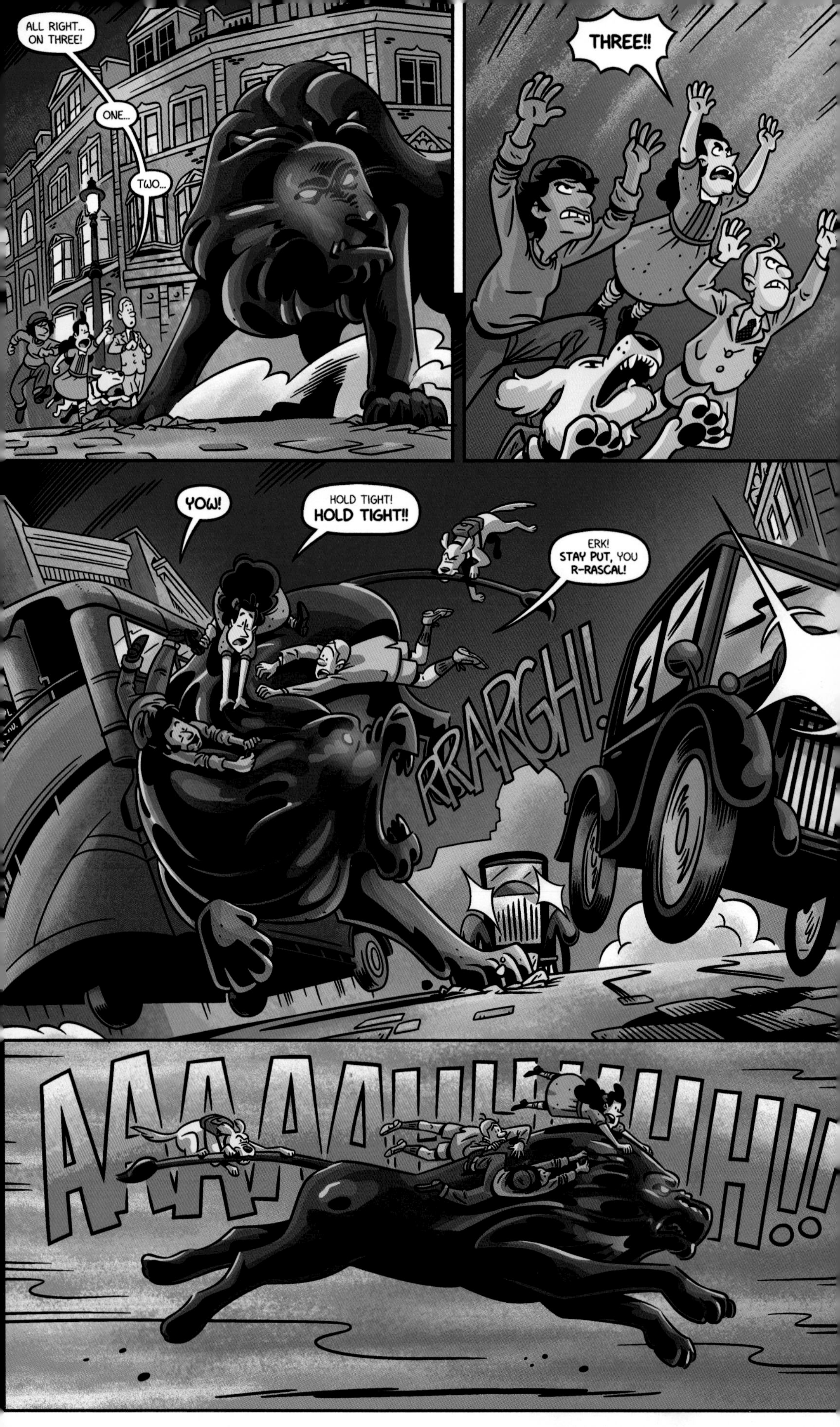
ALL RIGHT... ON THREE!
ONE...
TWO...
THREE!!
YOW!
HOLD TIGHT! HOLD TIGHT!!
ERK! STAY PUT, YOU R-RASCAL!
RRARGH!
AAAAHHHHHH!!!

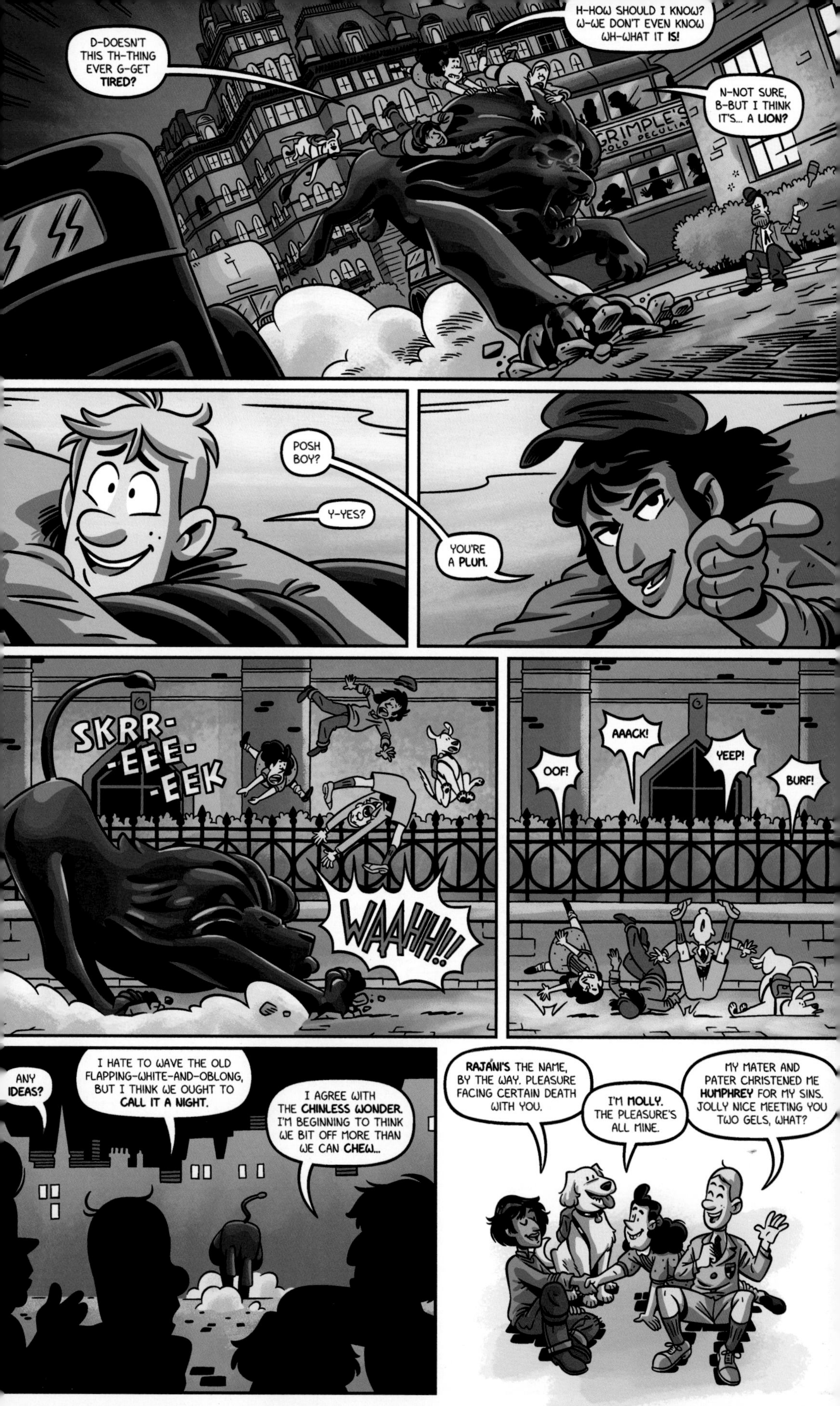
D-DOESN'T THIS TH-THING EVER G-GET TIRED?
H-HOW SHOULD I KNOW? W-WE DON'T EVEN KNOW WH-WHAT IT IS!
N-NOT SURE, B-BUT I THINK IT'S... A LION?
GRIMPLE'S
POSH BOY?
Y-YES?
YOU'RE A PLUM.
SKRR- -EEE- -EEK
WAAHH!!
OOF!
AAACK!
YEEP!
BURF!
ANY IDEAS?
I HATE TO WAVE THE OLD FLAPPING-WHITE-AND-OBLONG, BUT I THINK WE OUGHT TO CALL IT A NIGHT.
I AGREE WITH THE CHINLESS WONDER. I'M BEGINNING TO THINK WE BIT OFF MORE THAN WE CAN CHEW...
RAJANI'S THE NAME, BY THE WAY. PLEASURE FACING CERTAIN DEATH WITH YOU.
I'M MOLLY. THE PLEASURE'S ALL MINE.
MY MATER AND PATER CHRISTENED ME HUMPHREY FOR MY SINS. JOLLY NICE MEETING YOU TWO GELS, WHAT?

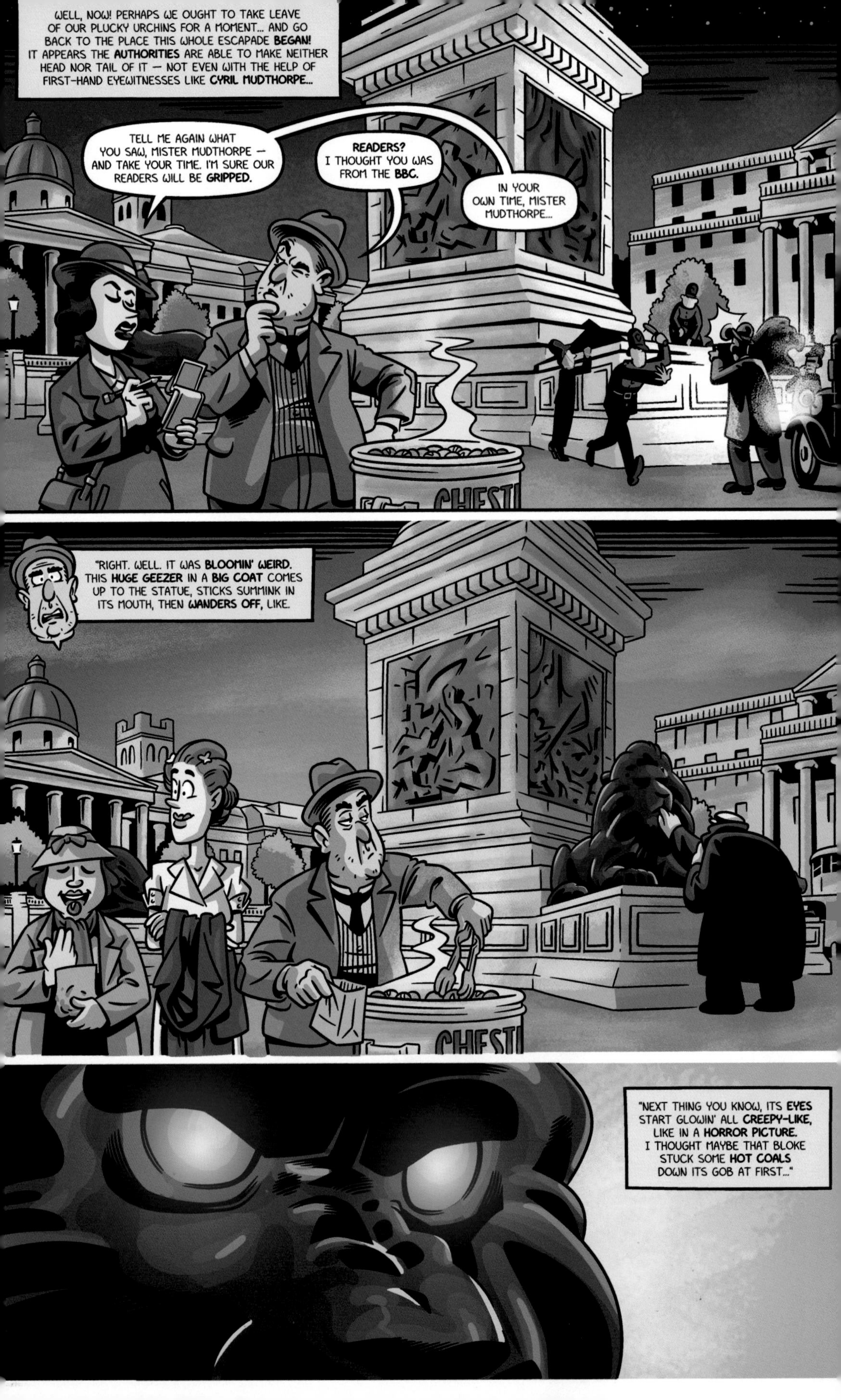
WELL, NOW! PERHAPS WE OUGHT TO TAKE LEAVE OF OUR PLUCKY URCHINS FOR A MOMENT... AND GO BACK TO THE PLACE THIS WHOLE ESCAPADE BEGAN! IT APPEARS THE AUTHORITIES ARE ABLE TO MAKE NEITHER HEAD NOR TAIL OF IT — NOT EVEN WITH THE HELP OF FIRST-HAND EYEWITNESSES LIKE CYRIL MUDTHORPE...
TELL ME AGAIN WHAT YOU SAW, MISTER MUDTHORPE — AND TAKE YOUR TIME. I'M SURE OUR READERS WILL BE GRIPPED.
READERS? I THOUGHT YOU WAS FROM THE BBC.
IN YOUR OWN TIME, MISTER MUDTHORPE...
CHEST
"RIGHT. WELL. IT WAS BLOOMIN' WEIRD. THIS HUGE GEEZER IN A BIG COAT COMES UP TO THE STATUE, STICKS SUMMINK IN ITS MOUTH, THEN WANDERS OFF, LIKE.
CHEST
"NEXT THING YOU KNOW, ITS EYES START GLOWIN' ALL CREEPY-LIKE, LIKE IN A HORROR PICTURE. I THOUGHT MAYBE THAT BLOKE STUCK SOME HOT COALS DOWN ITS GOB AT FIRST..."

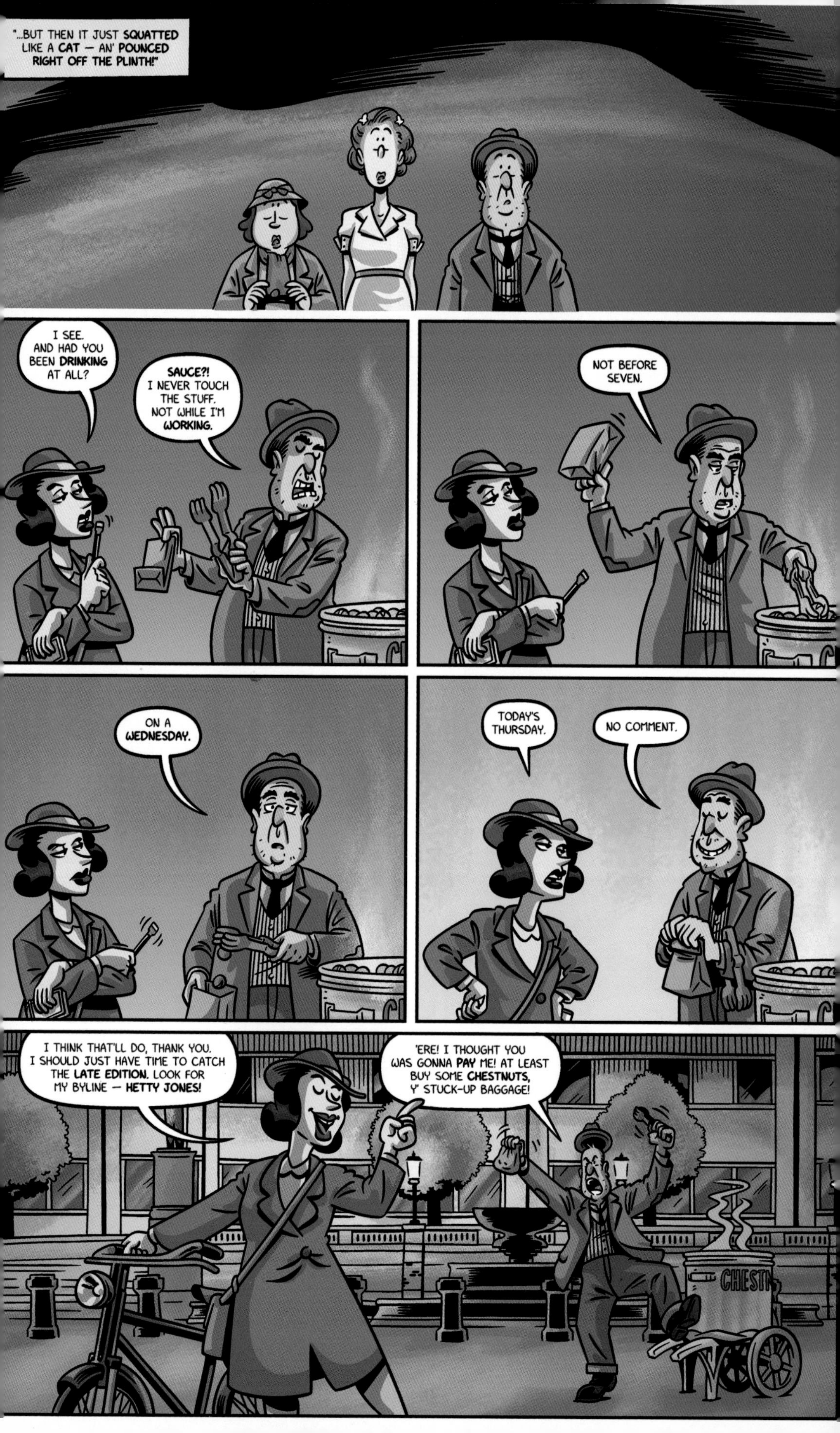
"...BUT THEN IT JUST SQUATTED LIKE A CAT — AN' POUNCED RIGHT OFF THE PLINTH!"
I SEE. AND HAD YOU BEEN DRINKING AT ALL?
SAUCE?! I NEVER TOUCH THE STUFF. NOT WHILE I'M WORKING.
NOT BEFORE SEVEN.
ON A WEDNESDAY.
TODAY'S THURSDAY.
NO COMMENT.
I THINK THAT'LL DO, THANK YOU. I SHOULD JUST HAVE TIME TO CATCH THE LATE EDITION. LOOK FOR MY BYLINE — HETTY JONES!
'ERE! I THOUGHT YOU WAS GONNA PAY ME! AT LEAST BUY SOME CHESTNUTS, Y' STUCK-UP BAGGAGE!

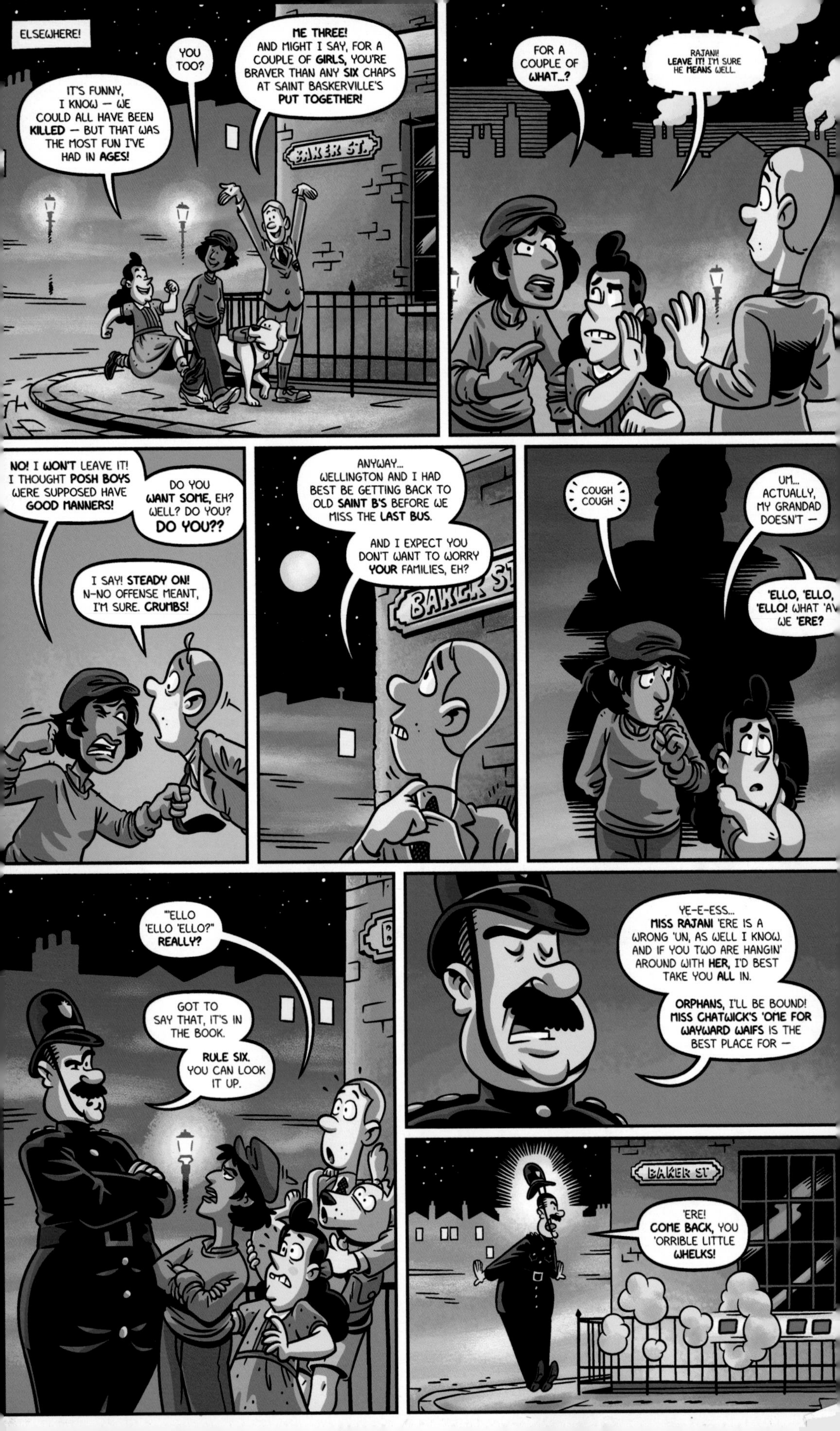
ELSEWHERE!
IT'S FUNNY, I KNOW — WE COULD ALL HAVE BEEN KILLED — BUT THAT WAS THE MOST FUN I'VE HAD IN AGES!
YOU TOO?
ME THREE! AND MIGHT I SAY, FOR A COUPLE OF GIRLS, YOU'RE BRAVER THAN ANY SIX CHAPS AT SAINT BASKERVILLE'S PUT TOGETHER!
BAKER ST.
FOR A COUPLE OF WHAT...?
RAJANI! LEAVE IT! I'M SURE HE MEANS WELL.
NO! I WON'T LEAVE IT! I THOUGHT POSH BOYS WERE SUPPOSED HAVE GOOD MANNERS!
DO YOU WANT SOME, EH? WELL? DO YOU? DO YOU??
I SAY! STEADY ON! N–NO OFFENSE MEANT, I'M SURE. CRUMBS!
ANYWAY... WELLINGTON AND I HAD BEST BE GETTING BACK TO OLD SAINT B'S BEFORE WE MISS THE LAST BUS.
AND I EXPECT YOU DON'T WANT TO WORRY YOUR FAMILIES, EH?
COUGH COUGH
UM... ACTUALLY, MY GRANDAD DOESN'T —
'ELLO, 'ELLO, 'ELLO! WHAT 'AV WE 'ERE?
"'ELLO 'ELLO 'ELLO?" REALLY?
GOT TO SAY THAT, IT'S IN THE BOOK.
RULE SIX. YOU CAN LOOK IT UP.
YE-E-ESS... MISS RAJANI 'ERE IS A WRONG 'UN, AS WELL I KNOW. AND IF YOU TWO ARE HANGIN' AROUND WITH HER, I'D BEST TAKE YOU ALL IN.
ORPHANS, I'LL BE BOUND! MISS CHATWICK'S 'OME FOR WAYWARD WAIFS IS THE BEST PLACE FOR —
BAKER ST
'ERE! COME BACK, YOU 'ORRIBLE LITTLE WHELKS!

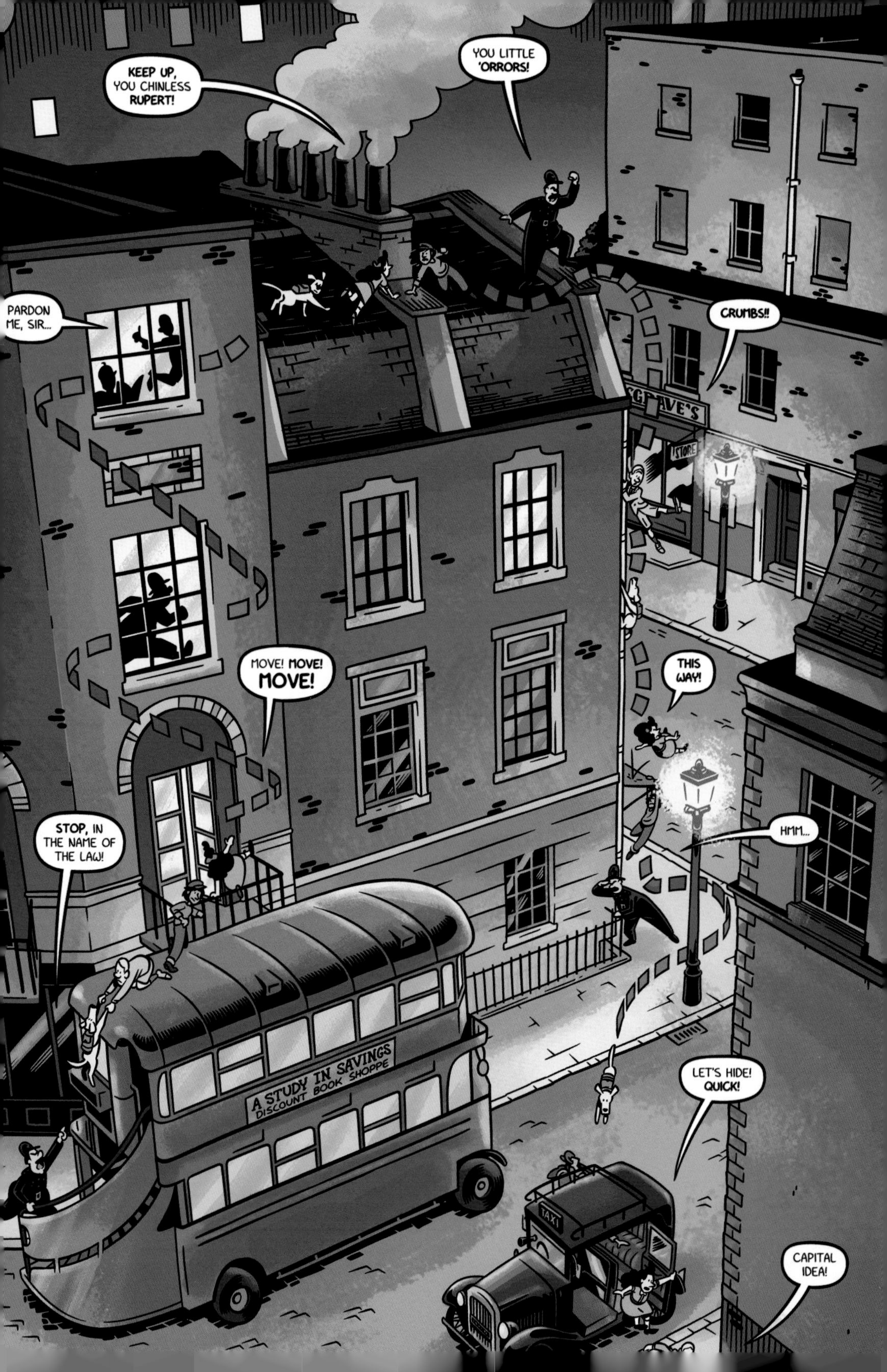
KEEP UP, YOU CHINLESS RUPERT!
YOU LITTLE 'ORRORS!
PARDON ME, SIR...
CRUMBS!!
MOVE! MOVE! MOVE!
THIS WAY!
STOP, IN THE NAME OF THE LAW!
HMM...
A STUDY IN SAVINGS DISCOUNT BOOK SHOPPE
LET'S HIDE! QUICK!
TAXI
CAPITAL IDEA!

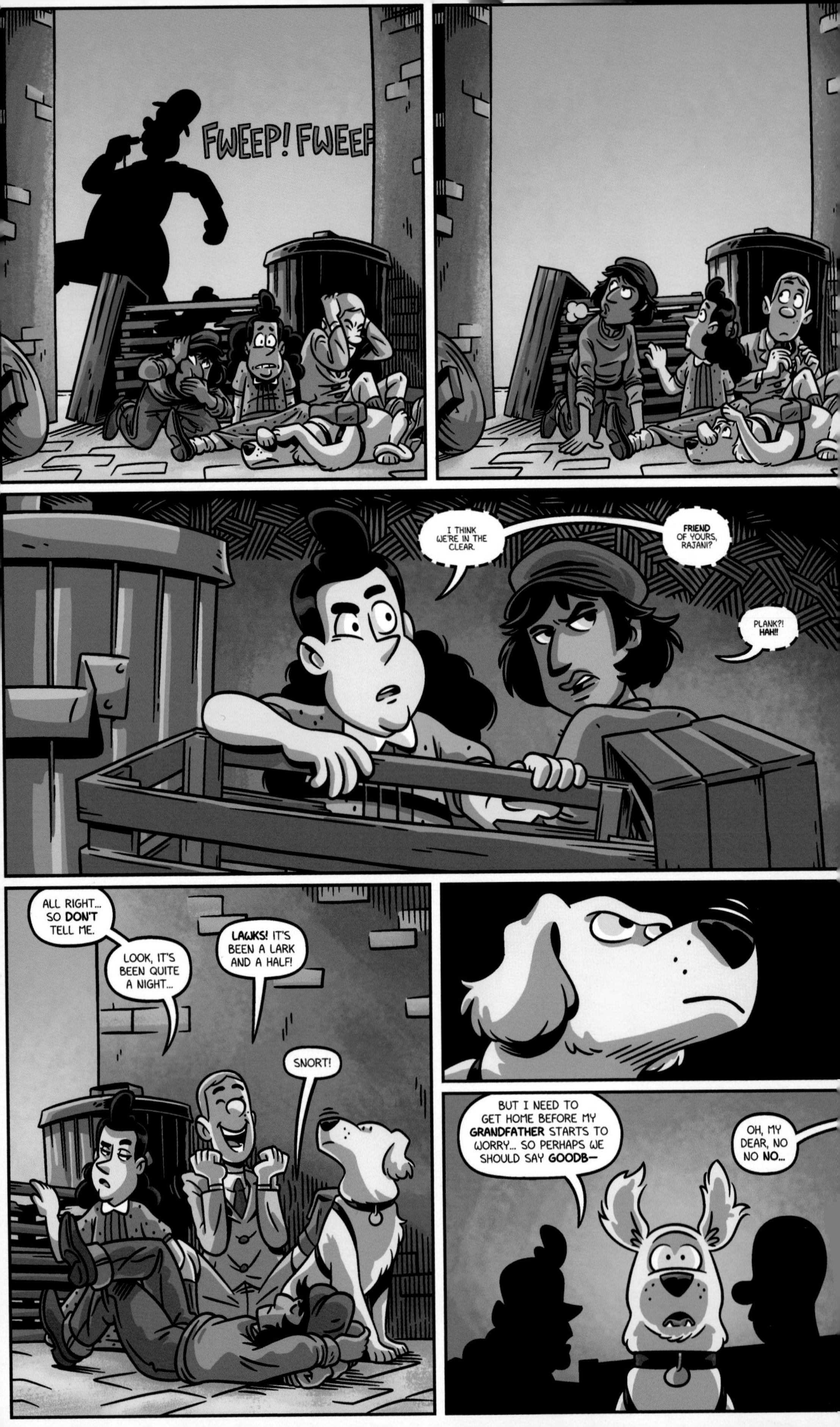
FWEEP! FWEEP
I THINK WE'RE IN THE CLEAR.
FRIEND OF YOURS, RAJANI?
PLANK?! HAH!!
ALL RIGHT... SO DON'T TELL ME.
LOOK, IT'S BEEN QUITE A NIGHT...
LAWKS! IT'S BEEN A LARK AND A HALF!
SNORT!
BUT I NEED TO GET HOME BEFORE MY GRANDFATHER STARTS TO WORRY... SO PERHAPS WE SHOULD SAY GOODB—
OH, MY DEAR, NO NO NO...

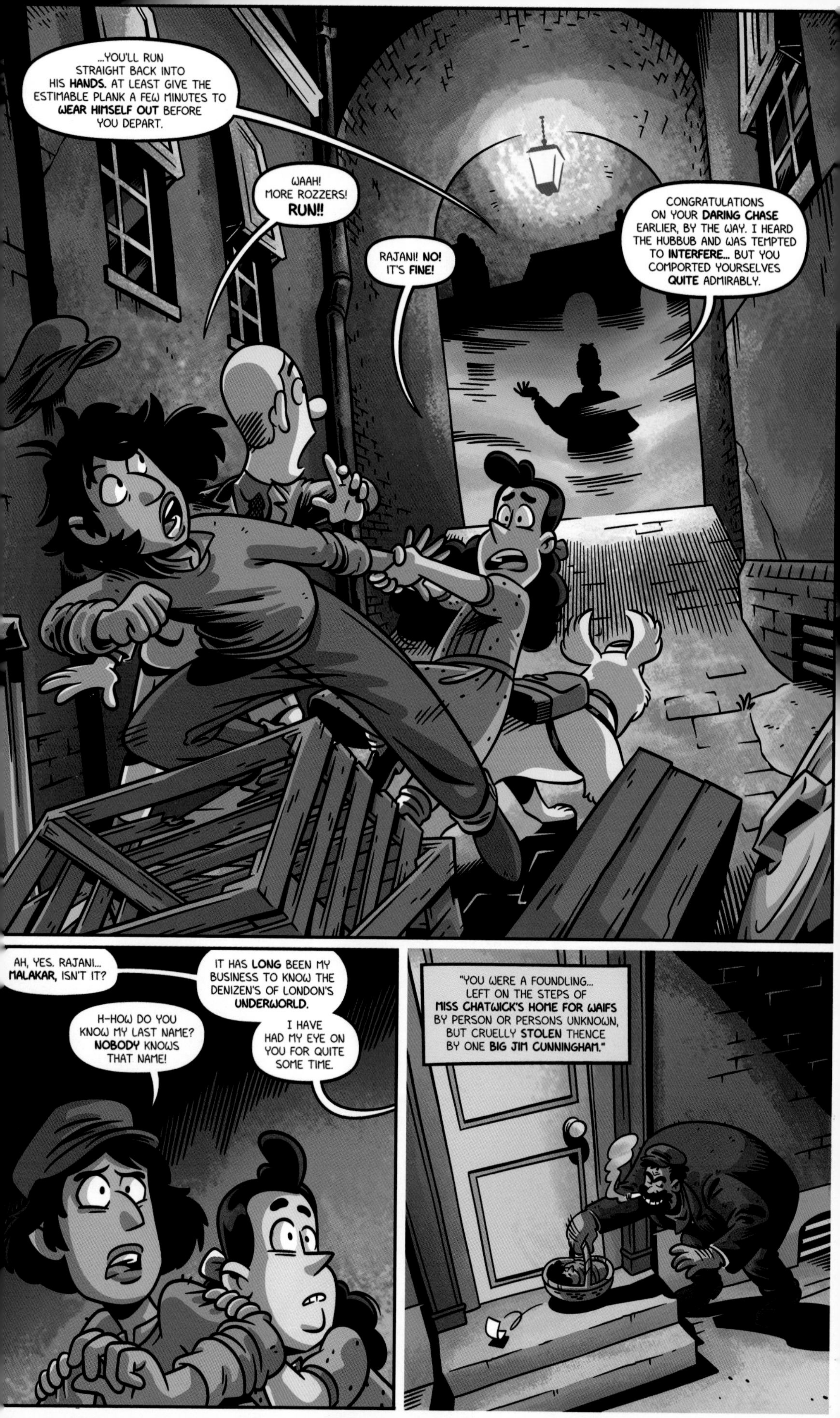
...YOU'LL RUN STRAIGHT BACK INTO HIS **HANDS.** AT LEAST GIVE THE ESTIMABLE PLANK A FEW MINUTES TO **WEAR HIMSELF OUT** BEFORE YOU DEPART.
WAAH! MORE ROZZERS! **RUN!!**
RAJANI! **NO!** IT'S **FINE!**
CONGRATULATIONS ON YOUR **DARING CHASE** EARLIER, BY THE WAY. I HEARD THE HUBBUB AND WAS TEMPTED TO **INTERFERE...** BUT YOU COMPORTED YOURSELVES **QUITE** ADMIRABLY.
AH, YES. RAJANI... **MALAKAR,** ISN'T IT?
H-HOW DO YOU KNOW MY LAST NAME? **NOBODY** KNOWS THAT NAME!
IT HAS **LONG** BEEN MY BUSINESS TO KNOW THE DENIZEN'S OF LONDON'S **UNDERWORLD.**
I HAVE HAD MY EYE ON YOU FOR QUITE SOME TIME.
"YOU WERE A FOUNDLING... LEFT ON THE STEPS OF **MISS CHATWICK'S HOME FOR WAIFS** BY PERSON OR PERSONS UNKNOWN, BUT CRUELLY **STOLEN** THENCE BY ONE **BIG JIM CUNNINGHAM.**"

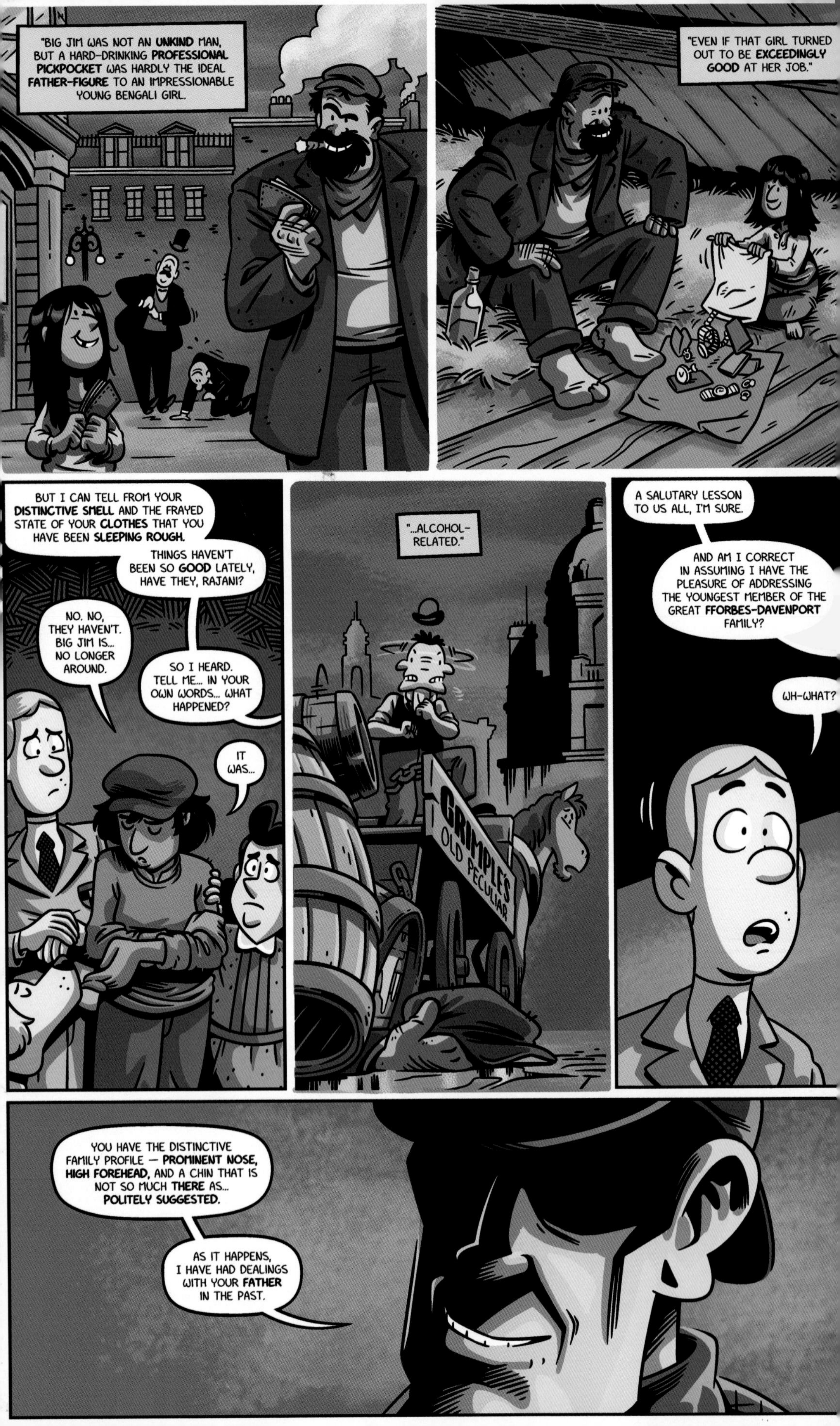
"BIG JIM WAS NOT AN **UNKIND** MAN, BUT A HARD-DRINKING **PROFESSIONAL PICKPOCKET** WAS HARDLY THE IDEAL **FATHER-FIGURE** TO AN IMPRESSIONABLE YOUNG BENGALI GIRL.
"EVEN IF THAT GIRL TURNED OUT TO BE **EXCEEDINGLY GOOD** AT HER JOB."
BUT I CAN TELL FROM YOUR **DISTINCTIVE SMELL** AND THE FRAYED STATE OF YOUR **CLOTHES** THAT YOU HAVE BEEN **SLEEPING ROUGH.**
THINGS HAVEN'T BEEN SO **GOOD** LATELY, HAVE THEY, RAJANI?
NO. NO, THEY HAVEN'T. BIG JIM IS... NO LONGER AROUND.
SO I HEARD. TELL ME... IN YOUR OWN WORDS... WHAT HAPPENED?
IT WAS...
"...ALCOHOL-RELATED."
GRIMPLE'S OLD PECULIAR
A SALUTARY LESSON TO US ALL, I'M SURE.
AND AM I CORRECT IN ASSUMING I HAVE THE PLEASURE OF ADDRESSING THE YOUNGEST MEMBER OF THE GREAT **FFORBES-DAVENPORT** FAMILY?
WH-WHAT?
YOU HAVE THE DISTINCTIVE FAMILY PROFILE — **PROMINENT NOSE, HIGH FOREHEAD,** AND A CHIN THAT IS NOT SO MUCH **THERE** AS... **POLITELY SUGGESTED.**
AS IT HAPPENS, I HAVE HAD DEALINGS WITH YOUR **FATHER** IN THE PAST.

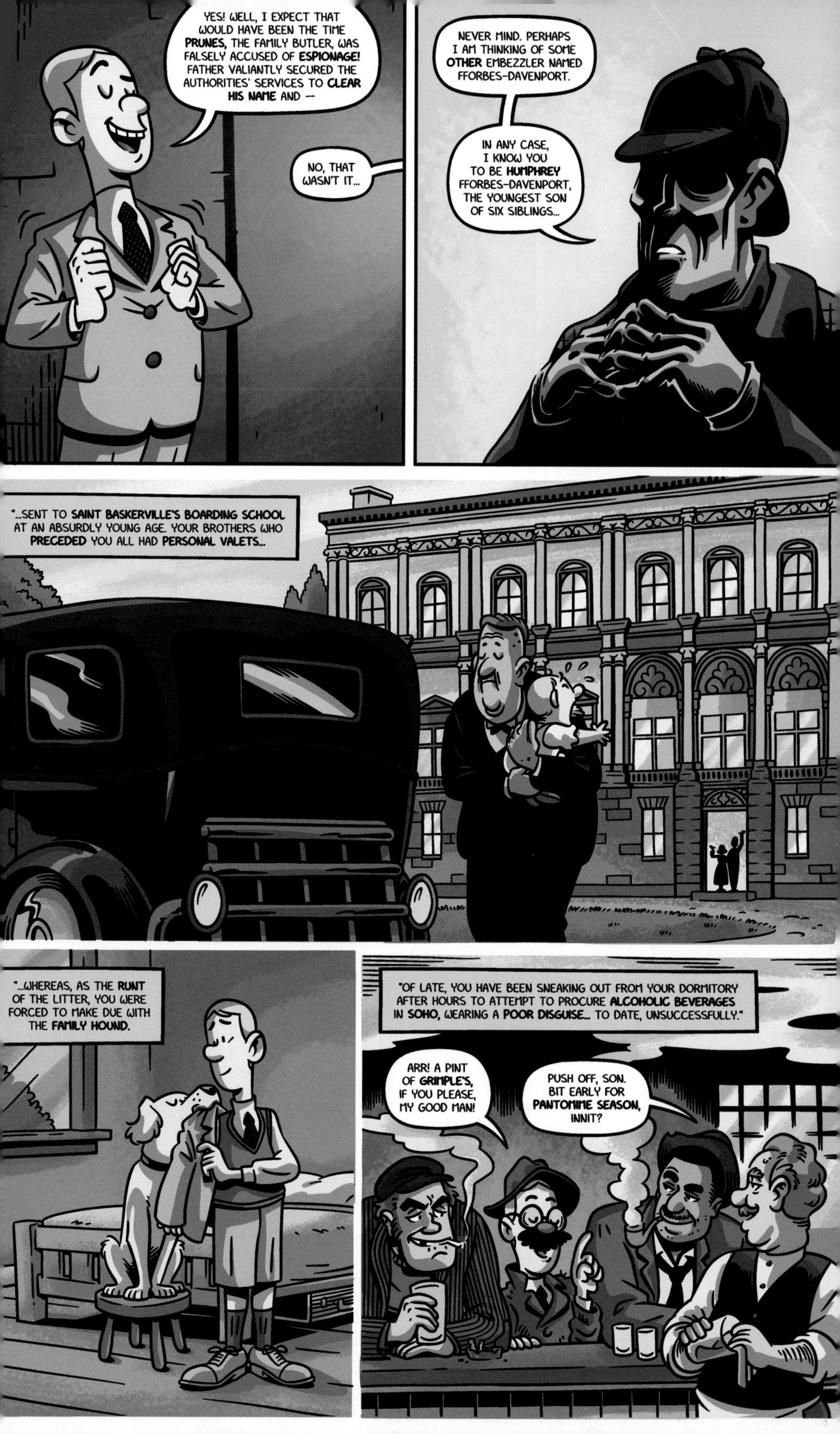
YES! WELL, I EXPECT THAT WOULD HAVE BEEN THE TIME PRUNES, THE FAMILY BUTLER, WAS FALSELY ACCUSED OF ESPIONAGE! FATHER VALIANTLY SECURED THE AUTHORITIES' SERVICES TO CLEAR HIS NAME AND —
NO, THAT WASN'T IT...
NEVER MIND. PERHAPS I AM THINKING OF SOME OTHER EMBEZZLER NAMED FFORBES-DAVENPORT.
IN ANY CASE, I KNOW YOU TO BE HUMPHREY FFORBES-DAVENPORT, THE YOUNGEST SON OF SIX SIBLINGS...
"...SENT TO SAINT BASKERVILLE'S BOARDING SCHOOL AT AN ABSURDLY YOUNG AGE. YOUR BROTHERS WHO PRECEDED YOU ALL HAD PERSONAL VALETS...
"...WHEREAS, AS THE RUNT OF THE LITTER, YOU WERE FORCED TO MAKE DUE WITH THE FAMILY HOUND.
"OF LATE, YOU HAVE BEEN SNEAKING OUT FROM YOUR DORMITORY AFTER HOURS TO ATTEMPT TO PROCURE ALCOHOLIC BEVERAGES IN SOHO, WEARING A POOR DISGUISE... TO DATE, UNSUCCESSFULLY."
ARR! A PINT OF GRIMPLE'S, IF YOU PLEASE, MY GOOD MAN!
PUSH OFF, SON. BIT EARLY FOR PANTOMIME SEASON, INNIT?

HOUND HE MAY BE, BUT **EXCELLENT VALET** HE MOST CERTAINLY IS! **NONE BETTER!** DON'T LISTEN TO THE NASTY MAN, WELLINGTON!

HUMOR ME, SIR... TELL ME HOW YOU KNEW THAT.

APART FROM THE **DAVENPORT CHIN,** YOU MEAN? HIS **CLASS** — AND THE SMELL OF **BOILED CABBAGE** — MADE BOARDING SCHOOL A CERTAINTY. SAWDUST ON HIS BOOTS INDICATE THE LOWER KIND OF **SOHO PUB...** AND YET THERE IS NO **ALCOHOL** ON HIS BREATH. I SMELL ONLY **SPIRIT GUM** FROM A POORLY-ATTACHED **FALSE BEARD.**

AND THE **DOG?**

DESPITE YOUR EVENING'S TREVAILS, YOU ARE STILL **IMMACULATELY GROOMED** — WHICH COULD ONLY BE THE CASE IF YOUR **VALET** WERE ACCOMPANYING YOU AT THIS VERY MOMENT.

OOH! **OOH!** DO ME NOW!

AH, YES — **ABNER ROSENBERG'S** GRANDDAUGHTER... **MOLLY,** IS IT? YOUR GRANDFATHER OWNS THE **SECOND-HAND CLOTHING SHOP** IN BRICK LANE. MANY'S THE TIME I HAVE VISITED THERE TO PROCURE MY **OWN** DISGUISES... IN **DISGUISE,** OF COURSE.

"I RECOGNIZE YOU FROM THE **PHOTOGRAPH** HE DISPLAYS THERE — AND FROM HIS **PROUD DESCRIPTION** OF YOU. PRESUMABLY THE ADULTS IN THE PICTURE WERE YOUR **PARENTS...** NOW DECEASED.

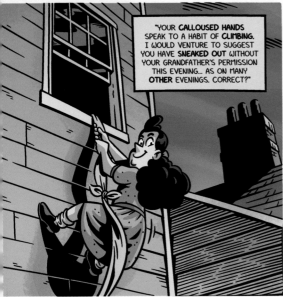

"YOUR **CALLOUSED HANDS** SPEAK TO A HABIT OF **CLIMBING.** I WOULD VENTURE TO SUGGEST YOU HAVE **SNEAKED OUT** WITHOUT YOUR GRANDFATHER'S PERMISSION THIS EVENING... AS ON MANY **OTHER** EVENINGS. CORRECT?"

IN **EVERY DETAIL!** BUT HOW DID YOU KNOW MY PARENTS WERE —?

YOUR GRANDFATHER KEEPS THE WEDDING RING YOUR MOTHER WEARS IN THE PHOTOGRAPH ON HIS **OWN** LITTLE FINGER... KEEPING IT SAFE FOR **YOU** ONE DAY, PRESUMABLY. I DOUBT SHE WOULD PART WITH IT OTHERWISE.

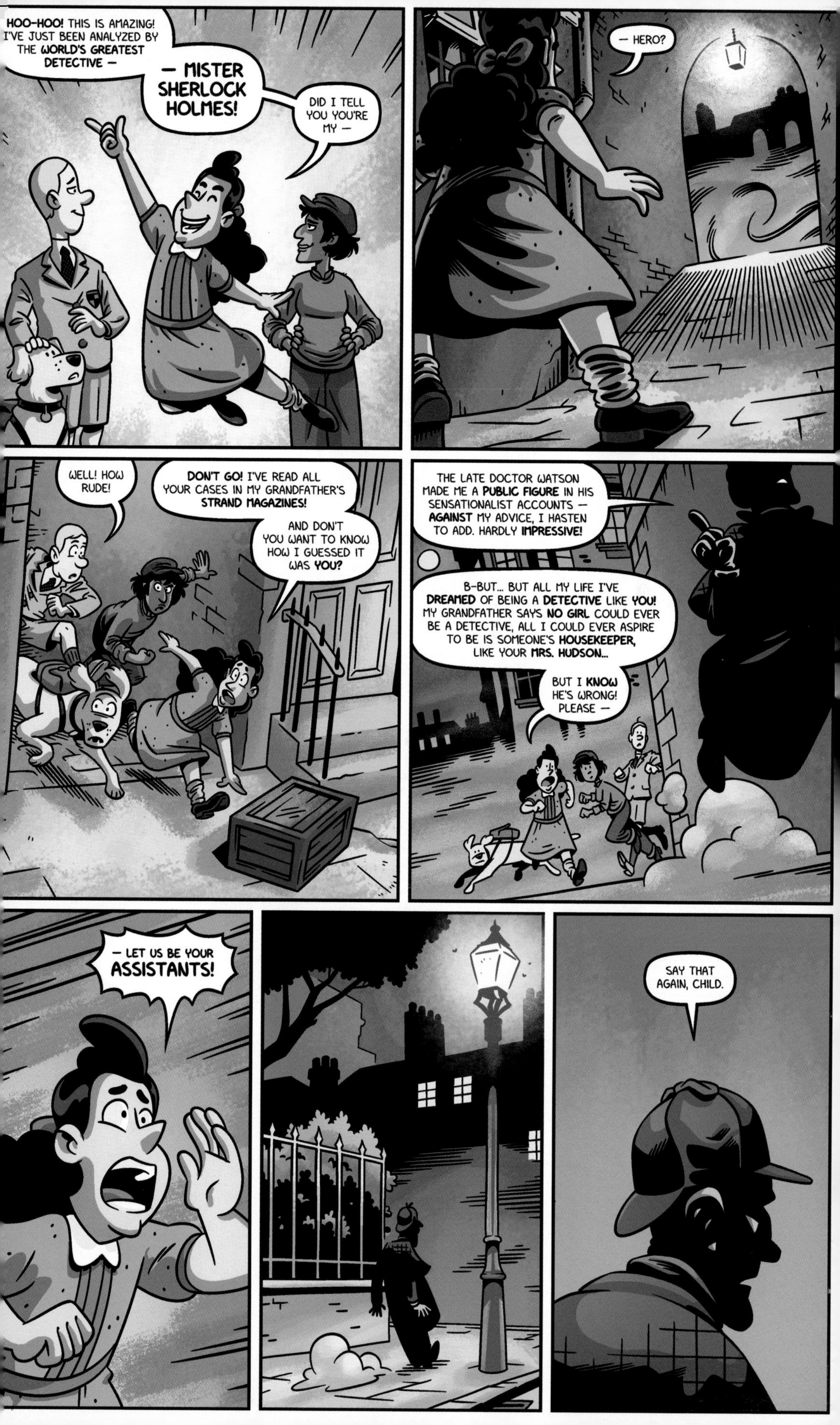

HOO-HOO! THIS IS AMAZING! I'VE JUST BEEN ANALYZED BY THE WORLD'S GREATEST DETECTIVE —
— MISTER SHERLOCK HOLMES!
DID I TELL YOU YOU'RE MY —
— HERO?
WELL! HOW RUDE!
DON'T GO! I'VE READ ALL YOUR CASES IN MY GRANDFATHER'S STRAND MAGAZINES!
AND DON'T YOU WANT TO KNOW HOW I GUESSED IT WAS YOU?
THE LATE DOCTOR WATSON MADE ME A PUBLIC FIGURE IN HIS SENSATIONALIST ACCOUNTS — AGAINST MY ADVICE, I HASTEN TO ADD. HARDLY IMPRESSIVE!
B-BUT... BUT ALL MY LIFE I'VE DREAMED OF BEING A DETECTIVE LIKE YOU! MY GRANDFATHER SAYS NO GIRL COULD EVER BE A DETECTIVE, ALL I COULD EVER ASPIRE TO BE IS SOMEONE'S HOUSEKEEPER, LIKE YOUR MRS. HUDSON...
BUT I KNOW HE'S WRONG! PLEASE —
— LET US BE YOUR ASSISTANTS!
SAY THAT AGAIN, CHILD.

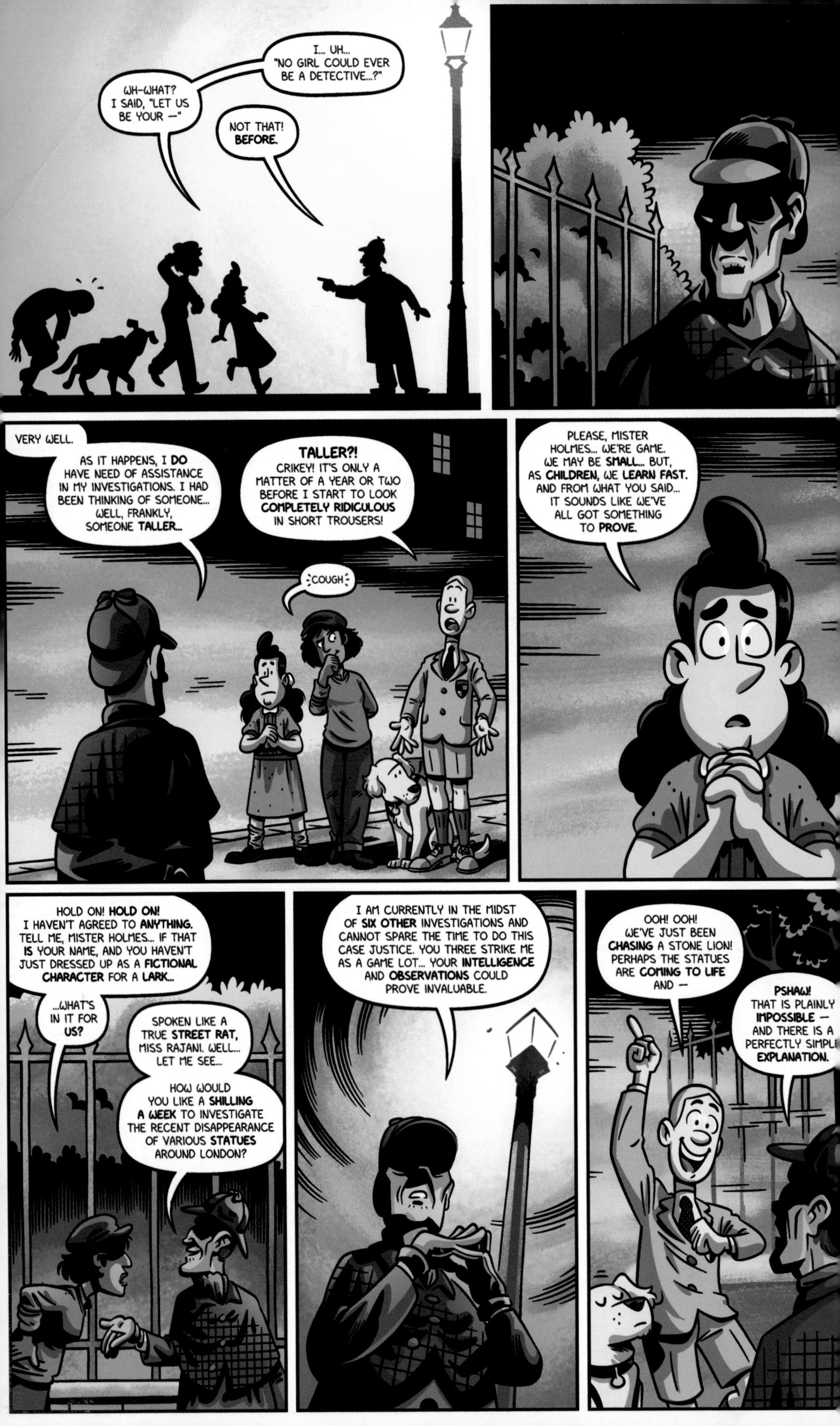
WH-WHAT? I SAID, "LET US BE YOUR —"
I... UH... "NO GIRL COULD EVER BE A DETECTIVE...?"
NOT THAT! BEFORE.
VERY WELL.
AS IT HAPPENS, I DO HAVE NEED OF ASSISTANCE IN MY INVESTIGATIONS. I HAD BEEN THINKING OF SOMEONE... WELL, FRANKLY, SOMEONE TALLER...
TALLER?! CRIKEY! IT'S ONLY A MATTER OF A YEAR OR TWO BEFORE I START TO LOOK COMPLETELY RIDICULOUS IN SHORT TROUSERS!
COUGH
PLEASE, MISTER HOLMES... WE'RE GAME. WE MAY BE SMALL... BUT, AS CHILDREN, WE LEARN FAST. AND FROM WHAT YOU SAID... IT SOUNDS LIKE WE'VE ALL GOT SOMETHING TO PROVE.
HOLD ON! HOLD ON! I HAVEN'T AGREED TO ANYTHING. TELL ME, MISTER HOLMES... IF THAT IS YOUR NAME, AND YOU HAVEN'T JUST DRESSED UP AS A FICTIONAL CHARACTER FOR A LARK...
...WHAT'S IN IT FOR US?
SPOKEN LIKE A TRUE STREET RAT, MISS RAJANI. WELL... LET ME SEE...
HOW WOULD YOU LIKE A SHILLING A WEEK TO INVESTIGATE THE RECENT DISAPPEARANCE OF VARIOUS STATUES AROUND LONDON?
I AM CURRENTLY IN THE MIDST OF SIX OTHER INVESTIGATIONS AND CANNOT SPARE THE TIME TO DO THIS CASE JUSTICE. YOU THREE STRIKE ME AS A GAME LOT... YOUR INTELLIGENCE AND OBSERVATIONS COULD PROVE INVALUABLE.
OOH! OOH! WE'VE JUST BEEN CHASING A STONE LION! PERHAPS THE STATUES ARE COMING TO LIFE AND —
PSHAW! THAT IS PLAINLY IMPOSSIBLE — AND THERE IS A PERFECTLY SIMPLE EXPLANATION.

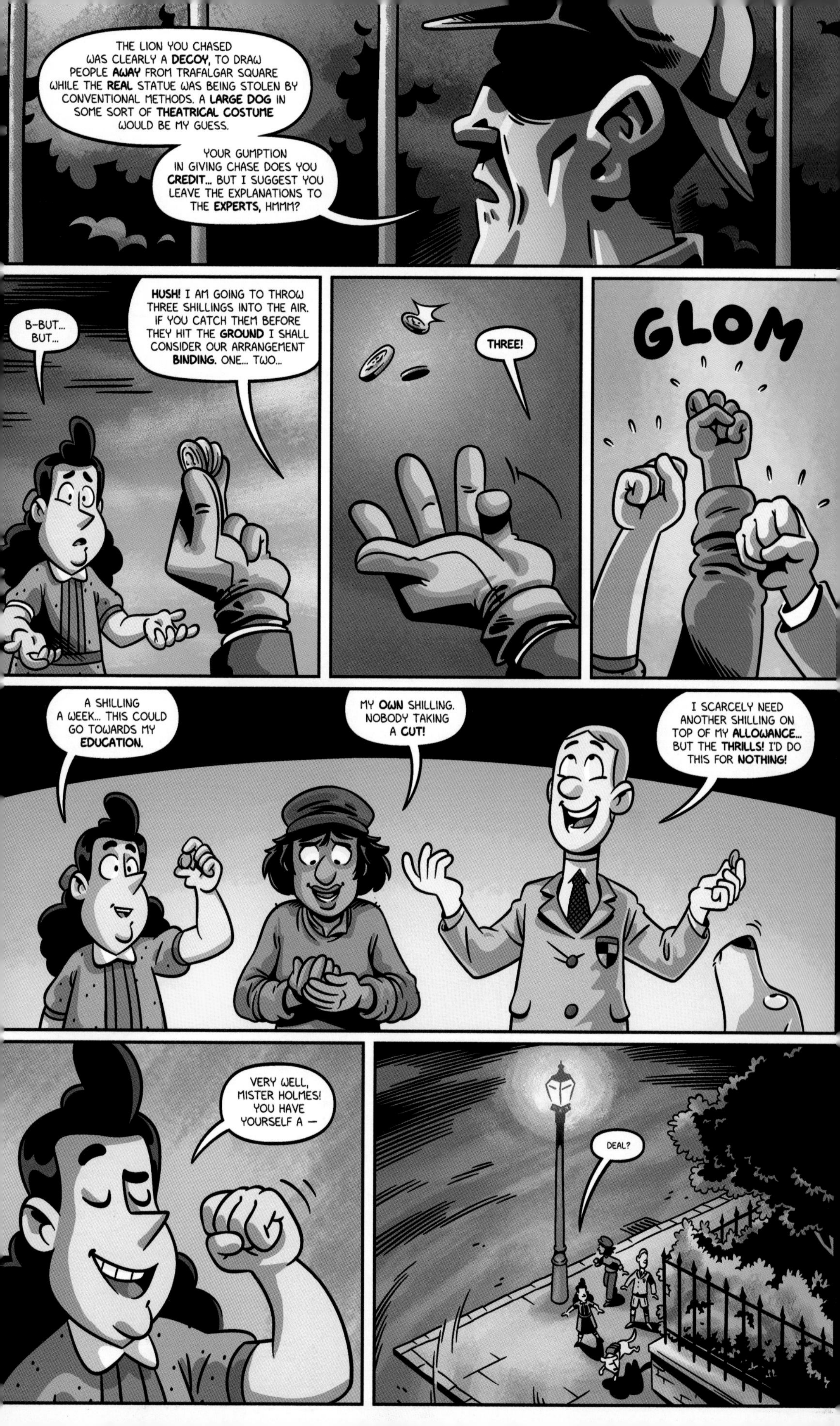
THE LION YOU CHASED WAS CLEARLY A **DECOY,** TO DRAW PEOPLE **AWAY** FROM TRAFALGAR SQUARE WHILE THE **REAL** STATUE WAS BEING STOLEN BY CONVENTIONAL METHODS. A **LARGE DOG** IN SOME SORT OF **THEATRICAL COSTUME** WOULD BE MY GUESS.
YOUR GUMPTION IN GIVING CHASE DOES YOU **CREDIT**... BUT I SUGGEST YOU LEAVE THE EXPLANATIONS TO THE **EXPERTS,** HMMM?
B-BUT... BUT...
HUSH! I AM GOING TO THROW THREE SHILLINGS INTO THE AIR. IF YOU CATCH THEM BEFORE THEY HIT THE **GROUND** I SHALL CONSIDER OUR ARRANGEMENT **BINDING.** ONE... TWO...
THREE!
GLOM
A SHILLING A WEEK... THIS COULD GO TOWARDS MY **EDUCATION.**
MY **OWN** SHILLING. NOBODY TAKING A **CUT!**
I SCARCELY NEED ANOTHER SHILLING ON TOP OF MY **ALLOWANCE**... BUT THE **THRILLS!** I'D DO THIS FOR **NOTHING!**
VERY WELL, MISTER HOLMES! YOU HAVE YOURSELF A —
DEAL?

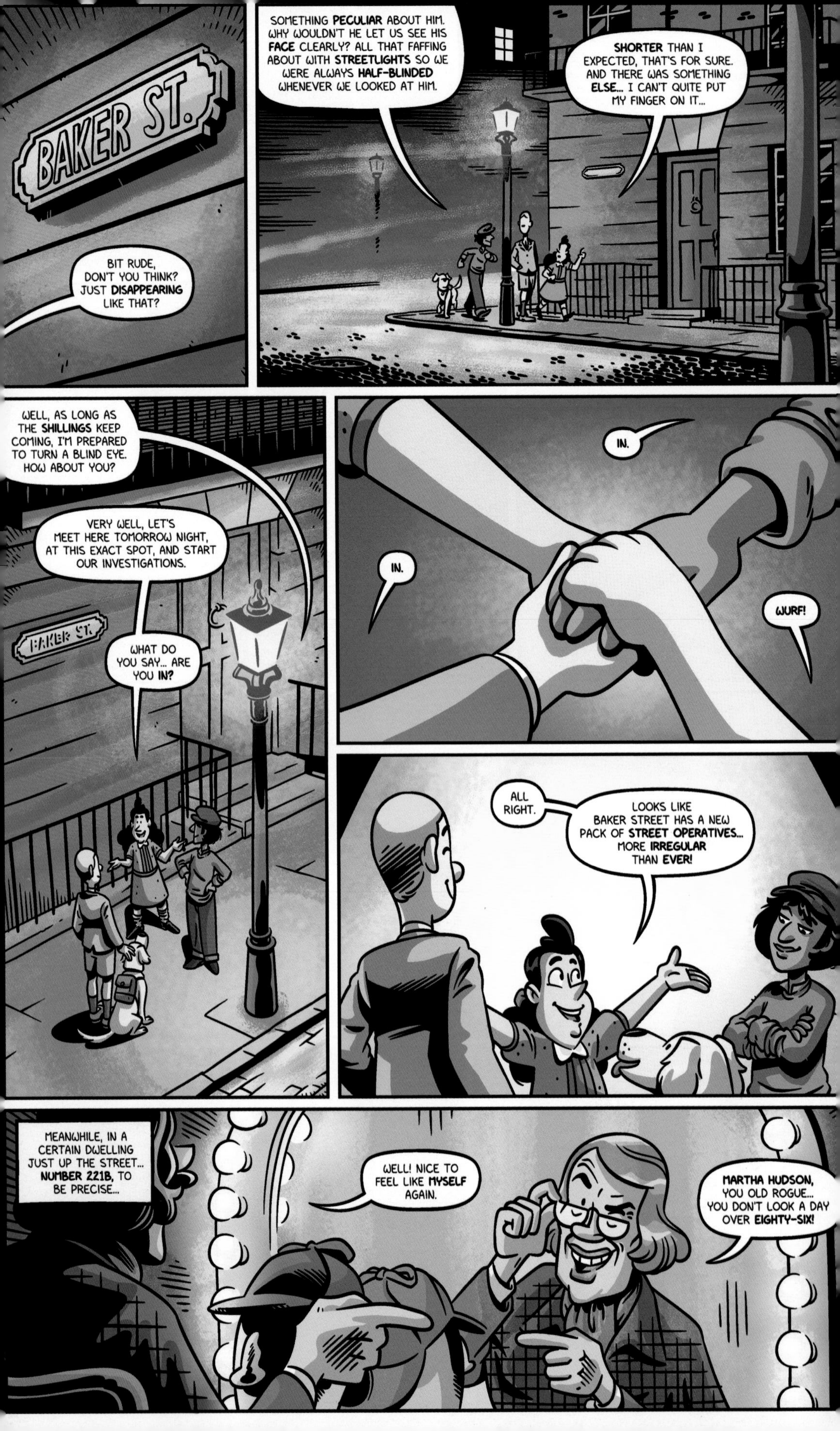
BAKER ST.
BIT RUDE, DON'T YOU THINK? JUST **DISAPPEARING** LIKE THAT?
SOMETHING **PECULIAR** ABOUT HIM. WHY WOULDN'T HE LET US SEE HIS **FACE** CLEARLY? ALL THAT FAFFING ABOUT WITH **STREETLIGHTS** SO WE WERE ALWAYS **HALF-BLINDED** WHENEVER WE LOOKED AT HIM.
SHORTER THAN I EXPECTED, THAT'S FOR SURE. AND THERE WAS SOMETHING **ELSE**... I CAN'T QUITE PUT MY FINGER ON IT...
WELL, AS LONG AS THE **SHILLINGS** KEEP COMING, I'M PREPARED TO TURN A BLIND EYE. HOW ABOUT YOU?
VERY WELL, LET'S MEET HERE TOMORROW NIGHT, AT THIS EXACT SPOT, AND START OUR INVESTIGATIONS.
BAKER ST.
WHAT DO YOU SAY... ARE YOU **IN?**
IN.
IN.
WURF!
ALL RIGHT.
LOOKS LIKE BAKER STREET HAS A NEW PACK OF **STREET OPERATIVES**... MORE **IRREGULAR** THAN **EVER!**
MEANWHILE, IN A CERTAIN DWELLING JUST UP THE STREET... **NUMBER 221B**, TO BE PRECISE...
WELL! NICE TO FEEL LIKE **MYSELF** AGAIN.
MARTHA HUDSON, YOU OLD ROGUE... YOU DON'T LOOK A DAY OVER **EIGHTY-SIX!**

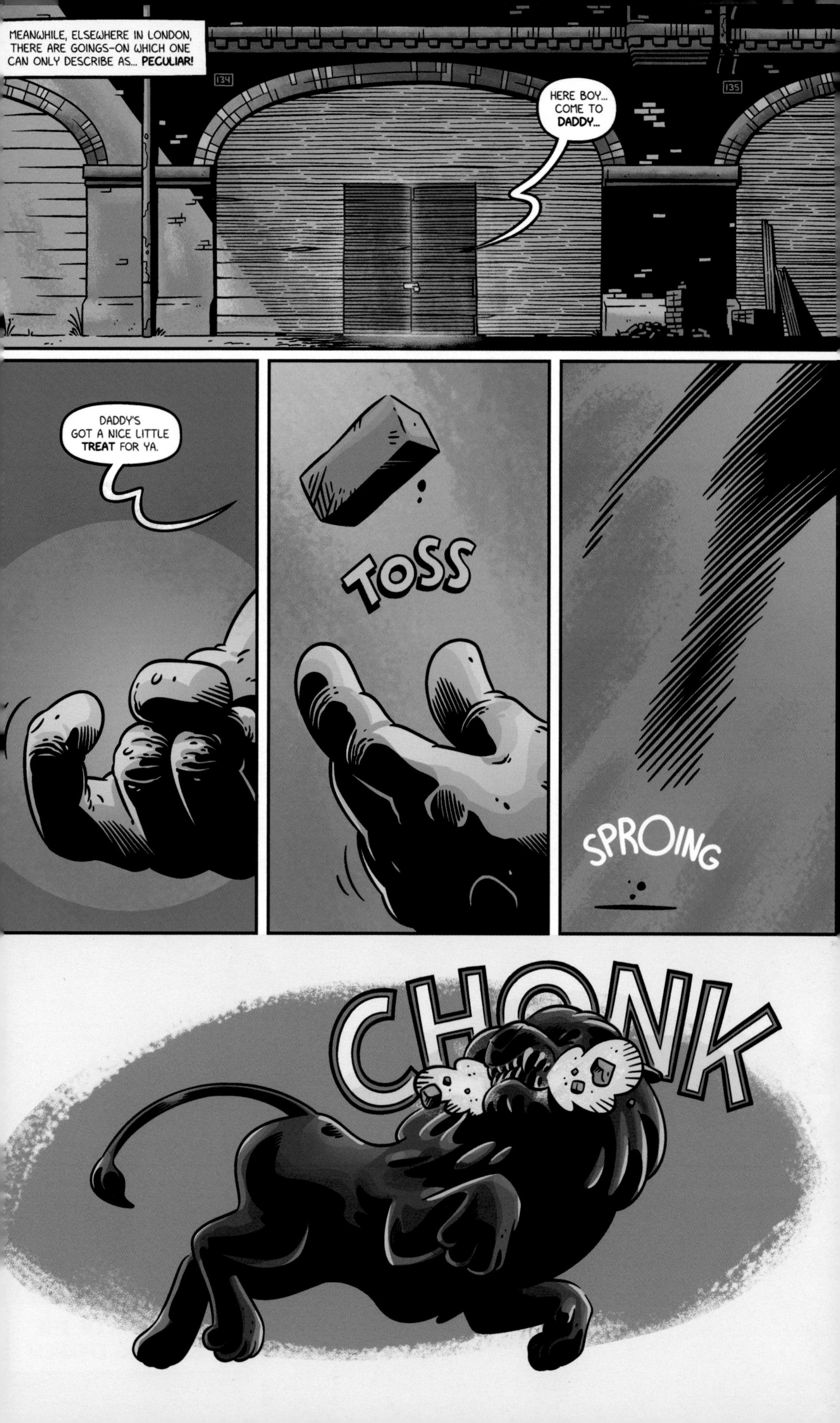
MEANWHILE, ELSEWHERE IN LONDON, THERE ARE GOINGS-ON WHICH ONE CAN ONLY DESCRIBE AS... PECULIAR!
134
135
HERE BOY... COME TO DADDY...
DADDY'S GOT A NICE LITTLE TREAT FOR YA.
TOSS
SPROING
CHONK

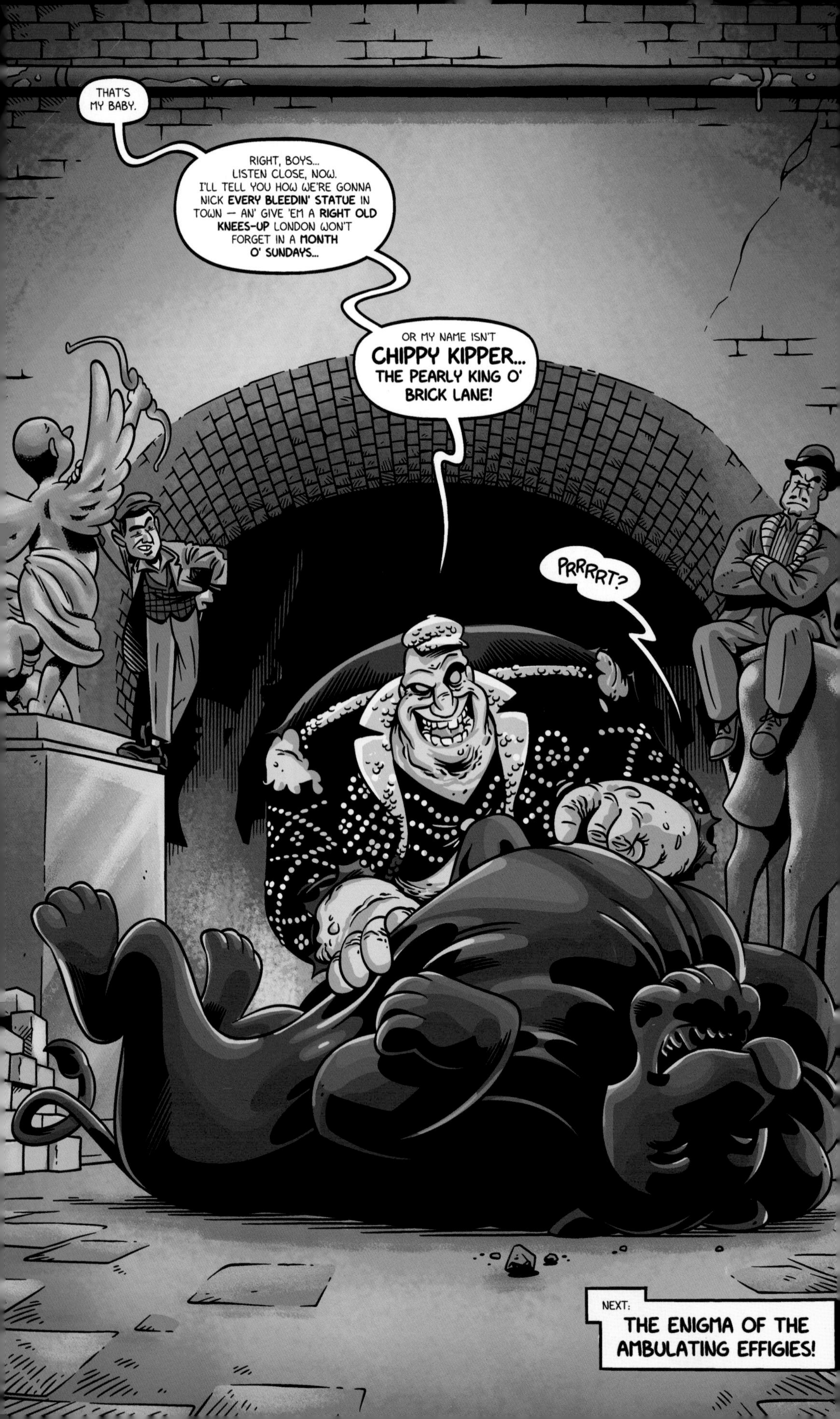
THAT'S MY BABY.
RIGHT, BOYS... LISTEN CLOSE, NOW. I'LL TELL YOU HOW WE'RE GONNA NICK **EVERY BLEEDIN' STATUE** IN TOWN — AN' GIVE 'EM A **RIGHT OLD KNEES-UP** LONDON WON'T FORGET IN A **MONTH O' SUNDAYS...**
OR MY NAME ISN'T **CHIPPY KIPPER... THE PEARLY KING O' BRICK LANE!**
PRRRRT?
NEXT: **THE ENIGMA OF THE AMBULATING EFFIGIES!**

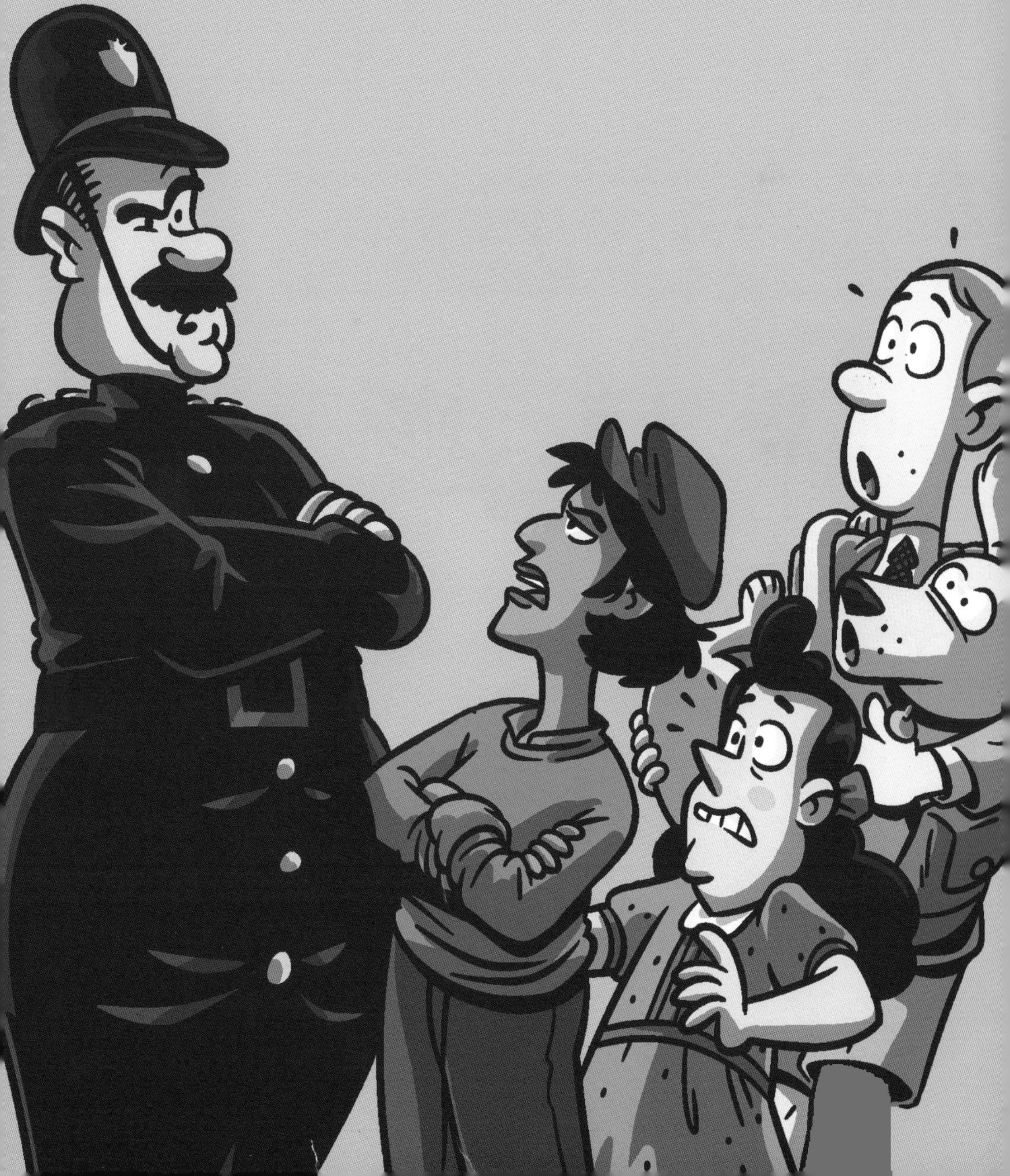

CHAPTER TWO

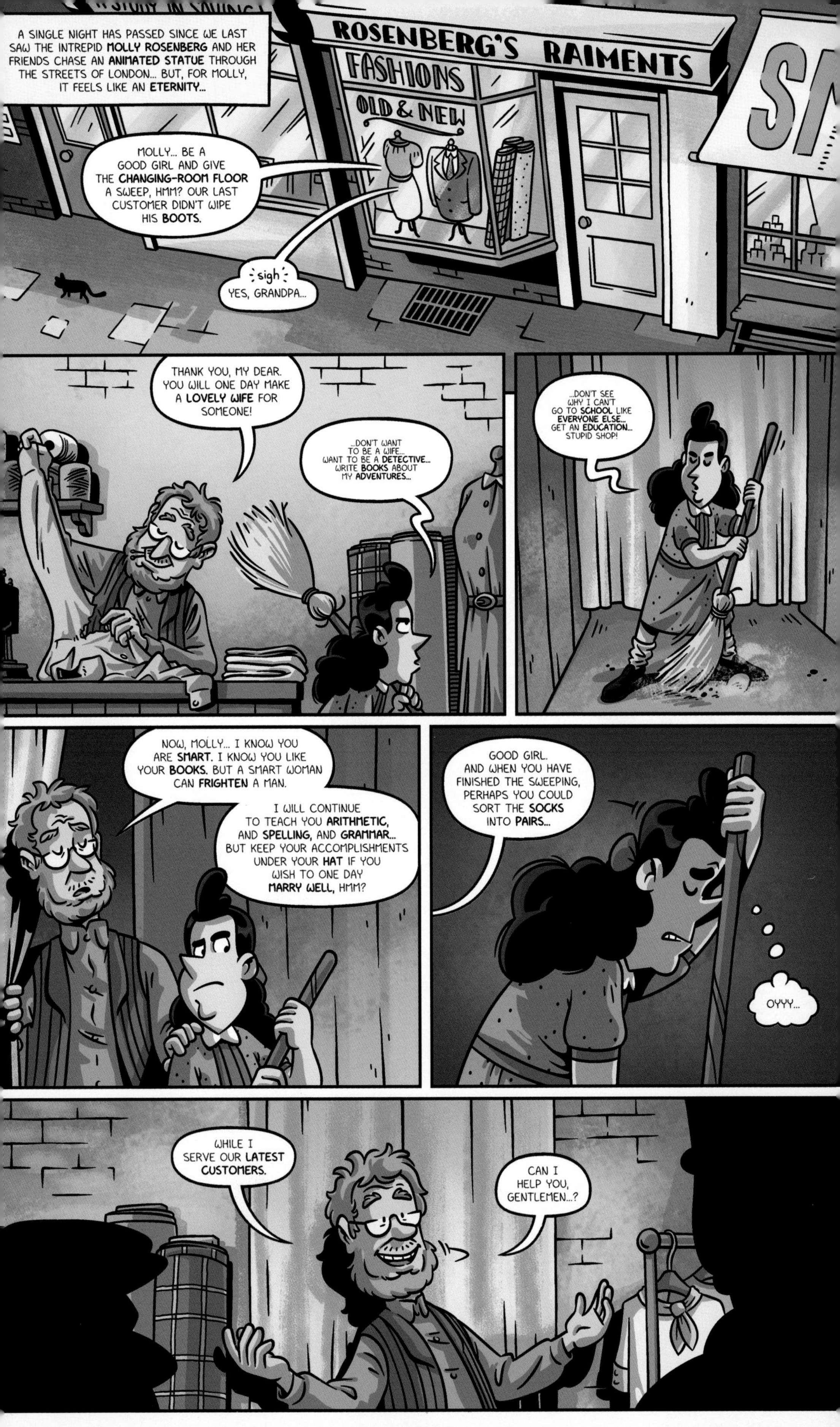

A SINGLE NIGHT HAS PASSED SINCE WE LAST SAW THE INTREPID MOLLY ROSENBERG AND HER FRIENDS CHASE AN ANIMATED STATUE THROUGH THE STREETS OF LONDON... BUT, FOR MOLLY, IT FEELS LIKE AN ETERNITY...
ROSENBERG'S RAIMENTS
FASHIONS
OLD & NEW
MOLLY... BE A GOOD GIRL AND GIVE THE CHANGING-ROOM FLOOR A SWEEP, HMM? OUR LAST CUSTOMER DIDN'T WIPE HIS BOOTS.
sigh
YES, GRANDPA...
THANK YOU, MY DEAR. YOU WILL ONE DAY MAKE A LOVELY WIFE FOR SOMEONE!
...DON'T WANT TO BE A WIFE... WANT TO BE A DETECTIVE... WRITE BOOKS ABOUT MY ADVENTURES...
...DON'T SEE WHY I CAN'T GO TO SCHOOL LIKE EVERYONE ELSE... GET AN EDUCATION... STUPID SHOP!
NOW, MOLLY... I KNOW YOU ARE SMART. I KNOW YOU LIKE YOUR BOOKS. BUT A SMART WOMAN CAN FRIGHTEN A MAN.
I WILL CONTINUE TO TEACH YOU ARITHMETIC, AND SPELLING, AND GRAMMAR... BUT KEEP YOUR ACCOMPLISHMENTS UNDER YOUR HAT IF YOU WISH TO ONE DAY MARRY WELL, HMM?
GOOD GIRL. AND WHEN YOU HAVE FINISHED THE SWEEPING, PERHAPS YOU COULD SORT THE SOCKS INTO PAIRS...
OYYY...
WHILE I SERVE OUR LATEST CUSTOMERS.
CAN I HELP YOU, GENTLEMEN...?

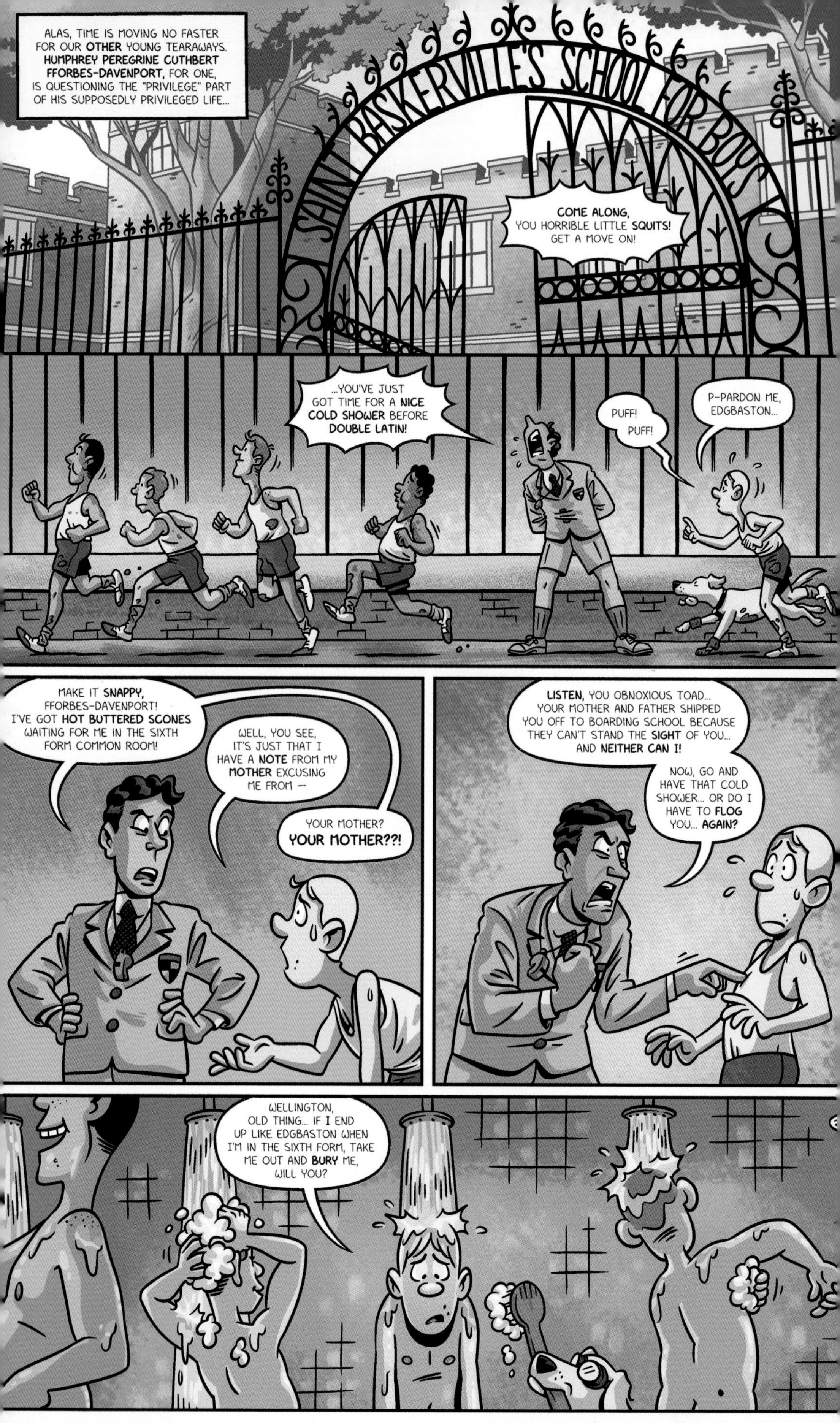
ALAS, TIME IS MOVING NO FASTER FOR OUR **OTHER** YOUNG TEARAWAYS. **HUMPHREY PEREGRINE CUTHBERT FFORBES-DAVENPORT,** FOR ONE, IS QUESTIONING THE "PRIVILEGE" PART OF HIS SUPPOSEDLY PRIVILEGED LIFE...
SAINT BASKERVILLE'S SCHOOL FOR BOYS
COME ALONG, YOU HORRIBLE LITTLE **SQUITS!** GET A MOVE ON!
...YOU'VE JUST GOT TIME FOR A **NICE COLD SHOWER** BEFORE **DOUBLE LATIN!**
PUFF! PUFF!
P-PARDON ME, EDGBASTON...
MAKE IT **SNAPPY,** FFORBES-DAVENPORT! I'VE GOT **HOT BUTTERED SCONES** WAITING FOR ME IN THE SIXTH FORM COMMON ROOM!
WELL, YOU SEE, IT'S JUST THAT I HAVE A **NOTE** FROM MY **MOTHER** EXCUSING ME FROM —
YOUR MOTHER? **YOUR MOTHER??!**
LISTEN, YOU OBNOXIOUS TOAD... YOUR MOTHER AND FATHER SHIPPED YOU OFF TO BOARDING SCHOOL BECAUSE THEY CAN'T STAND THE **SIGHT** OF YOU... AND **NEITHER CAN I!**
NOW, GO AND HAVE THAT COLD SHOWER... OR DO I HAVE TO **FLOG** YOU... **AGAIN?**
WELLINGTON, OLD THING... IF **I** END UP LIKE EDGBASTON WHEN I'M IN THE SIXTH FORM, TAKE ME OUT AND **BURY** ME, WILL YOU?

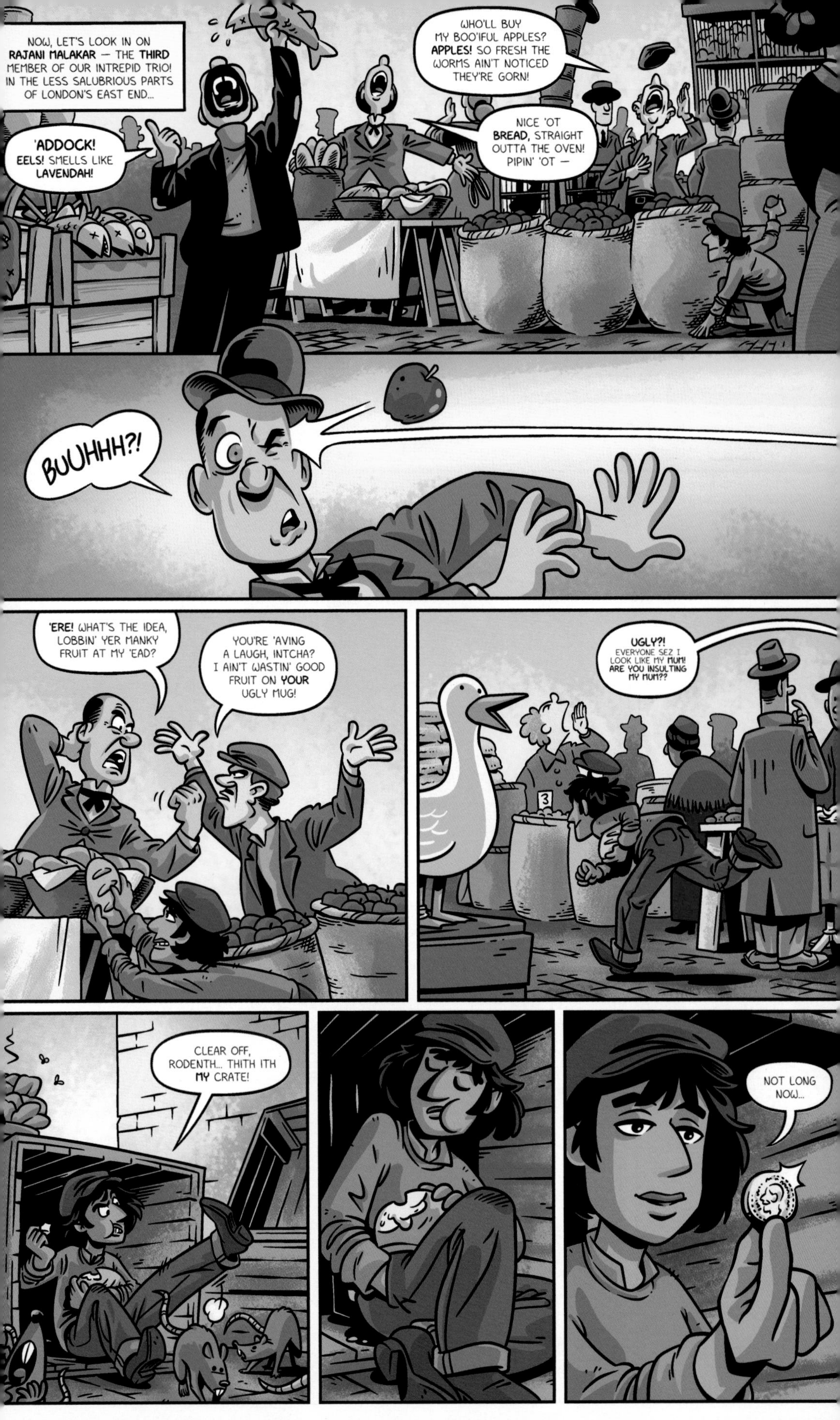
NOW, LET'S LOOK IN ON RAJANI MALAKAR — THE THIRD MEMBER OF OUR INTREPID TRIO! IN THE LESS SALUBRIOUS PARTS OF LONDON'S EAST END...
'ADDOCK! EELS! SMELLS LIKE LAVENDAH!
WHO'LL BUY MY BOO'IFUL APPLES? APPLES! SO FRESH THE WORMS AIN'T NOTICED THEY'RE GORN!
NICE 'OT BREAD, STRAIGHT OUTTA THE OVEN! PIPIN' 'OT —
BUUHHH?!
'ERE! WHAT'S THE IDEA, LOBBIN' YER MANKY FRUIT AT MY 'EAD?
YOU'RE 'AVING A LAUGH, INTCHA? I AIN'T WASTIN' GOOD FRUIT ON YOUR UGLY MUG!
UGLY?! EVERYONE SEZ I LOOK LIKE MY MUM! ARE YOU INSULTING MY MUM??
3
CLEAR OFF, RODENTH... THITH ITH MY CRATE!
NOT LONG NOW...

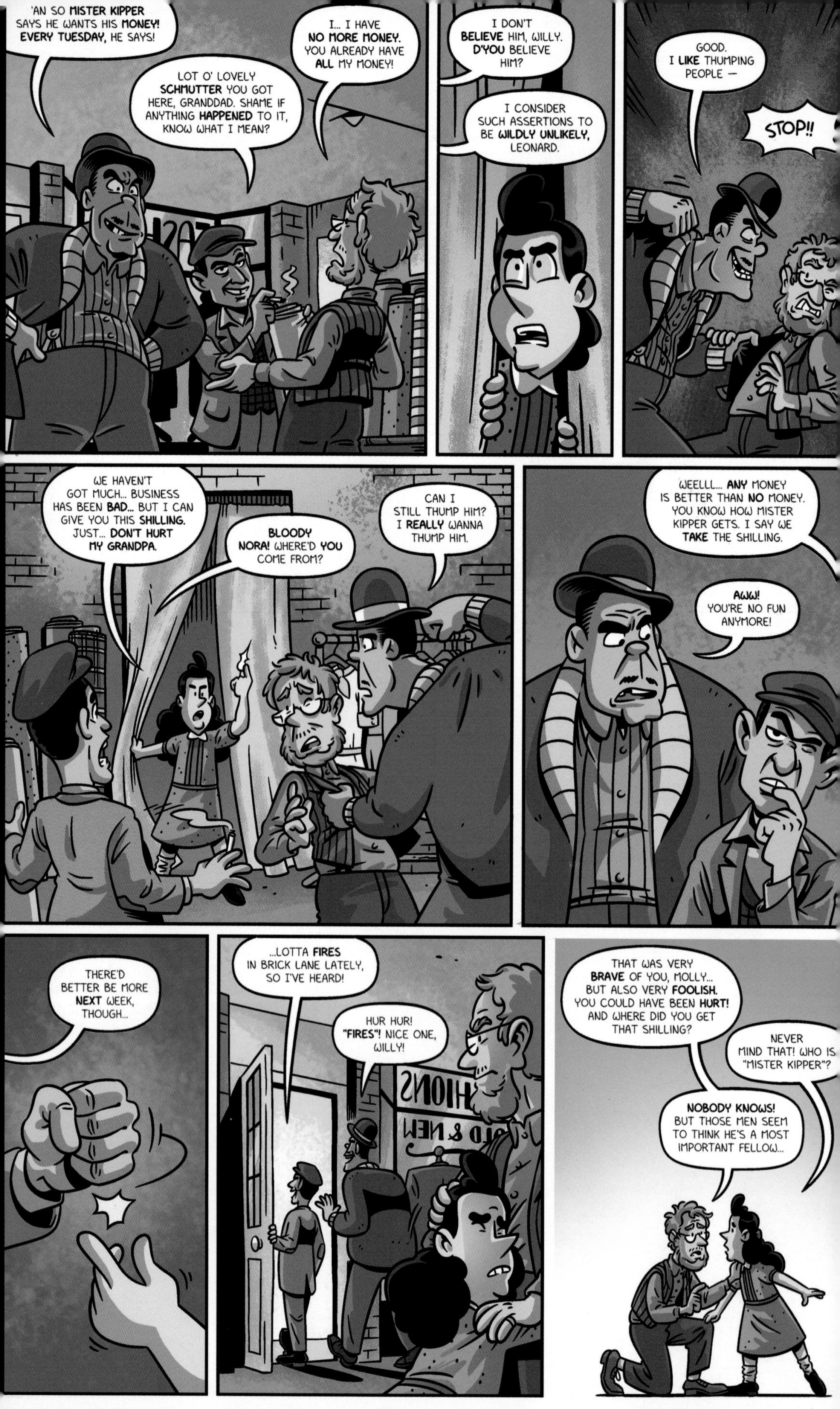
'AN SO MISTER KIPPER SAYS HE WANTS HIS MONEY! EVERY TUESDAY, HE SAYS!
LOT O' LOVELY SCHMUTTER YOU GOT HERE, GRANDDAD. SHAME IF ANYTHING HAPPENED TO IT, KNOW WHAT I MEAN?
I... I HAVE NO MORE MONEY. YOU ALREADY HAVE ALL MY MONEY!
I DON'T BELIEVE HIM, WILLY. D'YOU BELIEVE HIM?
I CONSIDER SUCH ASSERTIONS TO BE WILDLY UNLIKELY, LEONARD.
GOOD. I LIKE THUMPING PEOPLE —
STOP!!
WE HAVEN'T GOT MUCH... BUSINESS HAS BEEN BAD... BUT I CAN GIVE YOU THIS SHILLING. JUST... DON'T HURT MY GRANDPA.
BLOODY NORA! WHERE'D YOU COME FROM?
CAN I STILL THUMP HIM? I REALLY WANNA THUMP HIM.
WEELLL... ANY MONEY IS BETTER THAN NO MONEY. YOU KNOW HOW MISTER KIPPER GETS. I SAY WE TAKE THE SHILLING.
AWW! YOU'RE NO FUN ANYMORE!
THERE'D BETTER BE MORE NEXT WEEK, THOUGH...
...LOTTA FIRES IN BRICK LANE LATELY, SO I'VE HEARD!
HUR HUR! "FIRES"! NICE ONE, WILLY!
THAT WAS VERY BRAVE OF YOU, MOLLY... BUT ALSO VERY FOOLISH. YOU COULD HAVE BEEN HURT! AND WHERE DID YOU GET THAT SHILLING?
NEVER MIND THAT! WHO IS "MISTER KIPPER"?
NOBODY KNOWS! BUT THOSE MEN SEEM TO THINK HE'S A MOST IMPORTANT FELLOW...

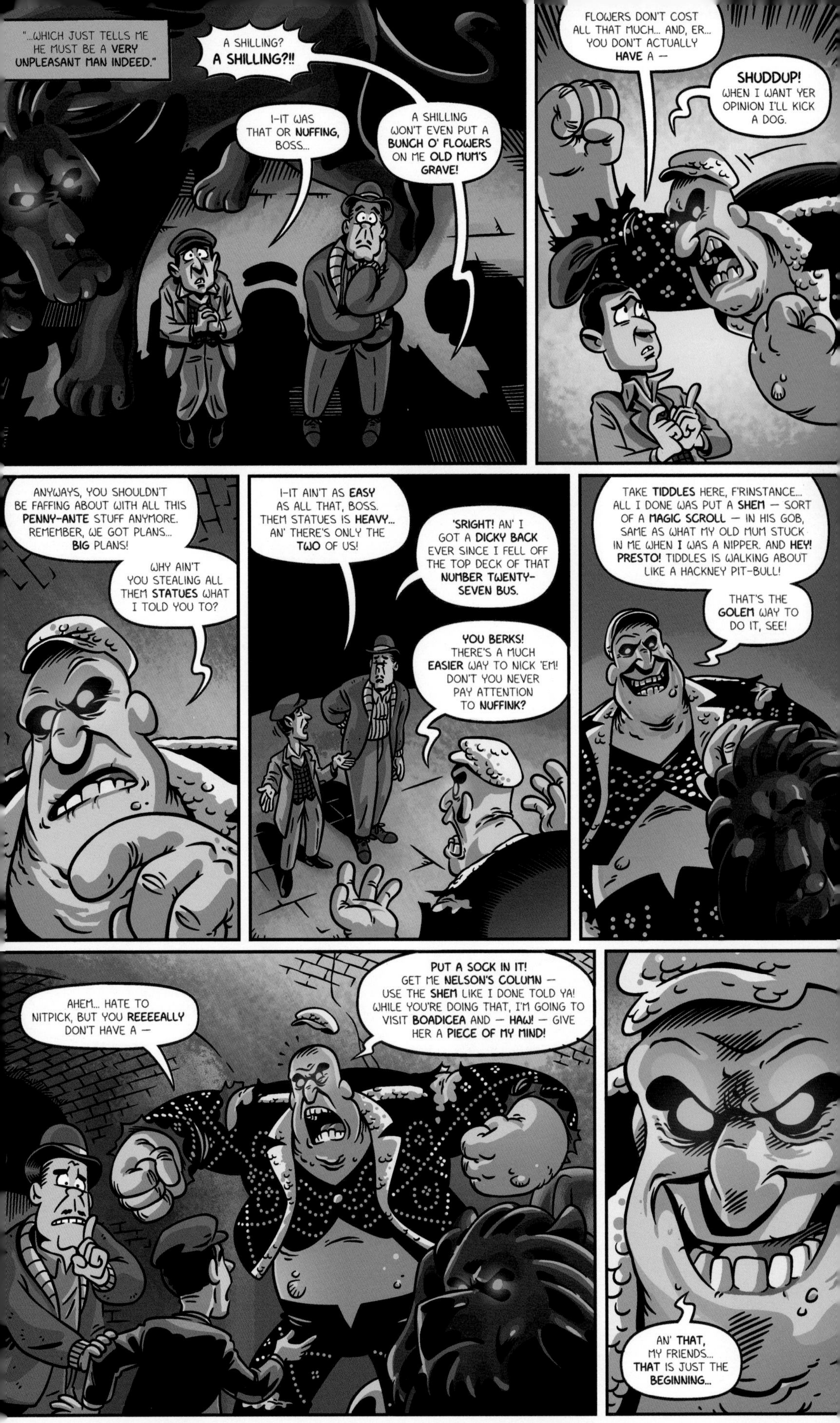
"...WHICH JUST TELLS ME HE MUST BE A VERY UNPLEASANT MAN INDEED."
A SHILLING? A SHILLING?!!
I-IT WAS THAT OR NUFFING, BOSS...
A SHILLING WON'T EVEN PUT A BUNCH O' FLOWERS ON ME OLD MUM'S GRAVE!
FLOWERS DON'T COST ALL THAT MUCH... AND, ER... YOU DON'T ACTUALLY HAVE A —
SHUDDUP! WHEN I WANT YER OPINION I'LL KICK A DOG.
ANYWAYS, YOU SHOULDN'T BE FAFFING ABOUT WITH ALL THIS PENNY-ANTE STUFF ANYMORE. REMEMBER, WE GOT PLANS... BIG PLANS!
WHY AIN'T YOU STEALING ALL THEM STATUES WHAT I TOLD YOU TO?
I-IT AIN'T AS EASY AS ALL THAT, BOSS. THEM STATUES IS HEAVY... AN' THERE'S ONLY THE TWO OF US!
'SRIGHT! AN' I GOT A DICKY BACK EVER SINCE I FELL OFF THE TOP DECK OF THAT NUMBER TWENTY-SEVEN BUS.
YOU BERKS! THERE'S A MUCH EASIER WAY TO NICK 'EM! DON'T YOU NEVER PAY ATTENTION TO NUFFINK?
TAKE TIDDLES HERE, F'RINSTANCE... ALL I DONE WAS PUT A SHEM — SORT OF A MAGIC SCROLL — IN HIS GOB, SAME AS WHAT MY OLD MUM STUCK IN ME WHEN I WAS A NIPPER. AND HEY! PRESTO! TIDDLES IS WALKING ABOUT LIKE A HACKNEY PIT-BULL!
THAT'S THE GOLEM WAY TO DO IT, SEE!
AHEM... HATE TO NITPICK, BUT YOU REEEEALLY DON'T HAVE A —
PUT A SOCK IN IT! GET ME NELSON'S COLUMN — USE THE SHEM LIKE I DONE TOLD YA! WHILE YOU'RE DOING THAT, I'M GOING TO VISIT BOADICEA AND — HAW! — GIVE HER A PIECE OF MY MIND!
AN' THAT, MY FRIENDS... THAT IS JUST THE BEGINNING...

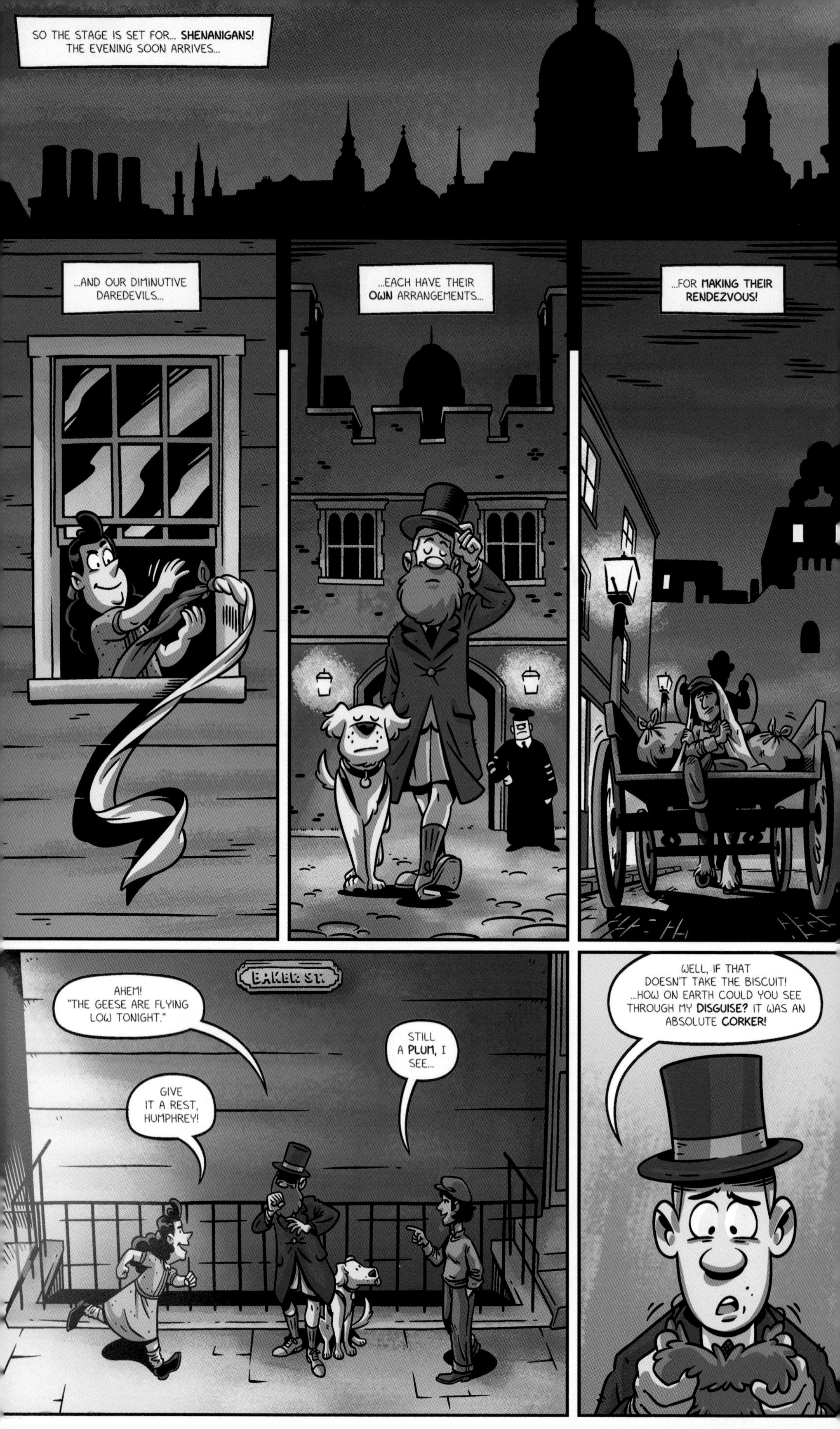
SO THE STAGE IS SET FOR... SHENANIGANS! THE EVENING SOON ARRIVES...
...AND OUR DIMINUTIVE DAREDEVILS...
...EACH HAVE THEIR OWN ARRANGEMENTS...
...FOR MAKING THEIR RENDEZVOUS!
BAKER ST.
AHEM! "THE GEESE ARE FLYING LOW TONIGHT."
GIVE IT A REST, HUMPHREY!
STILL A PLUM, I SEE...
WELL, IF THAT DOESN'T TAKE THE BISCUIT! ...HOW ON EARTH COULD YOU SEE THROUGH MY DISGUISE? IT WAS AN ABSOLUTE CORKER!

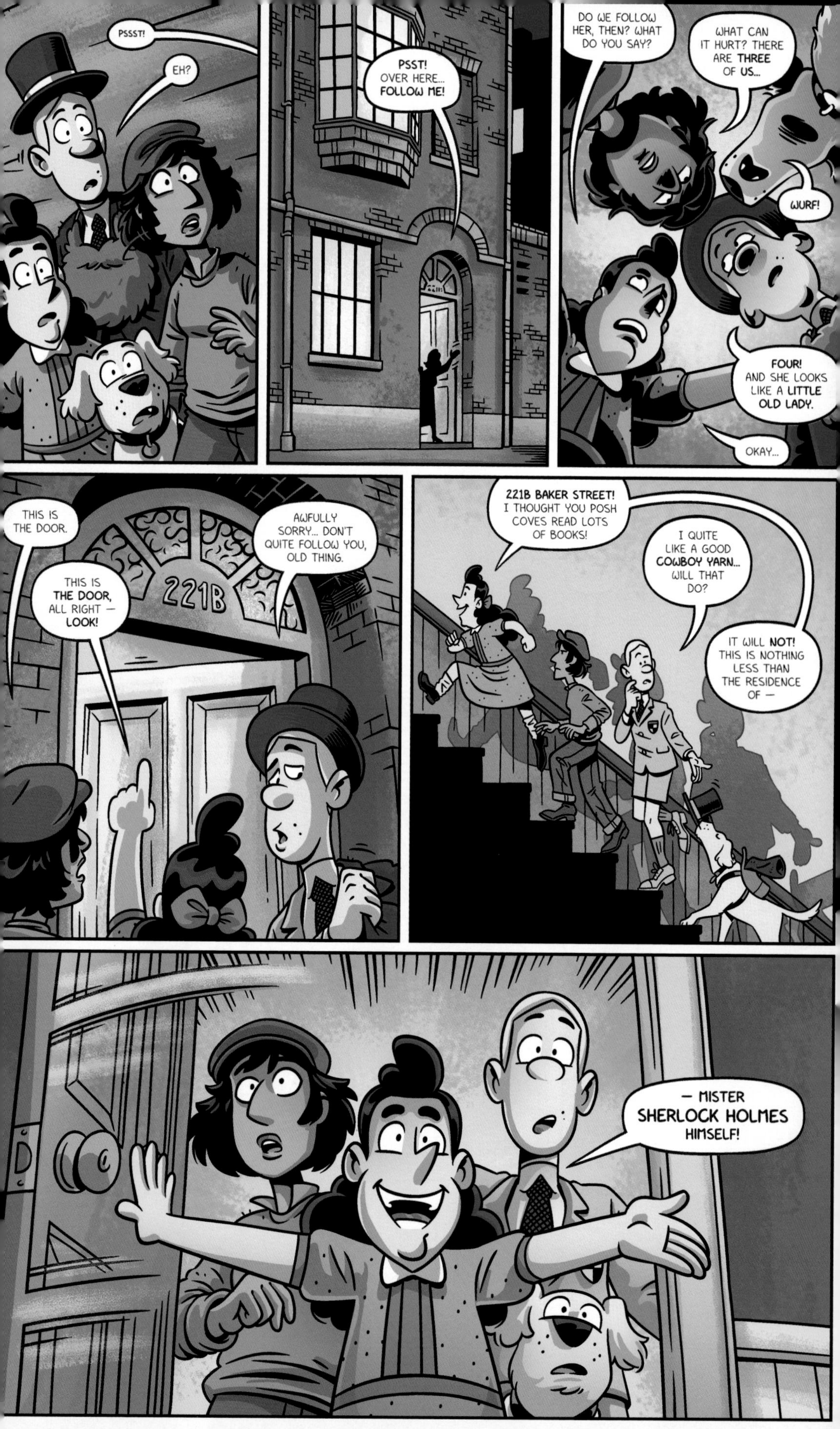
PSSST!
EH?
PSST! OVER HERE... FOLLOW ME!
DO WE FOLLOW HER, THEN? WHAT DO YOU SAY?
WHAT CAN IT HURT? THERE ARE THREE OF US...
WURF!
FOUR! AND SHE LOOKS LIKE A LITTLE OLD LADY.
OKAY...
THIS IS THE DOOR.
THIS IS THE DOOR, ALL RIGHT — LOOK!
221B
AWFULLY SORRY... DON'T QUITE FOLLOW YOU, OLD THING.
221B BAKER STREET! I THOUGHT YOU POSH COVES READ LOTS OF BOOKS!
I QUITE LIKE A GOOD COWBOY YARN... WILL THAT DO?
IT WILL NOT! THIS IS NOTHING LESS THAN THE RESIDENCE OF —
— MISTER SHERLOCK HOLMES HIMSELF!

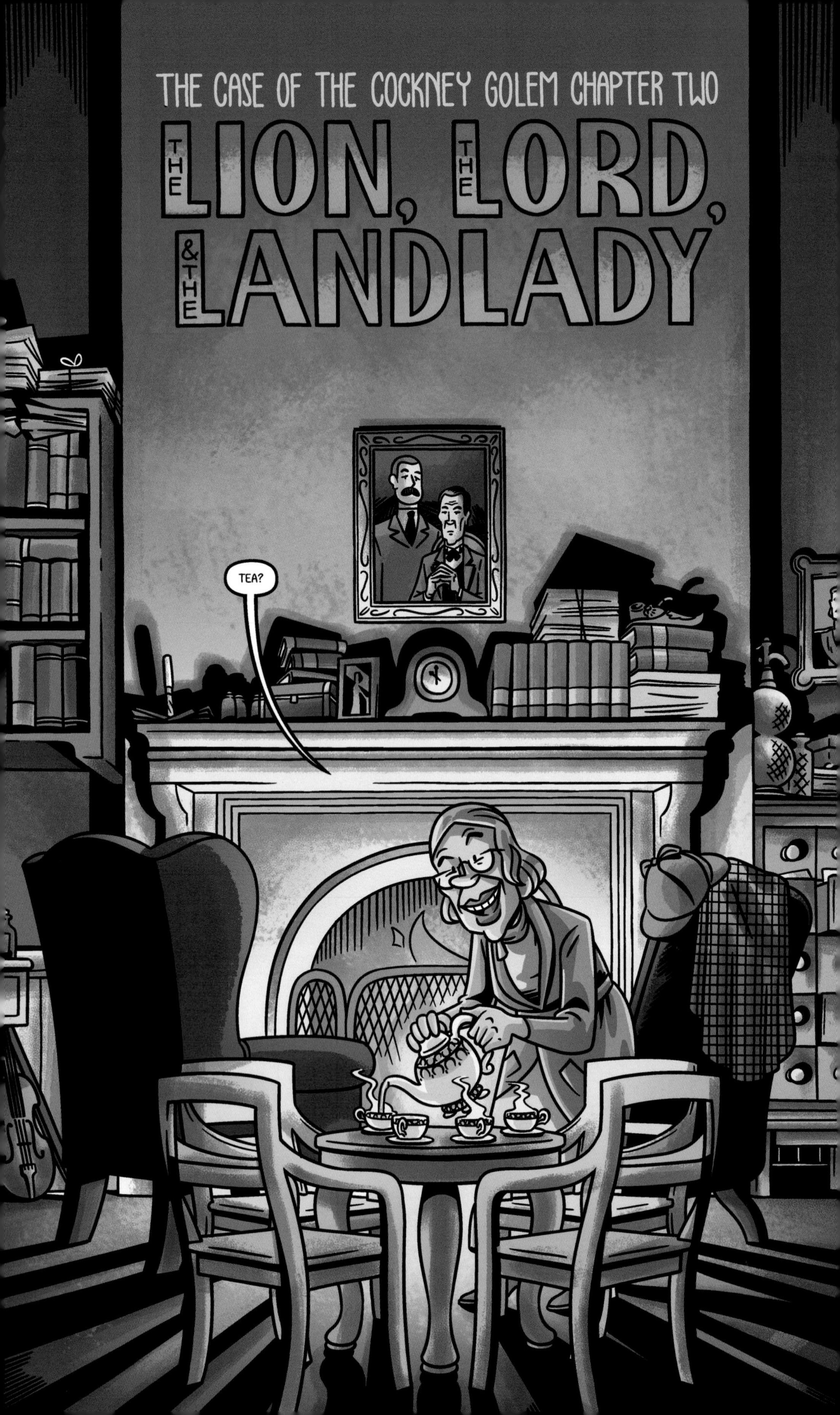
THE CASE OF THE COCKNEY GOLEM CHAPTER TWO
THE LION, THE LORD, & THE LANDLADY
TEA?

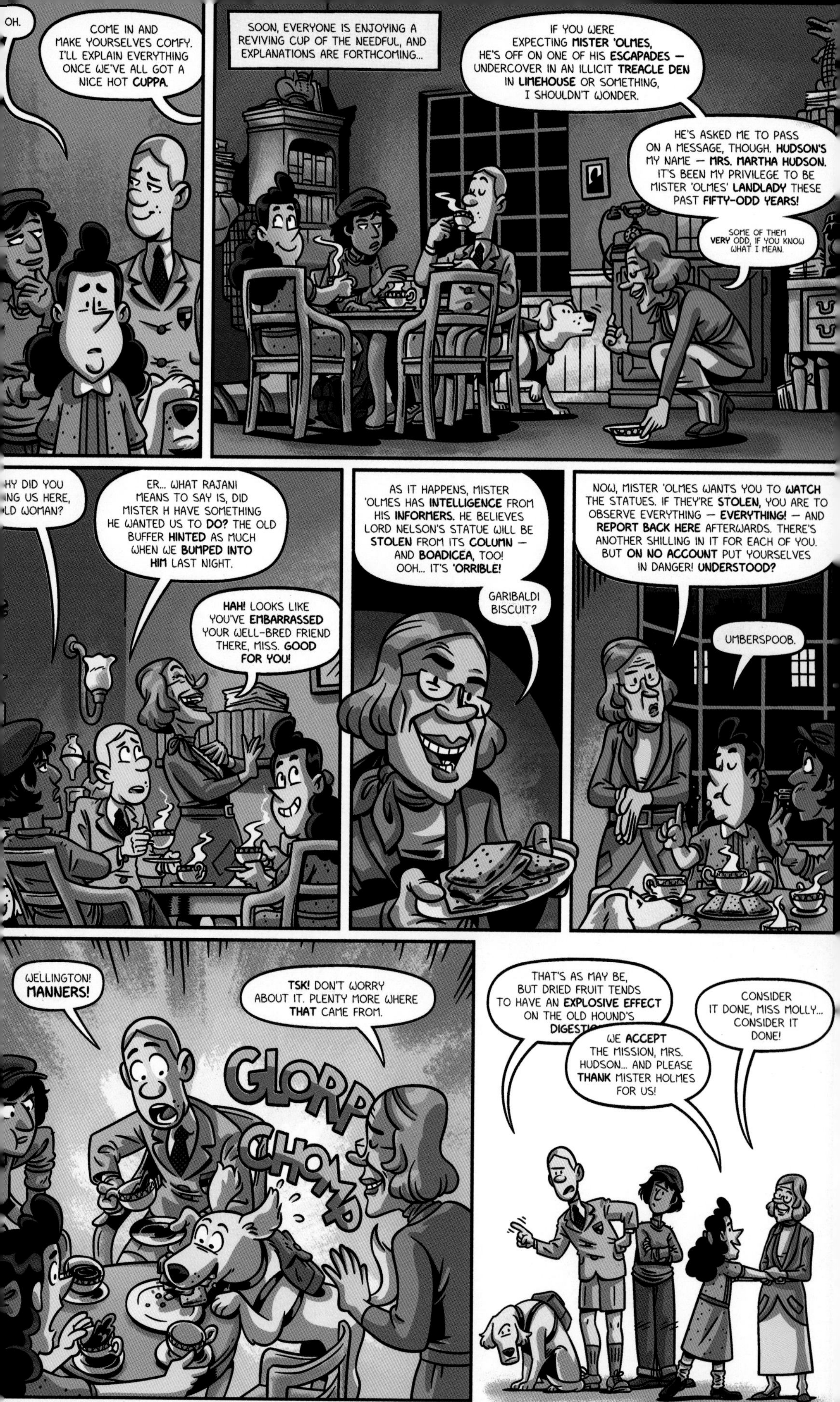
OH.
COME IN AND MAKE YOURSELVES COMFY. I'LL EXPLAIN EVERYTHING ONCE WE'VE ALL GOT A NICE HOT **CUPPA.**
SOON, EVERYONE IS ENJOYING A REVIVING CUP OF THE NEEDFUL, AND EXPLANATIONS ARE FORTHCOMING...
IF YOU WERE EXPECTING **MISTER 'OLMES,** HE'S OFF ON ONE OF HIS **ESCAPADES** — UNDERCOVER IN AN ILLICIT **TREACLE DEN** IN **LIMEHOUSE** OR SOMETHING, I SHOULDN'T WONDER.
HE'S ASKED ME TO PASS ON A MESSAGE, THOUGH. **HUDSON'S** MY NAME — **MRS. MARTHA HUDSON.** IT'S BEEN MY PRIVILEGE TO BE MISTER 'OLMES' **LANDLADY** THESE PAST **FIFTY-ODD YEARS!**
SOME OF THEM **VERY** ODD, IF YOU KNOW WHAT I MEAN.
HY DID YOU NG US HERE, LD WOMAN?
ER... WHAT RAJANI MEANS TO SAY IS, DID MISTER H HAVE SOMETHING HE WANTED US TO **DO?** THE OLD BUFFER **HINTED** AS MUCH WHEN WE **BUMPED INTO HIM** LAST NIGHT.
HAH! LOOKS LIKE YOU'VE **EMBARRASSED** YOUR WELL-BRED FRIEND THERE, MISS. **GOOD FOR YOU!**
AS IT HAPPENS, MISTER 'OLMES HAS **INTELLIGENCE** FROM HIS **INFORMERS.** HE BELIEVES LORD NELSON'S STATUE WILL BE **STOLEN** FROM ITS **COLUMN** — AND **BOADICEA,** TOO! OOH... IT'S **'ORRIBLE!**
GARIBALDI BISCUIT?
NOW, MISTER 'OLMES WANTS YOU TO **WATCH** THE STATUES. IF THEY'RE **STOLEN,** YOU ARE TO OBSERVE EVERYTHING — **EVERYTHING!** — AND **REPORT BACK HERE** AFTERWARDS. THERE'S ANOTHER SHILLING IN IT FOR EACH OF YOU. BUT **ON NO ACCOUNT** PUT YOURSELVES IN DANGER! **UNDERSTOOD?**
UMBERSPOOB.
WELLINGTON! **MANNERS!**
TSK! DON'T WORRY ABOUT IT. PLENTY MORE WHERE **THAT** CAME FROM.
GLORP
CHOMP
THAT'S AS MAY BE, BUT DRIED FRUIT TENDS TO HAVE AN **EXPLOSIVE EFFECT** ON THE OLD HOUND'S **DIGESTI**
WE **ACCEPT** THE MISSION, MRS. HUDSON... AND PLEASE **THANK** MISTER HOLMES FOR US!
CONSIDER IT DONE, MISS MOLLY... CONSIDER IT DONE!

AND SO OUR HEROES DIVIDE THE DUTIES BETWEEN THEM — MOLLY AND WELLINGTON HEADING FOR WESTMINSTER BRIDGE TO SPY ON BOADICEA...

BE CAREFUL!

YOU TOO, OLD THING!

DON'T WORRY, I'LL SEE POSH BOY DOESN'T GET BROKEN!

...WHILE RAJANI AND HUMPHREY HEAD BACK TO THE SCENE OF THE PREVIOUS NIGHT'S ADVENTURE!

...IT'S JUST THAT, WHEN WELLINGTON EATS CURRANTS, HE LETS LOOSE THE FOULEST, MOST TOXIC —

SHUT IT, YOU PLUM... WE'RE HERE!

YOINK! HERE THEY COME — GET BACK THERE!

EEP!

I TRUST WE'RE NOT BEING FOLLOWED, LEONARD.

DIDN'T SEE NUFFINK.

DELIGHTED TO HEAR IT. ALLOW ME TO ATTACH MYSELF TO THE APPARATUS WHILE YOU DO THE NECESSARY.

NO WORRIES.

YES, INDEED, LEONARD... IN A FEW MINUTES, YOU AND I WILL BE RESPONSIBLE FOR BRINGING BACK TO LIFE —

SQUEEEK
SQUIK SQUIK SQUII
FFFOP JJJ
SSHHSSSCH HHHPP
FF H
SS
SSSSSSI

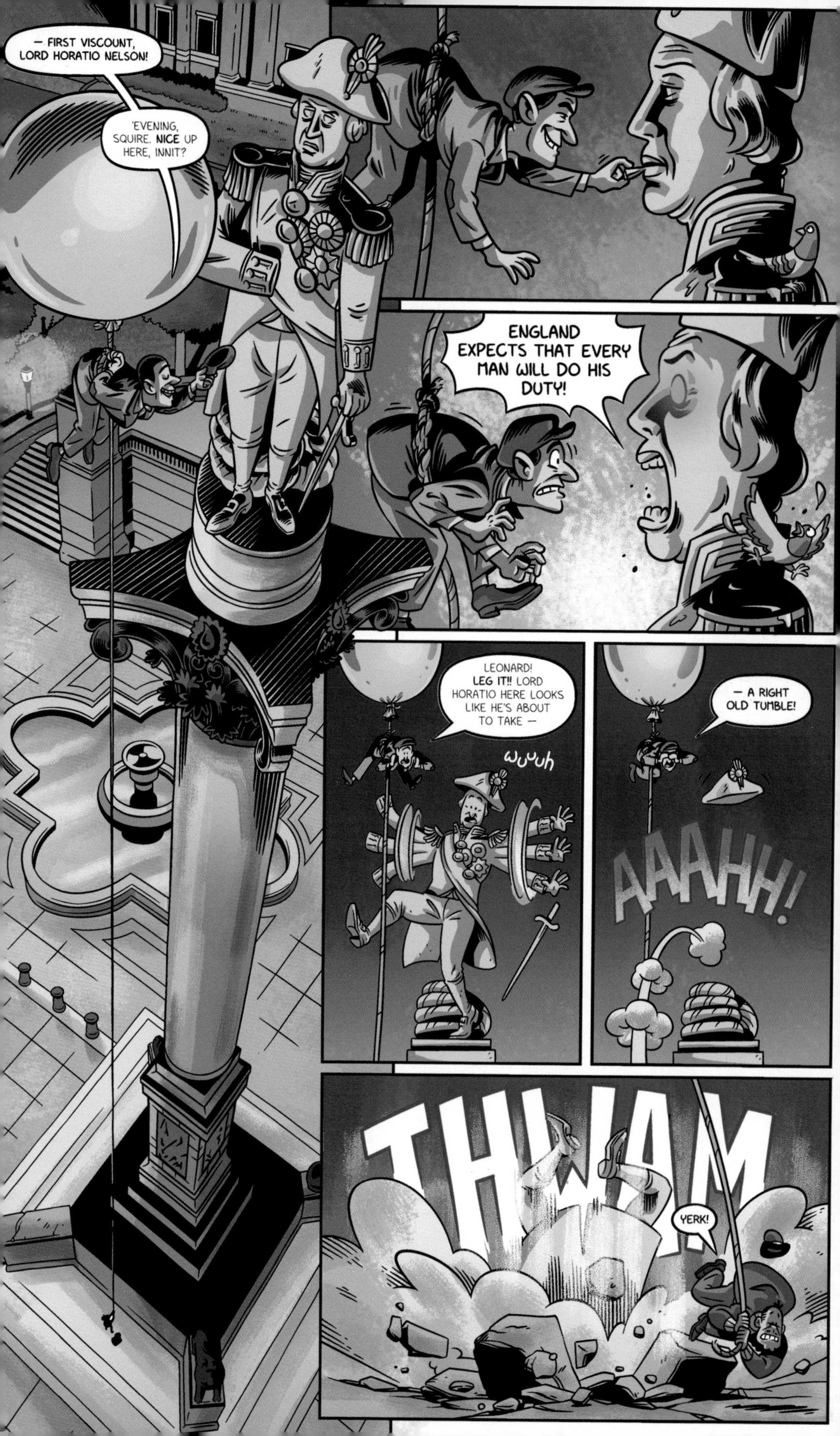
— FIRST VISCOUNT, LORD HORATIO NELSON!
'EVENING, SQUIRE. NICE UP HERE, INNIT?
ENGLAND EXPECTS THAT EVERY MAN WILL DO HIS DUTY!
LEONARD! LEG IT!! LORD HORATIO HERE LOOKS LIKE HE'S ABOUT TO TAKE —
WUUUH
— A RIGHT OLD TUMBLE!
AAAHH!
THWAM
YERK!

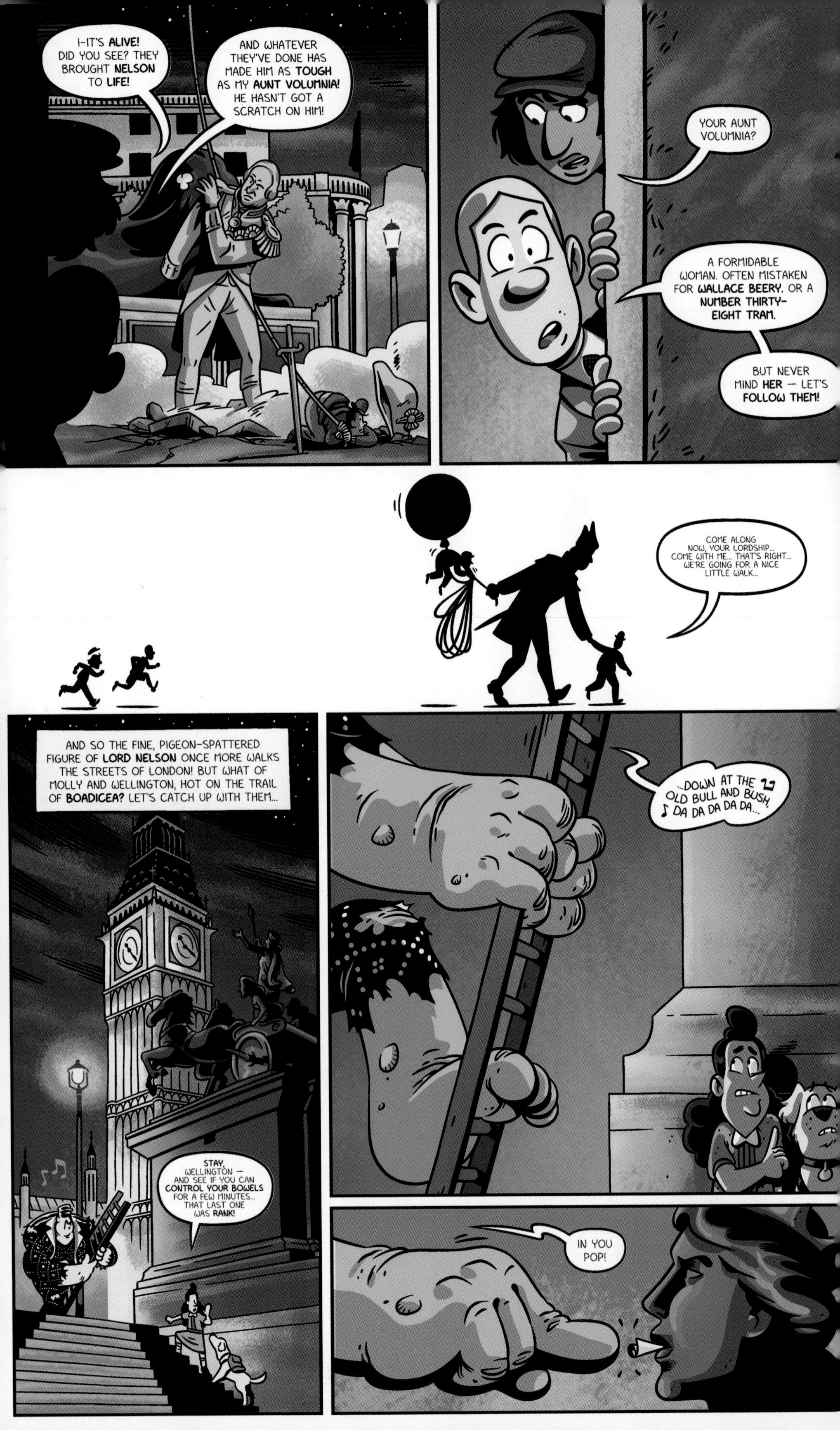
I-IT'S ALIVE! DID YOU SEE? THEY BROUGHT NELSON TO LIFE!
AND WHATEVER THEY'VE DONE HAS MADE HIM AS TOUGH AS MY AUNT VOLUMNIA! HE HASN'T GOT A SCRATCH ON HIM!
YOUR AUNT VOLUMNIA?
A FORMIDABLE WOMAN. OFTEN MISTAKEN FOR WALLACE BEERY. OR A NUMBER THIRTY-EIGHT TRAM.
BUT NEVER MIND HER — LET'S FOLLOW THEM!
COME ALONG NOW, YOUR LORDSHIP... COME WITH ME... THAT'S RIGHT... WE'RE GOING FOR A NICE LITTLE WALK...
AND SO THE FINE, PIGEON-SPATTERED FIGURE OF LORD NELSON ONCE MORE WALKS THE STREETS OF LONDON! BUT WHAT OF MOLLY AND WELLINGTON, HOT ON THE TRAIL OF BOADICEA? LET'S CATCH UP WITH THEM...
STAY, WELLINGTON — AND SEE IF YOU CAN CONTROL YOUR BOWELS FOR A FEW MINUTES... THAT LAST ONE WAS RANK!
...DOWN AT THE OLD BULL AND BUSH, DA DA DA DA DA...
IN YOU POP!

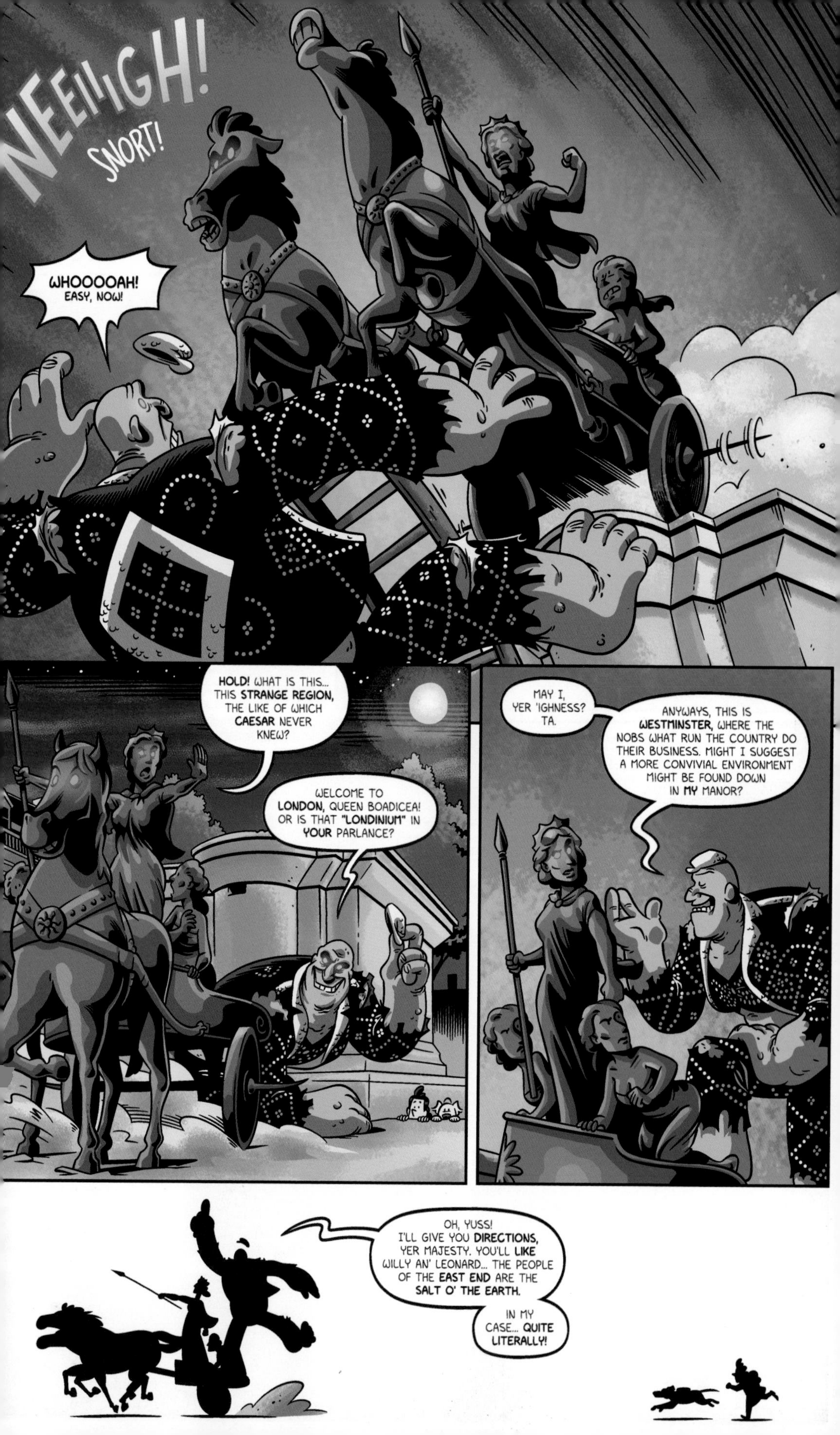
NEEIIIGH!
SNORT!
WHOOOOAH! EASY, NOW!
HOLD! WHAT IS THIS... THIS STRANGE REGION, THE LIKE OF WHICH CAESAR NEVER KNEW?
WELCOME TO LONDON, QUEEN BOADICEA! OR IS THAT "LONDINIUM" IN YOUR PARLANCE?
MAY I, YER 'IGHNESS? TA.
ANYWAYS, THIS IS WESTMINSTER, WHERE THE NOBS WHAT RUN THE COUNTRY DO THEIR BUSINESS. MIGHT I SUGGEST A MORE CONVIVIAL ENVIRONMENT MIGHT BE FOUND DOWN IN MY MANOR?
OH, YUSS! I'LL GIVE YOU DIRECTIONS, YER MAJESTY. YOU'LL LIKE WILLY AN' LEONARD... THE PEOPLE OF THE EAST END ARE THE SALT O' THE EARTH.
IN MY CASE... QUITE LITERALLY!

SO OUR INTREPID BAND HAVE BOTH WITNESSED THE **ASTONISHING**... NOT TO SAY THE **DOWNRIGHT PECULIAR!**... AND ARE **HOT ON THE TRAIL!**

AND, INEVITABLY, THEIR PATHS EVENTUALLY **CONVERGE**...

RAJANI! HUMPHREY! YOU'LL NEVER BELIEVE WHAT ME AND WELLINGTON JUST —

STATUES COMING TO LIFE, YOU MEAN?

RATHER **AHEAD** OF YOU THERE, OLD SAUSAGE! AND I DON'T KNOW ABOUT **YOURS**, BUT **OURS** ENDED UP...

...THERE!

HMM... YOU KNOW WHAT I THINK? I THINK THEY'RE MAKING **GOLEMS**!

"GOLEMS"? WHAT ON EARTH ARE YOU GIBBERING ABOUT? AND WELLINGTON, **MUST** YOU MAKE THOSE BEASTLY SMELLS?

IGNORE THE PLUM. WE'RE LISTENING...

"THERE'S AN OLD STORY ABOUT HOW A **RABBI** IN **PRAGUE** ONCE BUILT A **CLAY STATUE** TO PROTECT THE JEWISH PEOPLE...

"...THERE ARE DIFFERENT VERSIONS OF THE TALE...

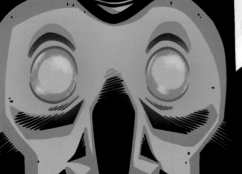

"...BUT IN THE ONE MY **GRANDPA** TOLD ME, HE **BROUGHT IT TO LIF** BY PLACING A MYSTICAL SCROLL CALLED A **SHEM** IN ITS MOUTH!"

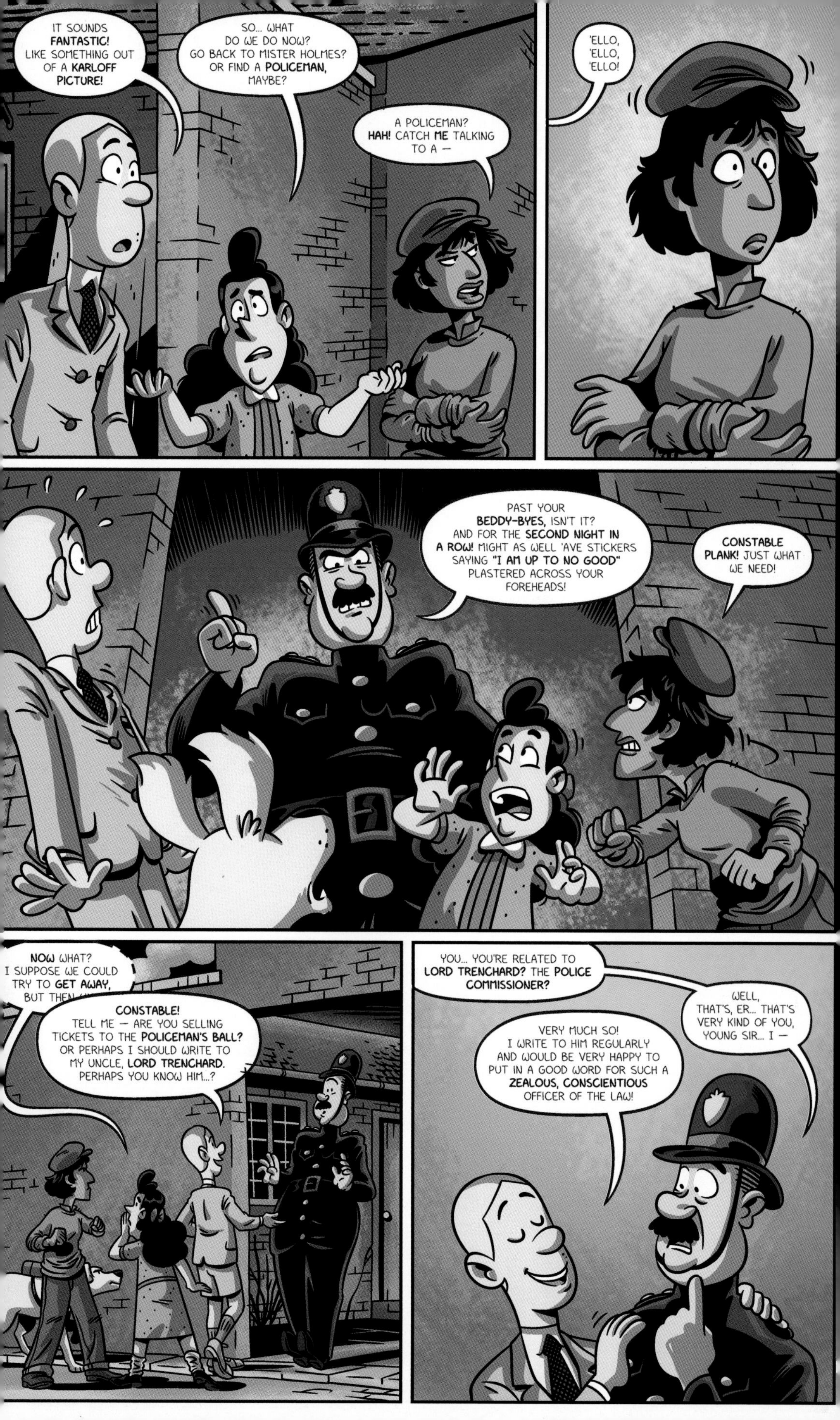
IT SOUNDS FANTASTIC! LIKE SOMETHING OUT OF A KARLOFF PICTURE!
SO... WHAT DO WE DO NOW? GO BACK TO MISTER HOLMES? OR FIND A POLICEMAN, MAYBE?
A POLICEMAN? HAH! CATCH ME TALKING TO A —
'ELLO, 'ELLO, 'ELLO!
PAST YOUR BEDDY-BYES, ISN'T IT? AND FOR THE SECOND NIGHT IN A ROW! MIGHT AS WELL 'AVE STICKERS SAYING "I AM UP TO NO GOOD" PLASTERED ACROSS YOUR FOREHEADS!
CONSTABLE PLANK! JUST WHAT WE NEED!
NOW WHAT? I SUPPOSE WE COULD TRY TO GET AWAY, BUT THEN
CONSTABLE! TELL ME — ARE YOU SELLING TICKETS TO THE POLICEMAN'S BALL? OR PERHAPS I SHOULD WRITE TO MY UNCLE, LORD TRENCHARD. PERHAPS YOU KNOW HIM...?
YOU... YOU'RE RELATED TO LORD TRENCHARD? THE POLICE COMMISSIONER?
VERY MUCH SO! I WRITE TO HIM REGULARLY AND WOULD BE VERY HAPPY TO PUT IN A GOOD WORD FOR SUCH A ZEALOUS, CONSCIENTIOUS OFFICER OF THE LAW!
WELL, THAT'S, ER... THAT'S VERY KIND OF YOU, YOUNG SIR... I —

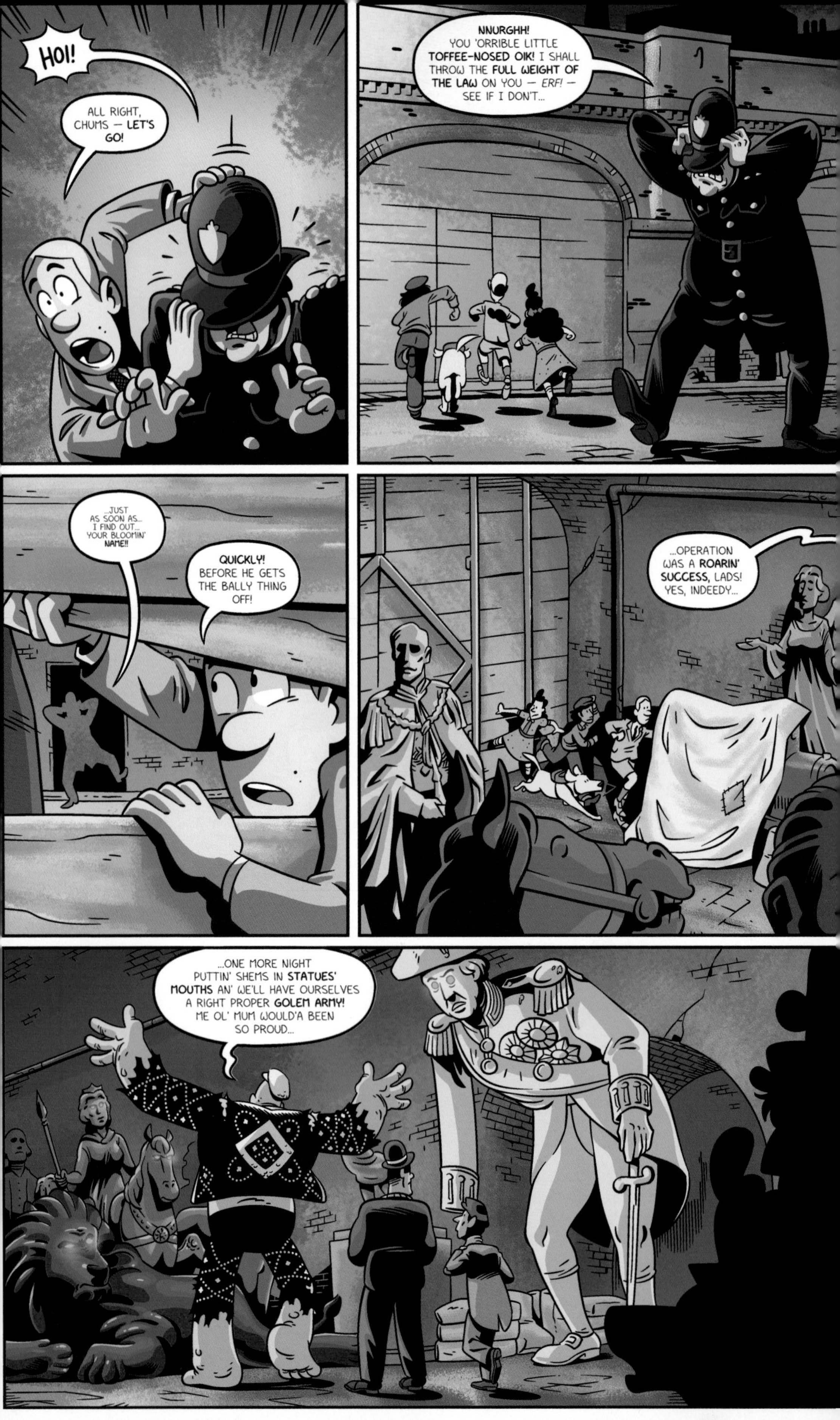
HOI!
ALL RIGHT, CHUMS — LET'S GO!
NNURGHH! YOU 'ORRIBLE LITTLE TOFFEE-NOSED OIK! I SHALL THROW THE FULL WEIGHT OF THE LAW ON YOU — ERF! — SEE IF I DON'T...
...JUST AS SOON AS... I FIND OUT... YOUR BLOOMIN' NAME!!
QUICKLY! BEFORE HE GETS THE BALLY THING OFF!
...OPERATION WAS A ROARIN' SUCCESS, LADS! YES, INDEEDY...
...ONE MORE NIGHT PUTTIN' SHEMS IN STATUES' MOUTHS AN' WE'LL HAVE OURSELVES A RIGHT PROPER GOLEM ARMY! ME OL' MUM WOULD'A BEEN SO PROUD...

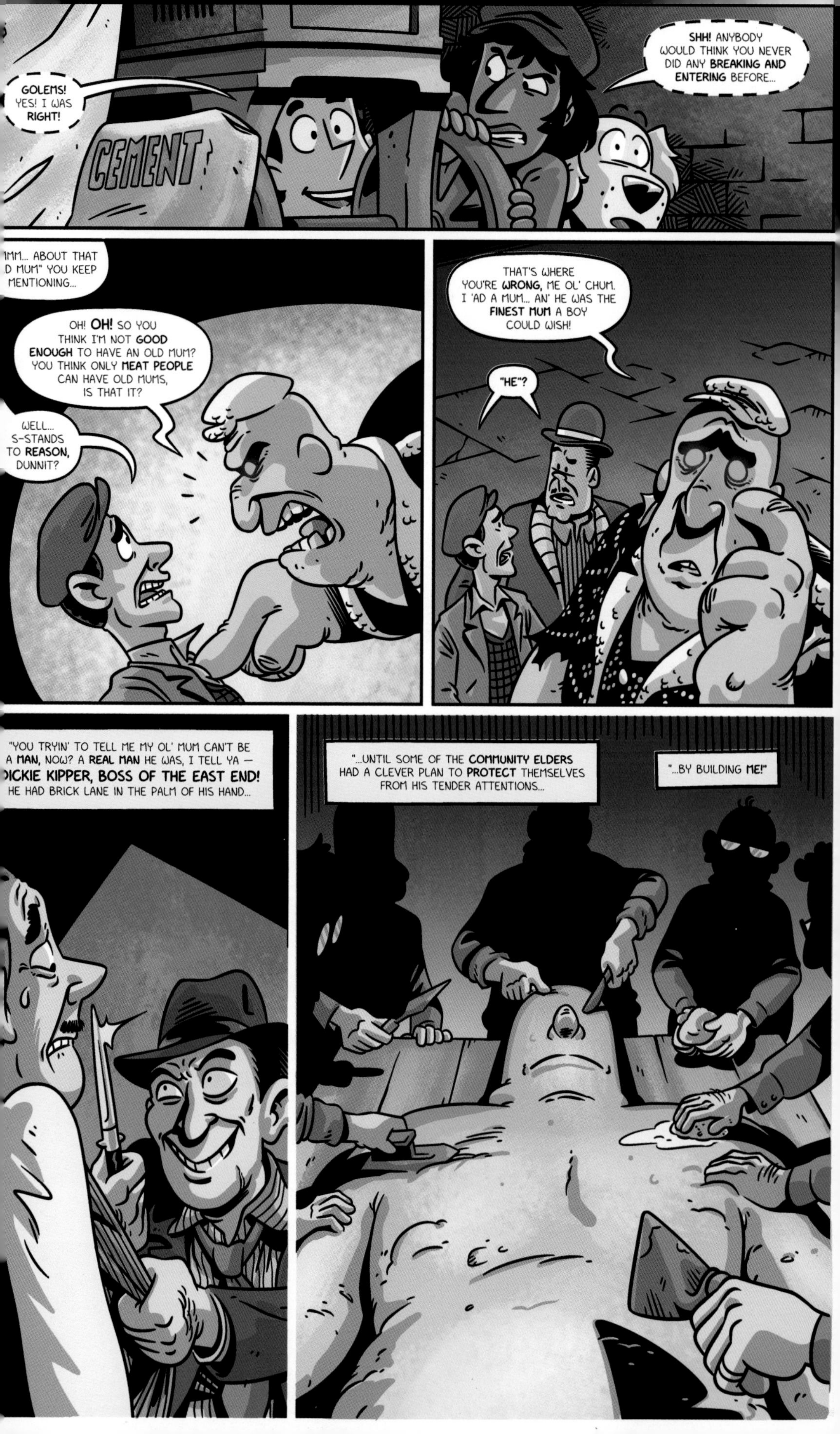
GOLEMS! YES! I WAS RIGHT!
CEMENT
SHH! ANYBODY WOULD THINK YOU NEVER DID ANY BREAKING AND ENTERING BEFORE...
MM... ABOUT THAT D MUM" YOU KEEP MENTIONING...
OH! OH! SO YOU THINK I'M NOT GOOD ENOUGH TO HAVE AN OLD MUM? YOU THINK ONLY MEAT PEOPLE CAN HAVE OLD MUMS, IS THAT IT?
WELL... S-STANDS TO REASON, DUNNIT?
THAT'S WHERE YOU'RE WRONG, ME OL' CHUM. I 'AD A MUM... AN' HE WAS THE FINEST MUM A BOY COULD WISH!
"HE"?
"YOU TRYIN' TO TELL ME MY OL' MUM CAN'T BE A MAN, NOW? A REAL MAN HE WAS, I TELL YA — DICKIE KIPPER, BOSS OF THE EAST END! HE HAD BRICK LANE IN THE PALM OF HIS HAND...
"...UNTIL SOME OF THE COMMUNITY ELDERS HAD A CLEVER PLAN TO PROTECT THEMSELVES FROM HIS TENDER ATTENTIONS...
"...BY BUILDING ME!"

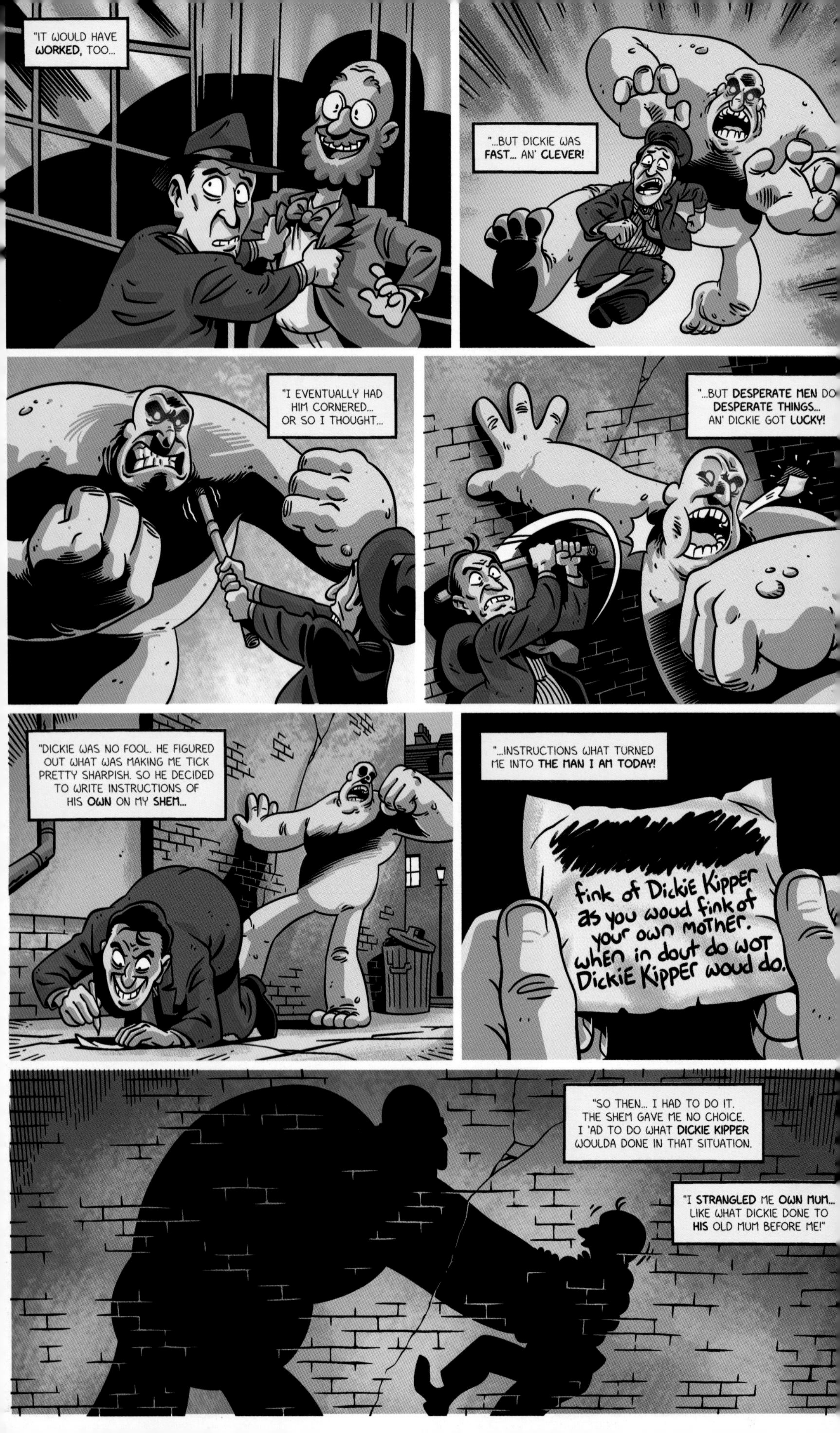

"IT WOULD HAVE **WORKED**, TOO...
"...BUT DICKIE WAS **FAST**... AN' **CLEVER**!
"I EVENTUALLY HAD HIM CORNERED... OR SO I THOUGHT...
"...BUT **DESPERATE MEN** DO **DESPERATE THINGS**... AN' DICKIE GOT **LUCKY**!
"DICKIE WAS NO FOOL. HE FIGURED OUT WHAT WAS MAKING ME TICK PRETTY SHARPISH. SO HE DECIDED TO WRITE INSTRUCTIONS OF HIS **OWN** ON MY **SHEM**...
"...INSTRUCTIONS WHAT TURNED ME INTO **THE MAN I AM TODAY**!
fink of Dickie Kipper as you woud fink of your own mother. when in dout do wot Dickie Kipper woud do.
"SO THEN... I HAD TO DO IT. THE SHEM GAVE ME NO CHOICE. I 'AD TO DO WHAT **DICKIE KIPPER** WOULDA DONE IN THAT SITUATION.
"I **STRANGLED** ME **OWN MUM**... LIKE WHAT DICKIE DONE TO **HIS** OLD MUM BEFORE ME!"

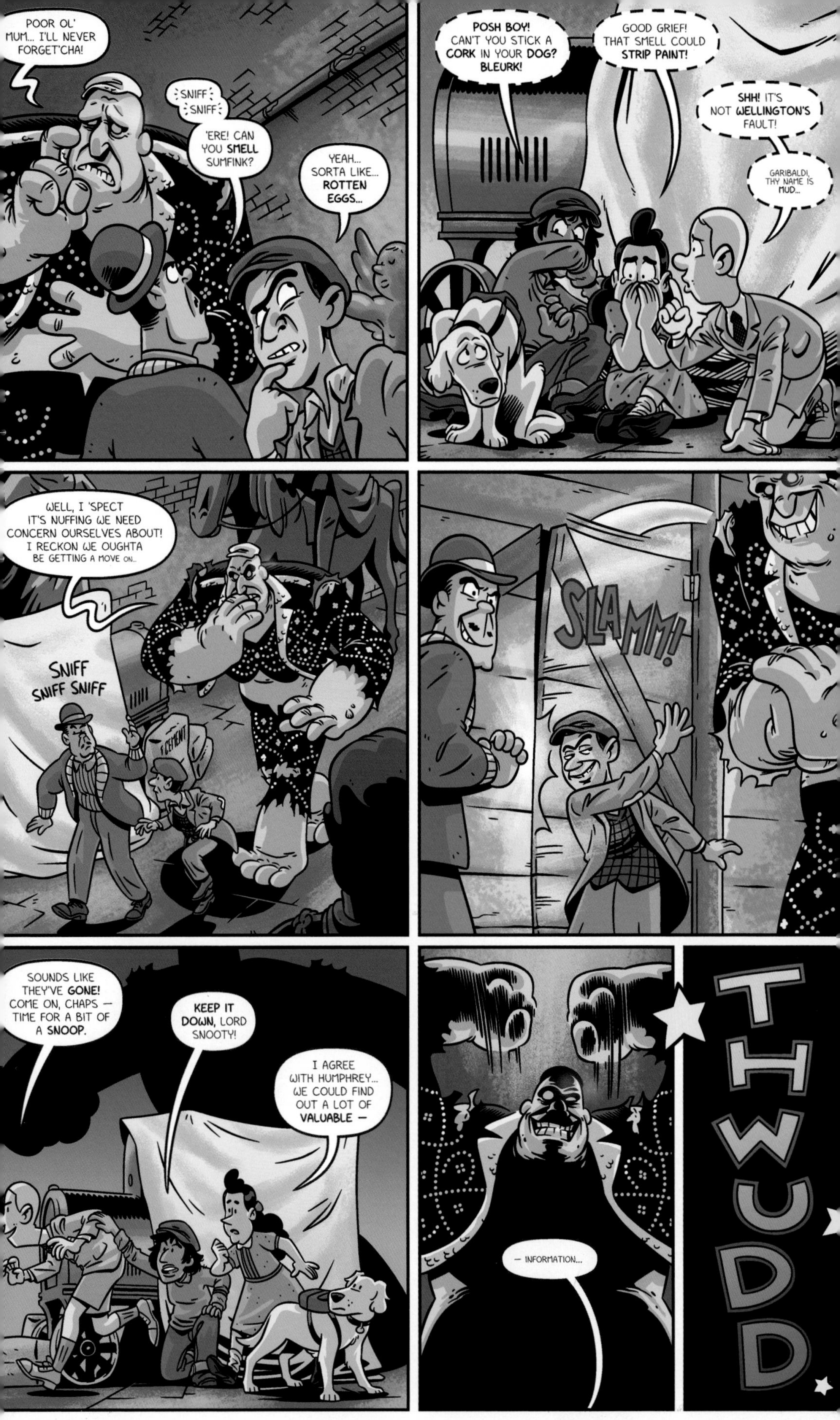
POOR OL' MUM... I'LL NEVER FORGET'CHA!
SNIFF SNIFF
'ERE! CAN YOU SMELL SUMFINK?
YEAH... SORTA LIKE... ROTTEN EGGS...
POSH BOY! CAN'T YOU STICK A CORK IN YOUR DOG? BLEURK!
GOOD GRIEF! THAT SMELL COULD STRIP PAINT!
SHH! IT'S NOT WELLINGTON'S FAULT!
GARIBALDI, THY NAME IS MUD...
WELL, I 'SPECT IT'S NUFFING WE NEED CONCERN OURSELVES ABOUT! I RECKON WE OUGHTA BE GETTING A MOVE ON...
SNIFF SNIFF SNIFF
CEMENT
SLAMM!
SOUNDS LIKE THEY'VE GONE! COME ON, CHAPS — TIME FOR A BIT OF A SNOOP.
KEEP IT DOWN, LORD SNOOTY!
I AGREE WITH HUMPHREY... WE COULD FIND OUT A LOT OF VALUABLE —
— INFORMATION...
THWUDD

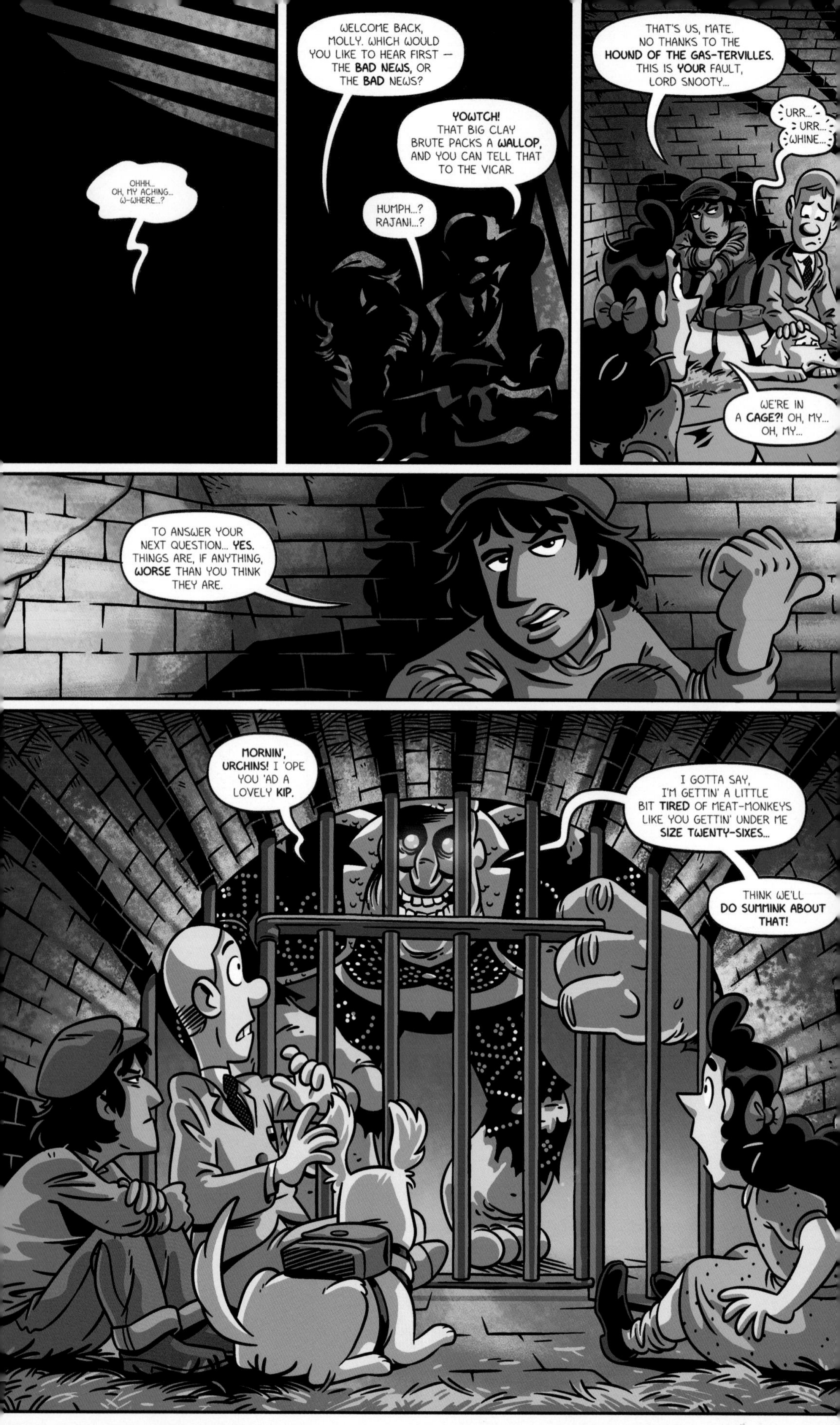
OHHH... OH, MY ACHING... W-WHERE...?
WELCOME BACK, MOLLY. WHICH WOULD YOU LIKE TO HEAR FIRST — THE BAD NEWS, OR THE BAD NEWS?
YOWTCH! THAT BIG CLAY BRUTE PACKS A WALLOP, AND YOU CAN TELL THAT TO THE VICAR.
HUMPH...? RAJANI...?
THAT'S US, MATE. NO THANKS TO THE HOUND OF THE GAS-TERVILLES. THIS IS YOUR FAULT, LORD SNOOTY...
URR... URR... WHINE...
WE'RE IN A CAGE?! OH, MY... OH, MY...
TO ANSWER YOUR NEXT QUESTION... YES. THINGS ARE, IF ANYTHING, WORSE THAN YOU THINK THEY ARE.
MORNIN', URCHINS! I 'OPE YOU 'AD A LOVELY KIP.
I GOTTA SAY, I'M GETTIN' A LITTLE BIT TIRED OF MEAT-MONKEYS LIKE YOU GETTIN' UNDER ME SIZE TWENTY-SIXES...
THINK WE'LL DO SUMMINK ABOUT THAT!

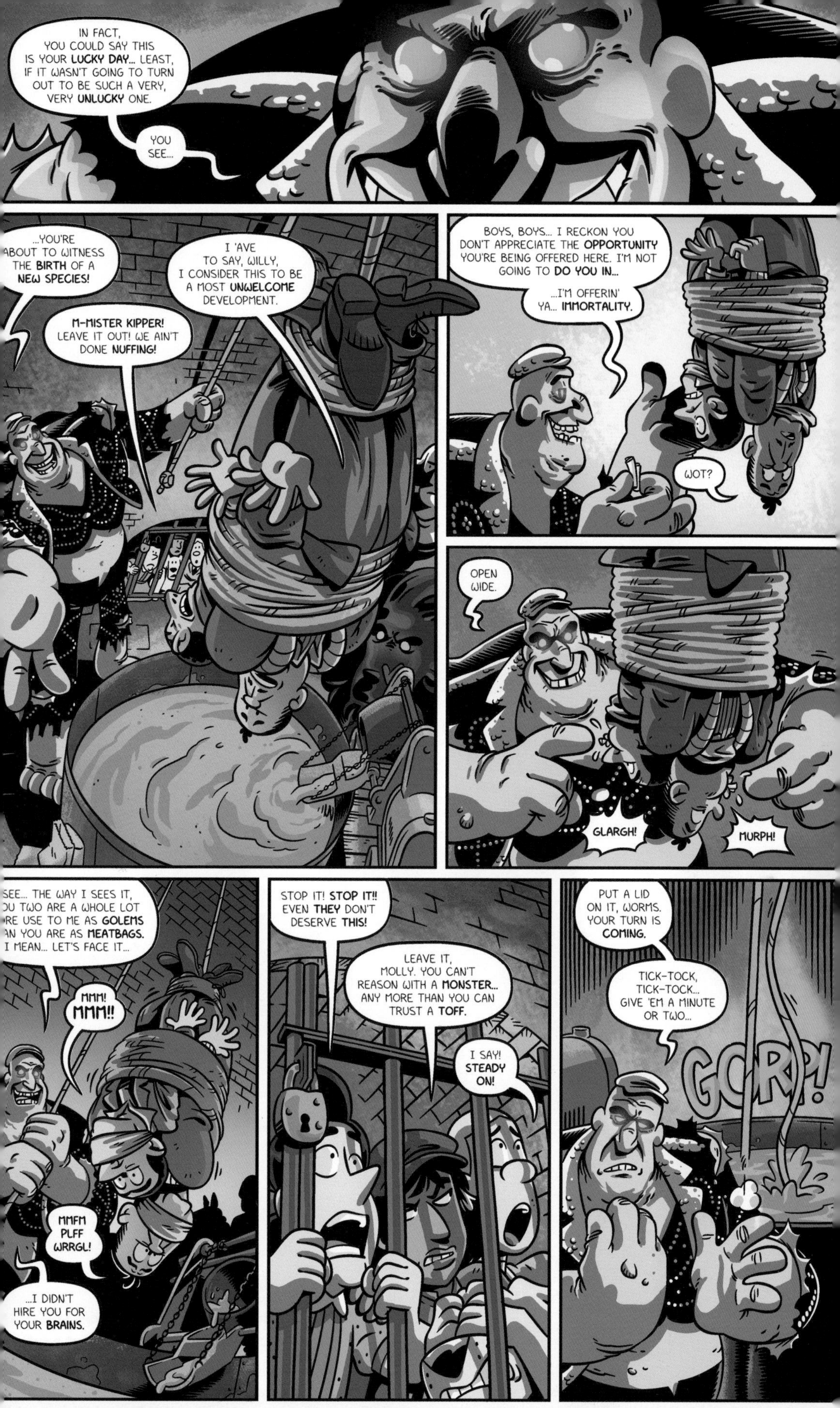
IN FACT, YOU COULD SAY THIS IS YOUR LUCKY DAY... LEAST, IF IT WASN'T GOING TO TURN OUT TO BE SUCH A VERY, VERY UNLUCKY ONE.
YOU SEE...
...YOU'RE ABOUT TO WITNESS THE BIRTH OF A NEW SPECIES!
M-MISTER KIPPER! LEAVE IT OUT! WE AIN'T DONE NUFFING!
I 'AVE TO SAY, WILLY, I CONSIDER THIS TO BE A MOST UNWELCOME DEVELOPMENT.
BOYS, BOYS... I RECKON YOU DON'T APPRECIATE THE OPPORTUNITY YOU'RE BEING OFFERED HERE. I'M NOT GOING TO DO YOU IN...
...I'M OFFERIN' YA... IMMORTALITY.
WOT?
OPEN WIDE.
GLARGH!
MURPH!
SEE... THE WAY I SEES IT, OU TWO ARE A WHOLE LOT RE USE TO ME AS GOLEMS AN YOU ARE AS MEATBAGS. I MEAN... LET'S FACE IT...
MMM! MMM!!
MMFM PLFF WRRGL!
...I DIDN'T HIRE YOU FOR YOUR BRAINS.
STOP IT! STOP IT!! EVEN THEY DON'T DESERVE THIS!
LEAVE IT, MOLLY. YOU CAN'T REASON WITH A MONSTER... ANY MORE THAN YOU CAN TRUST A TOFF.
I SAY! STEADY ON!
PUT A LID ON IT, WORMS. YOUR TURN IS COMING.
TICK-TOCK, TICK-TOCK... GIVE 'EM A MINUTE OR TWO...
GORP!

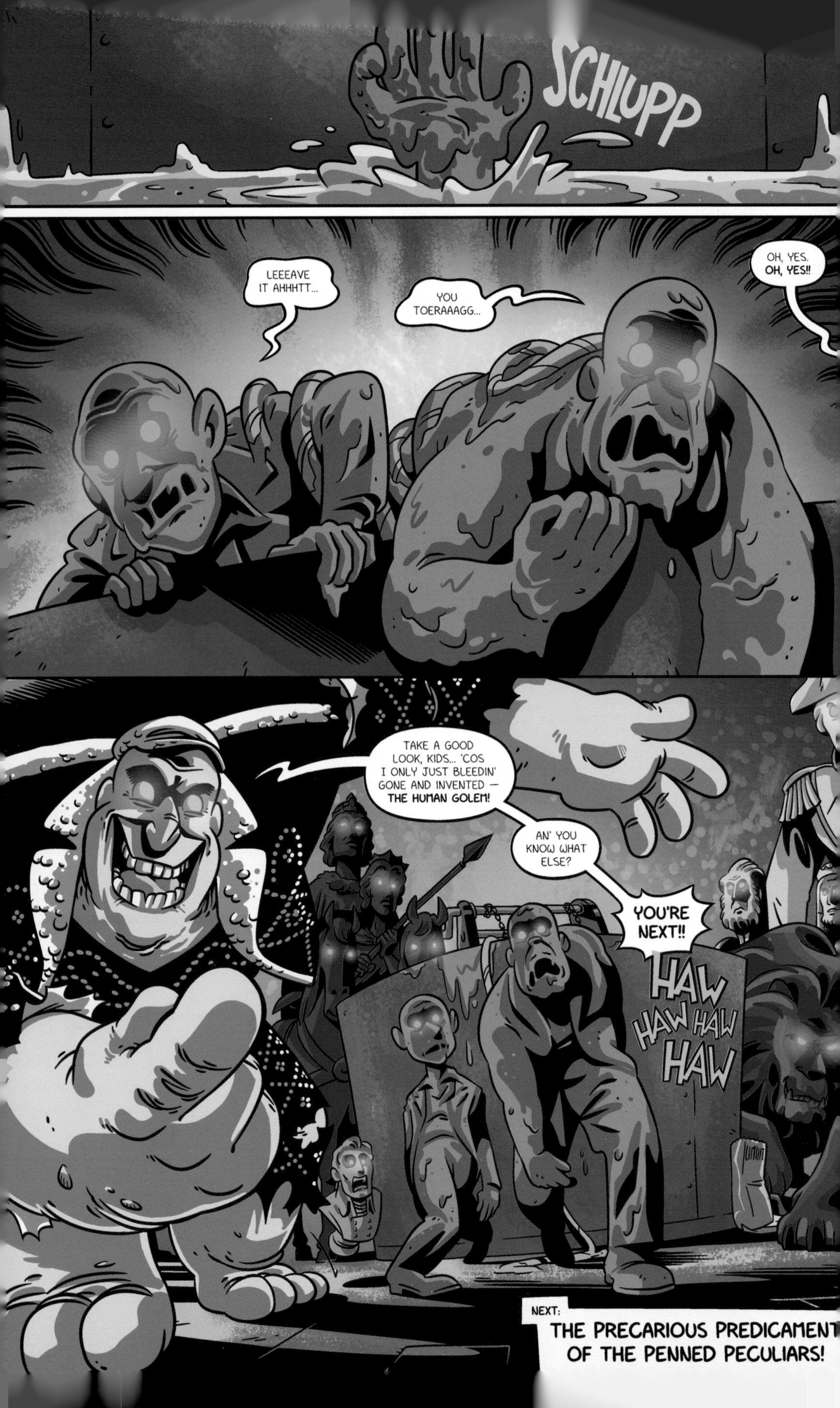
SCHLUPP
LEEEAVE IT AHHHTT...
YOU TOERAAAGG...
OH, YES. OH, YES!!
TAKE A GOOD LOOK, KIDS... 'COS I ONLY JUST BLEEDIN' GONE AND INVENTED — THE HUMAN GOLEM!
AN' YOU KNOW WHAT ELSE?
YOU'RE NEXT!!
HAW HAW HAW HAW
NEXT:
THE PRECARIOUS PREDICAMENT OF THE PENNED PECULIARS!

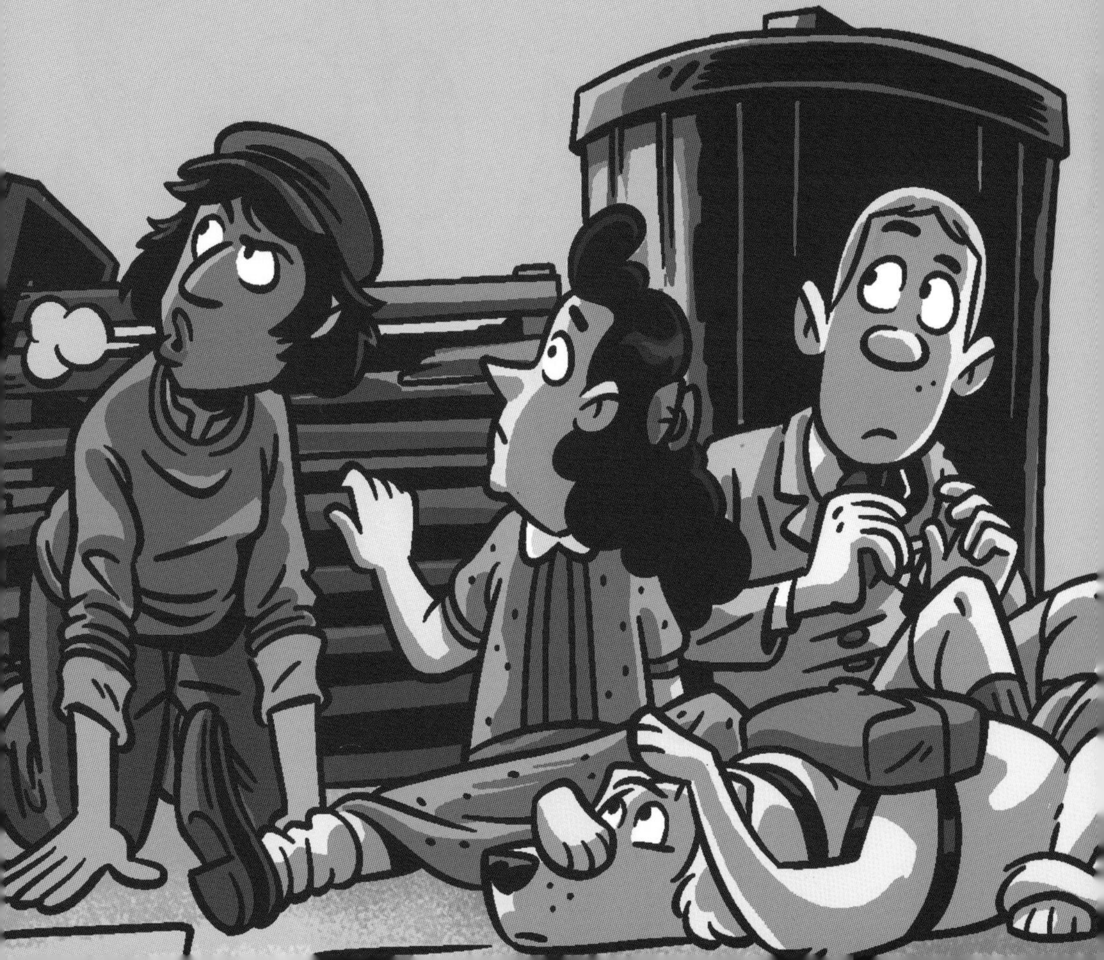

CHAPTER THREE

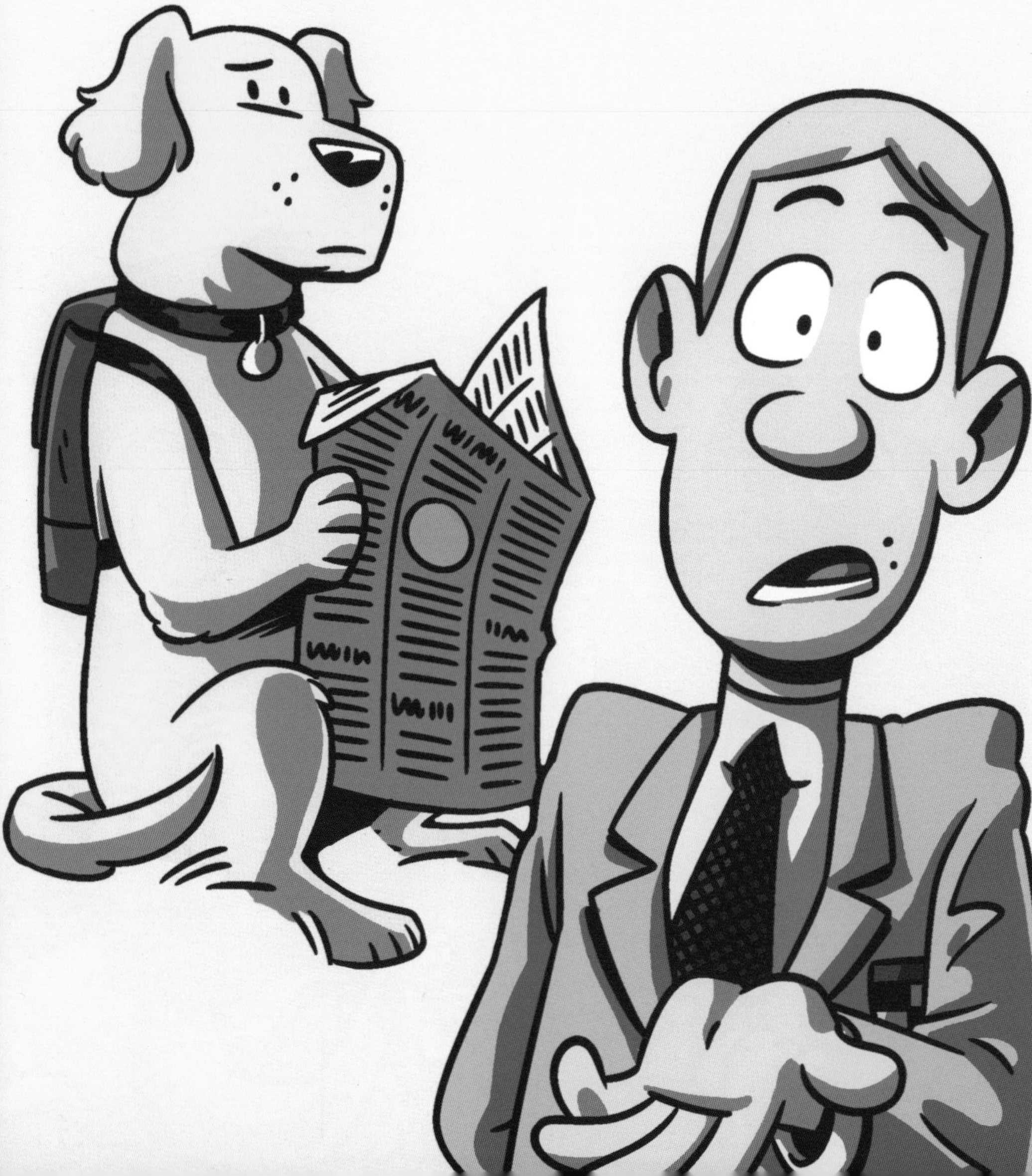

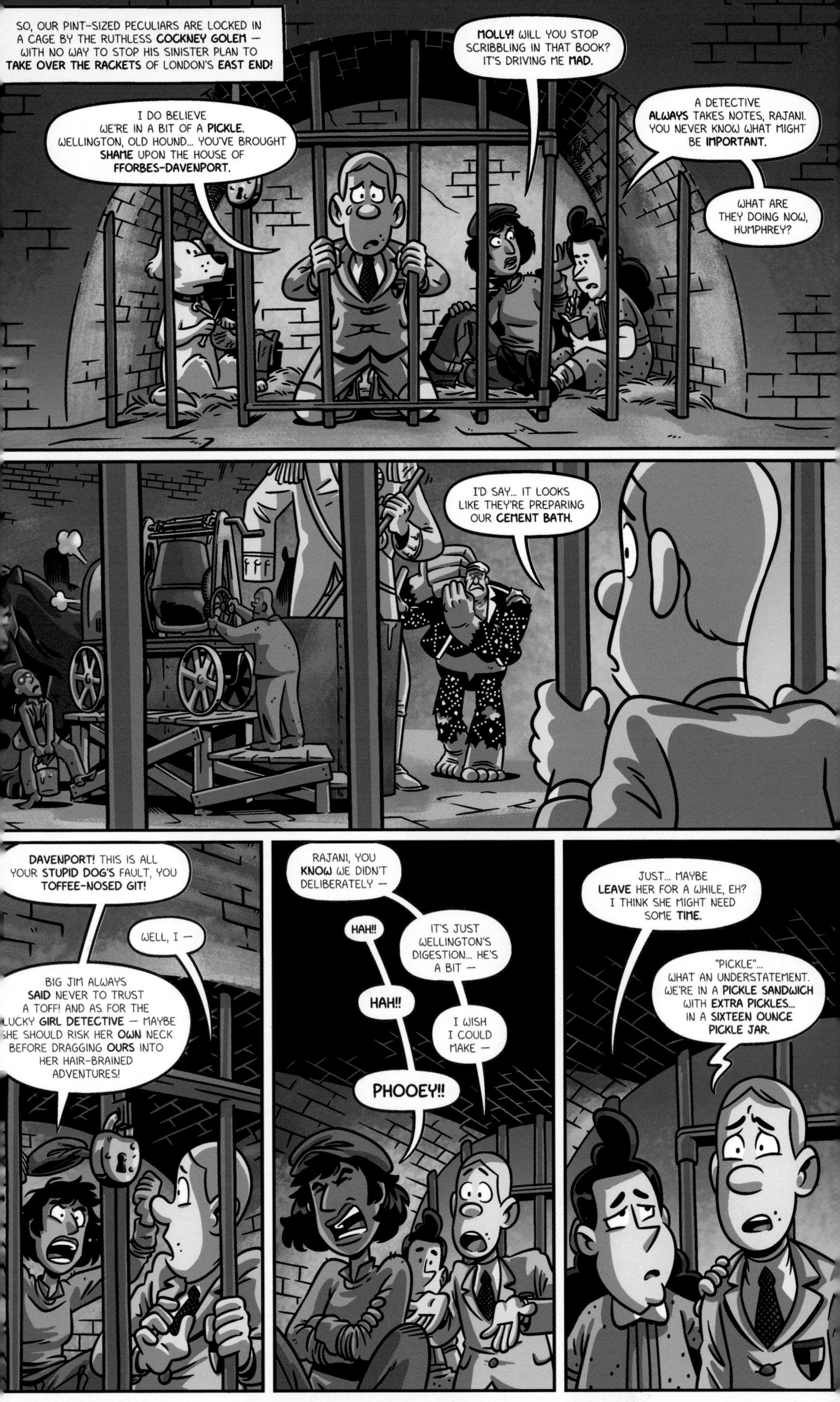
SO, OUR PINT-SIZED PECULIARS ARE LOCKED IN A CAGE BY THE RUTHLESS COCKNEY GOLEM — WITH NO WAY TO STOP HIS SINISTER PLAN TO TAKE OVER THE RACKETS OF LONDON'S EAST END!
I DO BELIEVE WE'RE IN A BIT OF A PICKLE. WELLINGTON, OLD HOUND... YOU'VE BROUGHT SHAME UPON THE HOUSE OF FFORBES-DAVENPORT.
MOLLY! WILL YOU STOP SCRIBBLING IN THAT BOOK? IT'S DRIVING ME MAD.
A DETECTIVE ALWAYS TAKES NOTES, RAJANI. YOU NEVER KNOW WHAT MIGHT BE IMPORTANT.
WHAT ARE THEY DOING NOW, HUMPHREY?
I'D SAY... IT LOOKS LIKE THEY'RE PREPARING OUR CEMENT BATH.
DAVENPORT! THIS IS ALL YOUR STUPID DOG'S FAULT, YOU TOFFEE-NOSED GIT!
WELL, I —
BIG JIM ALWAYS SAID NEVER TO TRUST A TOFF! AND AS FOR THE LUCKY GIRL DETECTIVE — MAYBE SHE SHOULD RISK HER OWN NECK BEFORE DRAGGING OURS INTO HER HAIR-BRAINED ADVENTURES!
RAJANI, YOU KNOW WE DIDN'T DELIBERATELY —
HAH!!
IT'S JUST WELLINGTON'S DIGESTION... HE'S A BIT —
HAH!!
I WISH I COULD MAKE —
PHOOEY!!
JUST... MAYBE LEAVE HER FOR A WHILE, EH? I THINK SHE MIGHT NEED SOME TIME.
"PICKLE"... WHAT AN UNDERSTATEMENT. WE'RE IN A PICKLE SANDWICH WITH EXTRA PICKLES... IN A SIXTEEN OUNCE PICKLE JAR.

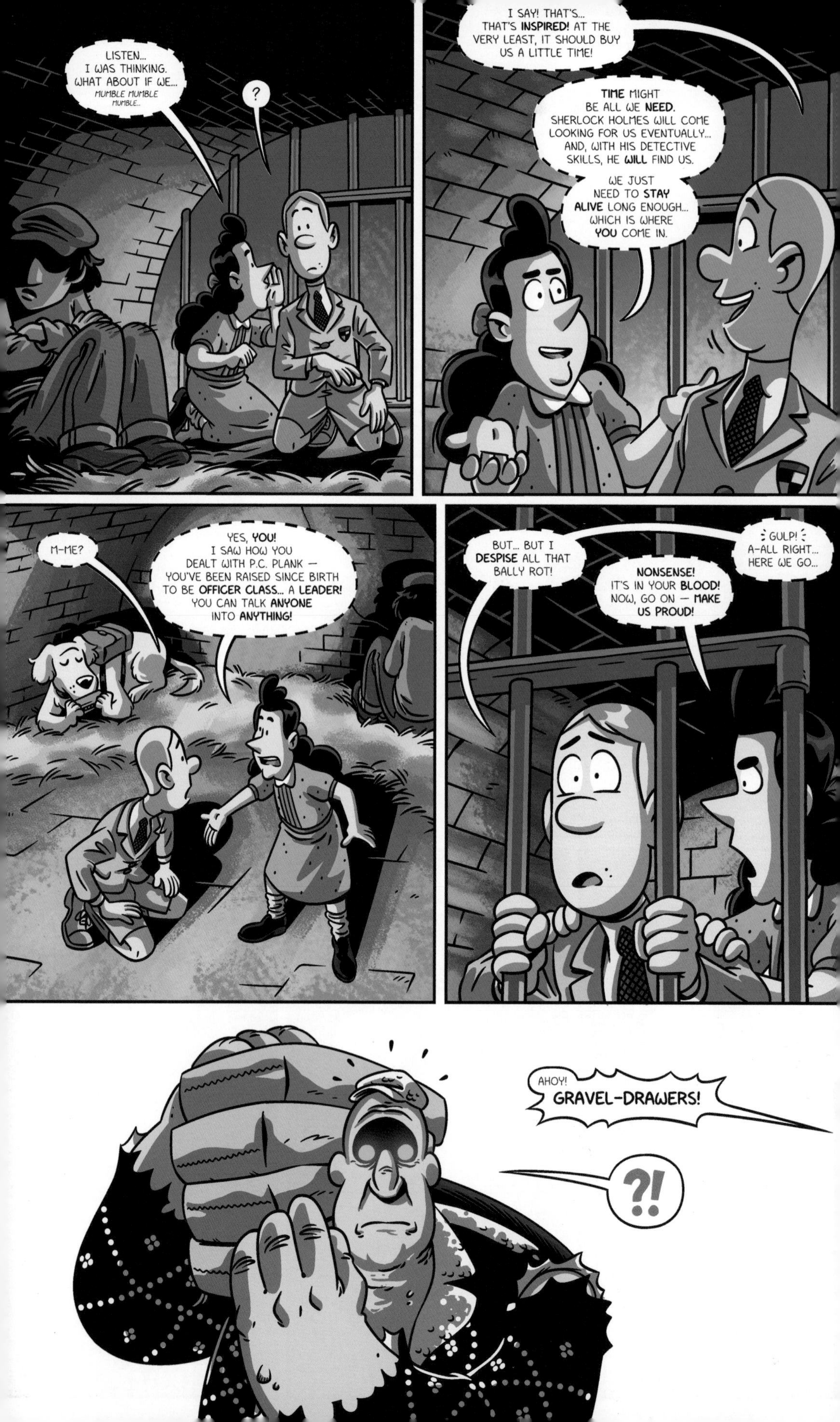
LISTEN... I WAS THINKING. WHAT ABOUT IF WE... MUMBLE MUMBLE MUMBLE...
?
I SAY! THAT'S... THAT'S INSPIRED! AT THE VERY LEAST, IT SHOULD BUY US A LITTLE TIME!
TIME MIGHT BE ALL WE NEED. SHERLOCK HOLMES WILL COME LOOKING FOR US EVENTUALLY... AND, WITH HIS DETECTIVE SKILLS, HE WILL FIND US.
WE JUST NEED TO STAY ALIVE LONG ENOUGH... WHICH IS WHERE YOU COME IN.
M-ME?
YES, YOU! I SAW HOW YOU DEALT WITH P.C. PLANK — YOU'VE BEEN RAISED SINCE BIRTH TO BE OFFICER CLASS... A LEADER! YOU CAN TALK ANYONE INTO ANYTHING!
BUT... BUT I DESPISE ALL THAT BALLY ROT!
NONSENSE! IT'S IN YOUR BLOOD! NOW, GO ON — MAKE US PROUD!
GULP! A-ALL RIGHT... HERE WE GO...
AHOY! GRAVEL-DRAWERS!
?!

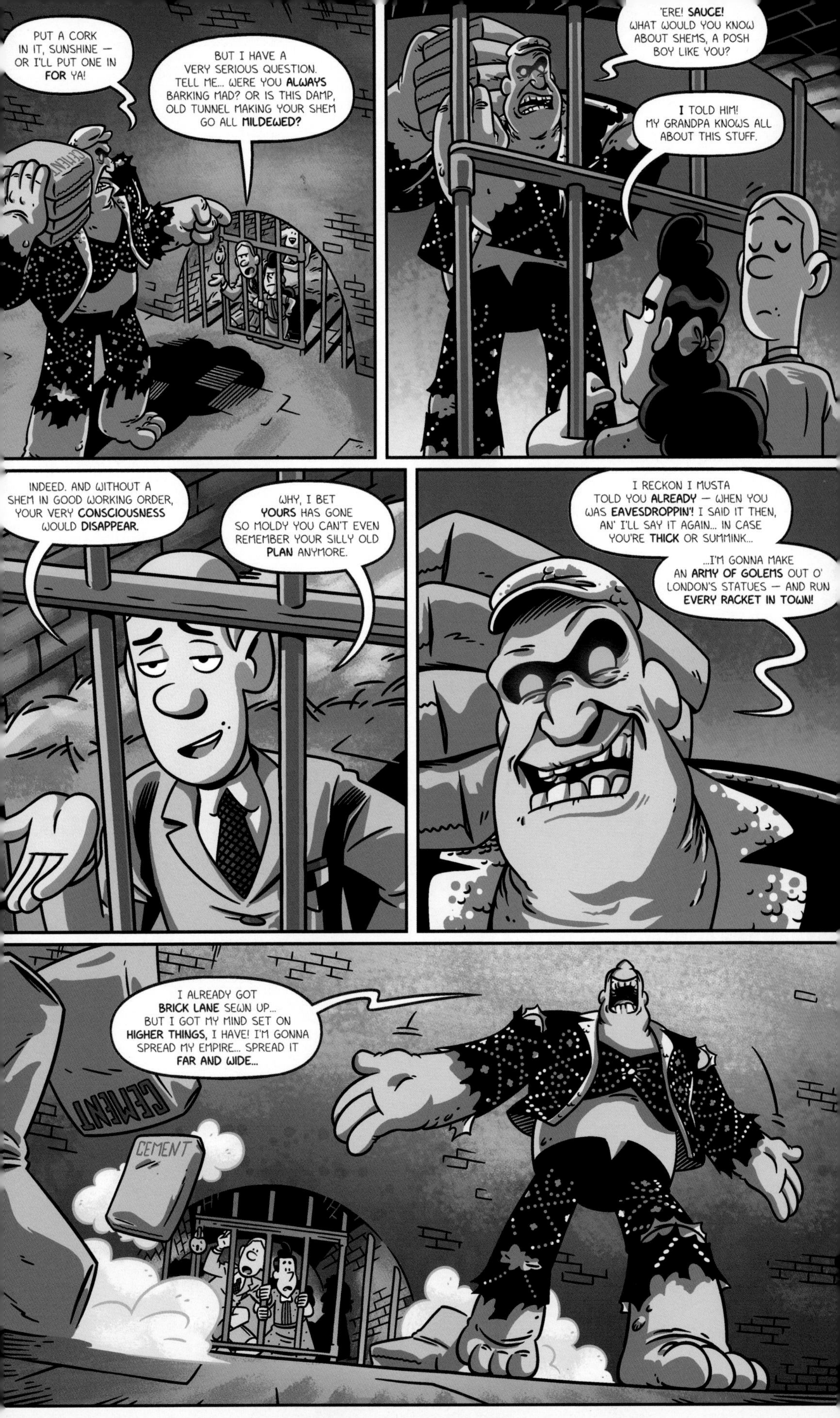
PUT A CORK IN IT, SUNSHINE — OR I'LL PUT ONE IN **FOR** YA!
BUT I HAVE A VERY SERIOUS QUESTION. TELL ME... WERE YOU **ALWAYS** BARKING MAD? OR IS THIS DAMP, OLD TUNNEL MAKING YOUR SHEM GO ALL **MILDEWED?**
CEMENT
'ERE! **SAUCE!** WHAT WOULD YOU KNOW ABOUT SHEMS, A POSH BOY LIKE YOU?
I TOLD HIM! MY GRANDPA KNOWS ALL ABOUT THIS STUFF.
INDEED. AND WITHOUT A SHEM IN GOOD WORKING ORDER, YOUR VERY **CONSCIOUSNESS** WOULD **DISAPPEAR.**
WHY, I BET **YOURS** HAS GONE SO MOLDY YOU CAN'T EVEN REMEMBER YOUR SILLY OLD **PLAN** ANYMORE.
I RECKON I MUSTA TOLD YOU **ALREADY** — WHEN YOU WAS **EAVESDROPPIN'!** I SAID IT THEN, AN' I'LL SAY IT AGAIN... IN CASE YOU'RE **THICK** OR SUMMINK...
...I'M GONNA MAKE AN **ARMY OF GOLEMS** OUT O' LONDON'S STATUES — AND RUN **EVERY RACKET IN TOWN!**
I ALREADY GOT **BRICK LANE** SEWN UP... BUT I GOT MY MIND SET ON **HIGHER THINGS,** I HAVE! I'M GONNA SPREAD MY EMPIRE... SPREAD IT **FAR AND WIDE...**
CEMENT
CEMENT

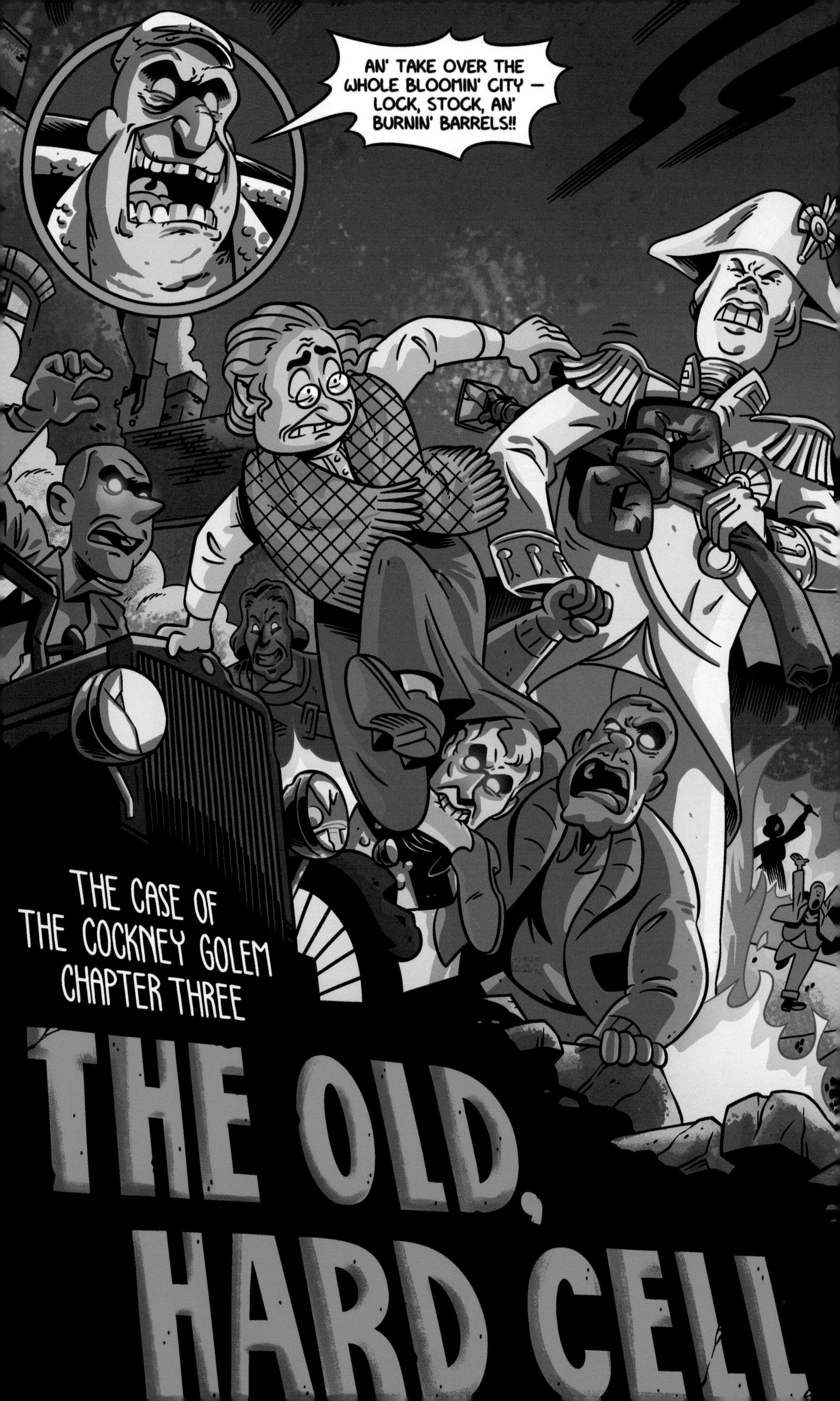
AN' TAKE OVER THE WHOLE BLOOMIN' CITY — LOCK, STOCK, AN' BURNIN' BARRELS!!
THE CASE OF
THE COCKNEY GOLEM
CHAPTER THREE
THE OLD, HARD CELL

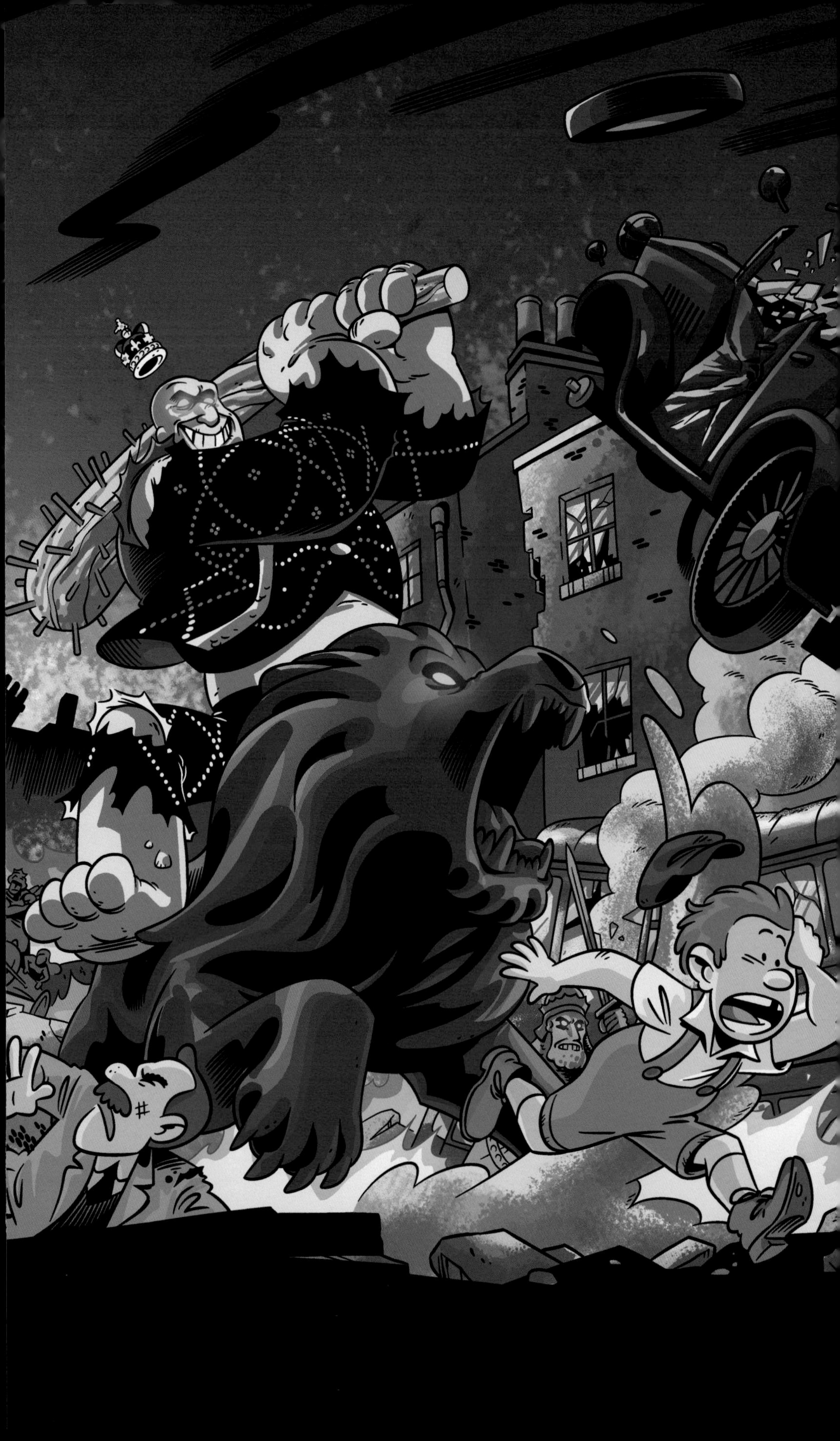

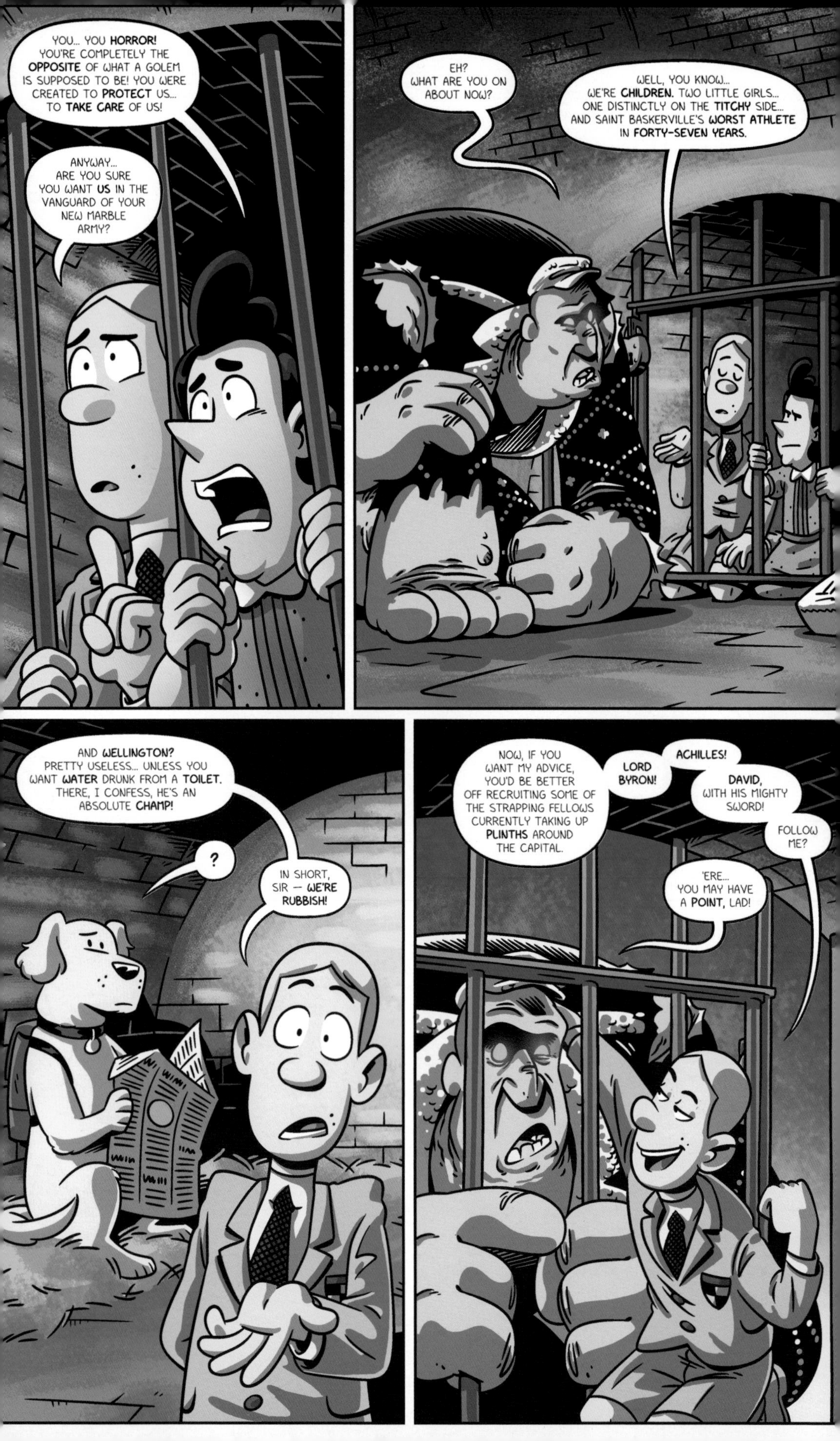

YOU... YOU **HORROR!** YOU'RE COMPLETELY THE **OPPOSITE** OF WHAT A GOLEM IS SUPPOSED TO BE! YOU WERE CREATED TO **PROTECT** US... TO **TAKE CARE** OF US!
ANYWAY... ARE YOU SURE YOU WANT **US** IN THE VANGUARD OF YOUR NEW MARBLE ARMY?
EH? WHAT ARE YOU ON ABOUT NOW?
WELL, YOU KNOW... WE'RE **CHILDREN.** TWO LITTLE GIRLS... ONE DISTINCTLY ON THE **TITCHY** SIDE... AND SAINT BASKERVILLE'S **WORST ATHLETE** IN **FORTY-SEVEN YEARS.**
AND **WELLINGTON?** PRETTY USELESS... UNLESS YOU WANT **WATER** DRUNK FROM A **TOILET**. THERE, I CONFESS, HE'S AN ABSOLUTE **CHAMP!**
?
IN SHORT, SIR — **WE'RE RUBBISH!**
NOW, IF YOU WANT MY ADVICE, YOU'D BE BETTER OFF RECRUITING SOME OF THE STRAPPING FELLOWS CURRENTLY TAKING UP **PLINTHS** AROUND THE CAPITAL.
LORD BYRON!
ACHILLES!
DAVID, WITH HIS MIGHTY SWORD!
FOLLOW ME?
'ERE... YOU MAY HAVE A **POINT,** LAD!

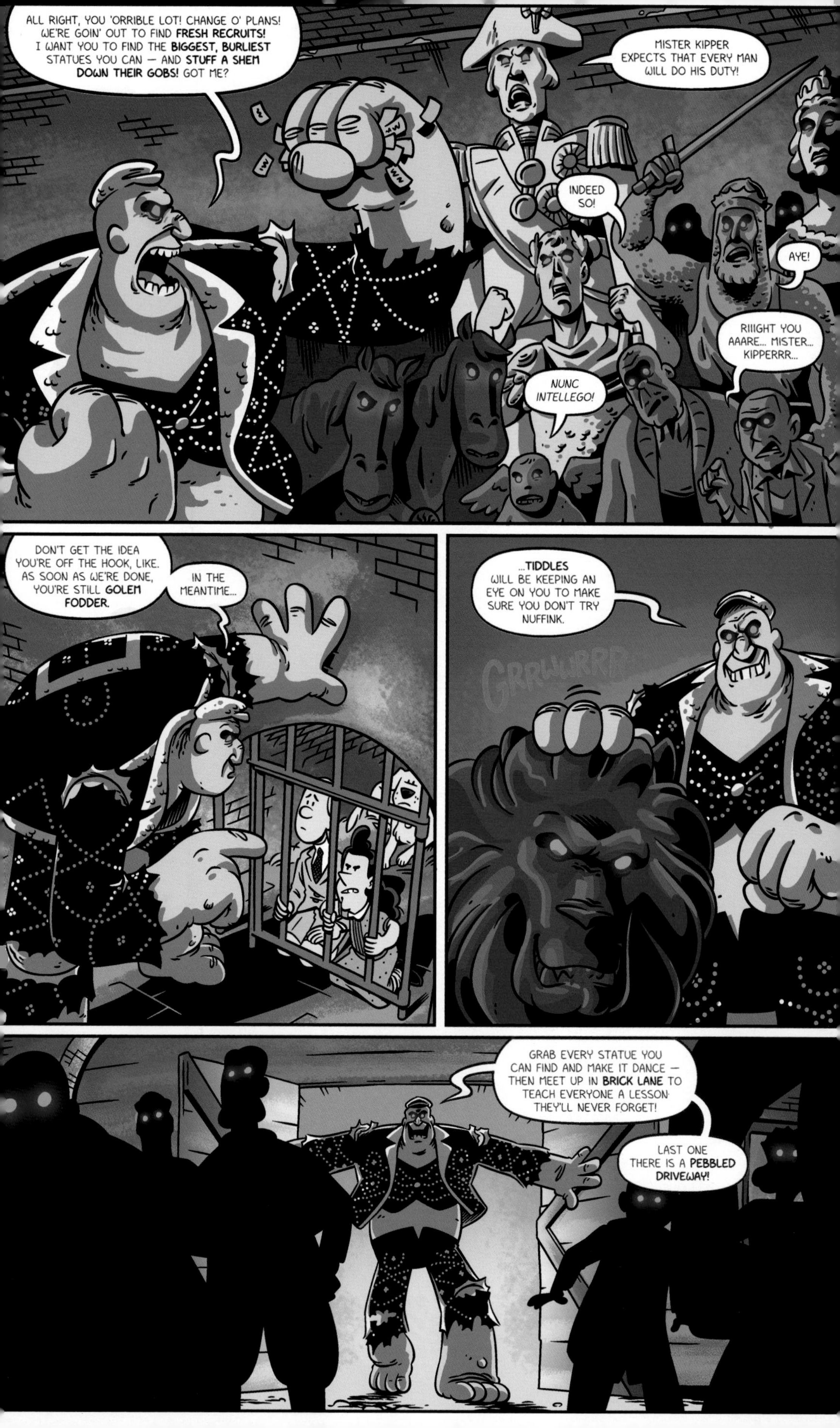
ALL RIGHT, YOU 'ORRIBLE LOT! CHANGE O' PLANS! WE'RE GOIN' OUT TO FIND FRESH RECRUITS! I WANT YOU TO FIND THE BIGGEST, BURLIEST STATUES YOU CAN — AND STUFF A SHEM DOWN THEIR GOBS! GOT ME?
MISTER KIPPER EXPECTS THAT EVERY MAN WILL DO HIS DUTY!
INDEED SO!
AYE!
RIIIGHT YOU AAARE... MISTER... KIPPERRR...
NUNC INTELLEGO!
DON'T GET THE IDEA YOU'RE OFF THE HOOK, LIKE. AS SOON AS WE'RE DONE, YOU'RE STILL GOLEM FODDER.
IN THE MEANTIME...
...TIDDLES WILL BE KEEPING AN EYE ON YOU TO MAKE SURE YOU DON'T TRY NUFFINK.
GRRWURRR
GRAB EVERY STATUE YOU CAN FIND AND MAKE IT DANCE — THEN MEET UP IN BRICK LANE TO TEACH EVERYONE A LESSON THEY'LL NEVER FORGET!
LAST ONE THERE IS A PEBBLED DRIVEWAY!

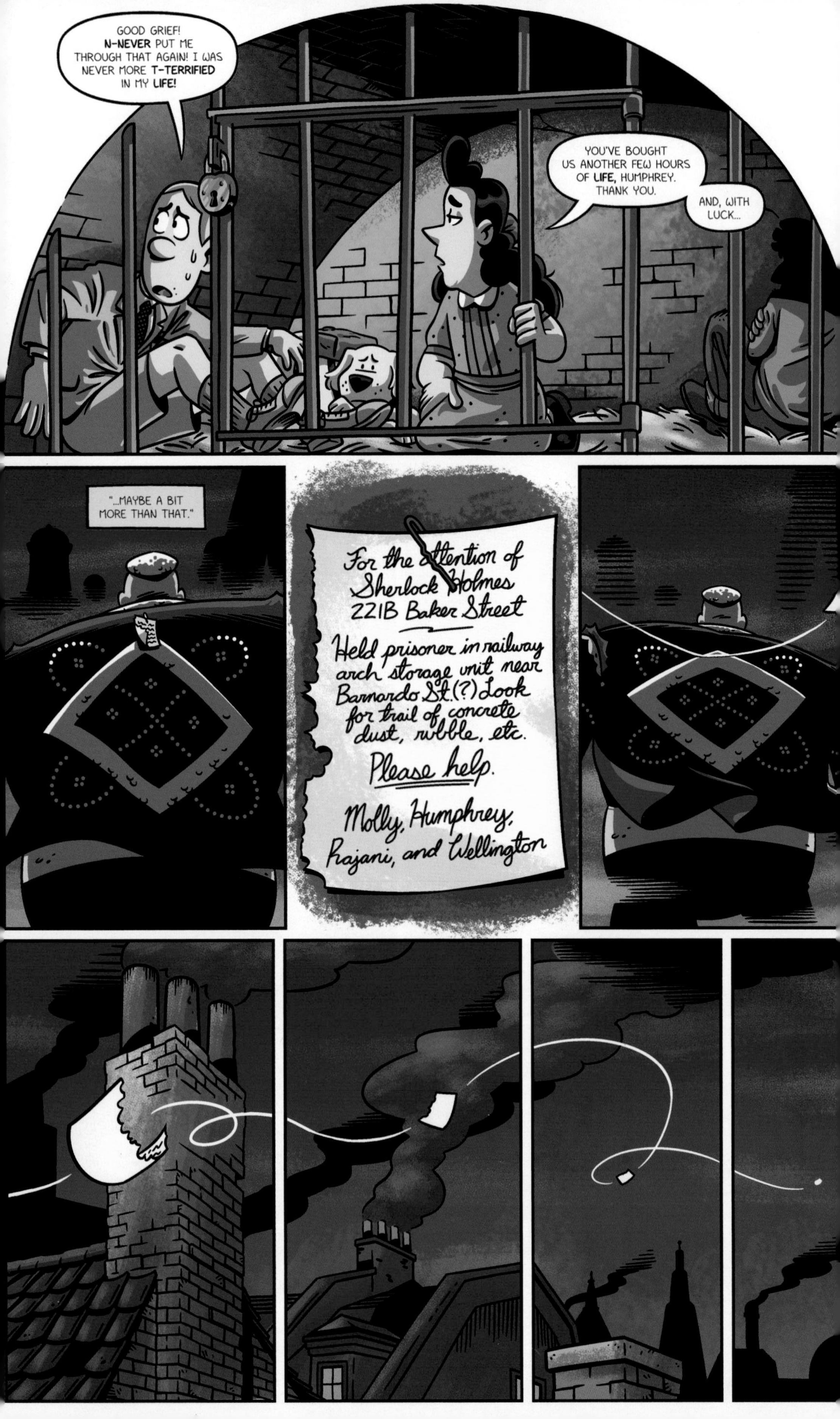
GOOD GRIEF! N-NEVER PUT ME THROUGH THAT AGAIN! I WAS NEVER MORE T-TERRIFIED IN MY LIFE!
YOU'VE BOUGHT US ANOTHER FEW HOURS OF LIFE, HUMPHREY. THANK YOU.
AND, WITH LUCK...
"...MAYBE A BIT MORE THAN THAT."
For the attention of Sherlock Holmes 221B Baker Street
Held prisoner in railway arch storage unit near Barnardo St.(?) Look for trail of concrete dust, rubble, etc.
Please help.
Molly, Humphrey, Rajani, and Wellington

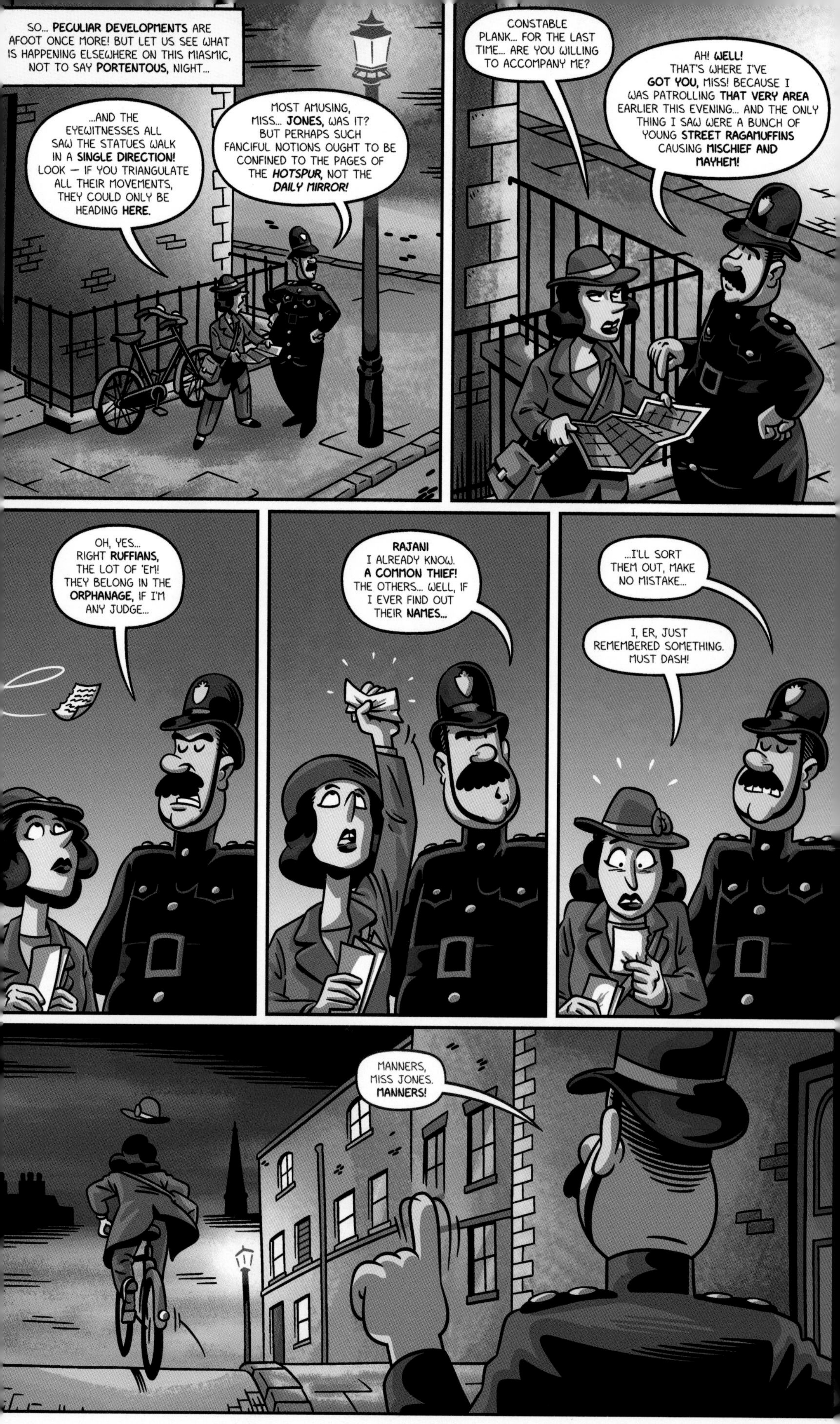
SO... **PECULIAR DEVELOPMENTS** ARE AFOOT ONCE MORE! BUT LET US SEE WHAT IS HAPPENING ELSEWHERE ON THIS MIASMIC, NOT TO SAY **PORTENTOUS**, NIGHT...
...AND THE EYEWITNESSES ALL SAW THE STATUES WALK IN A **SINGLE DIRECTION!** LOOK — IF YOU TRIANGULATE ALL THEIR MOVEMENTS, THEY COULD ONLY BE HEADING **HERE**.
MOST AMUSING, MISS... **JONES**, WAS IT? BUT PERHAPS SUCH FANCIFUL NOTIONS OUGHT TO BE CONFINED TO THE PAGES OF THE ***HOTSPUR***, NOT THE ***DAILY MIRROR!***
CONSTABLE PLANK... FOR THE LAST TIME... ARE YOU WILLING TO ACCOMPANY ME?
AH! **WELL!** THAT'S WHERE I'VE **GOT YOU**, MISS! BECAUSE I WAS PATROLLING **THAT VERY AREA** EARLIER THIS EVENING... AND THE ONLY THING I SAW WERE A BUNCH OF YOUNG **STREET RAGAMUFFINS** CAUSING **MISCHIEF AND MAYHEM!**
OH, YES... RIGHT **RUFFIANS**, THE LOT OF 'EM! THEY BELONG IN THE **ORPHANAGE**, IF I'M ANY JUDGE...
RAJANI I ALREADY KNOW. **A COMMON THIEF!** THE OTHERS... WELL, IF I EVER FIND OUT THEIR **NAMES**...
...I'LL SORT THEM OUT, MAKE NO MISTAKE...
I, ER, JUST REMEMBERED SOMETHING. MUST DASH!
MANNERS, MISS JONES. **MANNERS!**

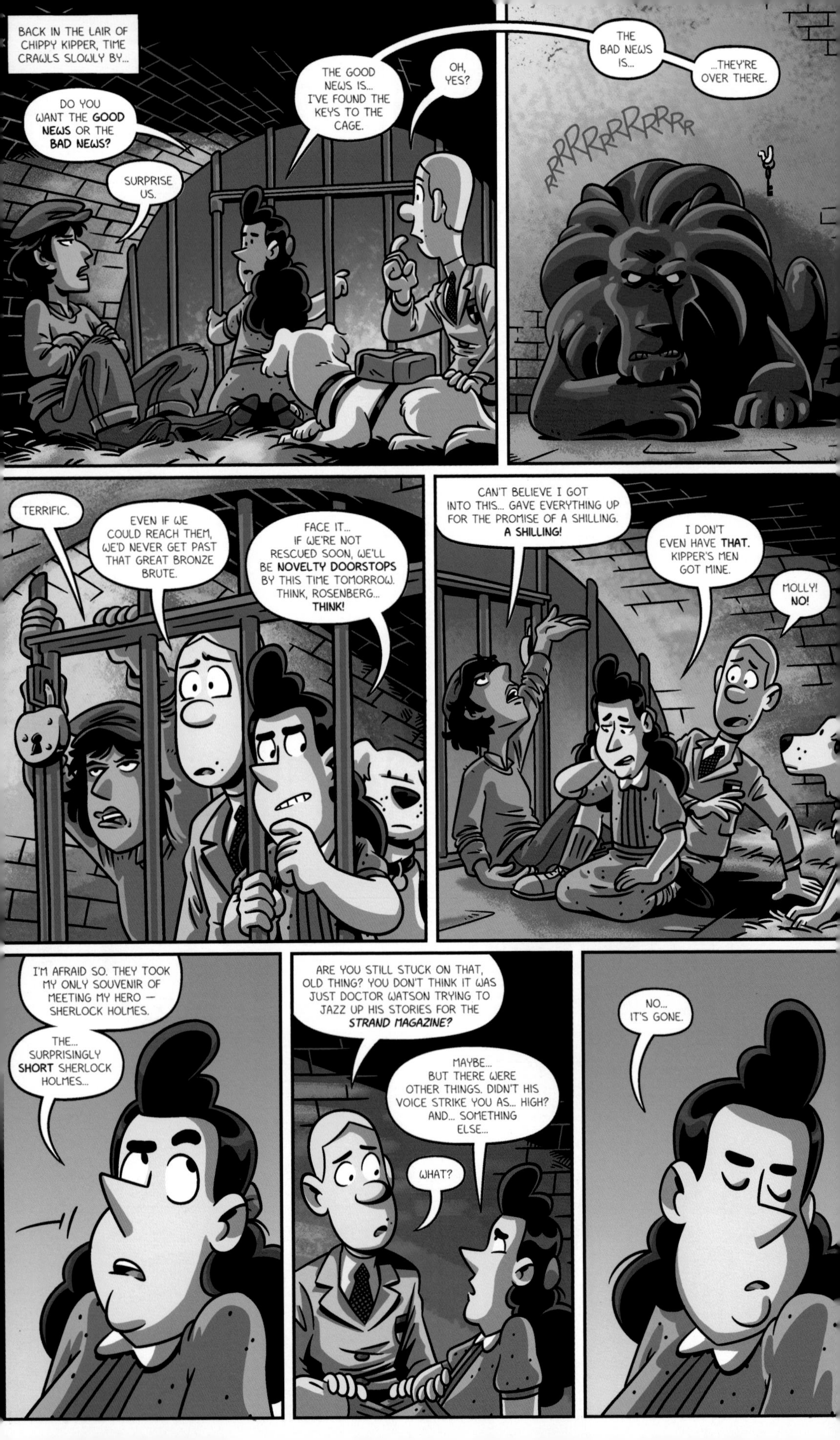
BACK IN THE LAIR OF CHIPPY KIPPER, TIME CRAWLS SLOWLY BY...
DO YOU WANT THE **GOOD NEWS** OR THE **BAD NEWS?**
SURPRISE US.
THE GOOD NEWS IS... I'VE FOUND THE KEYS TO THE CAGE.
OH, YES?
THE BAD NEWS IS...
...THEY'RE OVER THERE.
RRRRRRRRRRRR
TERRIFIC.
EVEN IF WE COULD REACH THEM, WE'D NEVER GET PAST THAT GREAT BRONZE BRUTE.
FACE IT... IF WE'RE NOT RESCUED SOON, WE'LL BE **NOVELTY DOORSTOPS** BY THIS TIME TOMORROW. THINK, ROSENBERG... **THINK!**
CAN'T BELIEVE I GOT INTO THIS... GAVE EVERYTHING UP FOR THE PROMISE OF A SHILLING. **A SHILLING!**
I DON'T EVEN HAVE **THAT.** KIPPER'S MEN GOT MINE.
MOLLY! **NO!**
I'M AFRAID SO. THEY TOOK MY ONLY SOUVENIR OF MEETING MY HERO — SHERLOCK HOLMES.
THE... SURPRISINGLY **SHORT** SHERLOCK HOLMES...
ARE YOU STILL STUCK ON THAT, OLD THING? YOU DON'T THINK IT WAS JUST DOCTOR WATSON TRYING TO JAZZ UP HIS STORIES FOR THE ***STRAND MAGAZINE?***
MAYBE... BUT THERE WERE OTHER THINGS. DIDN'T HIS VOICE STRIKE YOU AS... HIGH? AND... SOMETHING ELSE...
WHAT?
NO... IT'S GONE.

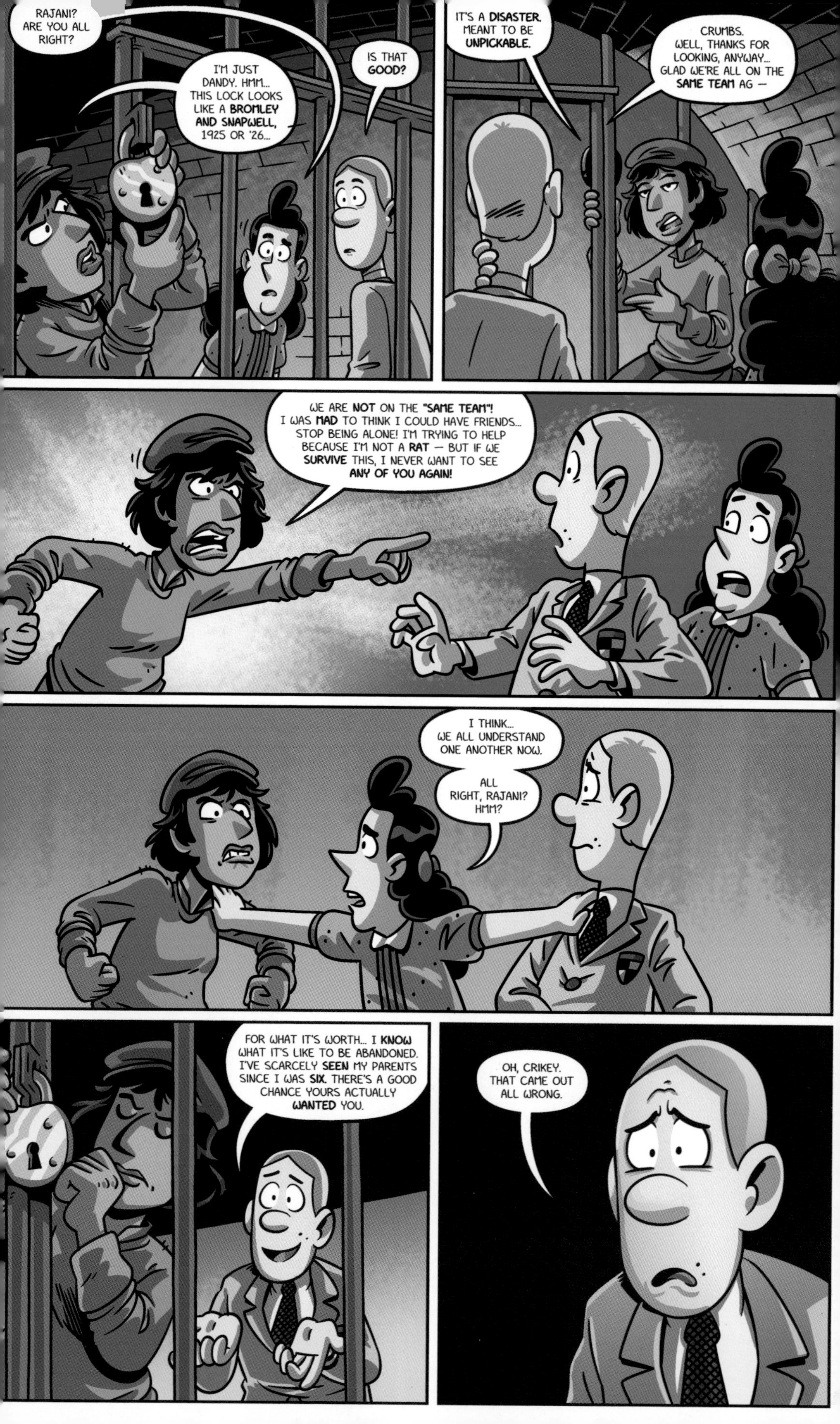
RAJANI? ARE YOU ALL RIGHT?
I'M JUST DANDY. HMM... THIS LOCK LOOKS LIKE A **BROMLEY AND SNAPWELL,** 1925 OR '26...
IS THAT **GOOD?**
IT'S A **DISASTER.** MEANT TO BE **UNPICKABLE.**
CRUMBS. WELL, THANKS FOR LOOKING, ANYWAY... GLAD WE'RE ALL ON THE **SAME TEAM** AG —
WE ARE **NOT** ON THE **"SAME TEAM"!** I WAS **MAD** TO THINK I COULD HAVE FRIENDS... STOP BEING ALONE! I'M TRYING TO HELP BECAUSE I'M NOT A **RAT** — BUT IF WE **SURVIVE** THIS, I NEVER WANT TO SEE **ANY OF YOU AGAIN!**
I THINK... WE ALL UNDERSTAND ONE ANOTHER NOW.
ALL RIGHT, RAJANI? HMM?
FOR WHAT IT'S WORTH... I **KNOW** WHAT IT'S LIKE TO BE ABANDONED. I'VE SCARCELY **SEEN** MY PARENTS SINCE I WAS **SIX.** THERE'S A GOOD CHANCE YOURS ACTUALLY **WANTED** YOU.
OH, CRIKEY. THAT CAME OUT ALL WRONG.

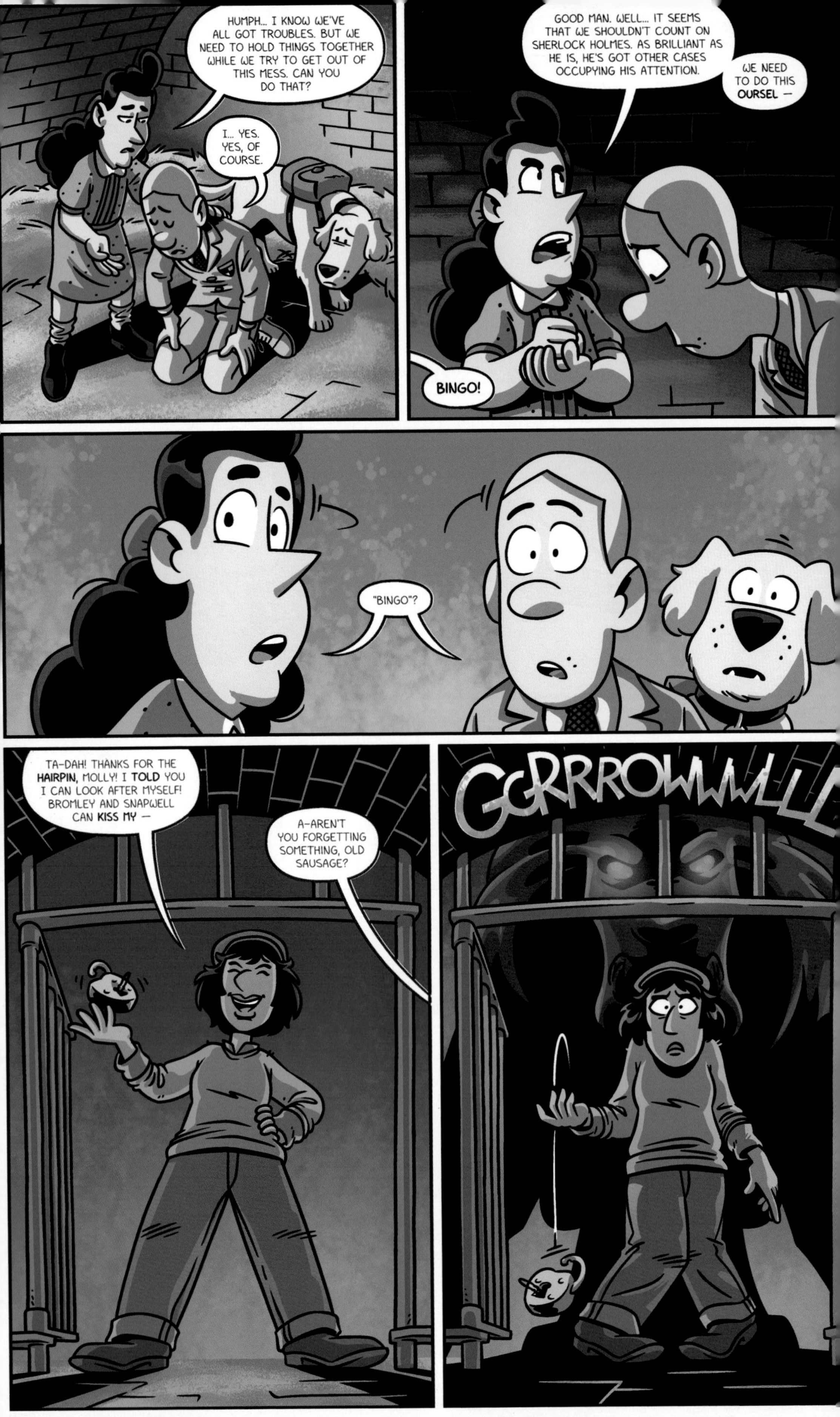
HUMPH... I KNOW WE'VE ALL GOT TROUBLES. BUT WE NEED TO HOLD THINGS TOGETHER WHILE WE TRY TO GET OUT OF THIS MESS. CAN YOU DO THAT?
I... YES. YES, OF COURSE.
GOOD MAN. WELL... IT SEEMS THAT WE SHOULDN'T COUNT ON SHERLOCK HOLMES. AS BRILLIANT AS HE IS, HE'S GOT OTHER CASES OCCUPYING HIS ATTENTION.
WE NEED TO DO THIS OURSEL —
BINGO!
"BINGO"?
TA-DAH! THANKS FOR THE HAIRPIN, MOLLY! I TOLD YOU I CAN LOOK AFTER MYSELF! BROMLEY AND SNAPWELL CAN KISS MY —
A-AREN'T YOU FORGETTING SOMETHING, OLD SAUSAGE?
GGRRROWWLLL

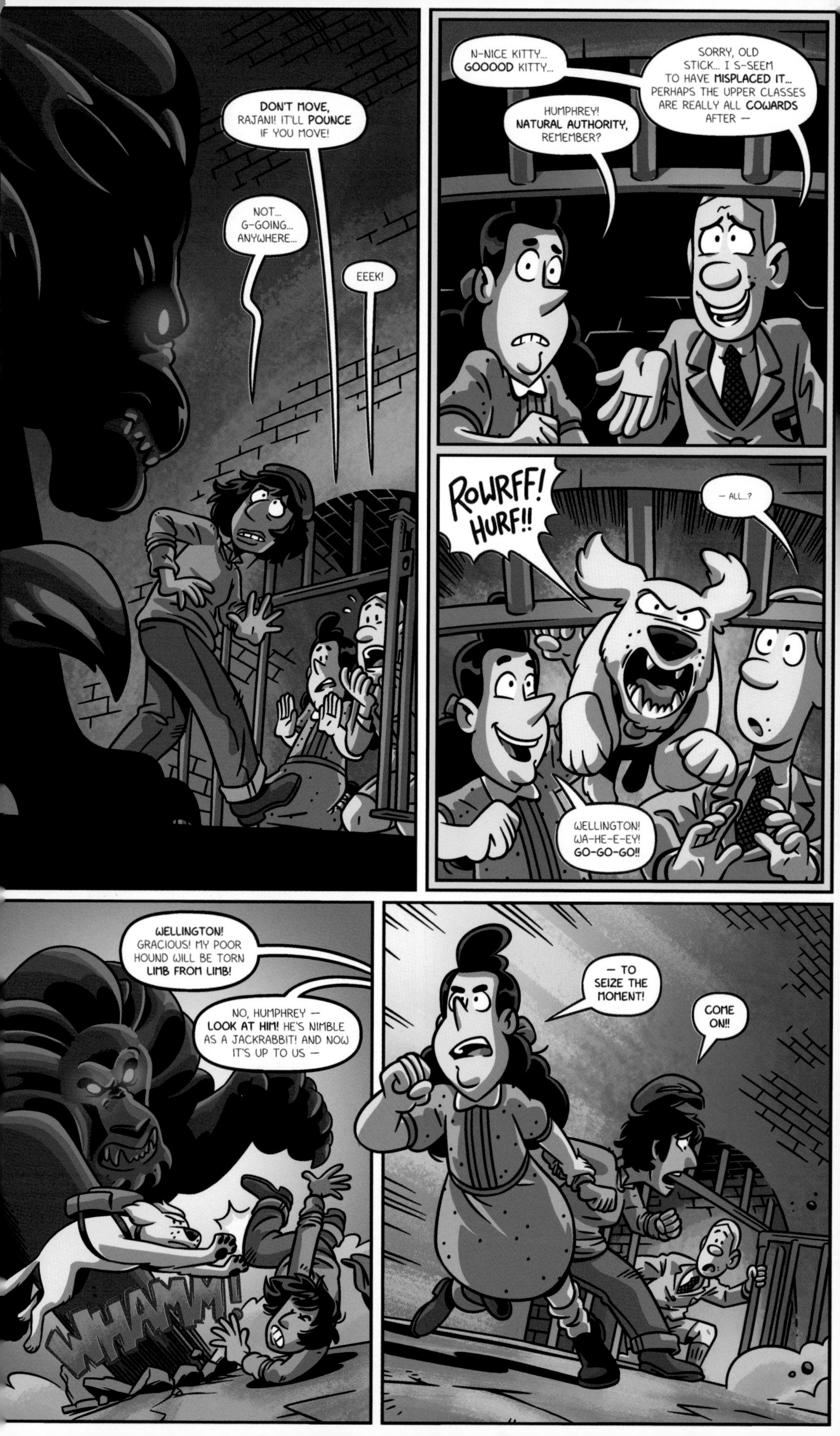
DON'T MOVE, RAJANI! IT'LL POUNCE IF YOU MOVE!
NOT... G-GOING... ANYWHERE...
EEEK!
N-NICE KITTY... GOOOOD KITTY...
HUMPHREY! NATURAL AUTHORITY, REMEMBER?
SORRY, OLD STICK... I S-SEEM TO HAVE MISPLACED IT... PERHAPS THE UPPER CLASSES ARE REALLY ALL COWARDS AFTER —
ROWRFF! HURF!!
— ALL...?
WELLINGTON! WA-HE-E-EY! GO-GO-GO!!
WELLINGTON! GRACIOUS! MY POOR HOUND WILL BE TORN LIMB FROM LIMB!
NO, HUMPHREY — LOOK AT HIM! HE'S NIMBLE AS A JACKRABBIT! AND NOW IT'S UP TO US —
WHAMM!
— TO SEIZE THE MOMENT!
COME ON!!

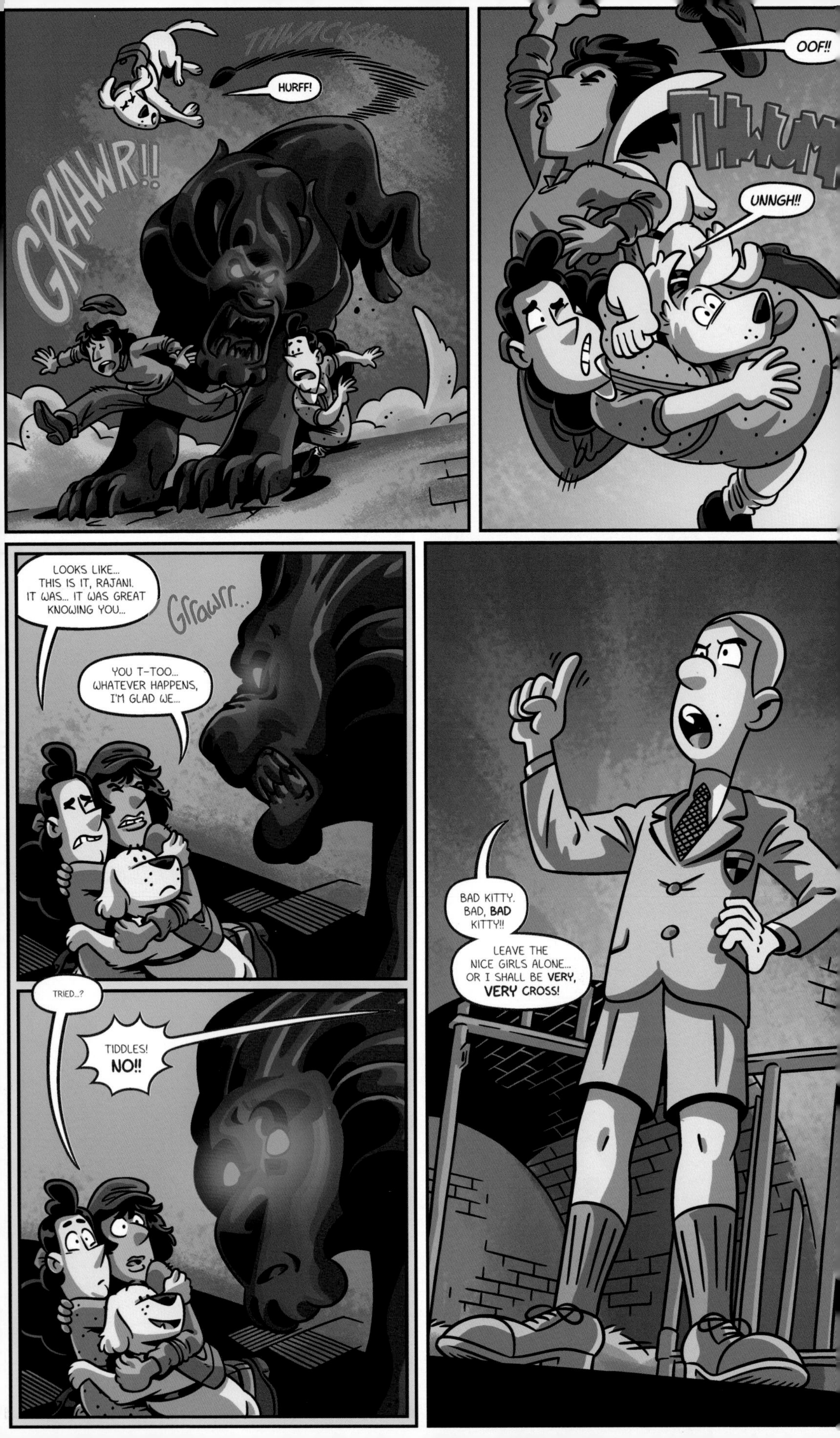
THWACK!!
HURFF!
GRAAWR!!
OOF!!
THWUMP
UNNGH!!
LOOKS LIKE... THIS IS IT, RAJANI. IT WAS... IT WAS GREAT KNOWING YOU...
Grrawrr...
YOU T-TOO... WHATEVER HAPPENS, I'M GLAD WE...
TRIED...?
TIDDLES! NO!!
BAD KITTY. BAD, BAD KITTY!!
LEAVE THE NICE GIRLS ALONE... OR I SHALL BE VERY, VERY CROSS!

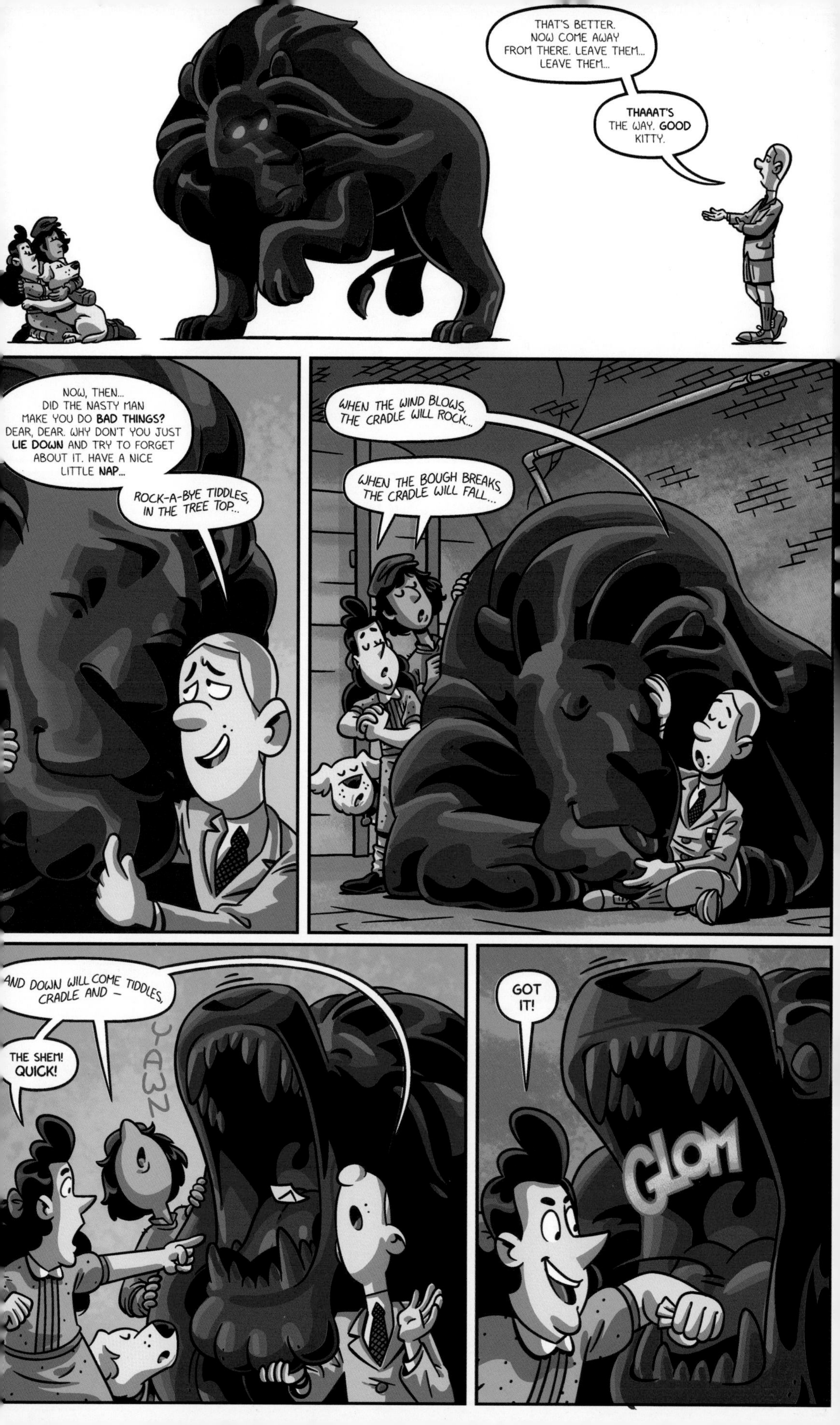
THAT'S BETTER. NOW COME AWAY FROM THERE. LEAVE THEM... LEAVE THEM...
THAAAT'S THE WAY. **GOOD** KITTY.
NOW, THEN... DID THE NASTY MAN MAKE YOU DO **BAD THINGS?** DEAR, DEAR. WHY DON'T YOU JUST **LIE DOWN** AND TRY TO FORGET ABOUT IT. HAVE A NICE LITTLE **NAP**...
ROCK-A-BYE TIDDLES, IN THE TREE TOP...
WHEN THE WIND BLOWS, THE CRADLE WILL ROCK...
WHEN THE BOUGH BREAKS, THE CRADLE WILL FALL...
AND DOWN WILL COME TIDDLES, CRADLE AND –
THE SHEM! **QUICK!**
YAWN
GOT IT!
GLOM

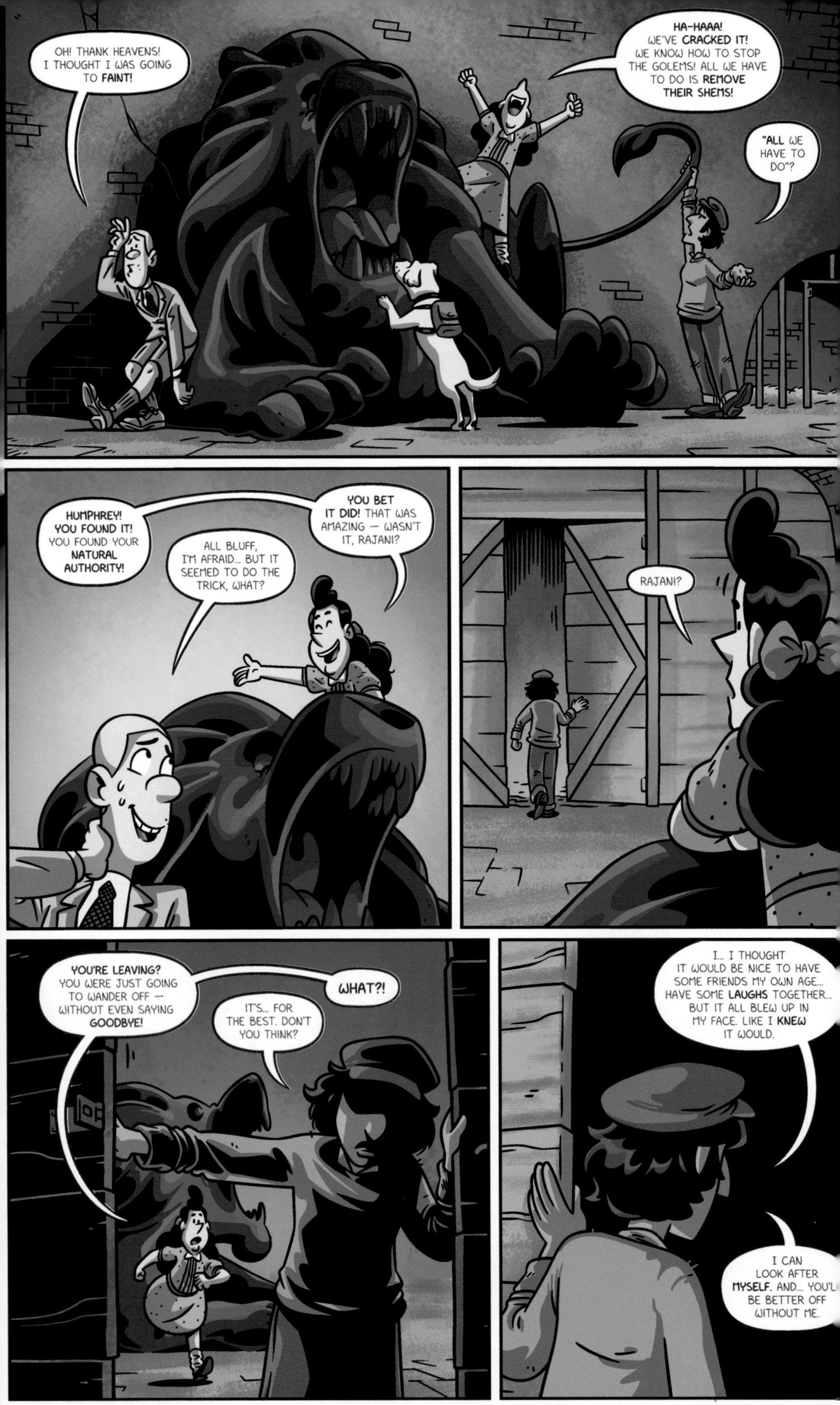
OH! THANK HEAVENS! I THOUGHT I WAS GOING TO FAINT!
HA-HAAA! WE'VE CRACKED IT! WE KNOW HOW TO STOP THE GOLEMS! ALL WE HAVE TO DO IS REMOVE THEIR SHEMS!
"ALL WE HAVE TO DO"?
HUMPHREY! YOU FOUND IT! YOU FOUND YOUR NATURAL AUTHORITY!
ALL BLUFF, I'M AFRAID... BUT IT SEEMED TO DO THE TRICK, WHAT?
YOU BET IT DID! THAT WAS AMAZING — WASN'T IT, RAJANI?
RAJANI?
YOU'RE LEAVING? YOU WERE JUST GOING TO WANDER OFF — WITHOUT EVEN SAYING GOODBYE!
WHAT?!
IT'S... FOR THE BEST. DON'T YOU THINK?
I... I THOUGHT IT WOULD BE NICE TO HAVE SOME FRIENDS MY OWN AGE... HAVE SOME LAUGHS TOGETHER... BUT IT ALL BLEW UP IN MY FACE. LIKE I KNEW IT WOULD.
I CAN LOOK AFTER MYSELF. AND... YOU'LL BE BETTER OFF WITHOUT ME.

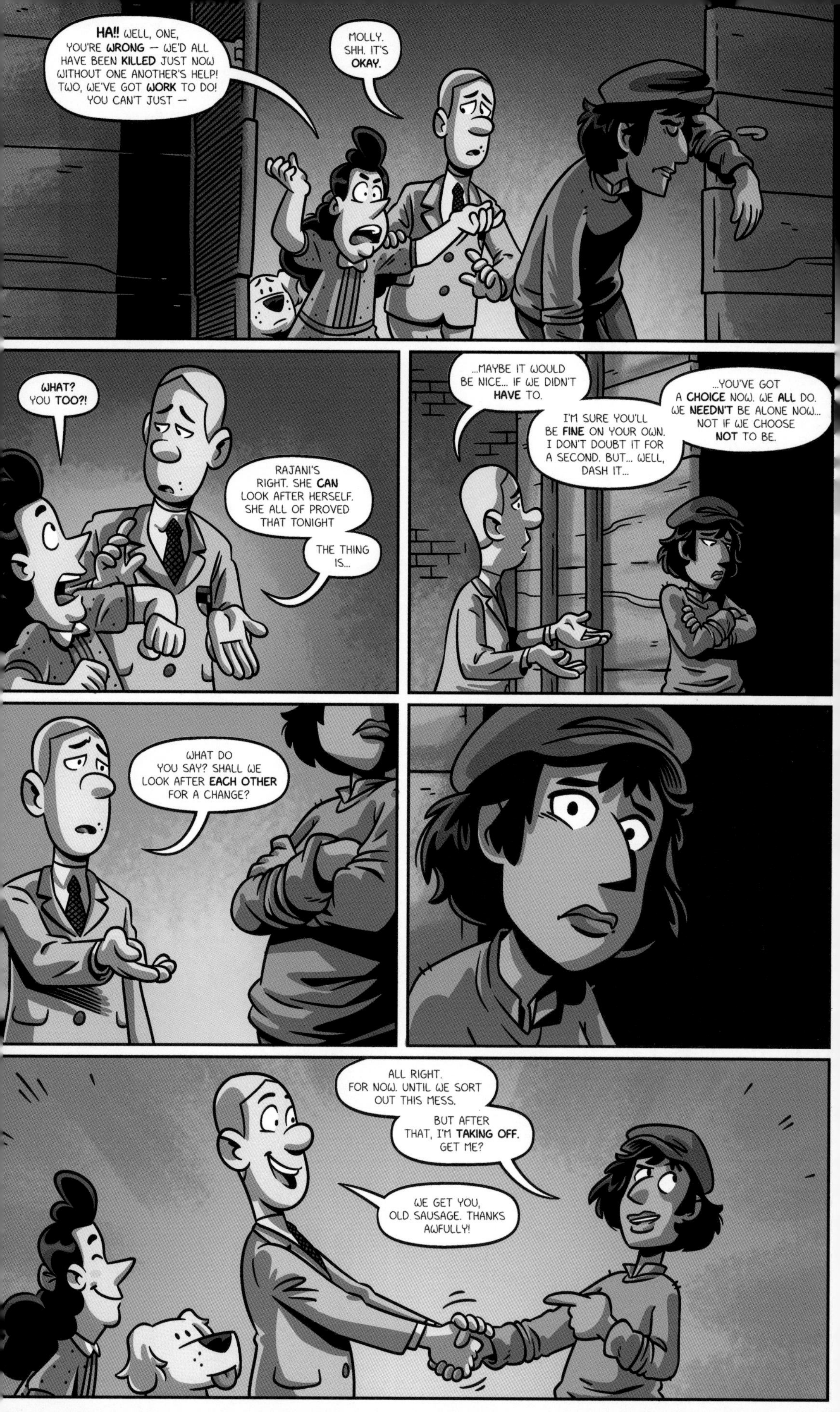
HA!! WELL, ONE, YOU'RE WRONG — WE'D ALL HAVE BEEN KILLED JUST NOW WITHOUT ONE ANOTHER'S HELP! TWO, WE'VE GOT WORK TO DO! YOU CAN'T JUST —
MOLLY. SHH. IT'S OKAY.
WHAT? YOU TOO?!
RAJANI'S RIGHT. SHE CAN LOOK AFTER HERSELF. SHE ALL OF PROVED THAT TONIGHT
THE THING IS...
...MAYBE IT WOULD BE NICE... IF WE DIDN'T HAVE TO.
I'M SURE YOU'LL BE FINE ON YOUR OWN. I DON'T DOUBT IT FOR A SECOND. BUT... WELL, DASH IT...
...YOU'VE GOT A CHOICE NOW. WE ALL DO. WE NEEDN'T BE ALONE NOW... NOT IF WE CHOOSE NOT TO BE.
WHAT DO YOU SAY? SHALL WE LOOK AFTER EACH OTHER FOR A CHANGE?
ALL RIGHT. FOR NOW. UNTIL WE SORT OUT THIS MESS.
BUT AFTER THAT, I'M TAKING OFF. GET ME?
WE GET YOU, OLD SAUSAGE. THANKS AWFULLY!

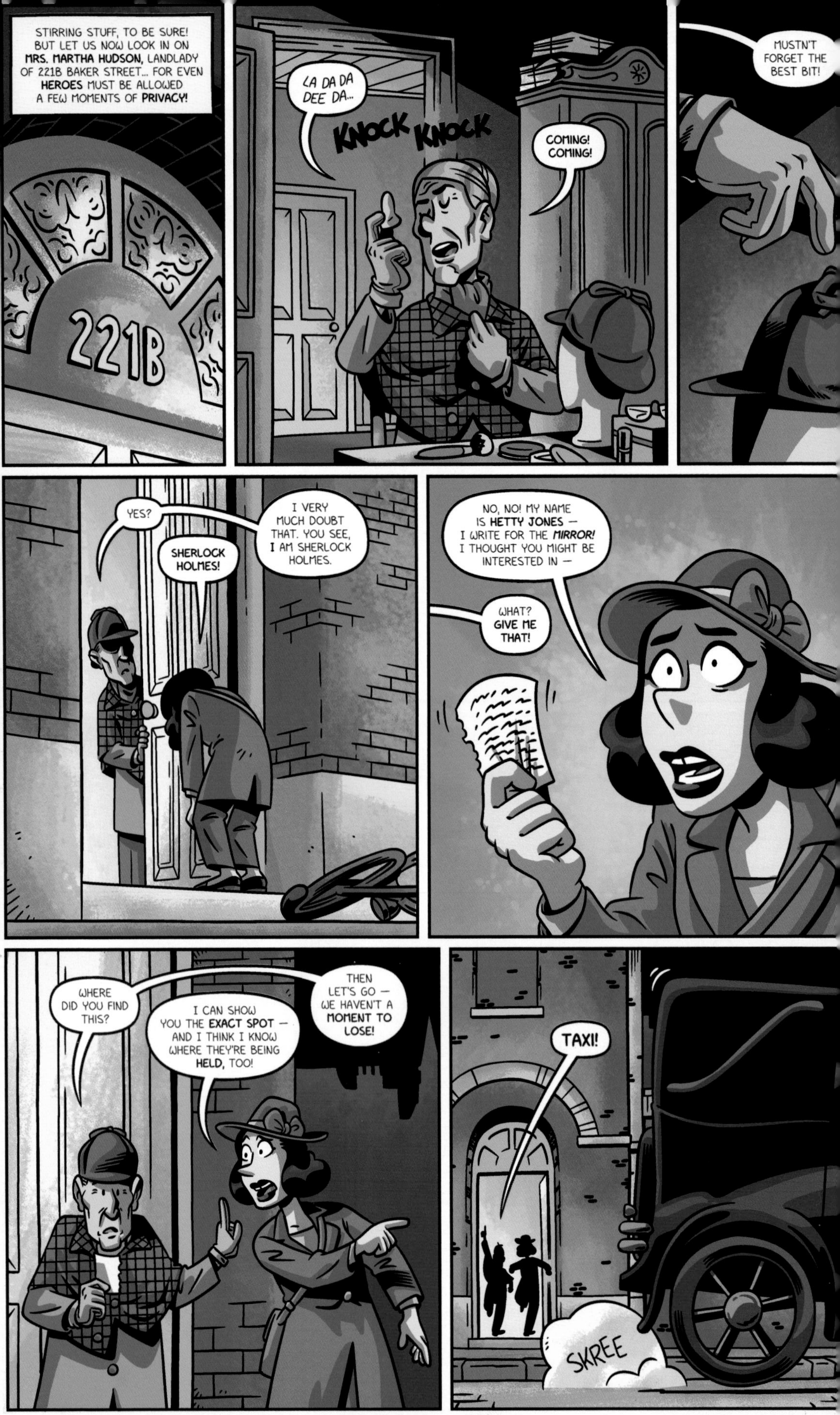
STIRRING STUFF, TO BE SURE! BUT LET US NOW LOOK IN ON MRS. MARTHA HUDSON, LANDLADY OF 221B BAKER STREET... FOR EVEN HEROES MUST BE ALLOWED A FEW MOMENTS OF PRIVACY!
221B
LA DA DA DEE DA...
KNOCK KNOCK
COMING! COMING!
MUSTN'T FORGET THE BEST BIT!
YES?
SHERLOCK HOLMES!
I VERY MUCH DOUBT THAT. YOU SEE, I AM SHERLOCK HOLMES.
NO, NO! MY NAME IS HETTY JONES — I WRITE FOR THE MIRROR! I THOUGHT YOU MIGHT BE INTERESTED IN —
WHAT? GIVE ME THAT!
WHERE DID YOU FIND THIS?
I CAN SHOW YOU THE EXACT SPOT — AND I THINK I KNOW WHERE THEY'RE BEING HELD, TOO!
THEN LET'S GO — WE HAVEN'T A MOMENT TO LOSE!
TAXI!
SKREE

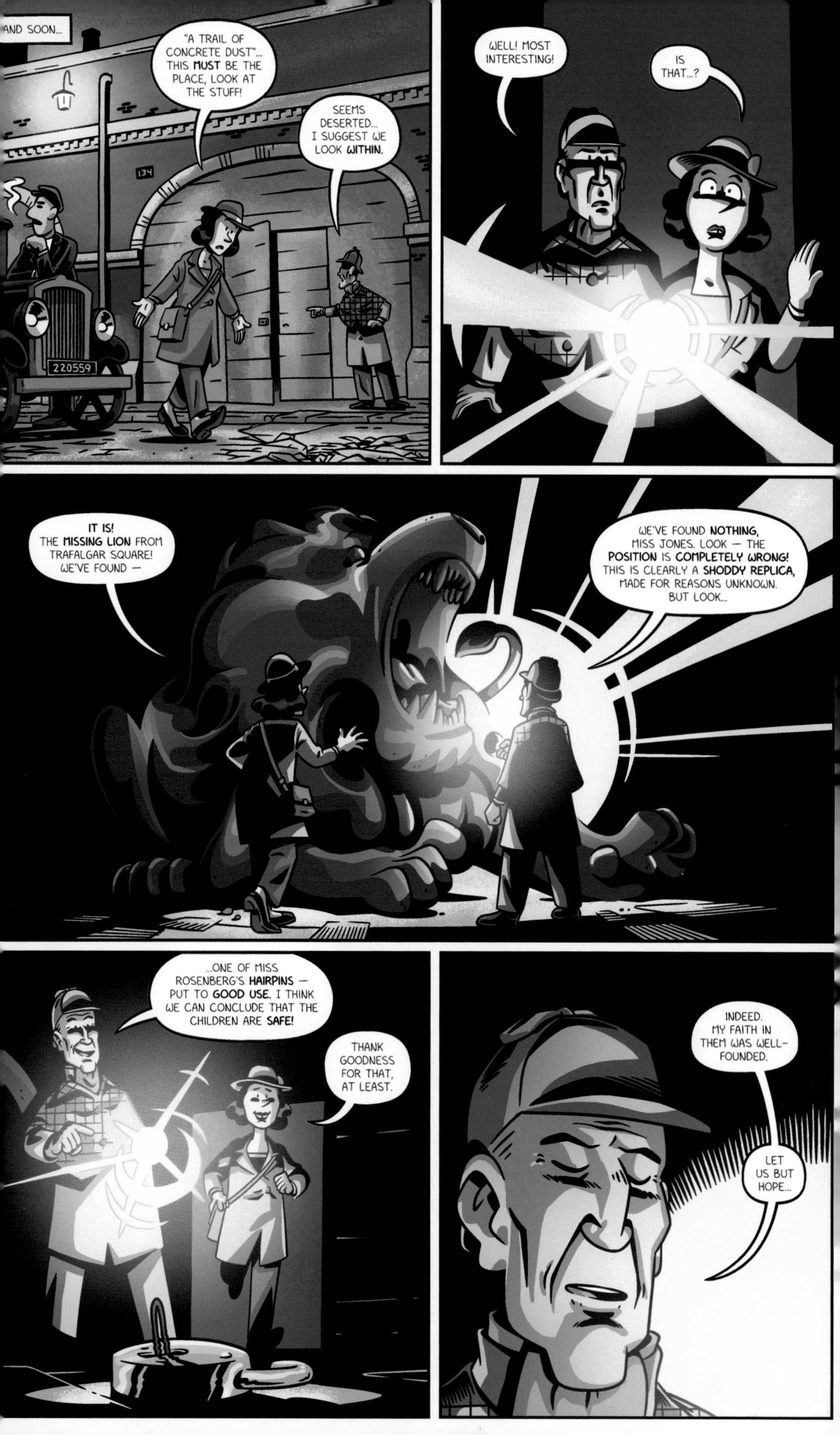
AND SOON...
"A TRAIL OF CONCRETE DUST"... THIS **MUST** BE THE PLACE, LOOK AT THE STUFF!
SEEMS DESERTED... I SUGGEST WE LOOK **WITHIN.**
134
220559
WELL! MOST INTERESTING!
IS THAT...?
IT IS! THE **MISSING LION** FROM TRAFALGAR SQUARE! WE'VE FOUND —
WE'VE FOUND **NOTHING,** MISS JONES. LOOK — THE **POSITION** IS **COMPLETELY WRONG!** THIS IS CLEARLY A **SHODDY REPLICA,** MADE FOR REASONS UNKNOWN. BUT LOOK...
...ONE OF MISS ROSENBERG'S **HAIRPINS** — PUT TO **GOOD USE.** I THINK WE CAN CONCLUDE THAT THE CHILDREN ARE **SAFE!**
THANK GOODNESS FOR THAT, AT LEAST.
INDEED. MY FAITH IN THEM WAS WELL-FOUNDED.
LET US BUT HOPE...

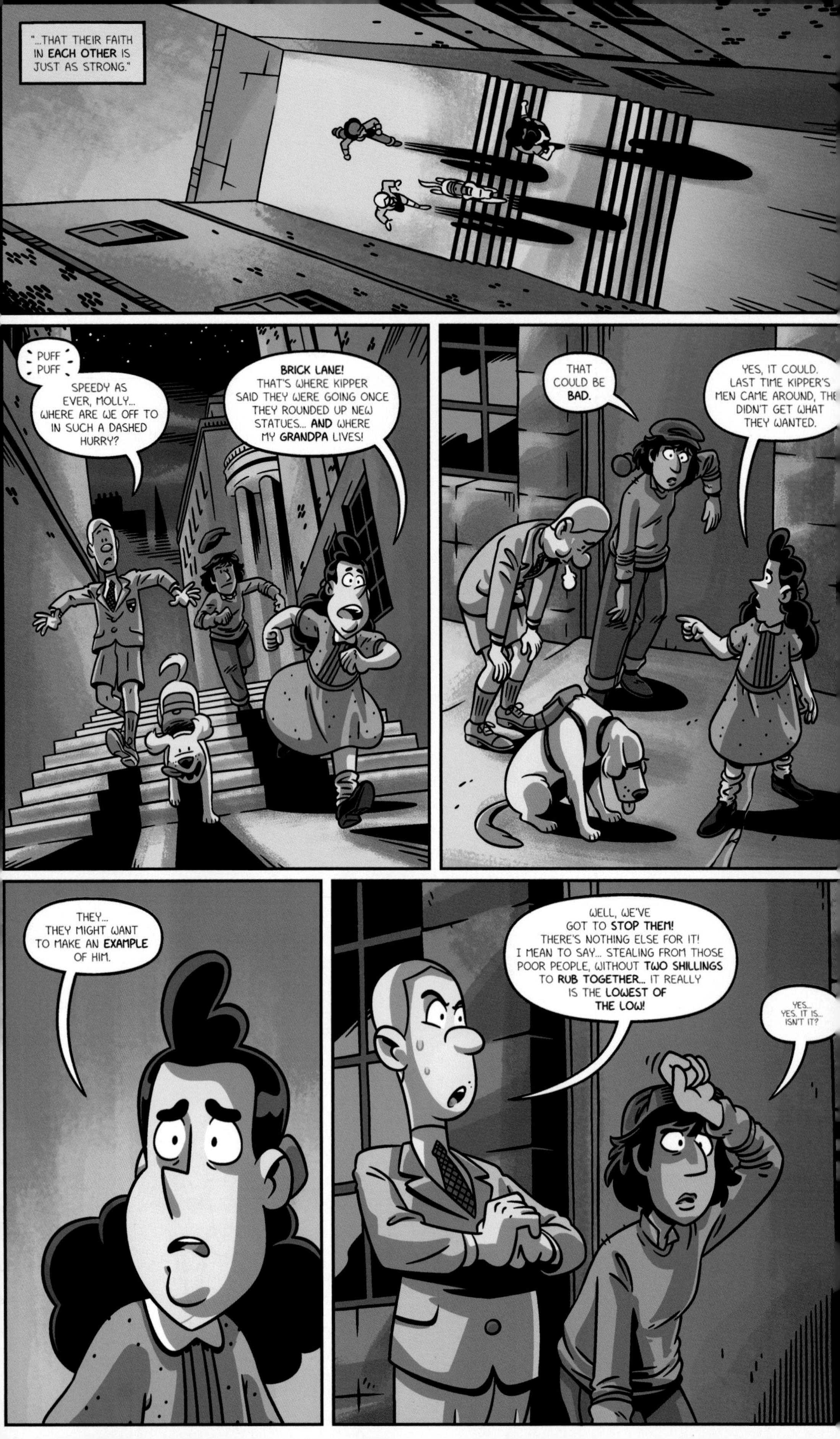
"...THAT THEIR FAITH IN **EACH OTHER** IS JUST AS STRONG."
PUFF PUFF
SPEEDY AS EVER, MOLLY... WHERE ARE WE OFF TO IN SUCH A DASHED HURRY?
BRICK LANE! THAT'S WHERE KIPPER SAID THEY WERE GOING ONCE THEY ROUNDED UP NEW STATUES... **AND** WHERE MY **GRANDPA** LIVES!
THAT COULD BE **BAD.**
YES, IT COULD. LAST TIME KIPPER'S MEN CAME AROUND, THE DIDN'T GET WHAT THEY WANTED.
THEY... THEY MIGHT WANT TO MAKE AN **EXAMPLE** OF HIM.
WELL, WE'VE GOT TO **STOP THEM!** THERE'S NOTHING ELSE FOR IT! I MEAN TO SAY... STEALING FROM THOSE POOR PEOPLE, WITHOUT **TWO SHILLINGS** TO **RUB TOGETHER...** IT REALLY IS THE **LOWEST OF THE LOW!**
YES... YES. IT IS... ISN'T IT?

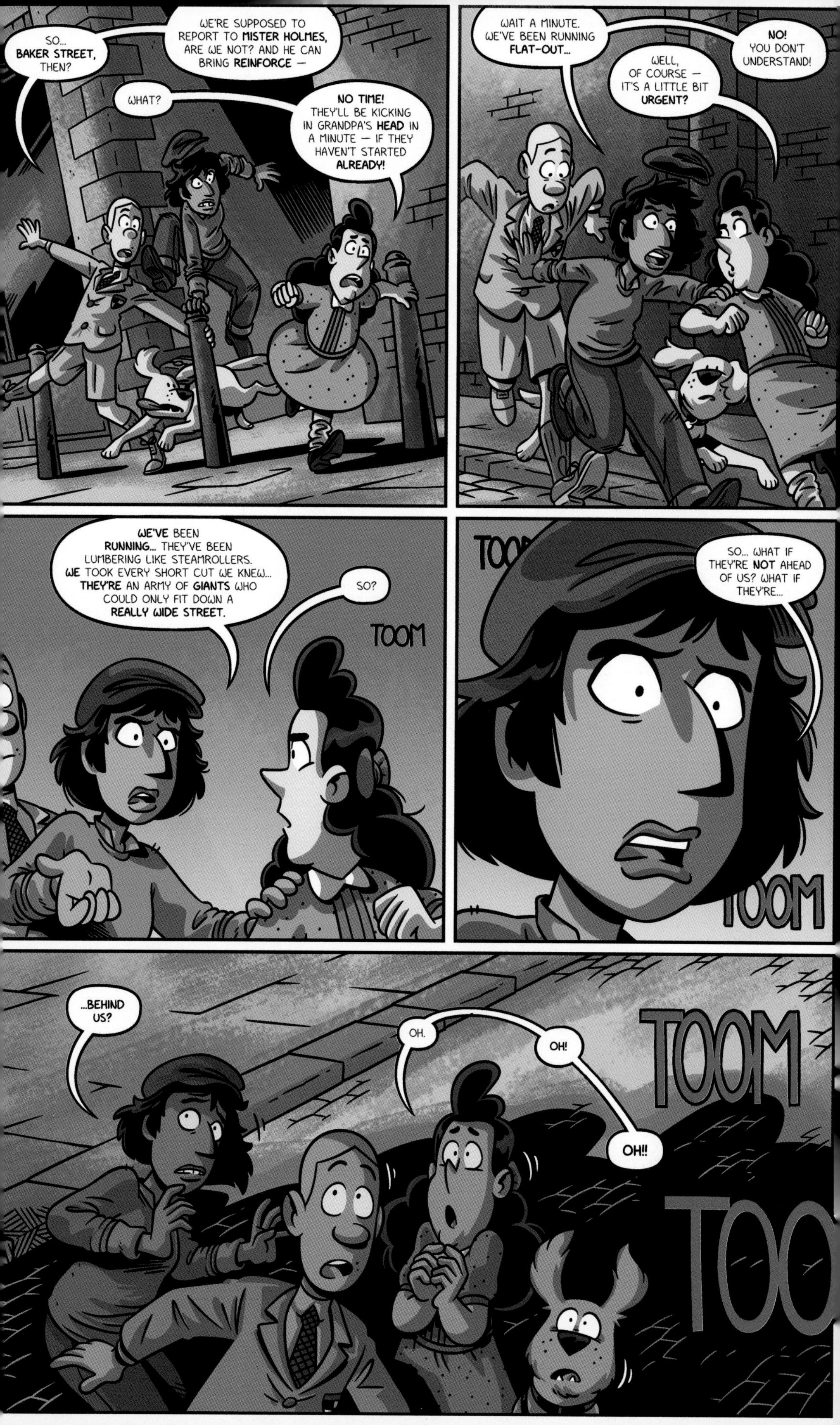

SO... BAKER STREET, THEN?
WE'RE SUPPOSED TO REPORT TO MISTER HOLMES, ARE WE NOT? AND HE CAN BRING REINFORCE —
WHAT?
NO TIME! THEY'LL BE KICKING IN GRANDPA'S HEAD IN A MINUTE — IF THEY HAVEN'T STARTED ALREADY!
WAIT A MINUTE. WE'VE BEEN RUNNING FLAT-OUT...
WELL, OF COURSE — IT'S A LITTLE BIT URGENT?
NO! YOU DON'T UNDERSTAND!
WE'VE BEEN RUNNING... THEY'VE BEEN LUMBERING LIKE STEAMROLLERS. WE TOOK EVERY SHORT CUT WE KNEW... THEY'RE AN ARMY OF GIANTS WHO COULD ONLY FIT DOWN A REALLY WIDE STREET.
SO?
TOOM
SO... WHAT IF THEY'RE NOT AHEAD OF US? WHAT IF THEY'RE...
TOOM
...BEHIND US?
OH.
OH!
OH!!
TOOM

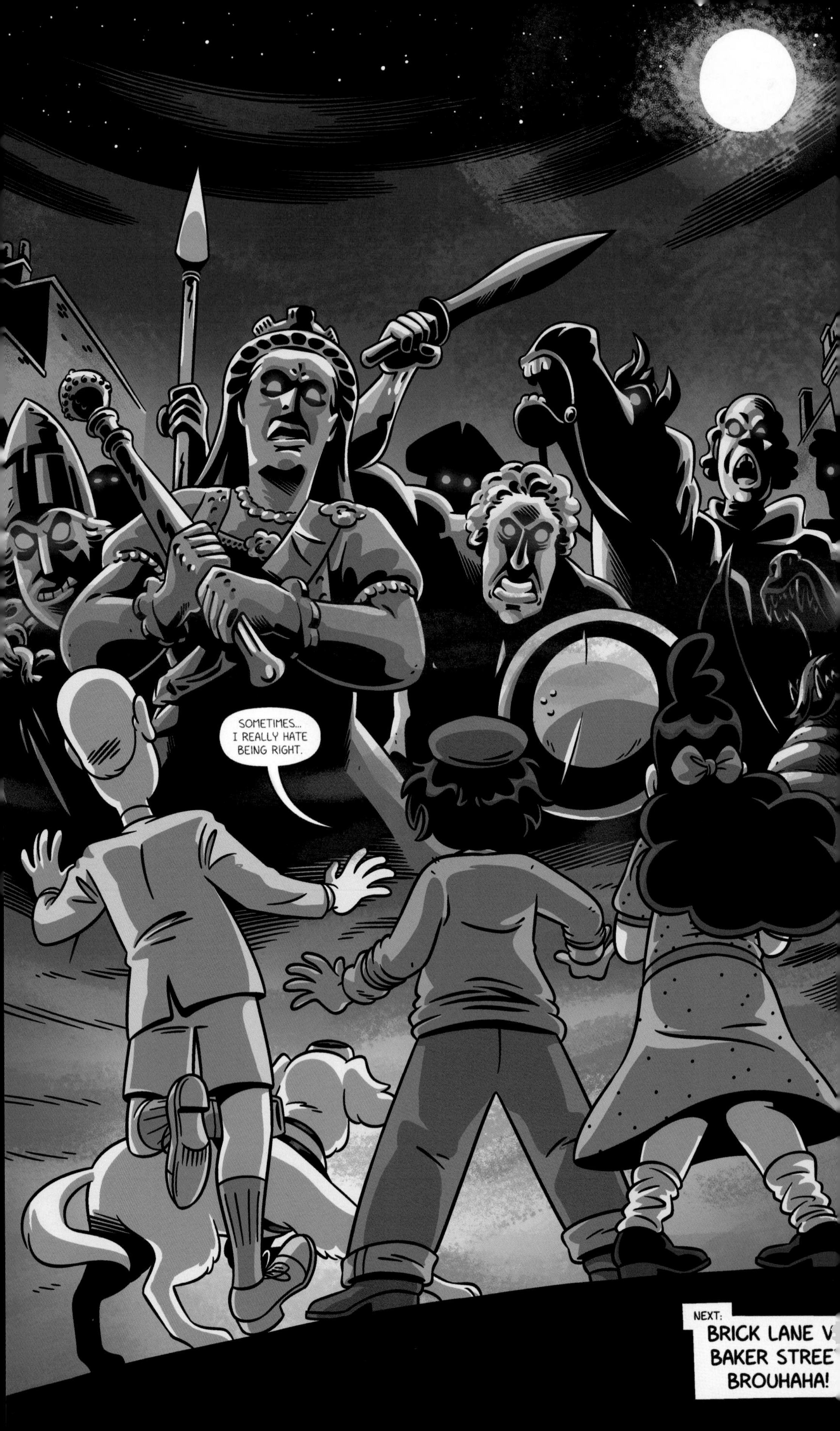
SOMETIMES... I REALLY HATE BEING RIGHT.
NEXT:
BRICK LANE V
BAKER STREE
BROUHAHA!

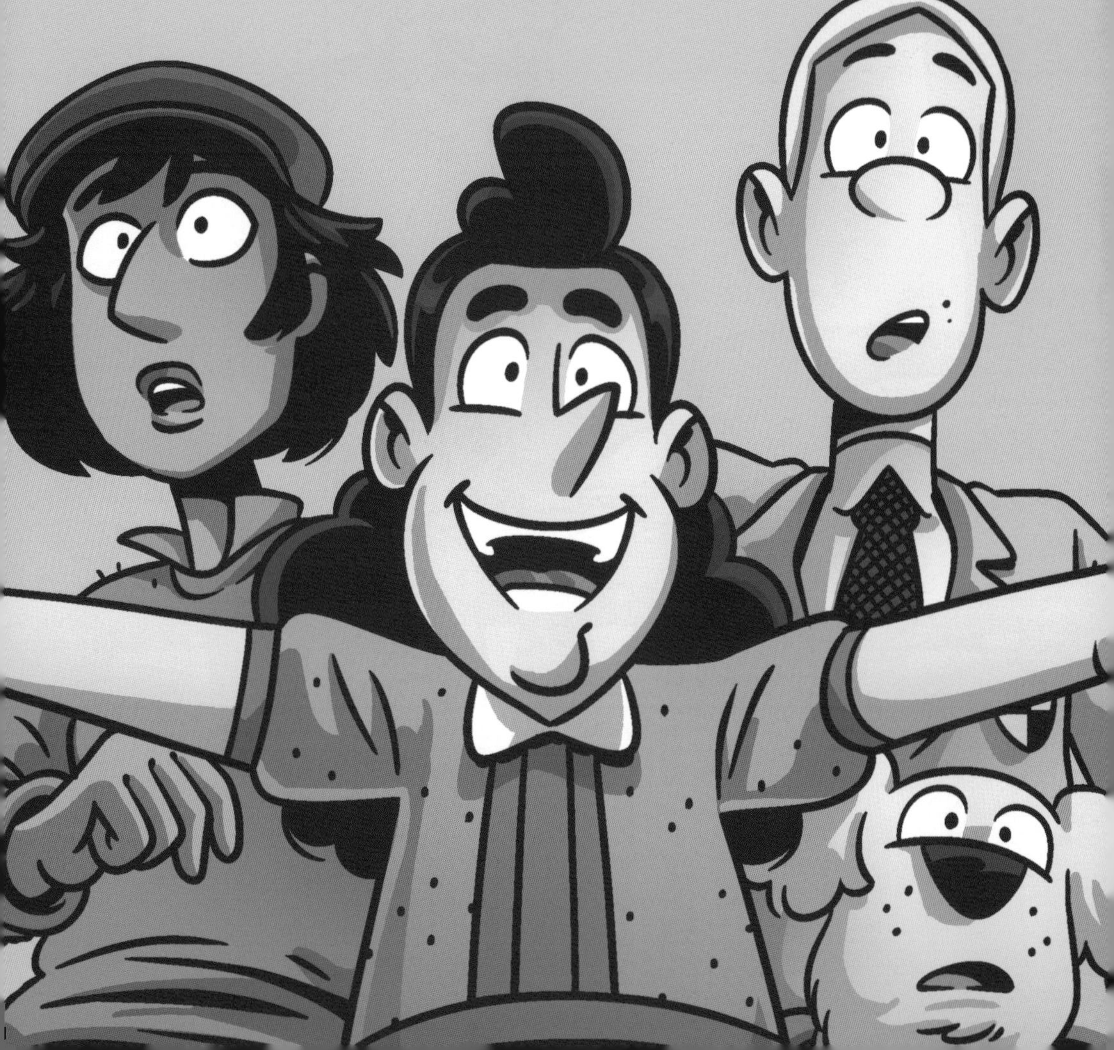

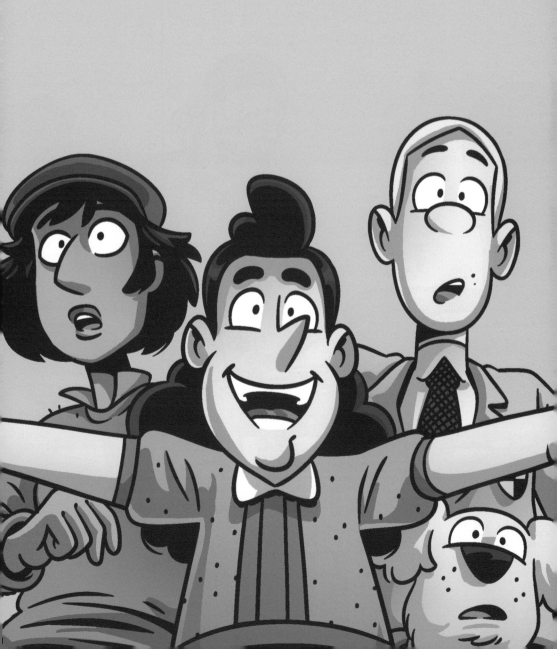

CHAPTER FOUR

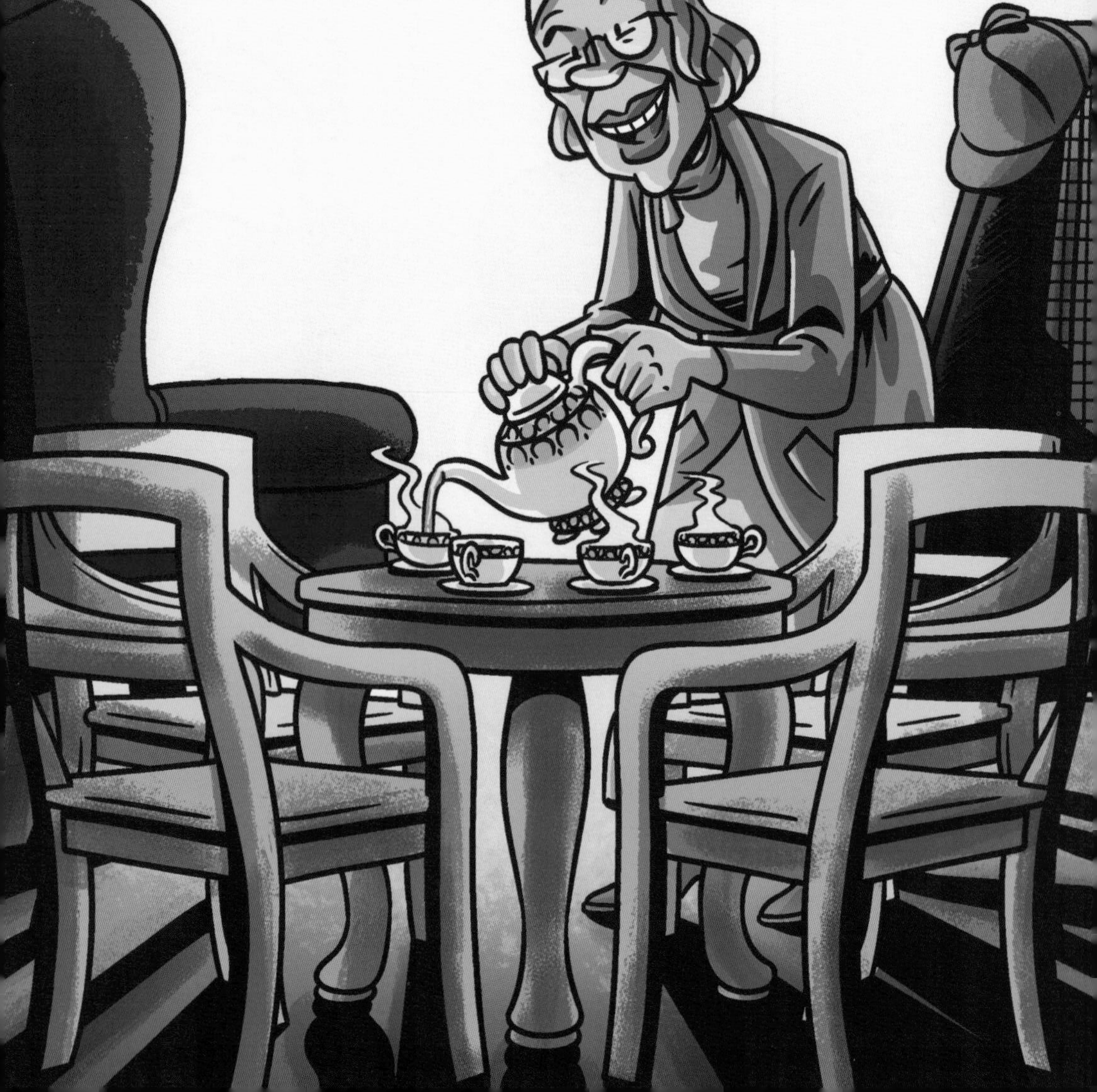

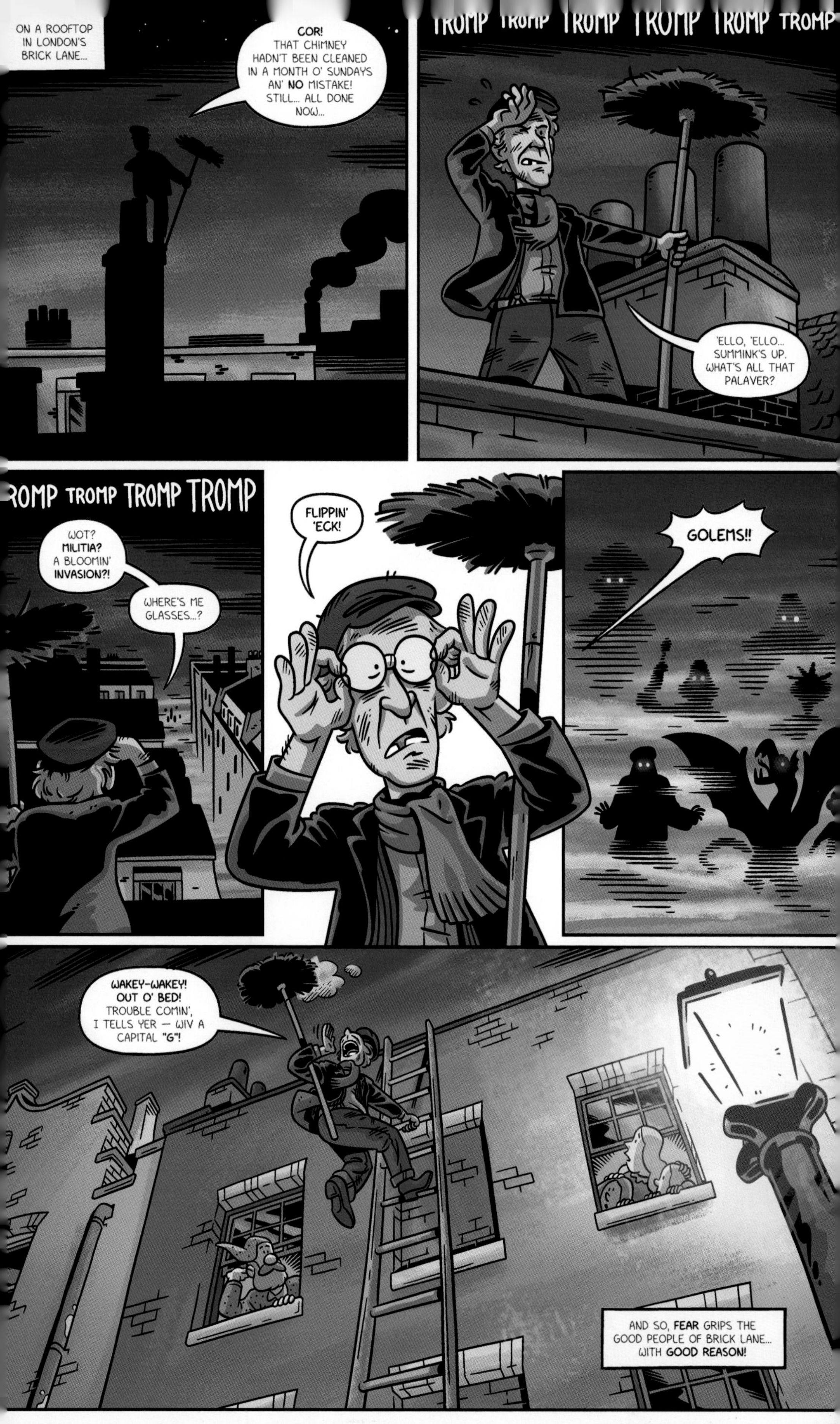
ON A ROOFTOP IN LONDON'S BRICK LANE...
COR! THAT CHIMNEY HADN'T BEEN CLEANED IN A MONTH O' SUNDAYS AN' NO MISTAKE! STILL... ALL DONE NOW...
TROMP TROMP TROMP TROMP TROMP TROMP
'ELLO, 'ELLO... SUMMINK'S UP. WHAT'S ALL THAT PALAVER?
TROMP TROMP TROMP TROMP
WOT? MILITIA? A BLOOMIN' INVASION?!
WHERE'S ME GLASSES...?
FLIPPIN' 'ECK!
GOLEMS!!
WAKEY-WAKEY! OUT O' BED! TROUBLE COMIN', I TELLS YER — WIV A CAPITAL "G"!
AND SO, FEAR GRIPS THE GOOD PEOPLE OF BRICK LANE... WITH GOOD REASON!

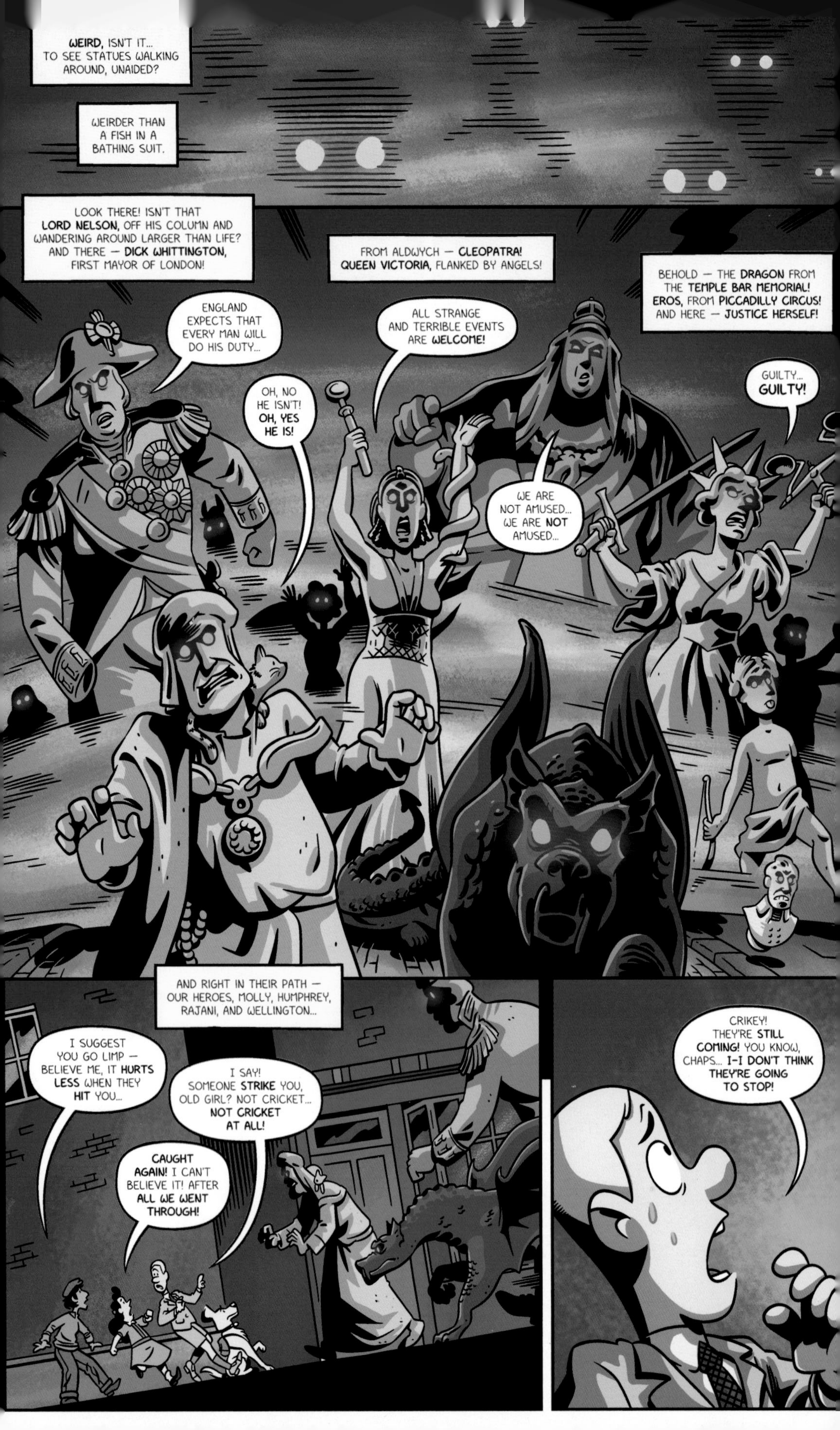
WEIRD, ISN'T IT... TO SEE STATUES WALKING AROUND, UNAIDED?
WEIRDER THAN A FISH IN A BATHING SUIT.
LOOK THERE! ISN'T THAT LORD NELSON, OFF HIS COLUMN AND WANDERING AROUND LARGER THAN LIFE? AND THERE — DICK WHITTINGTON, FIRST MAYOR OF LONDON!
FROM ALDWYCH — CLEOPATRA! QUEEN VICTORIA, FLANKED BY ANGELS!
BEHOLD — THE DRAGON FROM THE TEMPLE BAR MEMORIAL! EROS, FROM PICCADILLY CIRCUS! AND HERE — JUSTICE HERSELF!
ENGLAND EXPECTS THAT EVERY MAN WILL DO HIS DUTY...
OH, NO HE ISN'T! OH, YES HE IS!
ALL STRANGE AND TERRIBLE EVENTS ARE WELCOME!
WE ARE NOT AMUSED... WE ARE NOT AMUSED...
GUILTY... GUILTY!
AND RIGHT IN THEIR PATH — OUR HEROES, MOLLY, HUMPHREY, RAJANI, AND WELLINGTON...
I SUGGEST YOU GO LIMP — BELIEVE ME, IT HURTS LESS WHEN THEY HIT YOU...
I SAY! SOMEONE STRIKE YOU, OLD GIRL? NOT CRICKET... NOT CRICKET AT ALL!
CAUGHT AGAIN! I CAN'T BELIEVE IT! AFTER ALL WE WENT THROUGH!
CRIKEY! THEY'RE STILL COMING! YOU KNOW, CHAPS... I-I DON'T THINK THEY'RE GOING TO STOP!

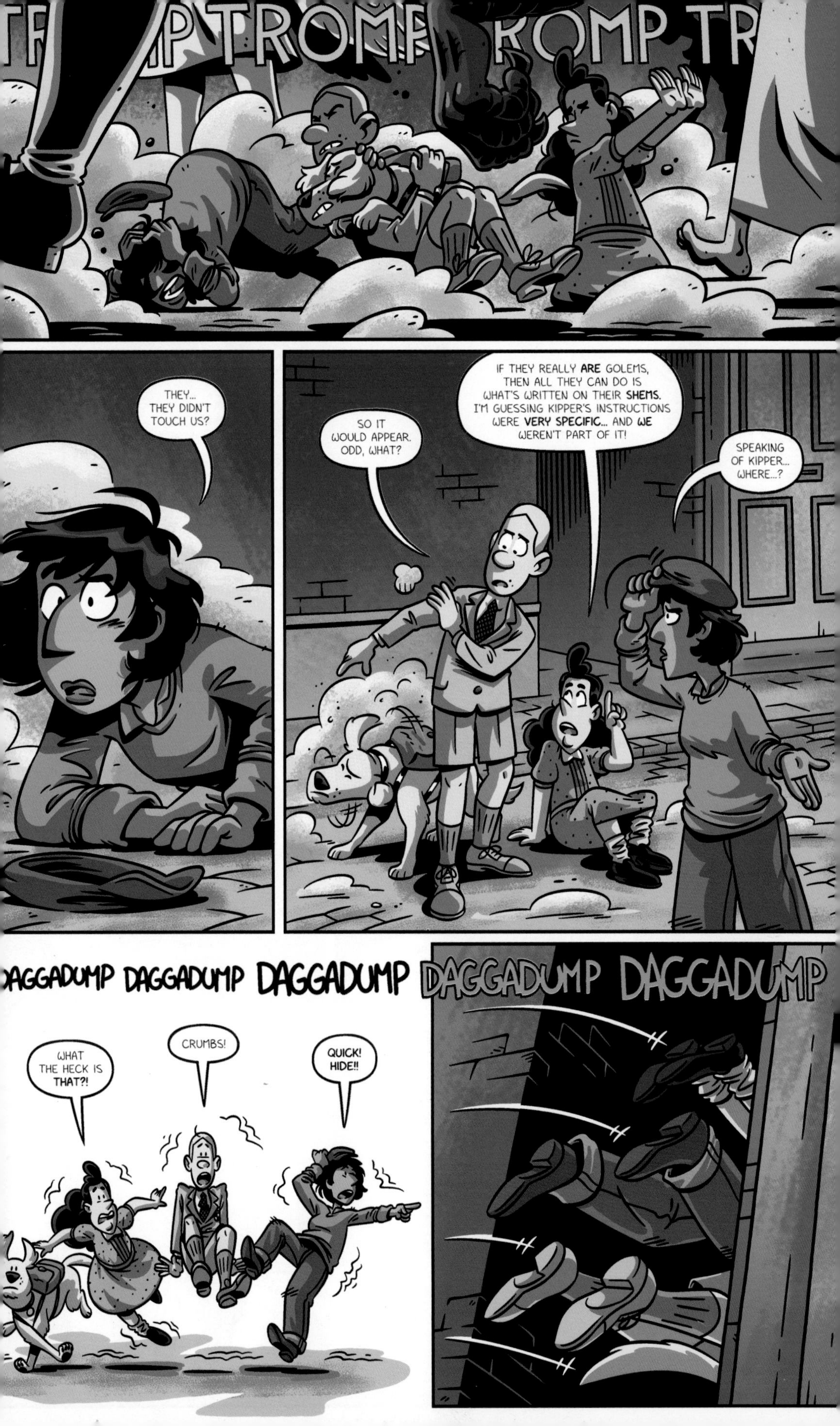
TROMP TROMP TROMP TR
THEY... THEY DIDN'T TOUCH US?
SO IT WOULD APPEAR. ODD, WHAT?
IF THEY REALLY ARE GOLEMS, THEN ALL THEY CAN DO IS WHAT'S WRITTEN ON THEIR SHEMS. I'M GUESSING KIPPER'S INSTRUCTIONS WERE VERY SPECIFIC... AND WE WEREN'T PART OF IT!
SPEAKING OF KIPPER... WHERE...?
DAGGADUMP DAGGADUMP DAGGADUMP DAGGADUMP DAGGADUMP
WHAT THE HECK IS THAT?!
CRUMBS!
QUICK! HIDE!!

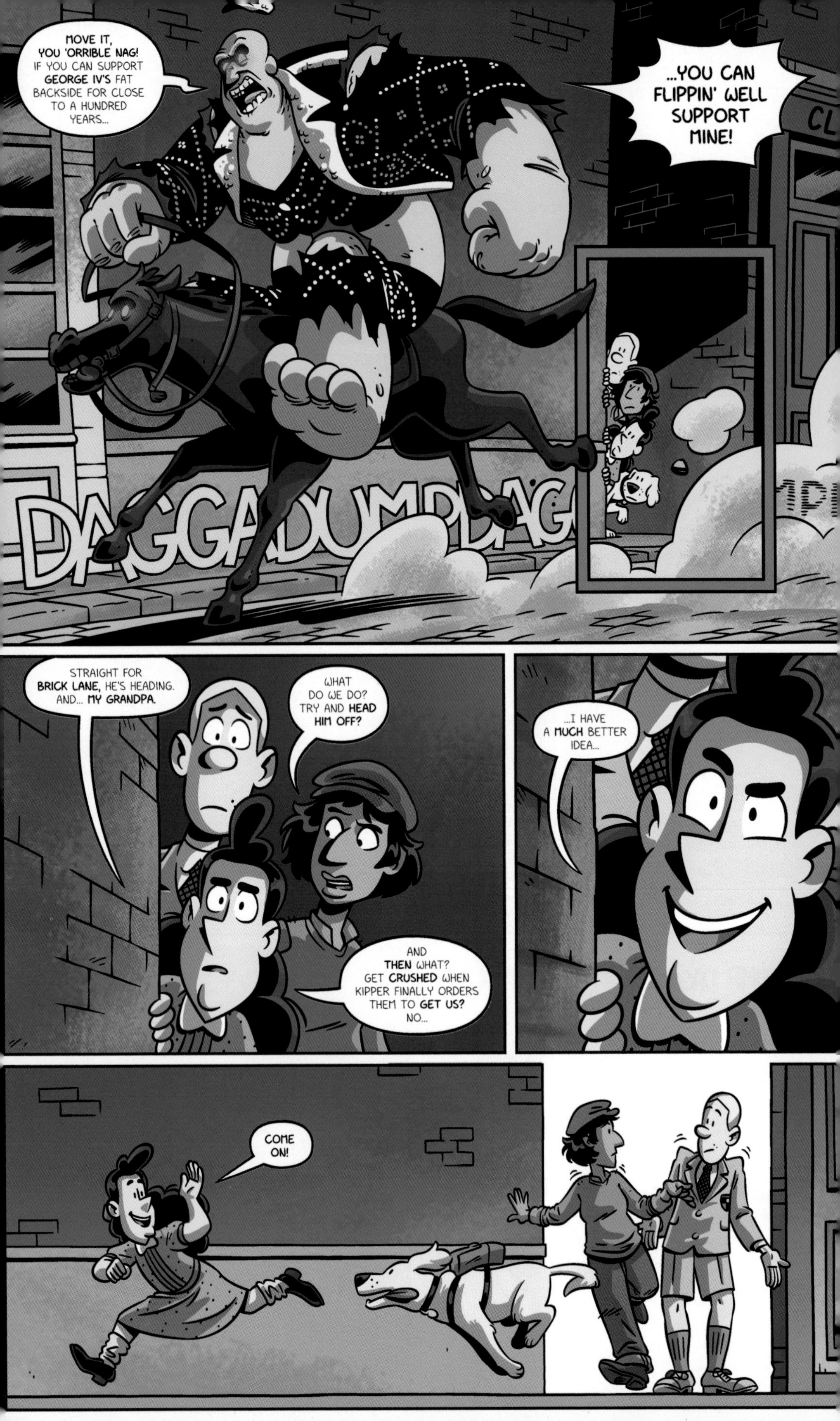
MOVE IT, YOU 'ORRIBLE NAG! IF YOU CAN SUPPORT GEORGE IV'S FAT BACKSIDE FOR CLOSE TO A HUNDRED YEARS...
...YOU CAN FLIPPIN' WELL SUPPORT MINE!
DAGGADUMPDAG
STRAIGHT FOR BRICK LANE, HE'S HEADING. AND... MY GRANDPA.
WHAT DO WE DO? TRY AND HEAD HIM OFF?
AND THEN WHAT? GET CRUSHED WHEN KIPPER FINALLY ORDERS THEM TO GET US? NO...
...I HAVE A MUCH BETTER IDEA...
COME ON!

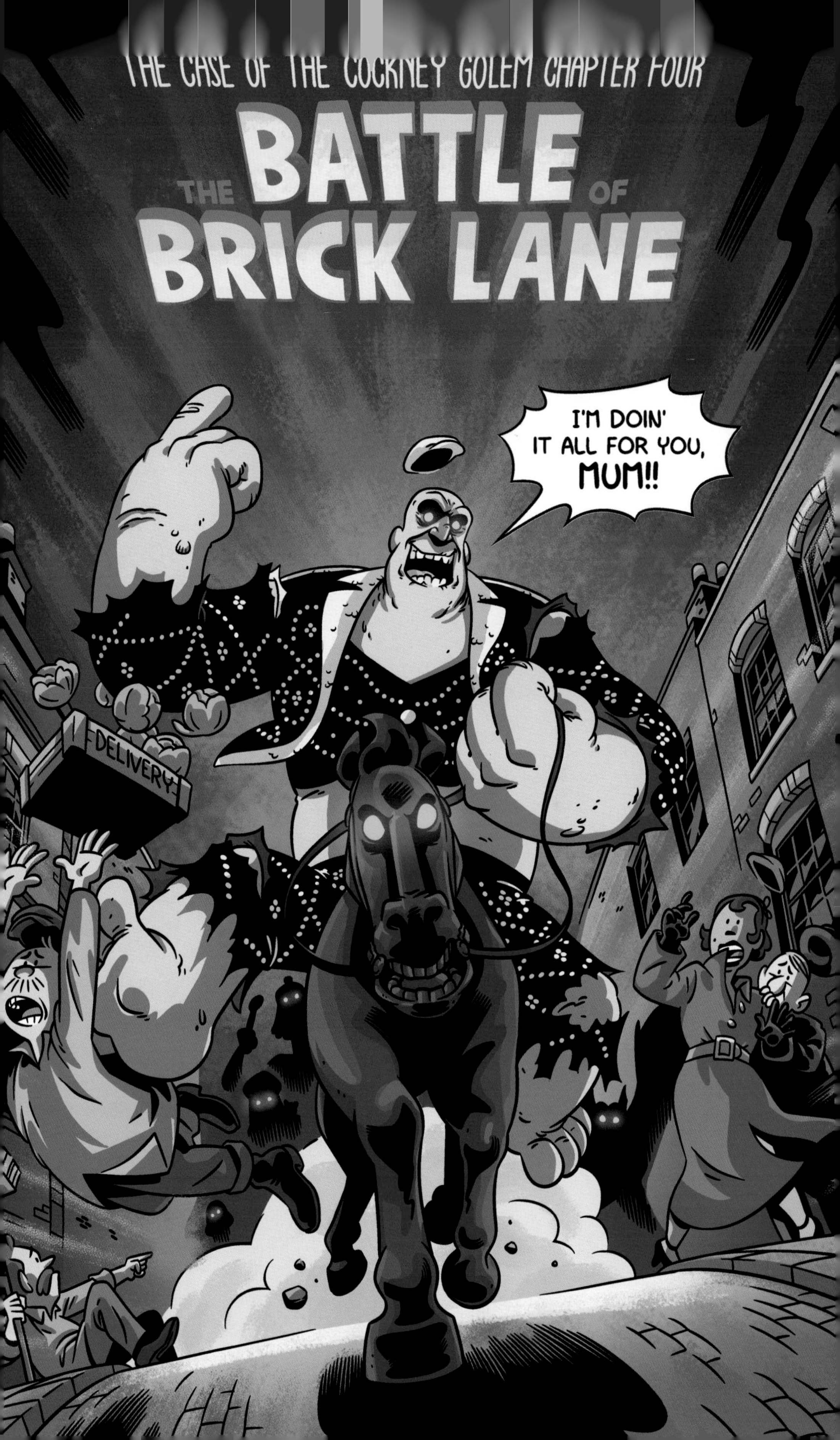
THE CASE OF THE COCKNEY GOLEM CHAPTER FOUR
THE BATTLE OF BRICK LANE
I'M DOIN' IT ALL FOR YOU, MUM!!
DELIVERY

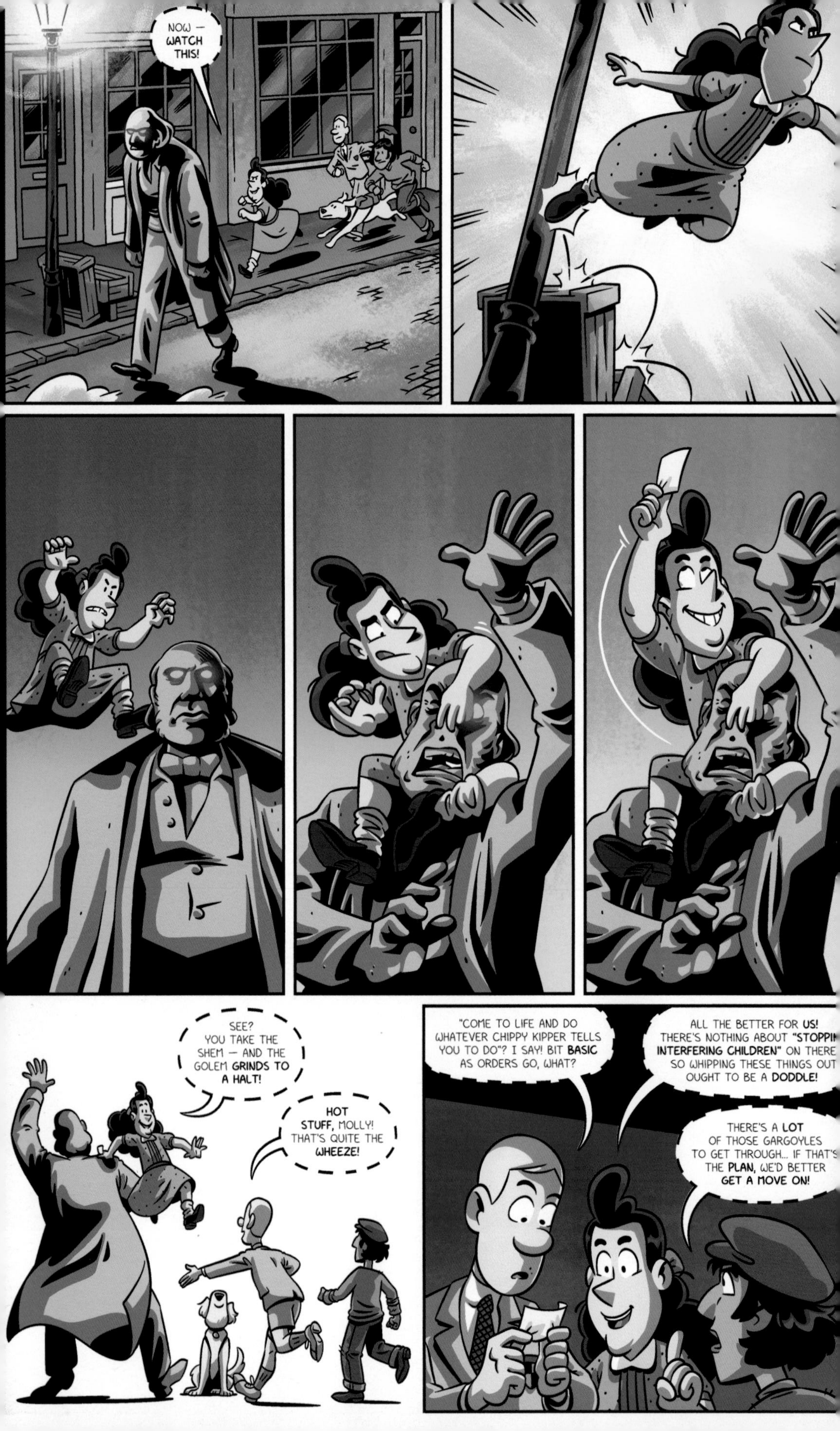
NOW — WATCH THIS!
SEE? YOU TAKE THE SHEM — AND THE GOLEM GRINDS TO A HALT!
HOT STUFF, MOLLY! THAT'S QUITE THE WHEEZE!
"COME TO LIFE AND DO WHATEVER CHIPPY KIPPER TELLS YOU TO DO"? I SAY! BIT BASIC AS ORDERS GO, WHAT?
ALL THE BETTER FOR US! THERE'S NOTHING ABOUT "STOPPI
INTERFERING CHILDREN" ON THERE
SO WHIPPING THESE THINGS OUT OUGHT TO BE A DODDLE!
THERE'S A LOT OF THOSE GARGOYLES TO GET THROUGH... IF THAT'S THE PLAN, WE'D BETTER GET A MOVE ON!

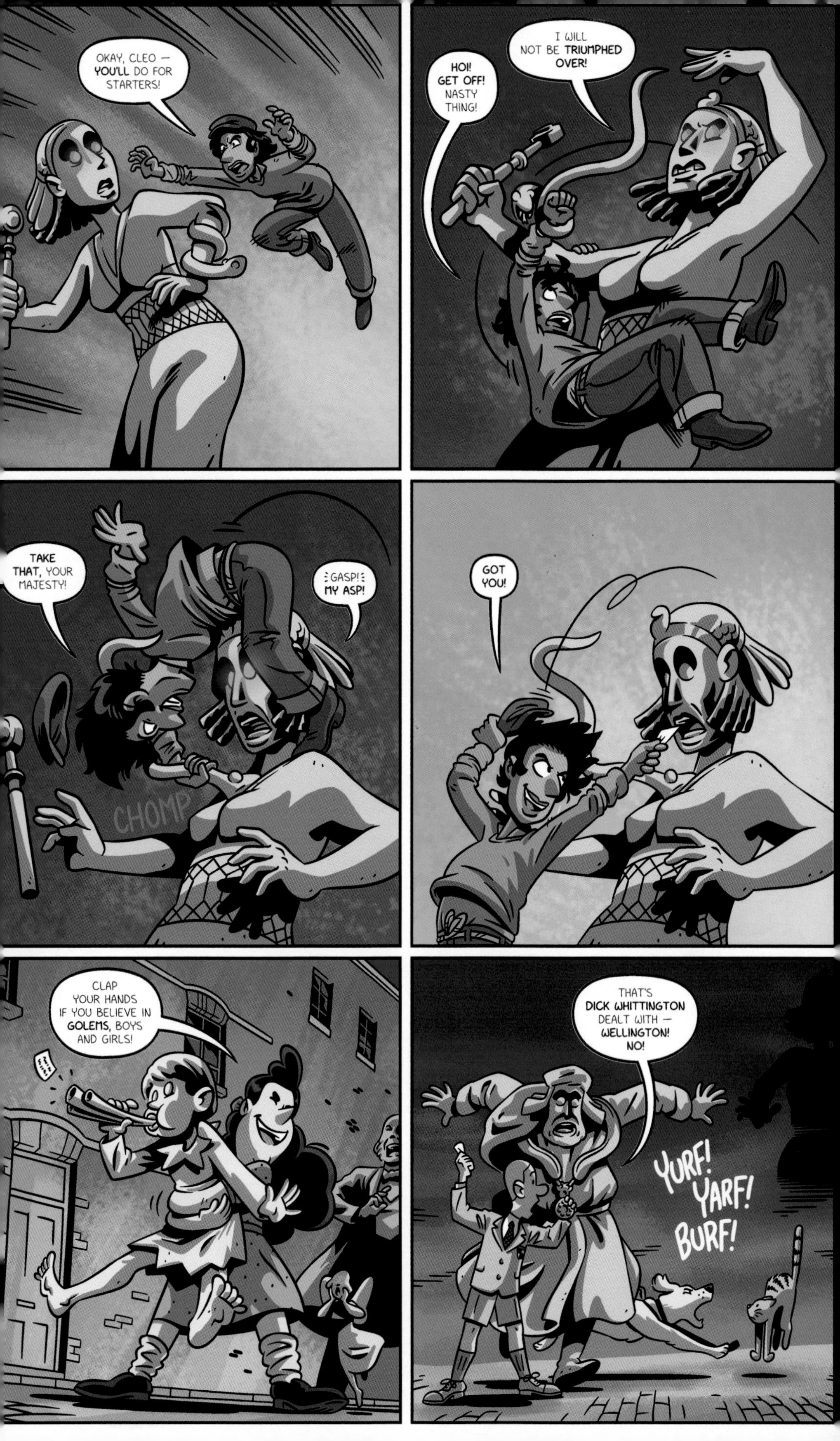
OKAY, CLEO — YOU'LL DO FOR STARTERS!
HOI! GET OFF! NASTY THING!
I WILL NOT BE TRIUMPHED OVER!
TAKE THAT, YOUR MAJESTY!
GASP! MY ASP!
CHOMP
GOT YOU!
CLAP YOUR HANDS IF YOU BELIEVE IN GOLEMS, BOYS AND GIRLS!
THAT'S DICK WHITTINGTON DEALT WITH — WELLINGTON! NO!
YURF! YARF! BURF!

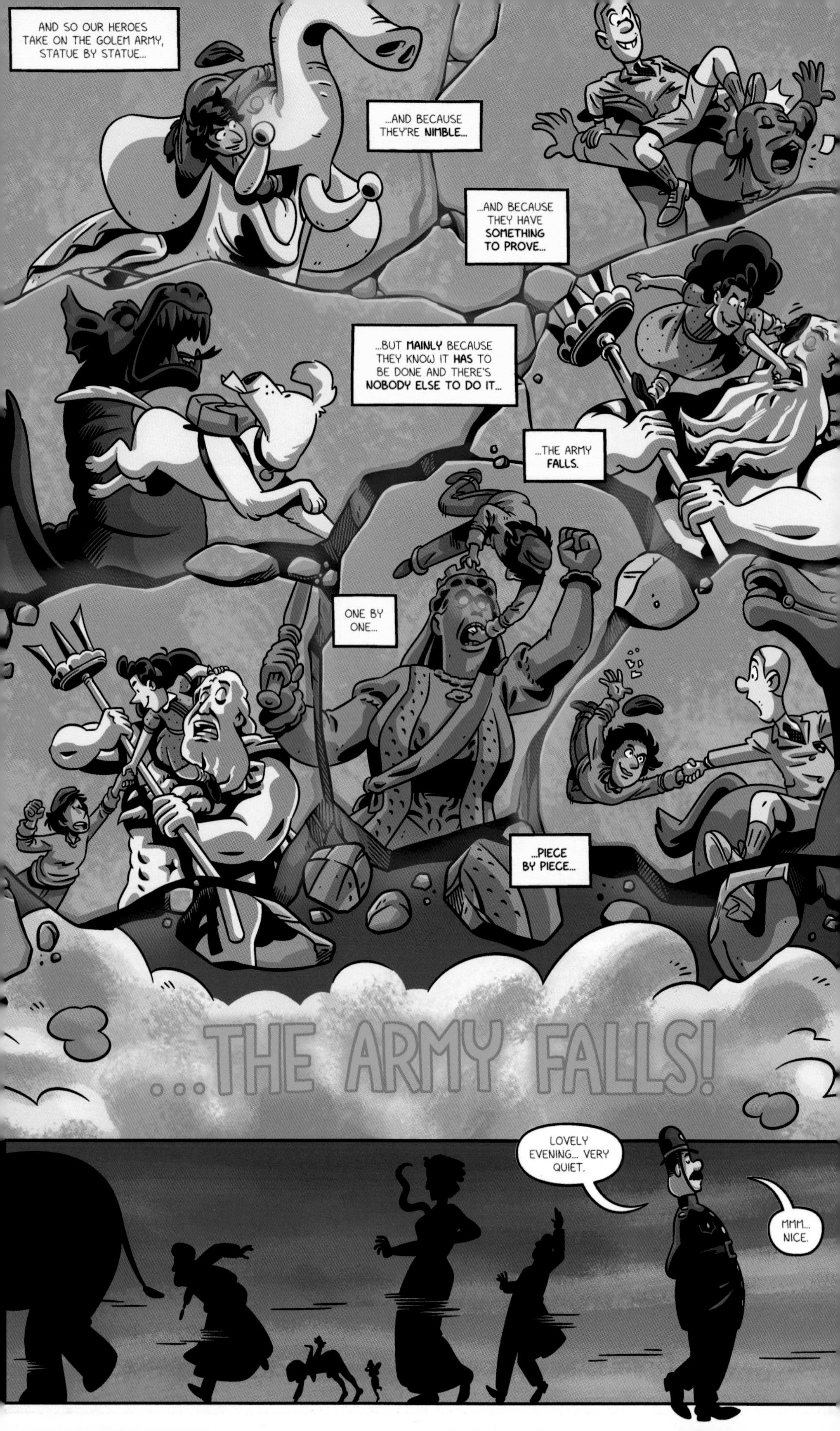

AND SO OUR HEROES TAKE ON THE GOLEM ARMY, STATUE BY STATUE...
...AND BECAUSE THEY'RE **NIMBLE**...
...AND BECAUSE THEY HAVE **SOMETHING TO PROVE**...
...BUT **MAINLY** BECAUSE THEY KNOW IT **HAS** TO BE DONE AND THERE'S **NOBODY ELSE TO DO IT**...
...THE ARMY **FALLS.**
ONE BY ONE...
...**PIECE BY PIECE**...
...THE ARMY FALLS!
LOVELY EVENING... VERY QUIET.
MMM... NICE.

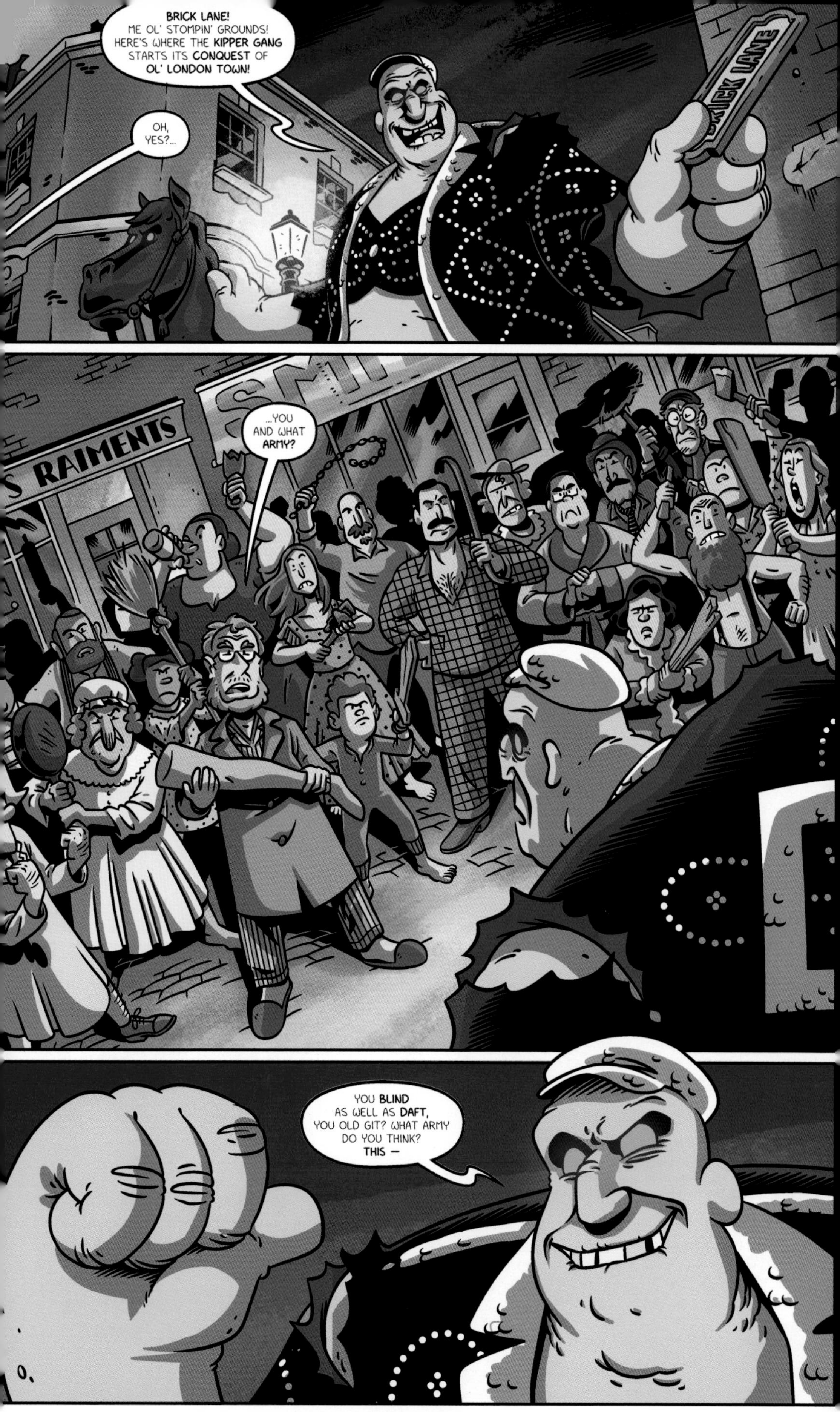
BRICK LANE! ME OL' STOMPIN' GROUNDS! HERE'S WHERE THE KIPPER GANG STARTS ITS CONQUEST OF OL' LONDON TOWN!
OH, YES?...
BRICK LANE
S RAIMENTS
...YOU AND WHAT ARMY?
YOU BLIND AS WELL AS DAFT, YOU OLD GIT? WHAT ARMY DO YOU THINK? THIS —

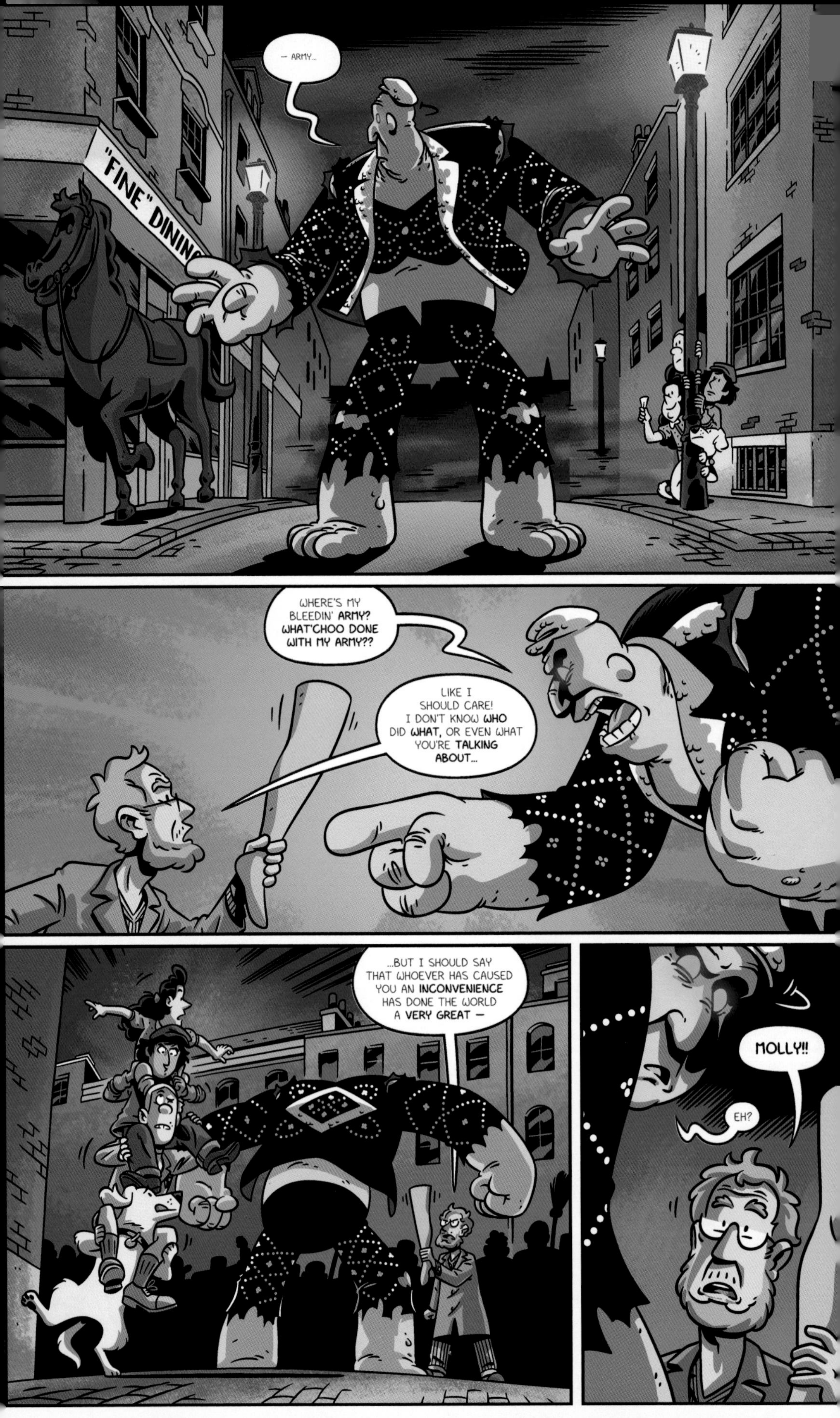
— ARMY...
"FINE" DINING
WHERE'S MY BLEEDIN' ARMY? WHAT'CHOO DONE WITH MY ARMY??
LIKE I SHOULD CARE! I DON'T KNOW WHO DID WHAT, OR EVEN WHAT YOU'RE TALKING ABOUT...
...BUT I SHOULD SAY THAT WHOEVER HAS CAUSED YOU AN INCONVENIENCE HAS DONE THE WORLD A VERY GREAT —
MOLLY!!
EH?

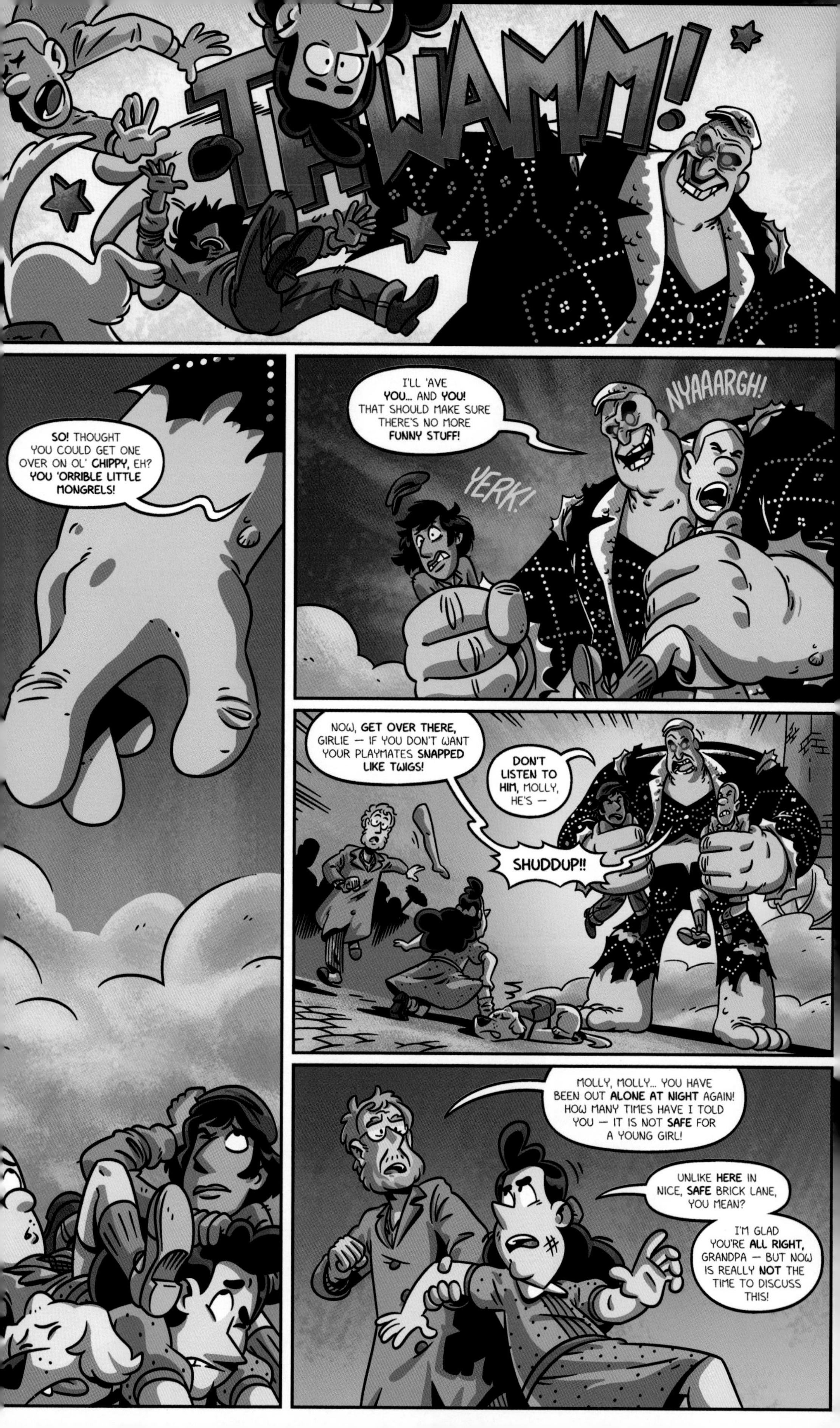
THWAMM!
SO! THOUGHT YOU COULD GET ONE OVER ON OL' CHIPPY, EH? YOU 'ORRIBLE LITTLE MONGRELS!
I'LL 'AVE YOU... AND YOU! THAT SHOULD MAKE SURE THERE'S NO MORE FUNNY STUFF!
NYAAARGH!
YERK!
NOW, GET OVER THERE, GIRLIE — IF YOU DON'T WANT YOUR PLAYMATES SNAPPED LIKE TWIGS!
DON'T LISTEN TO HIM, MOLLY, HE'S —
SHUDDUP!!
MOLLY, MOLLY... YOU HAVE BEEN OUT ALONE AT NIGHT AGAIN! HOW MANY TIMES HAVE I TOLD YOU — IT IS NOT SAFE FOR A YOUNG GIRL!
UNLIKE HERE IN NICE, SAFE BRICK LANE, YOU MEAN?
I'M GLAD YOU'RE ALL RIGHT, GRANDPA — BUT NOW IS REALLY NOT THE TIME TO DISCUSS THIS!

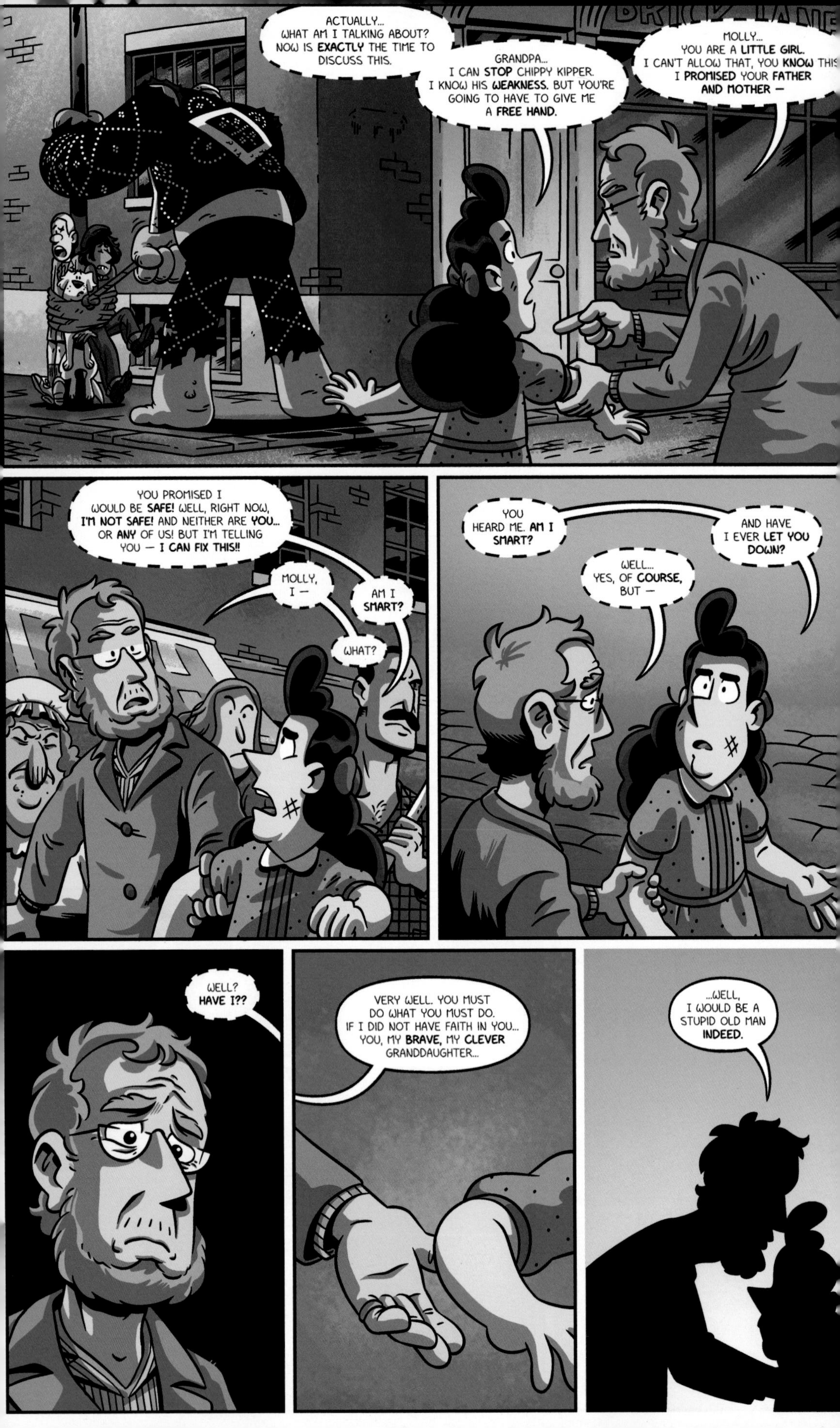
ACTUALLY... WHAT AM I TALKING ABOUT? NOW IS **EXACTLY** THE TIME TO DISCUSS THIS.
GRANDPA... I CAN **STOP** CHIPPY KIPPER. I KNOW HIS **WEAKNESS.** BUT YOU'RE GOING TO HAVE TO GIVE ME A **FREE HAND.**
MOLLY... YOU ARE A **LITTLE GIRL.** I CAN'T ALLOW THAT, YOU **KNOW** THIS. I **PROMISED** YOUR **FATHER AND MOTHER —**
YOU PROMISED I WOULD BE **SAFE!** WELL, RIGHT NOW, **I'M NOT SAFE!** AND NEITHER ARE **YOU**... OR **ANY** OF US! BUT I'M TELLING YOU — **I CAN FIX THIS!!**
MOLLY, I —
AM I **SMART?**
WHAT?
YOU HEARD ME. **AM I SMART?**
WELL... YES, OF **COURSE,** BUT —
AND HAVE I EVER **LET YOU DOWN?**
WELL? **HAVE I??**
VERY WELL. YOU MUST DO WHAT YOU MUST DO. IF I DID NOT HAVE FAITH IN YOU... YOU, MY **BRAVE,** MY **CLEVER** GRANDDAUGHTER...
...WELL, I WOULD BE A STUPID OLD MAN **INDEED.**

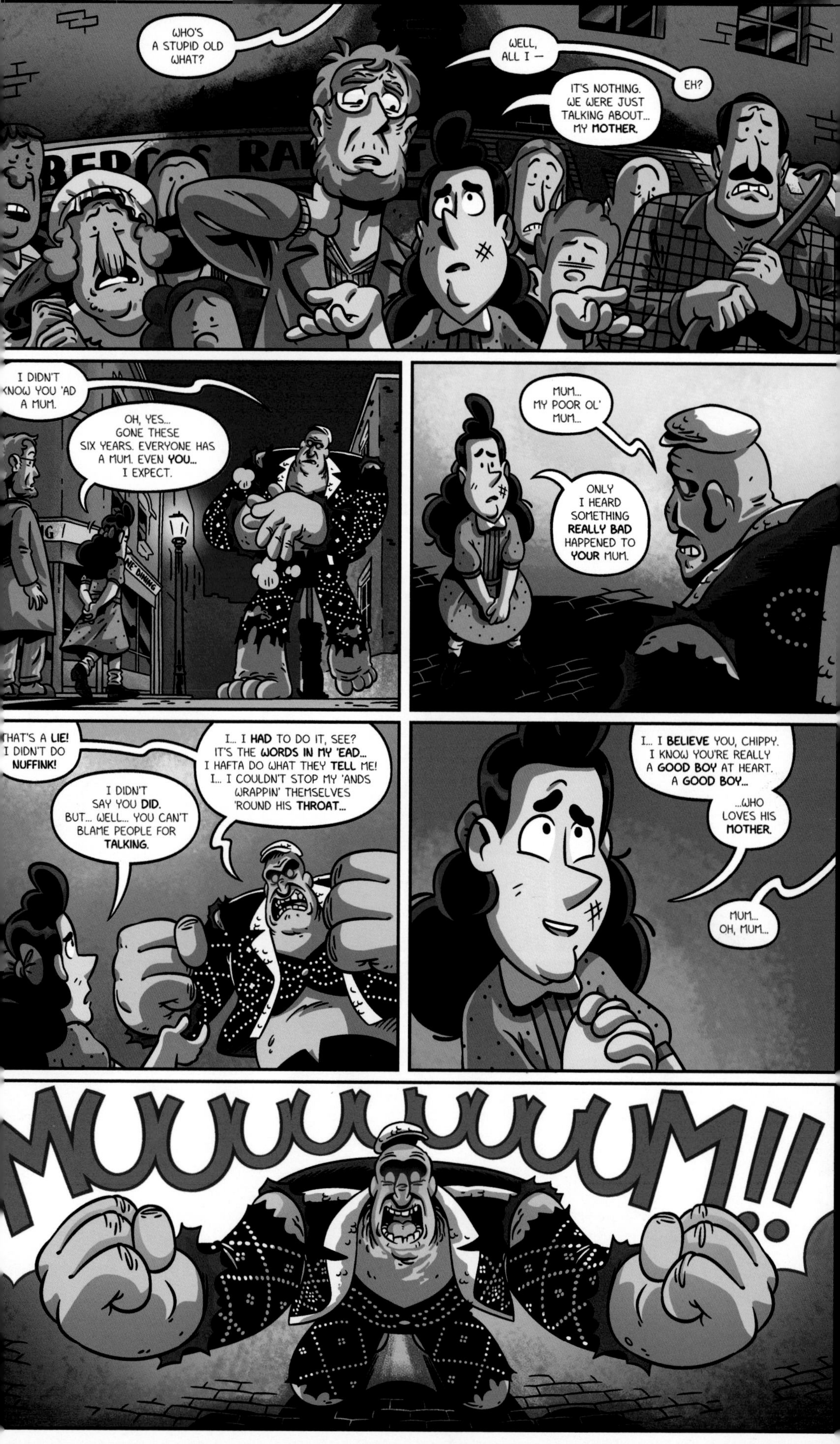
WHO'S A STUPID OLD WHAT?
WELL, ALL I —
EH?
IT'S NOTHING. WE WERE JUST TALKING ABOUT... MY MOTHER.
I DIDN'T KNOW YOU 'AD A MUM.
OH, YES... GONE THESE SIX YEARS. EVERYONE HAS A MUM. EVEN YOU... I EXPECT.
MUM... MY POOR OL' MUM...
ONLY I HEARD SOMETHING REALLY BAD HAPPENED TO YOUR MUM.
THAT'S A LIE! I DIDN'T DO NUFFINK!
I DIDN'T SAY YOU DID. BUT... WELL... YOU CAN'T BLAME PEOPLE FOR TALKING.
I... I HAD TO DO IT, SEE? IT'S THE WORDS IN MY 'EAD... I HAFTA DO WHAT THEY TELL ME! I... I COULDN'T STOP MY 'ANDS WRAPPIN' THEMSELVES 'ROUND HIS THROAT...
I... I BELIEVE YOU, CHIPPY. I KNOW YOU'RE REALLY A GOOD BOY AT HEART. A GOOD BOY...
...WHO LOVES HIS MOTHER.
MUM... OH, MUM...
MUUUUUUUUM!!

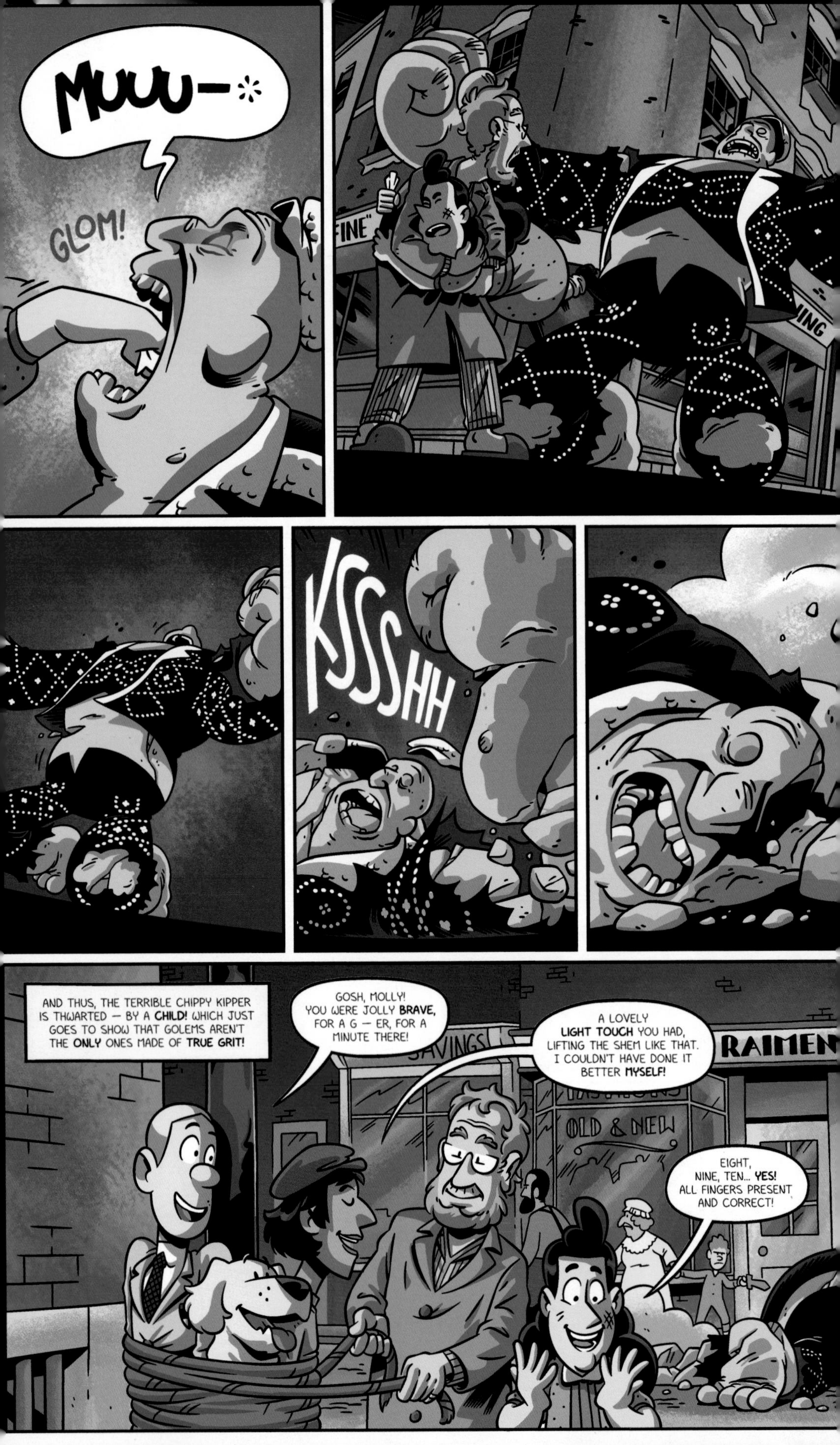
MUUU-
GLOM!
FINE
ING
KSSSHH
AND THUS, THE TERRIBLE CHIPPY KIPPER IS THWARTED — BY A CHILD! WHICH JUST GOES TO SHOW THAT GOLEMS AREN'T THE ONLY ONES MADE OF TRUE GRIT!
GOSH, MOLLY! YOU WERE JOLLY BRAVE, FOR A G — ER, FOR A MINUTE THERE!
A LOVELY LIGHT TOUCH YOU HAD, LIFTING THE SHEM LIKE THAT. I COULDN'T HAVE DONE IT BETTER MYSELF!
SAVINGS
RAIMEN
OLD & NEW
EIGHT, NINE, TEN... YES! ALL FINGERS PRESENT AND CORRECT!

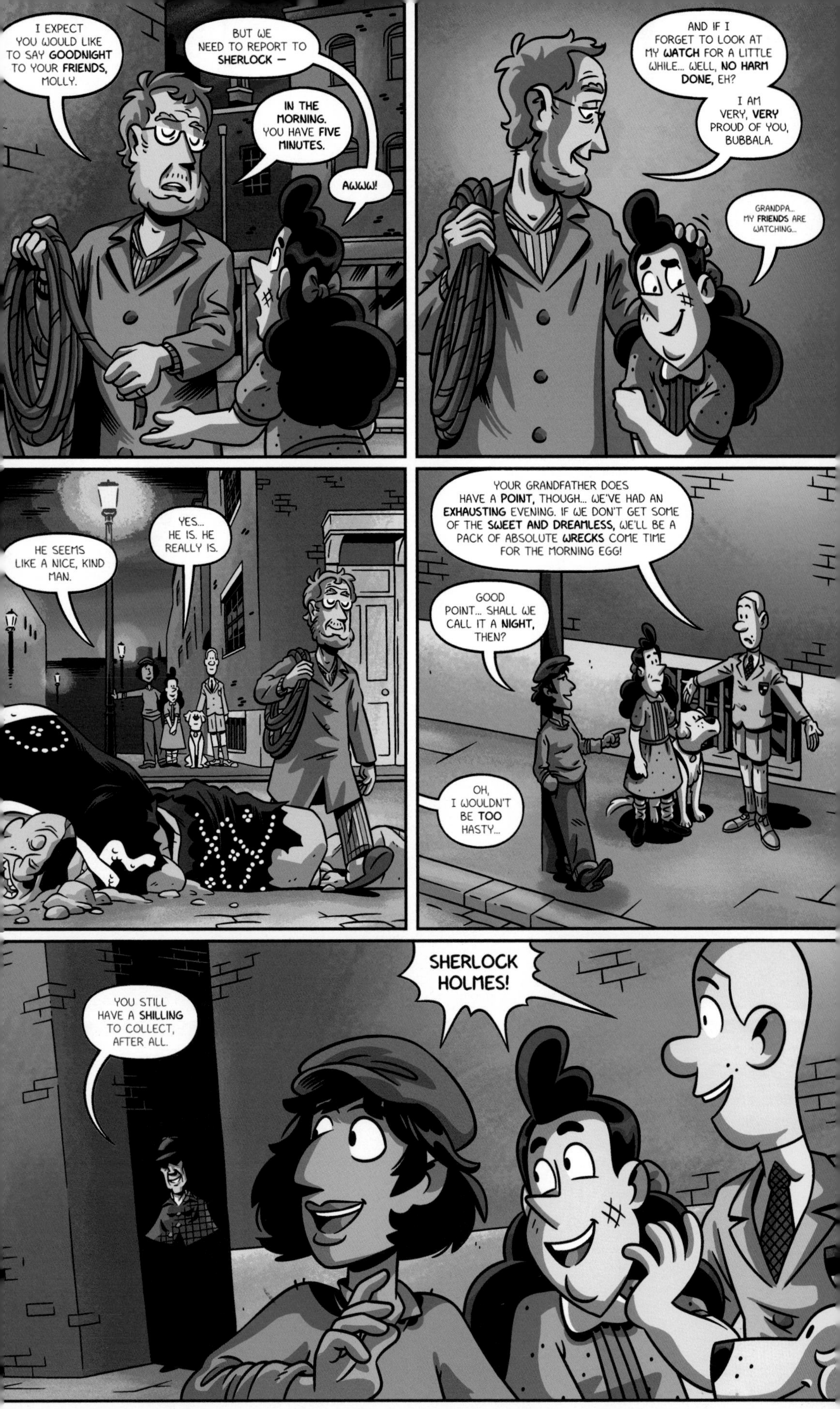
I EXPECT YOU WOULD LIKE TO SAY GOODNIGHT TO YOUR FRIENDS, MOLLY.
BUT WE NEED TO REPORT TO SHERLOCK —
IN THE MORNING. YOU HAVE FIVE MINUTES.
AWWW!
AND IF I FORGET TO LOOK AT MY WATCH FOR A LITTLE WHILE... WELL, NO HARM DONE, EH?
I AM VERY, VERY PROUD OF YOU, BUBBALA.
GRANDPA... MY FRIENDS ARE WATCHING...
HE SEEMS LIKE A NICE, KIND MAN.
YES... HE IS. HE REALLY IS.
YOUR GRANDFATHER DOES HAVE A POINT, THOUGH... WE'VE HAD AN EXHAUSTING EVENING. IF WE DON'T GET SOME OF THE SWEET AND DREAMLESS, WE'LL BE A PACK OF ABSOLUTE WRECKS COME TIME FOR THE MORNING EGG!
GOOD POINT... SHALL WE CALL IT A NIGHT, THEN?
OH, I WOULDN'T BE TOO HASTY...
YOU STILL HAVE A SHILLING TO COLLECT, AFTER ALL.
SHERLOCK HOLMES!

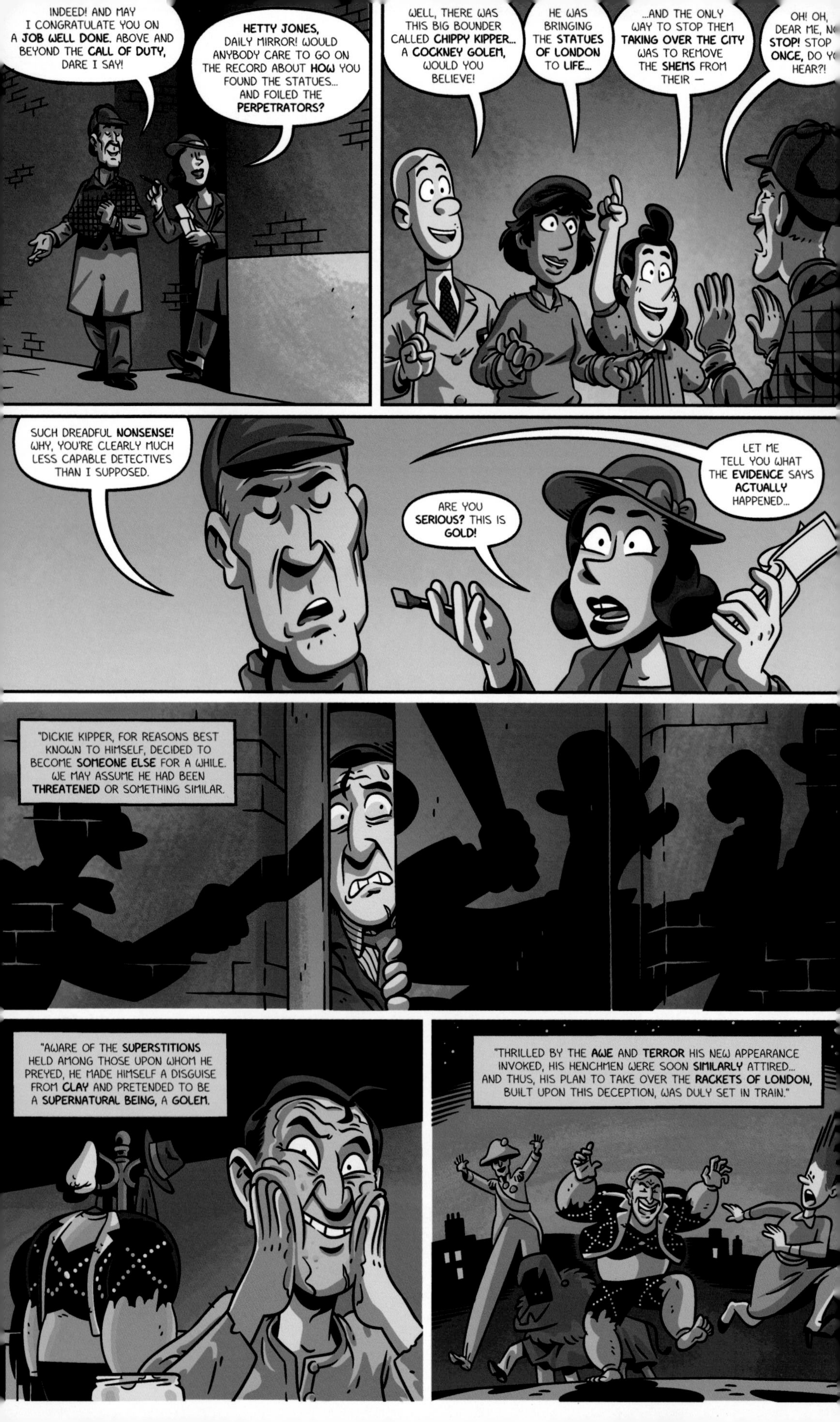
INDEED! AND MAY I CONGRATULATE YOU ON A JOB WELL DONE. ABOVE AND BEYOND THE CALL OF DUTY, DARE I SAY!
HETTY JONES, DAILY MIRROR! WOULD ANYBODY CARE TO GO ON THE RECORD ABOUT HOW YOU FOUND THE STATUES... AND FOILED THE PERPETRATORS?
WELL, THERE WAS THIS BIG BOUNDER CALLED CHIPPY KIPPER... A COCKNEY GOLEM, WOULD YOU BELIEVE!
HE WAS BRINGING THE STATUES OF LONDON TO LIFE...
...AND THE ONLY WAY TO STOP THEM TAKING OVER THE CITY WAS TO REMOVE THE SHEMS FROM THEIR —
OH! OH, DEAR ME, N STOP! STOP ONCE, DO Y HEAR?!
SUCH DREADFUL NONSENSE! WHY, YOU'RE CLEARLY MUCH LESS CAPABLE DETECTIVES THAN I SUPPOSED.
ARE YOU SERIOUS? THIS IS GOLD!
LET ME TELL YOU WHAT THE EVIDENCE SAYS ACTUALLY HAPPENED...
"DICKIE KIPPER, FOR REASONS BEST KNOWN TO HIMSELF, DECIDED TO BECOME SOMEONE ELSE FOR A WHILE. WE MAY ASSUME HE HAD BEEN THREATENED OR SOMETHING SIMILAR.
"AWARE OF THE SUPERSTITIONS HELD AMONG THOSE UPON WHOM HE PREYED, HE MADE HIMSELF A DISGUISE FROM CLAY AND PRETENDED TO BE A SUPERNATURAL BEING, A GOLEM.
"THRILLED BY THE AWE AND TERROR HIS NEW APPEARANCE INVOKED, HIS HENCHMEN WERE SOON SIMILARLY ATTIRED... AND THUS, HIS PLAN TO TAKE OVER THE RACKETS OF LONDON, BUILT UPON THIS DECEPTION, WAS DULY SET IN TRAIN."

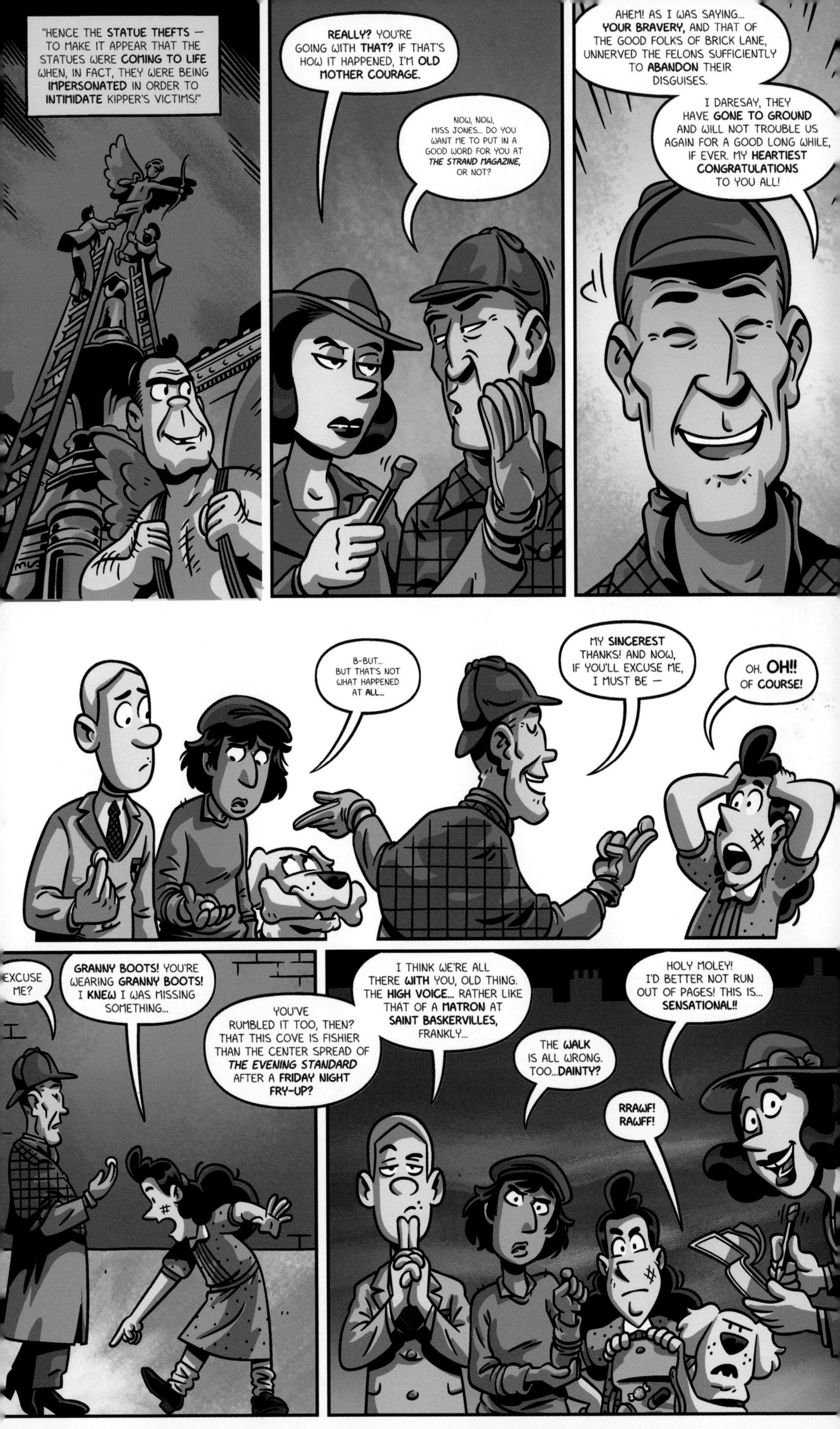
"HENCE THE **STATUE THEFTS** — TO MAKE IT APPEAR THAT THE STATUES WERE **COMING TO LIFE** WHEN, IN FACT, THEY WERE BEING **IMPERSONATED** IN ORDER TO **INTIMIDATE** KIPPER'S VICTIMS!"
REALLY? YOU'RE GOING WITH **THAT?** IF THAT'S HOW IT HAPPENED, I'M **OLD MOTHER COURAGE.**
NOW, NOW, MISS JONES... DO YOU WANT ME TO PUT IN A GOOD WORD FOR YOU AT ***THE STRAND MAGAZINE,*** OR NOT?
AHEM! AS I WAS SAYING... **YOUR BRAVERY,** AND THAT OF THE GOOD FOLKS OF BRICK LANE, UNNERVED THE FELONS SUFFICIENTLY TO **ABANDON** THEIR DISGUISES.
I DARESAY, THEY HAVE **GONE TO GROUND** AND WILL NOT TROUBLE US AGAIN FOR A GOOD LONG WHILE, IF EVER. MY **HEARTIEST CONGRATULATIONS** TO YOU ALL!
B-BUT... BUT THAT'S NOT WHAT HAPPENED AT **ALL**...
MY **SINCEREST** THANKS! AND NOW, IF YOU'LL EXCUSE ME, I MUST BE —
OH. **OH!!** OF **COURSE!**
EXCUSE ME?
GRANNY BOOTS! YOU'RE WEARING **GRANNY BOOTS!** I **KNEW** I WAS MISSING SOMETHING...
YOU'VE RUMBLED IT TOO, THEN? THAT THIS COVE IS FISHIER THAN THE CENTER SPREAD OF ***THE EVENING STANDARD*** AFTER A **FRIDAY NIGHT FRY-UP?**
I THINK WE'RE ALL THERE **WITH** YOU, OLD THING. THE **HIGH VOICE**... RATHER LIKE THAT OF A **MATRON** AT **SAINT BASKERVILLES,** FRANKLY...
THE **WALK** IS ALL WRONG. TOO...**DAINTY?**
RRAWF! RAWFF!
HOLY MOLEY! I'D BETTER NOT RUN OUT OF PAGES! THIS IS... **SENSATIONAL!!**

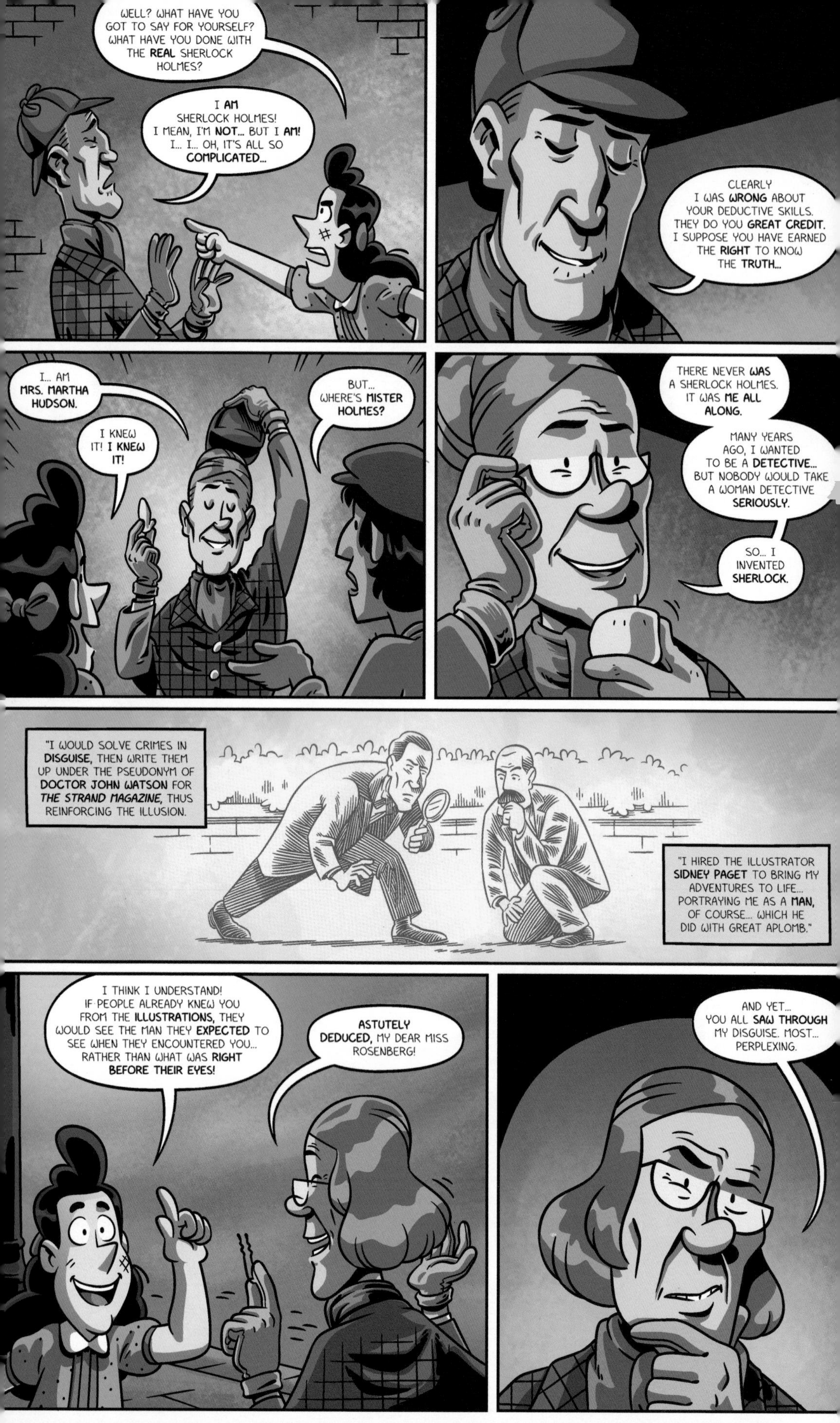
WELL? WHAT HAVE YOU GOT TO SAY FOR YOURSELF? WHAT HAVE YOU DONE WITH THE REAL SHERLOCK HOLMES?
I AM SHERLOCK HOLMES! I MEAN, I'M NOT... BUT I AM! I... I... OH, IT'S ALL SO COMPLICATED...
CLEARLY I WAS WRONG ABOUT YOUR DEDUCTIVE SKILLS. THEY DO YOU GREAT CREDIT. I SUPPOSE YOU HAVE EARNED THE RIGHT TO KNOW THE TRUTH...
I... AM MRS. MARTHA HUDSON.
I KNEW IT! I KNEW IT!
BUT... WHERE'S MISTER HOLMES?
THERE NEVER WAS A SHERLOCK HOLMES. IT WAS ME ALL ALONG.
MANY YEARS AGO, I WANTED TO BE A DETECTIVE... BUT NOBODY WOULD TAKE A WOMAN DETECTIVE SERIOUSLY.
SO... I INVENTED SHERLOCK.
"I WOULD SOLVE CRIMES IN DISGUISE, THEN WRITE THEM UP UNDER THE PSEUDONYM OF DOCTOR JOHN WATSON FOR THE STRAND MAGAZINE, THUS REINFORCING THE ILLUSION.
"I HIRED THE ILLUSTRATOR SIDNEY PAGET TO BRING MY ADVENTURES TO LIFE... PORTRAYING ME AS A MAN, OF COURSE... WHICH HE DID WITH GREAT APLOMB."
I THINK I UNDERSTAND! IF PEOPLE ALREADY KNEW YOU FROM THE ILLUSTRATIONS, THEY WOULD SEE THE MAN THEY EXPECTED TO SEE WHEN THEY ENCOUNTERED YOU... RATHER THAN WHAT WAS RIGHT BEFORE THEIR EYES!
ASTUTELY DEDUCED, MY DEAR MISS ROSENBERG!
AND YET... YOU ALL SAW THROUGH MY DISGUISE. MOST... PERPLEXING.

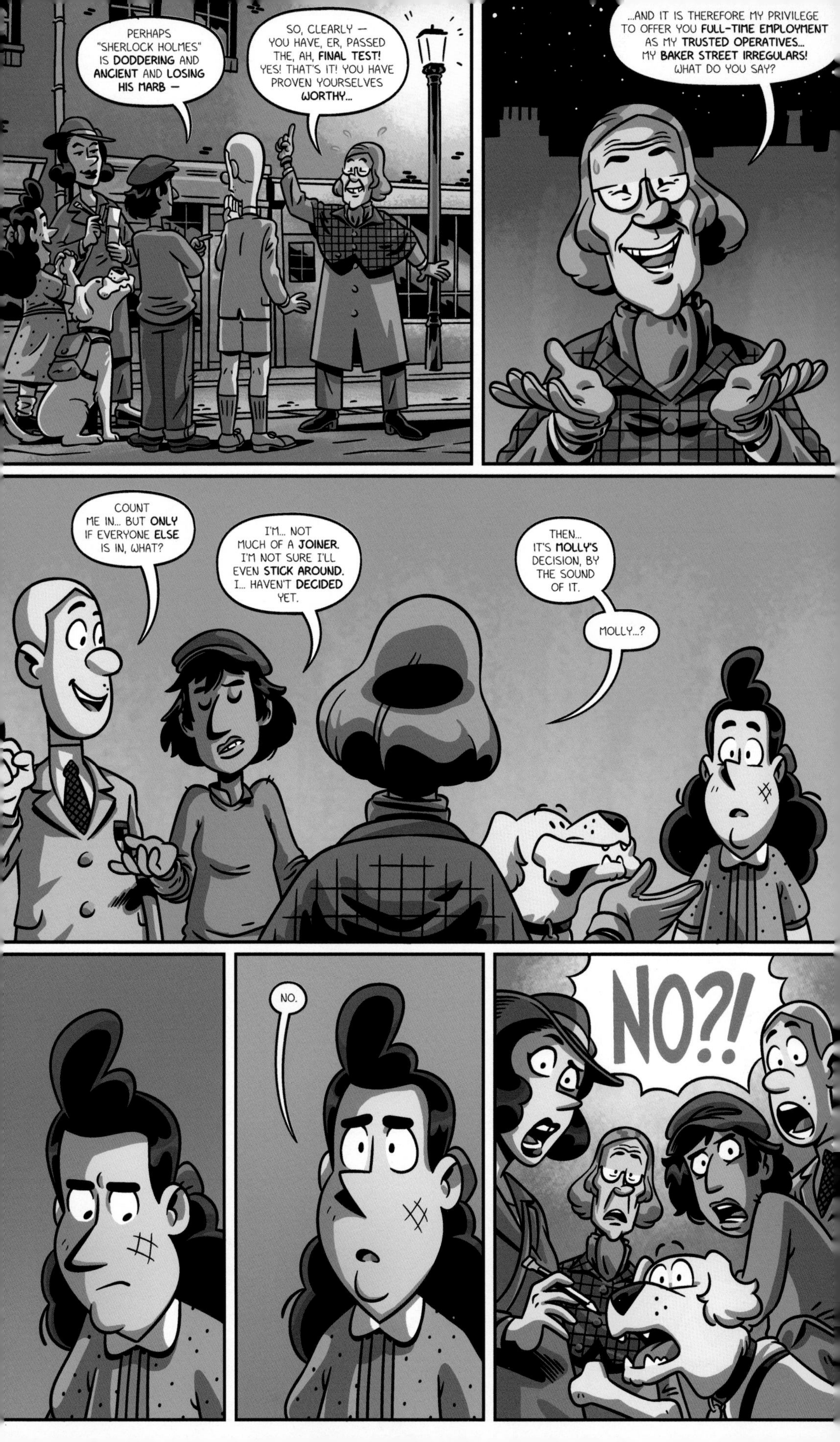
PERHAPS "SHERLOCK HOLMES" IS **DODDERING** AND **ANCIENT** AND **LOSING HIS MARB** —
SO, CLEARLY — YOU HAVE, ER, PASSED THE, AH, **FINAL TEST!** YES! THAT'S IT! YOU HAVE PROVEN YOURSELVES **WORTHY...**
...AND IT IS THEREFORE MY PRIVILEGE TO OFFER YOU **FULL-TIME EMPLOYMENT** AS MY **TRUSTED OPERATIVES...** MY **BAKER STREET IRREGULARS!** WHAT DO YOU SAY?
COUNT ME IN... BUT **ONLY** IF EVERYONE **ELSE** IS IN, WHAT?
I'M... NOT MUCH OF A **JOINER.** I'M NOT SURE I'LL EVEN **STICK AROUND.** I... HAVEN'T **DECIDED** YET.
THEN... IT'S **MOLLY'S** DECISION, BY THE SOUND OF IT.
MOLLY...?
NO.
NO?!

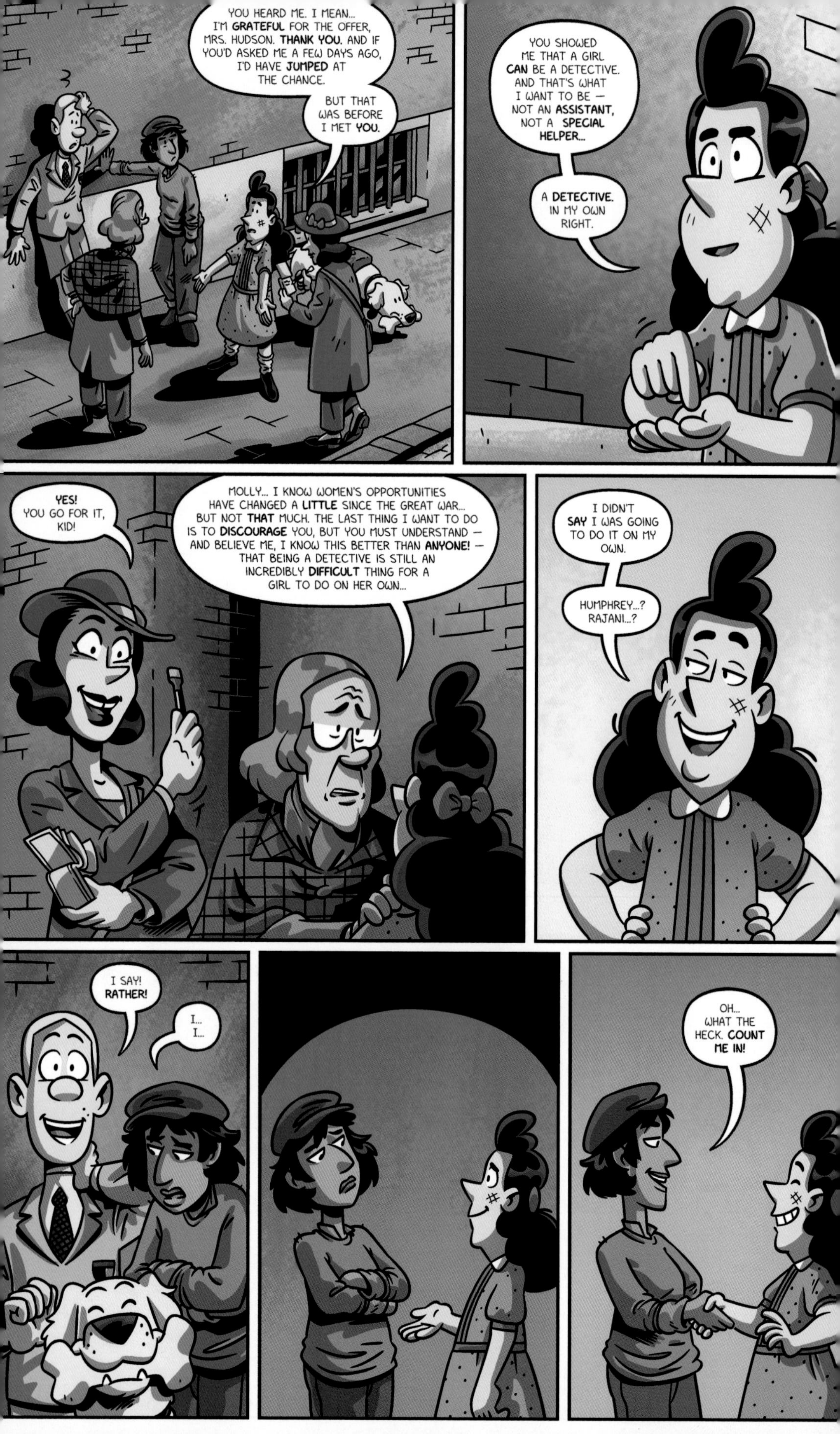
YOU HEARD ME. I MEAN... I'M **GRATEFUL** FOR THE OFFER, MRS. HUDSON. **THANK YOU.** AND IF YOU'D ASKED ME A FEW DAYS AGO, I'D HAVE **JUMPED** AT THE CHANCE.
BUT THAT WAS BEFORE I MET **YOU.**
YOU SHOWED ME THAT A GIRL **CAN** BE A DETECTIVE. AND THAT'S WHAT I WANT TO BE — NOT AN **ASSISTANT,** NOT A **SPECIAL HELPER...**
A **DETECTIVE.** IN MY OWN RIGHT.
YES! YOU GO FOR IT, KID!
MOLLY... I KNOW WOMEN'S OPPORTUNITIES HAVE CHANGED A **LITTLE** SINCE THE GREAT WAR... BUT NOT **THAT** MUCH. THE LAST THING I WANT TO DO IS TO **DISCOURAGE** YOU, BUT YOU MUST UNDERSTAND — AND BELIEVE ME, I KNOW THIS BETTER THAN **ANYONE!** — THAT BEING A DETECTIVE IS STILL AN INCREDIBLY **DIFFICULT** THING FOR A GIRL TO DO ON HER OWN...
I DIDN'T **SAY** I WAS GOING TO DO IT ON MY OWN.
HUMPHREY...? RAJANI...?
I SAY! **RATHER!**
I... I...
OH... WHAT THE HECK. **COUNT ME IN!**

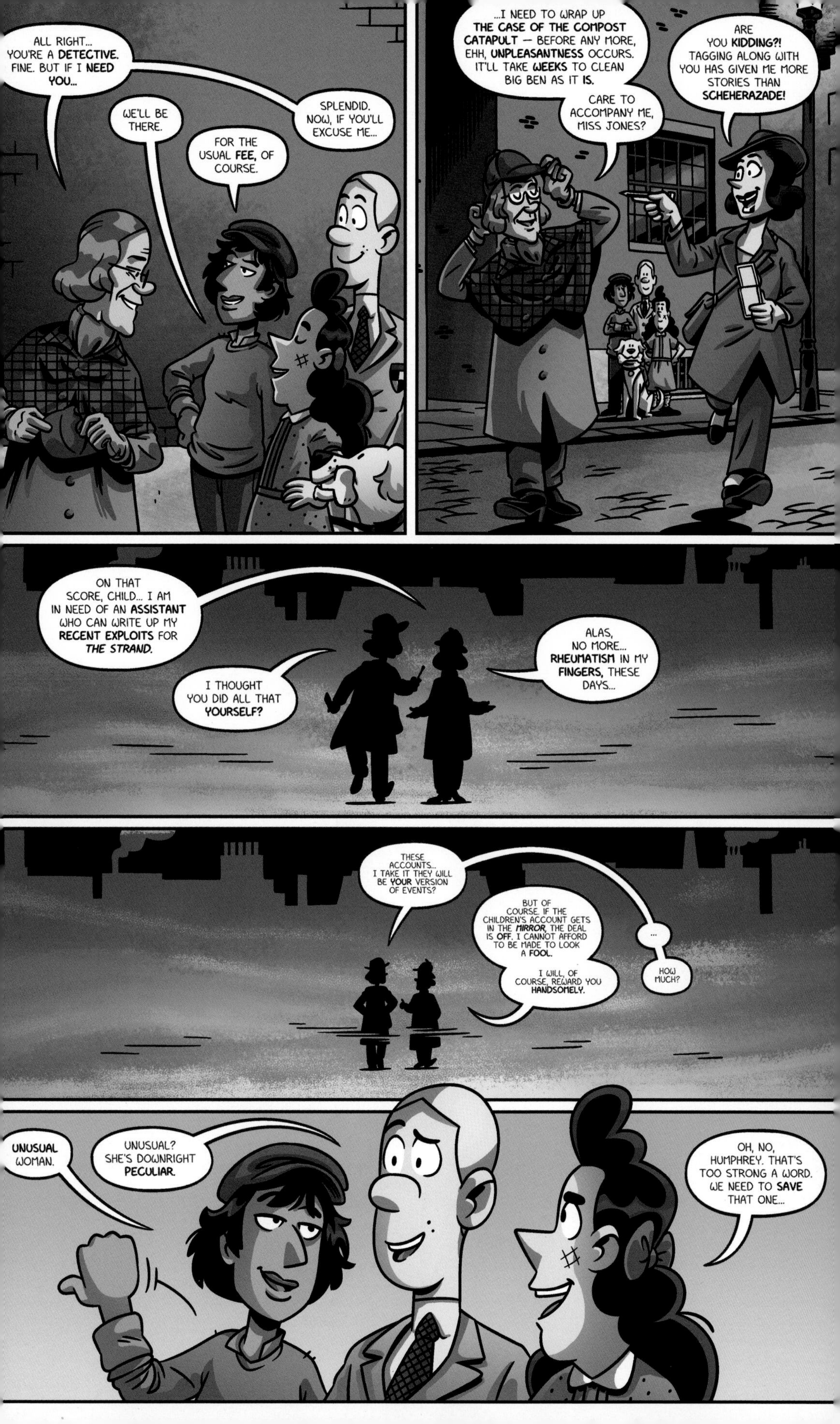
ALL RIGHT... YOU'RE A DETECTIVE. FINE. BUT IF I NEED YOU...
WE'LL BE THERE.
FOR THE USUAL FEE, OF COURSE.
SPLENDID. NOW, IF YOU'LL EXCUSE ME...
...I NEED TO WRAP UP THE CASE OF THE COMPOST CATAPULT — BEFORE ANY MORE, EHH, UNPLEASANTNESS OCCURS. IT'LL TAKE WEEKS TO CLEAN BIG BEN AS IT IS.
CARE TO ACCOMPANY ME, MISS JONES?
ARE YOU KIDDING?! TAGGING ALONG WITH YOU HAS GIVEN ME MORE STORIES THAN SCHEHERAZADE!
ON THAT SCORE, CHILD... I AM IN NEED OF AN ASSISTANT WHO CAN WRITE UP MY RECENT EXPLOITS FOR THE STRAND.
I THOUGHT YOU DID ALL THAT YOURSELF?
ALAS, NO MORE... RHEUMATISM IN MY FINGERS, THESE DAYS...
THESE ACCOUNTS... I TAKE IT THEY WILL BE YOUR VERSION OF EVENTS?
BUT OF COURSE. IF THE CHILDREN'S ACCOUNT GETS IN THE MIRROR, THE DEAL IS OFF. I CANNOT AFFORD TO BE MADE TO LOOK A FOOL.
I WILL, OF COURSE, REWARD YOU HANDSOMELY.
...
HOW MUCH?
UNUSUAL WOMAN.
UNUSUAL? SHE'S DOWNRIGHT PECULIAR.
OH, NO, HUMPHREY. THAT'S TOO STRONG A WORD. WE NEED TO SAVE THAT ONE...

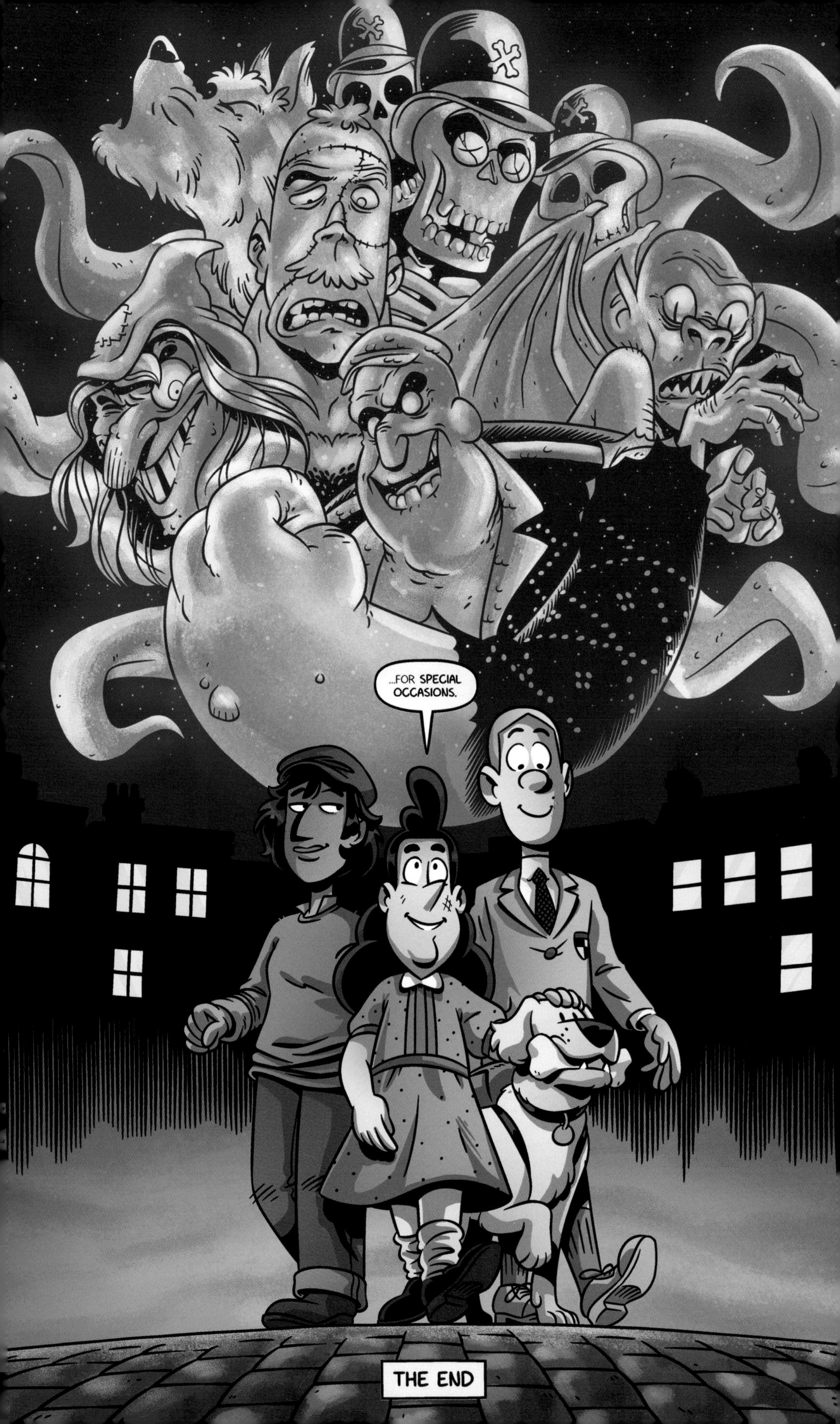
...FOR SPECIAL OCCASIONS.
THE END

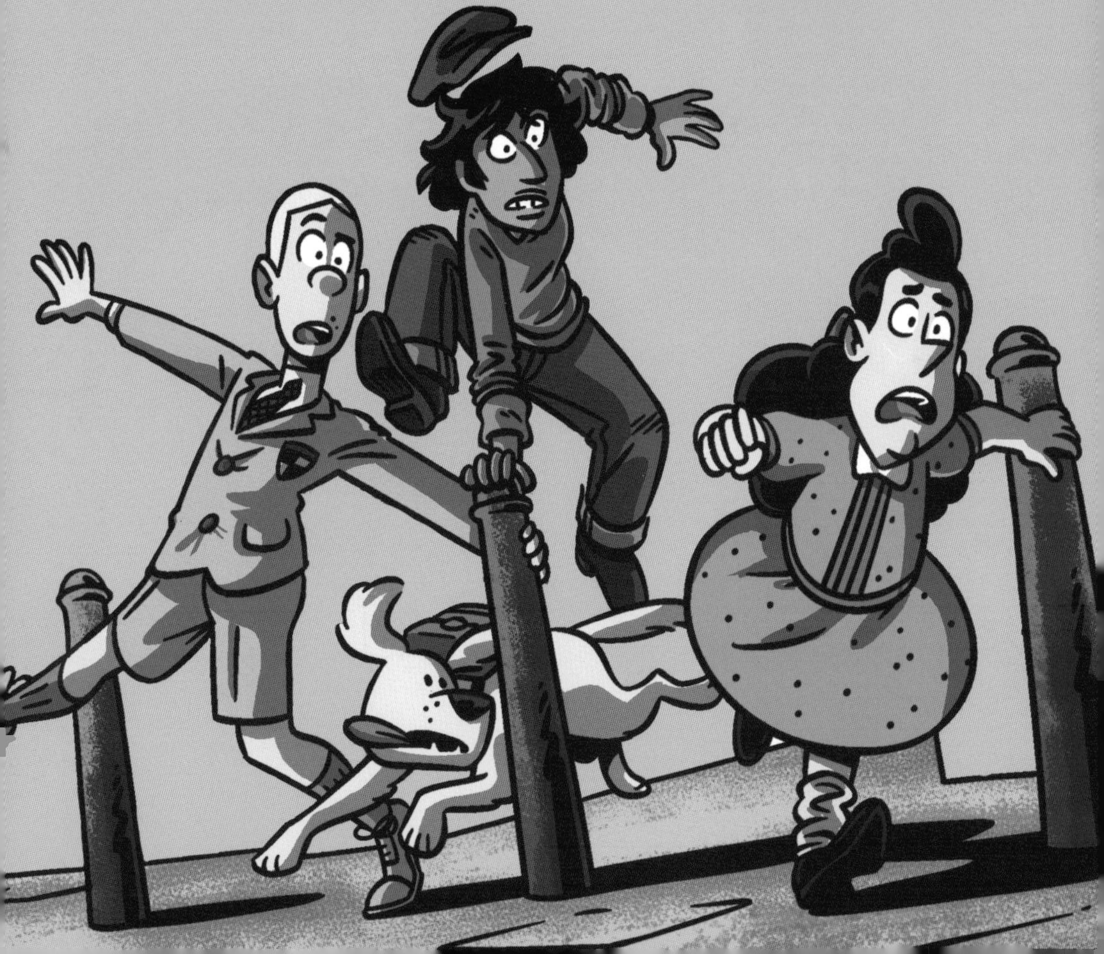

COVER GALLERY

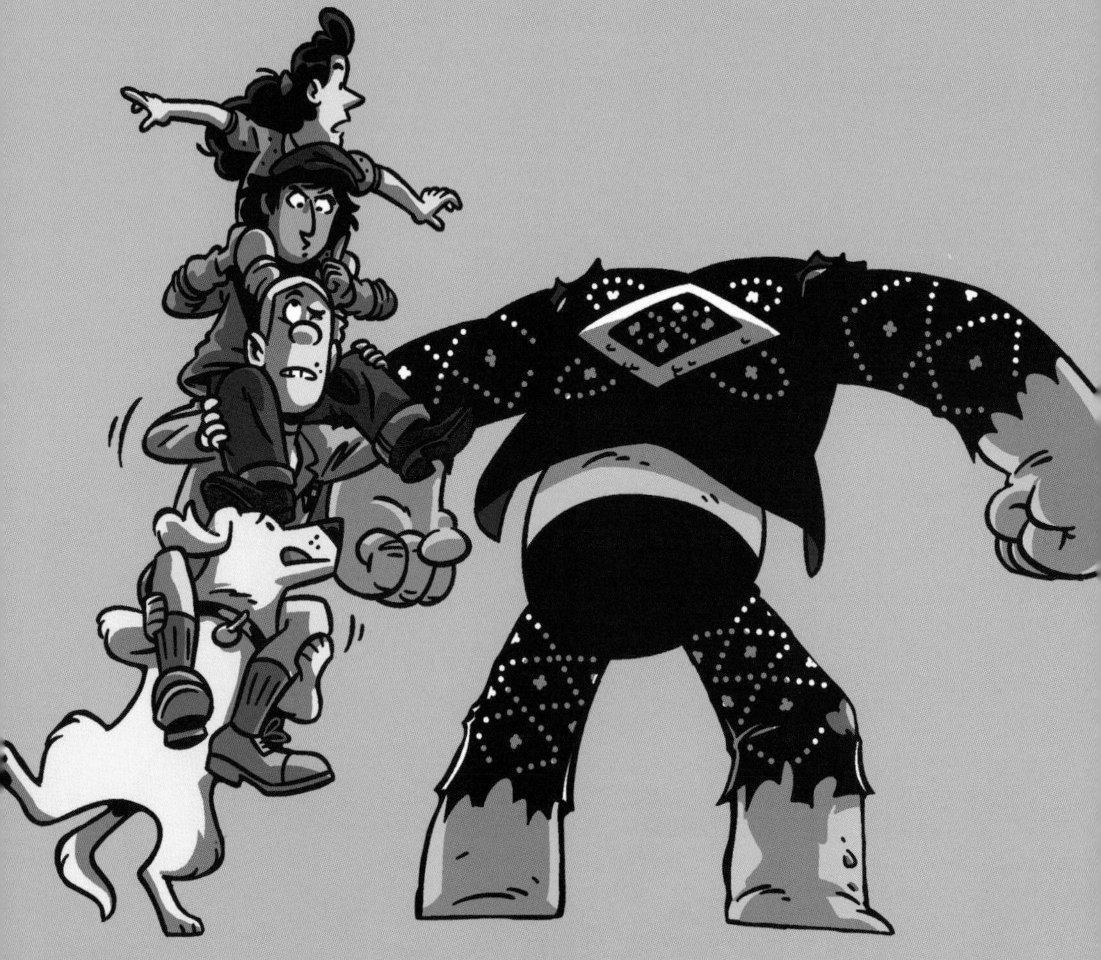

#1 Cover by
ANDY HIRSCH

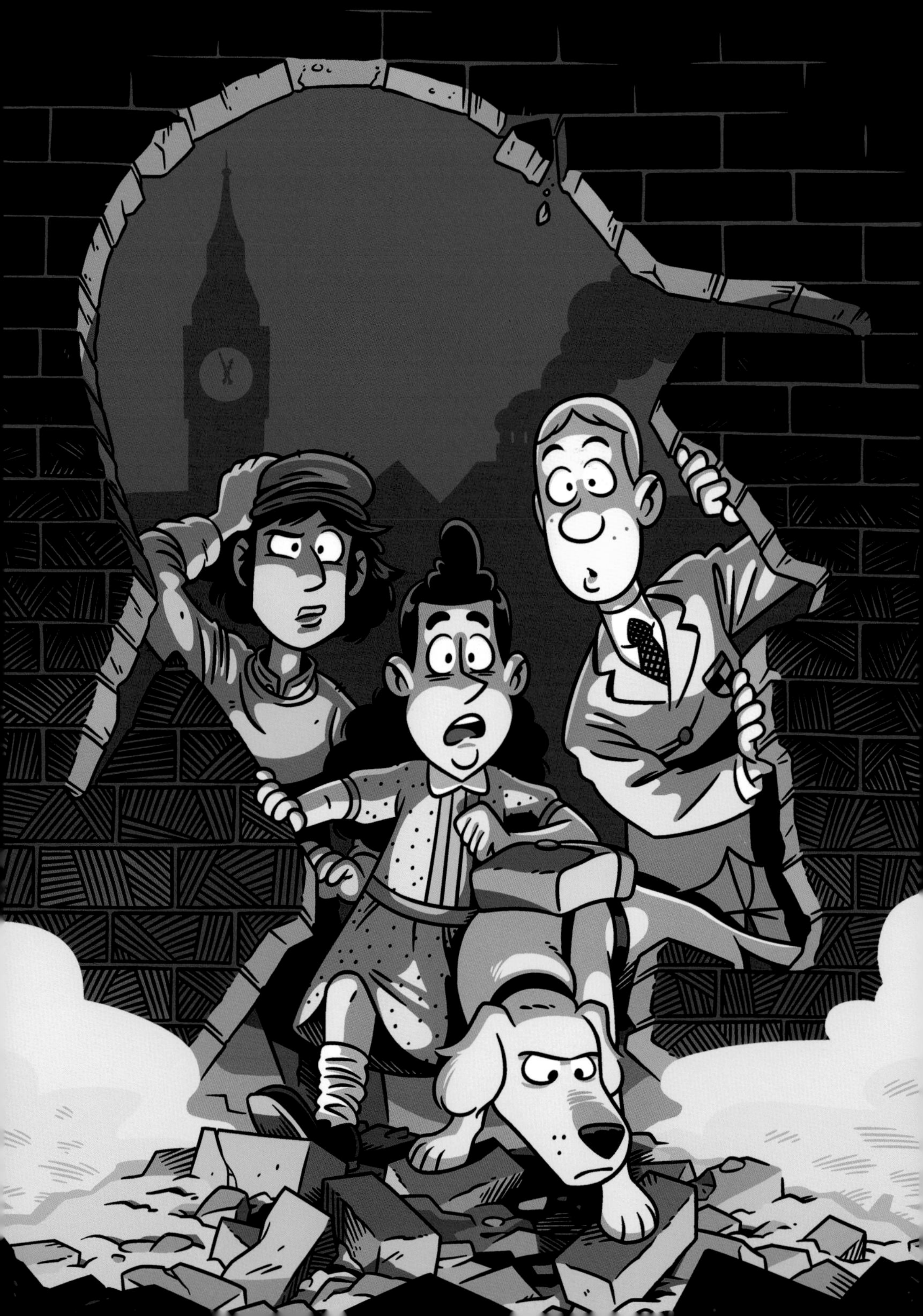

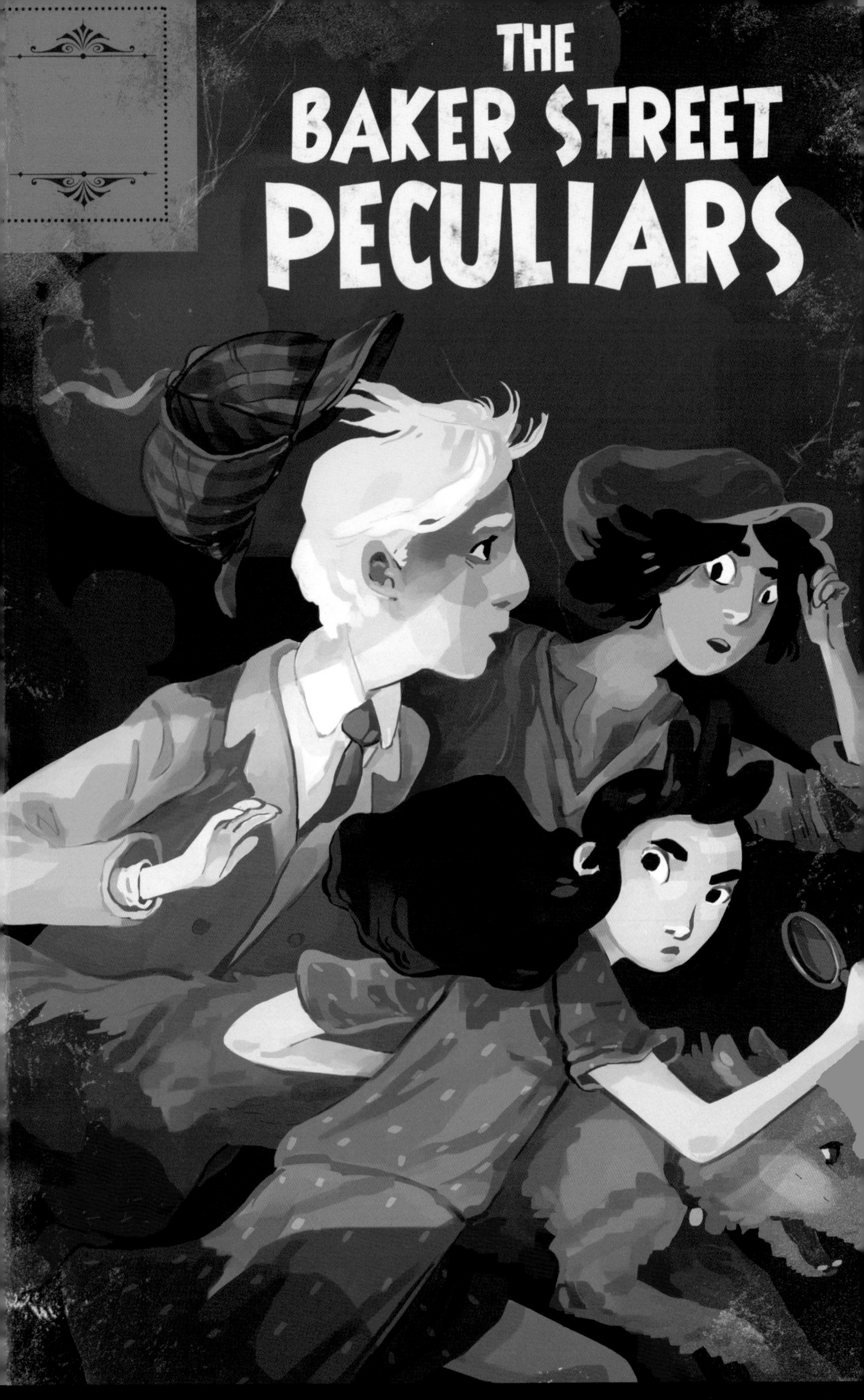
THE
BAKER STREET
PECULIARS

#1 Variant Cover by

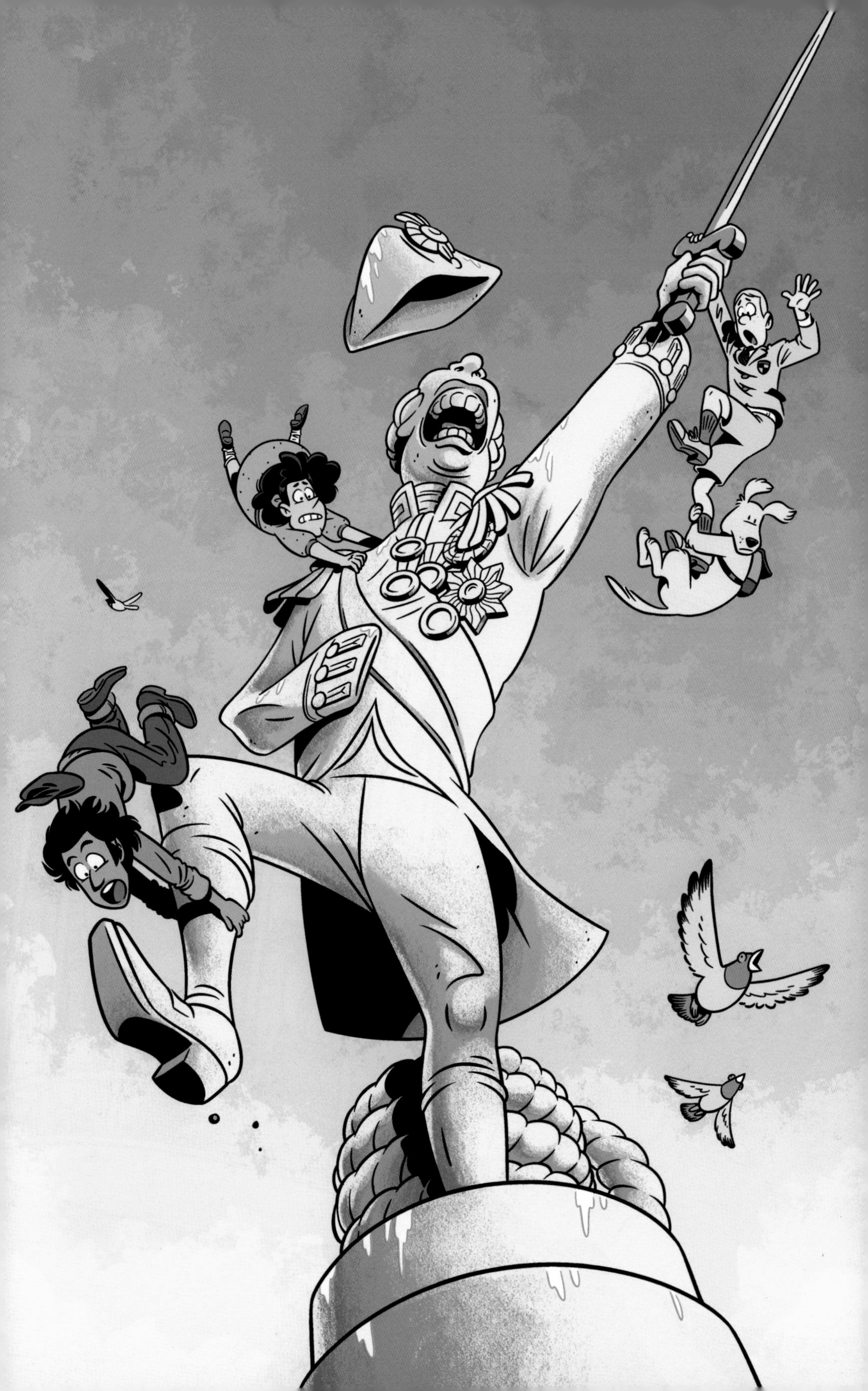

ANDY HIRSCH

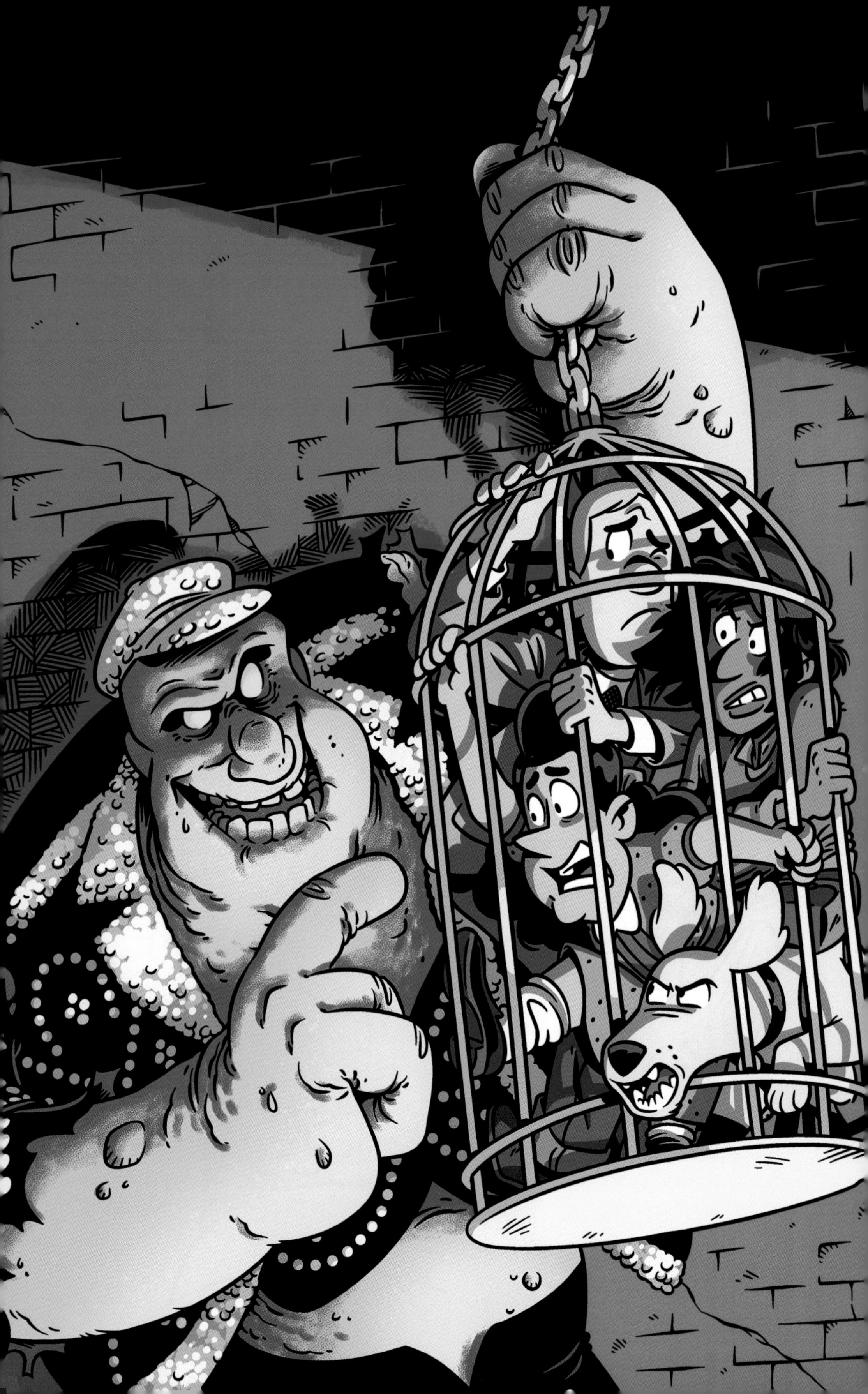

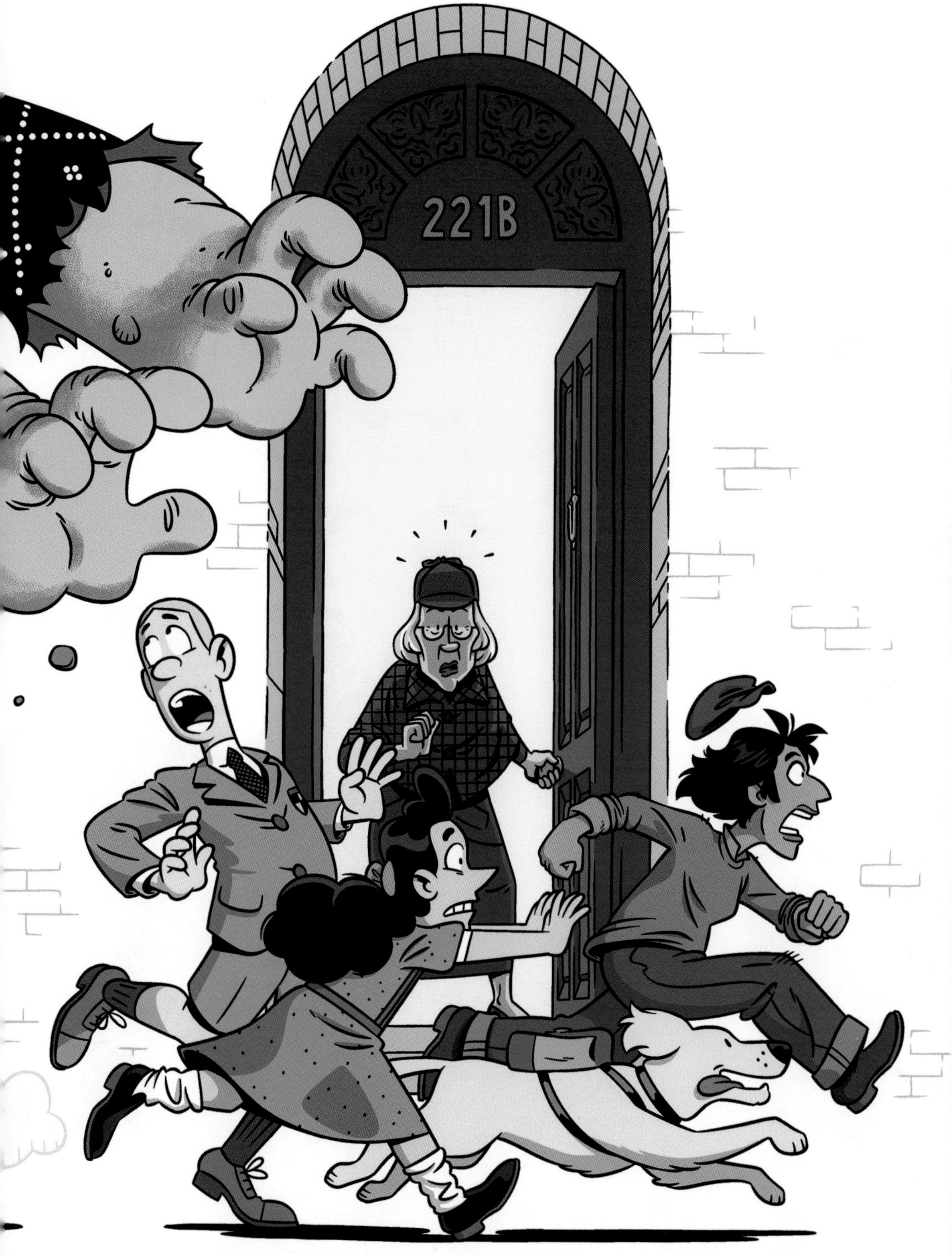
221B

MEET THE PECULIARS

A behind-the-scenes look at the original character designs by Andy Hirsch.

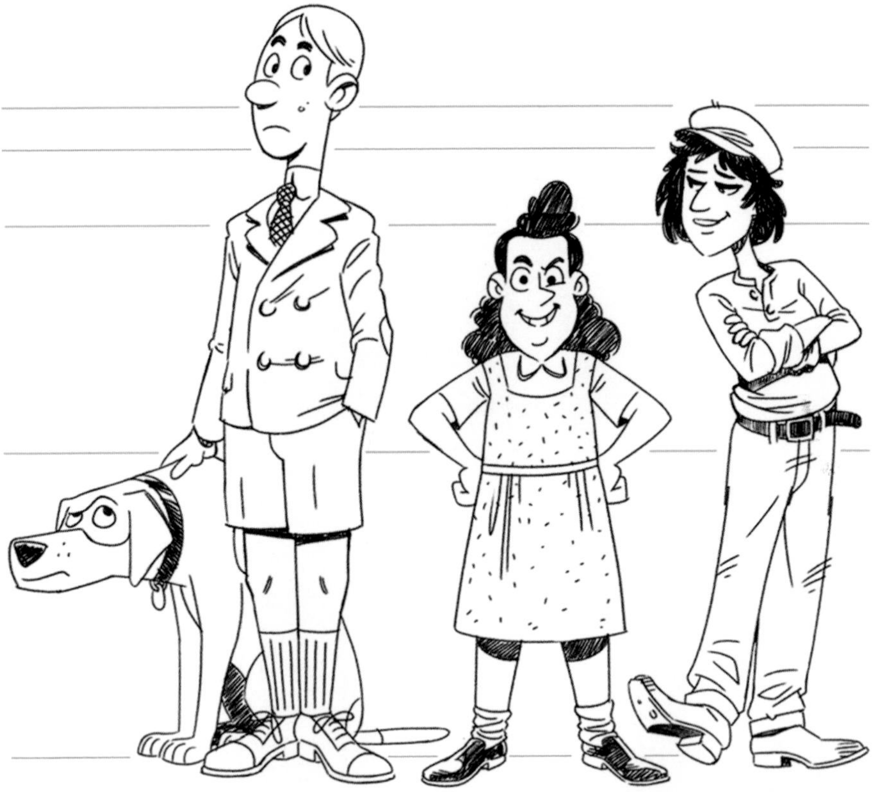

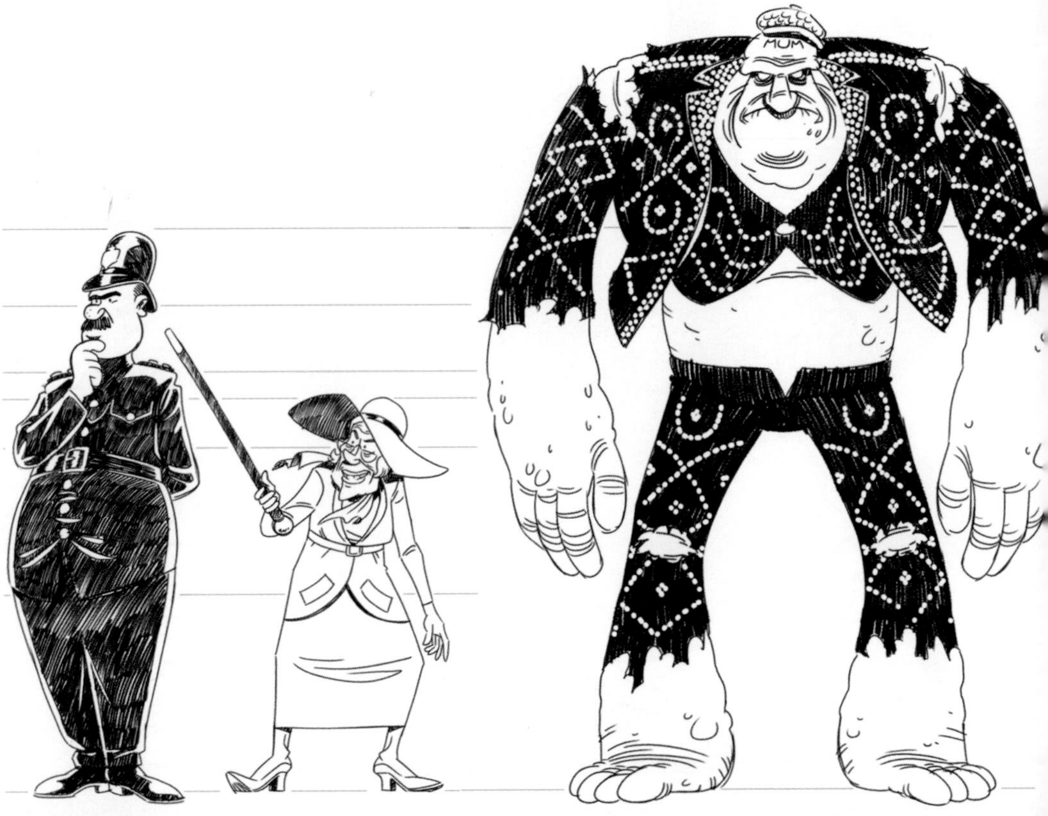
MUM

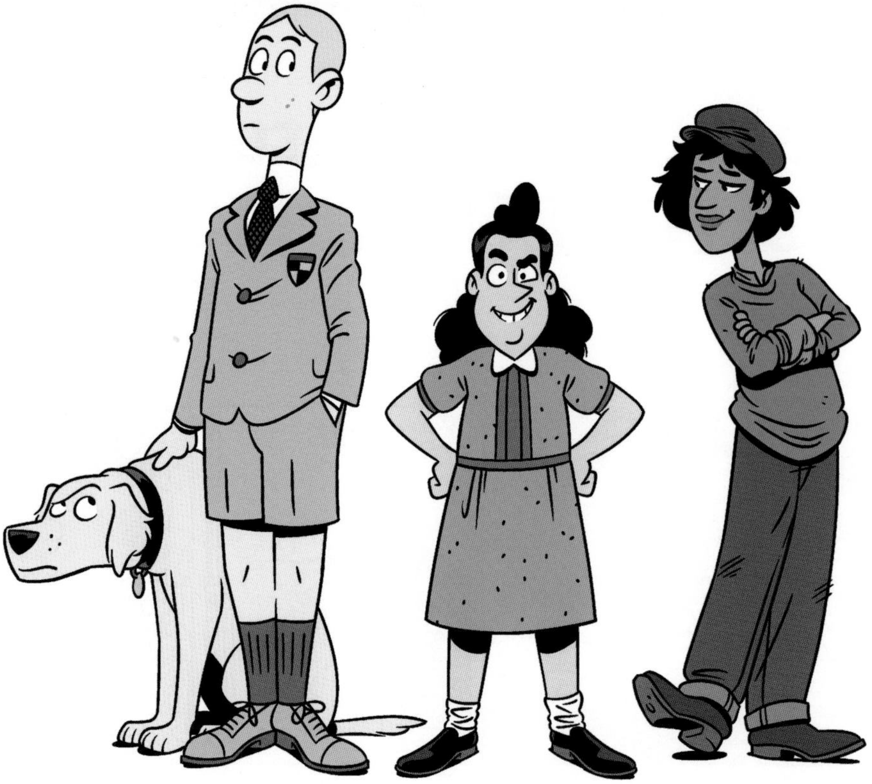

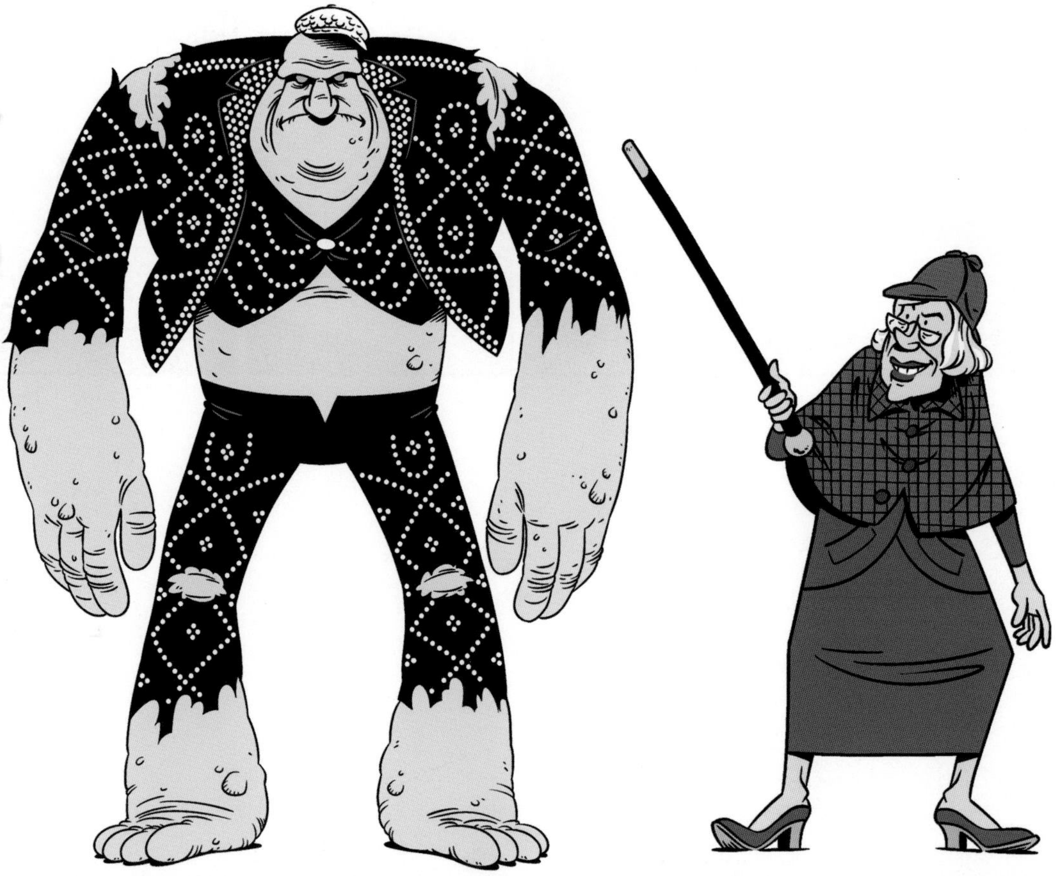

The Peculiar Adventures of SHERLOCK HOLMES

The case of the Spider in Aspic

Set Holmes on a chase quite fantastic.

You may think it uncouth, But the quick-thinking sleuth

Stopped the cad with her knicker elastic.

The thing about James Moriarty — His appetite's always quite hearty.

So the sleuth baked a pie

And the fiend found out why

SNAP

Holmes is always the life of the party!

CLAP CLAP CLAP CLAP

BY ROGER LANGRIDGE

The Baker Street cat, name of Spike, Was quite an unlovable tyke.

With a talent for death

And unbearable breath

And a face only Mother could like.

The footprints had led to the guest room...

The hostess had offered her best room.

But Sherlock was late! What excuse for the wait?

Well, there's always a line for the rest room.

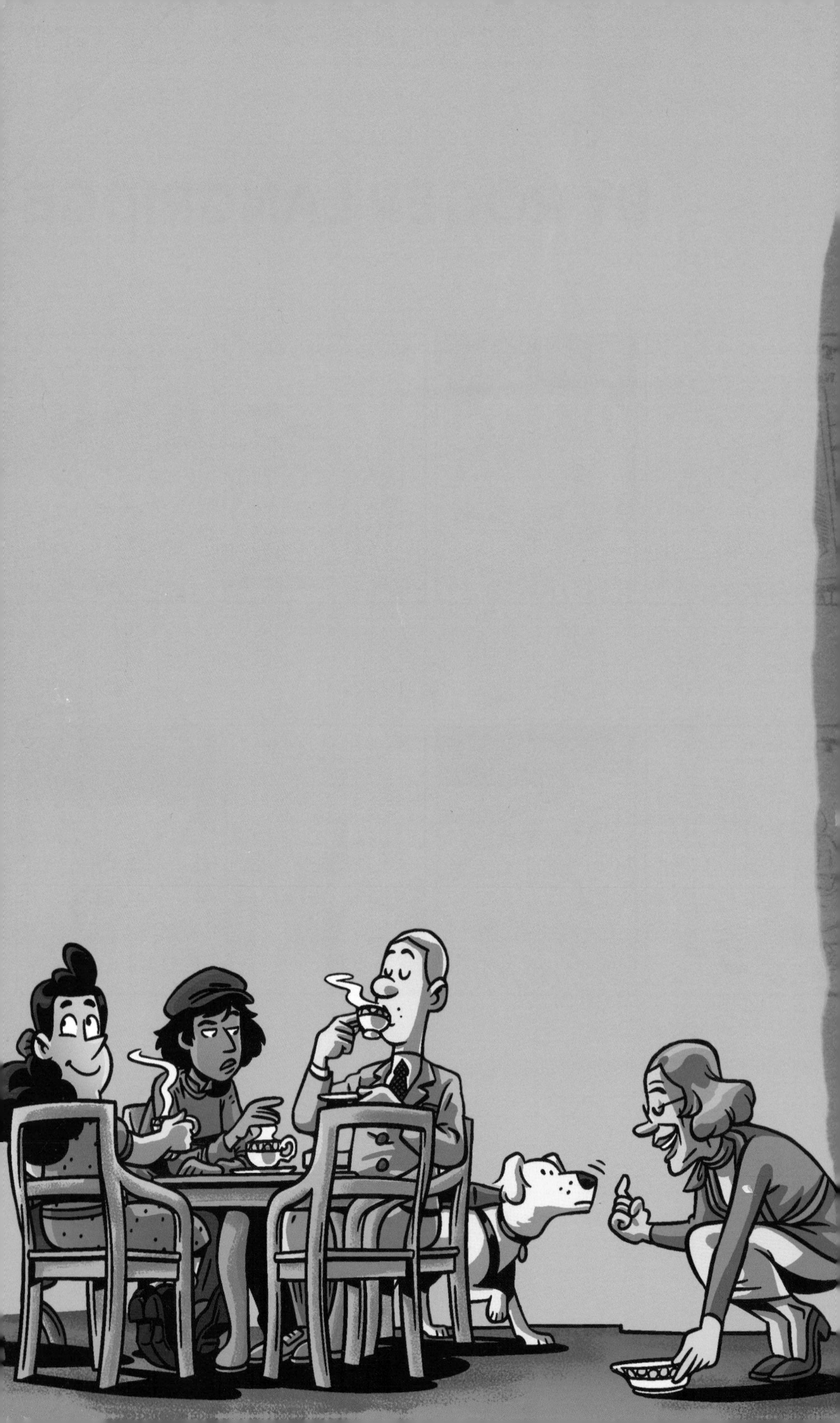